Asahel Kendrick

The life and letters of Mrs. Emily C. Judson

Asahel Kendrick

The life and letters of Mrs. Emily C. Judson

ISBN/EAN: 9783337135225

Printed in Europe, USA, Canada, Australia, Japan

Cover: Foto ©Raphael Reischuk / pixelio.de

More available books at **www.hansebooks.com**

THE

LIFE AND LETTERS

OF

MRS. EMILY C. JUDSON.

BY

A. C. KENDRICK,

PROFESSOR OF GREEK LITERATURE IN THE UNIVERSITY OF ROCHESTER.

NEW YORK:

SHELDON & COMPANY, 115 NASSAU ST.

BOSTON: GOULD & LINCOLN.

1860.

STEREOTYPED BY
SMITH & McDOUGAL,
82 & 84 Beekman-st. N. Y.

PRINTED BY
PUDNEY & RUSSELL
79 John-street, N. Y.

PREFACE.

IT is with unfeigned diffidence that the writer commits this work to the public. A man writing the memoir of a woman—a digger among Greek roots writing the life of a sensitive child of genius and song—a not very intimate acquaintance delineating a character to which the most thorough knowledge could hardly do justice, constitutes a triad of difficulties which he can scarcely hope to have overcome. The author undertook the work reluctantly, and he will be abundantly satisfied if it shall make upon the mind of the reader that impression of the rare excellence of its subject which the study of her life and letters has left upon his own.

Mrs. Judson was a very voluminous correspondent, and the selection from her letters, often of very nearly equal merit, was a matter of considerable difficulty. Sometimes, doubtless, the selection might have been made more wisely, and many have been omitted which, with larger limits, he would gladly have inserted. The reader should remember that Mrs. Judson's letters were written amidst the pressing duties of a very busy life; often from a sick bed; often when her brain was over-tasked, and well nigh exhausted by the drafts for the press; and her letters, therefore, could be hardly expected to be always a fair measure of her intellectual powers. Still they will not, I think, be found unworthy of her reputation.

The true lover of poetry will not, I trust, complain of the number of her poetical pieces inserted in the memoir, for most of these are such as will always find a welcome, and they will, in fact, enhance very considerably the interest of the volume. My chief apology, however, for inserting them is that they belong in a preëminent degree to her life. They grow directly out of the critical passages of her history, and they at once illustrate her feelings amidst these scenes, and derive from the circumstances under which they were written fresh force and beauty. They come from her heart more than from her intellect; they belong to her life even more than to her works.

In parting with the work, I would express my gratitude to the family and personal friends of Mrs. Judson, who have furnished valuable materials. To Rev. Dr. Bright I am under very peculiar obligations for his patient kindness in listening to the reading of my manuscript during the hot month of August, and for the important information and numerous valuable suggestions by which he has improved the work. With this I submit it to the public, earnestly hoping that it may subserve the great cause to which Mrs. Judson's life was devoted.

UNIVERSITY OF ROCHESTER, September, 1860.

CONTENTS.

CHAPTER I.

ALDERBROOK.

"THE floating clouds their state shall lend
  To her; for her the willow bend:
    Nor shall she fail to see,
  Even in the motions of the storm,
  Grace that shall mould the maiden's form,
    By silent sympathy.

  The stars of midnight shall be dear
  To her; and she shall lean her ear
    In many a secret place,
  Where rivulets dance their wayward round,
  And beauty, born of murmuring sound,
    Shall pass into her face."

ABOUT thirty miles south from Utica, in Central New York, on the head waters of the Chenango River, and at the head of the charming valley which follows the windings of that stream in its picturesque course to the Susquehanna, lies Hamilton, one of the most beautiful interior villages of the State, and the seat of the literary and theological institution known as Madison University. Here the parents of Mrs. Emily C. Judson spent nearly the last twenty years of their lives; here Mrs. Judson was married; and hither she finally came back to die. Bordering Hamilton on the southeast, lies the the broken and hilly township of Brookfield; to the

southwest a considerable range of hills separates it from
the neat and thriving village of Eaton, four miles distant.   North of this latter place, in the same town, lies
the somewhat larger village of Morrisville.   Northeast
of Morrisville is the small settlement of Pratt's Hollow,
or Prattsville ; Smithfield, with its pleasant village of
Peterboro', joins it on the north ; and about ten miles
west, on one of our lovely little inland lakes, is Cazenovia, the seat of a flourishing institution of learning,
founded by the Methodists.   These and many other villages lying in Madison county, dot the surface of an
elevated and broken, but picturesquely diversified, and
not unfruitful region—a region where winter holds a
long and rigorous sway, but which blooms into varied
and most attractive loveliness under the balmy influence
of summer.

About a mile and a half south of Eaton village, the
road passes through a sequestered and narrow valley,
where nestles in the hillside a small dwelling, known to
the readers of Fanny Forester's sketches as Underhill
Cottage.   The road which now winds at its foot formerly
ran above it, so that the roof of the cottage scarcely rose
above its level, and you did in truth feel half disposed
" to step from the road where you stood to the tip of the
chimney," that peeped out from its verdurous shelter.
For a description of the cottage as it was and is, I must
send the reader to Miss Forester's faithful portraiture.
Embosomed in trees and shrubbery, the clematis wreath-
ing itself about the humble portico ; the wild vine and
the eglantine clambering over the windows and the roof ;
the myrtle and the roses blending their green and fragrance, it amply justifies her description, and realizes our
ideal of a thoroughly rural residence.   At some distance

below, through the bottom of the valley, wound a small streamlet, fringed with alders, while beyond rises a range of hills, covered partly with forests, partly with wild briars—the whole forming a scene of romantic loveliness such as might have inspired the pen that portrayed the scenery of the Lady of the Lake. This spot—the cottage, the brook, the valley, the hills which embosom them—the pen of genius has consecrated to the world as Alderbrook. Some of the accessories to the picture, Emily, with a romancer's license, borrowed from the neighboring village of Morrisville, and her use of the term stretches over a somewhat fluctuating territory. But all the actual elements of the scene she has delineated with equal spirit and fidelity.

I said the streamlet wound—not winds—through the valley beneath the cottage ; for that, within a few years, has become a thing of the past. The ruthless march of improvement has invaded these sacred precincts ; the clang of machinery breaks the stillness of the secluded valley ; its broad tributary expanse of water now rolls over the little brook and its fringe of green ; and Alderbrook, touched by the magic of genius, is "Alderbrook," indeed, still, and for ever—but it is alder-brook no longer. Thus does the remorseless touch of enterprise brush away the golden hues of the ideal. So it is to be ; and in an age when omnibuses thunder by the olive garden of Plato, when the steam-whistle startles the hoary centuries that look down from the summits of the Pyramids, and threatens the sacred solitudes of Olivet and Tabor, so humble a bit of romance as Alderbrook may not hope to escape unprofaned. But the true "hallowed ground" of earth is in the human heart ; the consecrated spots of genius, driven from the dusty and noon-day

1*

glare of the actual, live inviolate in the haunted realm, the " dim, religious light" of the imagination.

In the little cottage thus signalized, **Emily** Chubbuck was—not born ; but in a small dwelling near by, now no longer standing. But here she spent most of **her** early childhood ; this she often afterward revisited, and ever cherished with peculiar affection ; and this, perhaps, beyond any other spot on earth, was endeared to **her** heart and her fancy by the sacred associations of home. In the shade of those embowering trees she and her sisters played ; along that murmuring brook they wandered in childish glee ; and among those wild and romantic hills they learned to love nature in all her varied aspects of sullenness and beauty.

She was born August 22, 1817, of poor, but reputable parents, who removed to this region from New Hampshire in 1816, when the country was comparatively new. They had formerly been in comfortable circumstances, though never wealthy. Her father was a man of more than ordinary intelligence ; but failed to combine with it much of that practical shrewdness and energy so necessary to worldly prosperity. Tried by life's lower, material standard, his life was a failure ; tried by its higher, spiritual standard, it was a gratifying success. Emily's mother also was a woman of fine intellect, and endowed with much of that force of will and practical sagacity in which her husband was deficient. Both, with all who knew them, were in character above any whisper of reproach. Beyond these brief statements, **Emily has** spared her biographer the labor of an extended record. The following little sketch of her parentage and childhood, drawn up for her husband, is too interesting to be withheld from the reader.

What its details may be thought to lack in dignity **will** be **more** than made up by the light which **they shed on** the hidden springs of her character and destiny They strike to the inner heart of her biography, and show us in what a school of suffering and self-denial God **was** fitting her for her life-work. They will be read with tearful interest by her admirers, and teach, we hope, to many youthful hearts lessons **of** thankful resignation **and** resolute purpose.

CHAPTER II.

AUTOBIOGRAPHY OF HER CHILDHOOD.

"The roots how bitter!—yet the fruits are sweet!"

"Sorrows that are sorrows still,
    Lose the bitter taste of woe;
Nothing 's altogether ill
    In the griefs of long ago."

NOTES OF MY EARLY LIFE, PREPARED PARTLY FROM MEMORY, AND PARTLY
FROM LETTERS AND PAPERS. (FOR MY HUSBAND.)

JOHN CHUBBUCK was a native of Wales, though of
English parentage. He emigrated to the American colonies somewhere about the year 1700. The vessel in
which he sailed being wrecked off Nantucket, he landed
and subsequently took up his permanent residence in
that vicinity. His son Jonathan, born near Nantucket,
was married to Hannah Marble, a worthy and pious
woman, by whom he had several children. Among
them was Simeon, my paternal grandfather. Simeon
Chubbuck was born at Bridgewater, Massachusetts. At
the breaking out of hostilities between England and
her colonies, he, though only sixteen years of age, enlisted as a volunteer in the colonial army, and continued
in the service until peace was restored, and the army
disbanded. He afterward married Lydia Pratt, a native
of Bridgewater, by whom he had five sons and five

daughters. Charles, the second son, was born at Bedford, New Hampshire, March 3, 1780.

James Richards, the father of my maternal grandfather, was a native of England, and a dissenter. His son Amos married Catharine McCartney, whose father was an Irishman, and her mother, Mary Bois, a French Huguenot. My maternal grandfather was also a boy-volunteer in the war of the Revolution, and a commissioned officer in the last war of the United States with England. Lavinia Richards, the eldest of the thirteen children of Amos and Catharine McCartney Richards, was born June 1, 1785, at Goffstown, New Hampshire. She was piously educated by an excellent mother, and at an early age united with the Presbyterian church.

Charles Chubbuck and Lavinia Richards were married November 17, 1805, at Goffstown, New Hampshire. They subsequently removed to Eaton, Madison county, New York, where they arrived September 27, 1816. While on a visit preparatory to removal, my father gained a hope in Christ, and was baptized May 19, 1816, and my mother followed him in the same ordinance the ensuing November. They brought with them to New York four children.

Lavinia Richards Chubbuck was born at Bedford, New Hampshire, September 28, 1806, and died at Pratt's Hollow, New York, June 22, 1829, after a lingering illness of about five weeks. She evinced from childhood singular energy and strength of character, which qualities increased as trials thickened round her path, and through her last years of suffering her activity and cheerfulness never failed. She was converted and baptized at the commencement of her illness, and from that time she daily grew in grace until the end of her life. Materials for a memoir (a journal, several poems, letters, etc.) were placed in the hands of the Rev. Dr. Nathaniel Kendrick, who arranged them for the press, and left them at a publishing house, but they were never heard of afterward.*

Benjamin Chubbuck was born at Bedford, New Hampshire, March 25, 1809. When about seven years of age he had an alarming attack of inflammation of the brain, from the effects of which he never fully recovered. His nervous system was permanently deranged, and some of the mental qualities entirely suspended, while others remained in full and healthful operation. He was on this account a source of constant anxiety up to the time of his death, which took place at the house of our mother's sister in Michigan, September 1, 1846. He left a wife and two children.

Harriet Chubbuck was born at Goffstown, New Hampshire, November 18, 1811, and died at Morrisville, New York, December 6, 1831. She was very beautiful in person, and fascinating in manners, and for a time was the pride of the family. After her conversion, less than a year previous to her death, her natural gaiety was to a great extent subdued ; and so beloved had she rendered herself, that her death, which was sudden, threw a gloom over the whole community, and the funeral services were disturbed by sobbings from different parts of the house. Her mind was much exercised on the subject of missions ; and she once told me, in strict confidence, that she had consecrated herself solemnly to

---

* Lavinia and her younger sister Harriet are beautifully commemorated by Mrs. Judson in the small volume entitled "My Two Sisters," written after her return from Burmah.

this cause—had made a vow which nothing but death could break.

John Walker Chubbuck was born September 24, 1815, at Goffstown, New Hampshire. He learned the business of printing at Morrisville, New York, and afterward conducted newspapers at Hamilton and Cazenovia. He removed to Milwaukee, Wisconsin Territory, in 1834, where he established, in connection with another man, a newspaper which has since been permanent. While residing there he was converted, and united with the Presbyterian church.

Sarah Catharine Chubbuck was born at Eaton, New York, October 25, 1816. She was baptized at Morrisville, April, 1840.

William Wallace Chubbuck was born at Eaton, New York, January 1, 1824. He learned printing, but has devoted his life principally thus far to editing papers and to teaching.

I was the fifth child, and the first born out of New England. I was born August 22, 1817, at Eaton, Madison county, New York. I was an exceedingly delicate child, and my mother was often warned that she could "have me with her but a short time." I remember being much petted and indulged during my first years (probably on account of the fragility of my constitution), and also being several times prostrated for a week or more after a day's visit with my little cousins. The first event of any importance which I remember is the conversion of my sister Lavinia, when I was about seven years of age. My little cot was in her room; and as she grew worse after her baptism, the young members of the church were in the habit of spending the night with her, partly in the character of watchers, partly because of a unity of interest and feeling. She and her visitors spent the greater part of the night in conversation and prayer, without any thought of disturbing so sound a sleeper as I seemed to be. I was a silent, sometimes tearful listener when they talked; and when they prayed, I used to kneel down in my bed, and with hands clasped and heart uplifted, follow them through to the end. I can not recall my exercises with any degree of distinctness; but I remember longing to go to heaven, and be with Christ; some moments of ecstacy, and some of deep depression on account of my childish delinquencies. My sister used often to converse with me on religious subjects; and I remember on one occasion her going to the next room and saying to my mother, "That child's talk is wonderful! I believe, if there is a Christian in the world, she is one." For a moment I felt a deep thrill of joy, and then I became alarmed lest I should have deceived them. The effect was to make me reserved and cautious.

April, 1828. Removed with my parents to Pratt's Hollow, a small village, where there was a woolen factory, and immediately commenced work at splicing rolls. We were at this time very poor, and did not know on one day what we should eat the next, otherwise I should not have been placed at such hard work. My parents, however, judiciously allowed me to spend half my wages (the whole was one dollar and twenty-five cents per week) as I thought proper; and in this way, with numerous incentives to economy, I first learned the use of money. My principal recollections during this summer are of noise and filth, bleeding hands and aching feet, and a very sad heart.

December, 1828. The ice stopped the water-wheel, and the factory was closed for a few months.

January, 1829. Entered the district school, and, I believe, acquitted myself to the satisfaction of everybody, my poor sick sister especially. She had taken great pains with my education while I was at work in the factory, though, as we worked twelve hours a day, and came home completely worn out with fatigue, I was not a very promising subject.

March, 1829. The factory reopened, and I left school and returned to my old employment.

May, 1829. It was some time in this month, but I do not recollect the day, that the carding-machine broke, and I had the afternoon to myself. I spent all my little stock of money in hiring a horse and wagon, and took poor Lavinia out driving. We spread a buffalo robe on a pretty, dry knoll, and father carried her to it in his arms. I shall never forget how happy she was, nor how Kate and I almost buried her in violets and other wild spring flowers. It was the last time that she ever went out.

June 23, 1829. This was the day of poor Lavinia's death. They released me from the factory four days on this occasion, and O, how long they seemed to me ! The first day she was in great agony, and I crept as much out of the way as I could, and scarcely moved. The next day she rallied, and took some notice of me ; but the women (very many neighbors had come in) appeared just as busy and anxious as ever, and mother wept incessantly. Every thing appeared strange and unnatural about the house, and I thought it must be unpleasant for her. She kissed me, and told me I must be a good girl ; but her voice sounded hollow, and her lips were cold. I longed to do something for her, and remembering her extreme fondness for flowers, I went to a neighbor's and begged an apron full of roses. When I returned the house was still as death. I entered her room; they were kneeling around her bed, and no one took any notice of me. In a moment, however, she beckoned to me with her finger, and when I put the flowers upon the bed she smiled. She tried again to turn her eye upon me, but it would not obey her will. She tried to speak, but her lips gave no sound. She lay quietly a few moments, then suddenly exclaimed, "Glory! glory! my Father! Jesus!" and never breathed again. She was buried at Eaton, being a member of the church there.

August, 1829. My health failed very perceptibly after my sister's death, and at last mother called in a physician. He said that I could not live where I was, but must have my freedom and fresh air—a home on a farm, if possible.

1828-9. I believe there was not a decidedly vicious person in the factory, and there were several, both men and women, who were pious. Indeed, there was less coarseness and vulgarity among them than would be supposed, though they were certainly far from being the society one would select for a child. The girls were, most of them, great novel readers, and they used to lend their novels to me, first exacting a promise that I would not tell my mother and sister. When I had finished one I used to carry out the story, and imagine my favorite character going on, on—but it always would end in *death*. Of what avail, then, was the beauty? Of what use the wealth and honor? At other times, while at my work, I used to make a heroine of myself. My

Uncle Jonathan (who was lost twenty years before on a voyage to India) would come home and make me an heiress ; or my face, which people used sometimes to praise, would become so beautiful as to bewitch the whole world ; or I should be a brilliant poetess (my verses were greatly admired by my brother and sisters), and my name would be famous while the world stood. But nothing satisfied me. Whatever I became, I should die and lose it all. Then common sense told me that these great things were unattainable, and I would moderate my plans, and confine my wishes within narrower limits. But all ended in the same way ; *death* would come at the end, and then, what good ?

One day I took up a little, dingy, coarse newspaper —the *Baptist Register* in its infancy—and my eye fell on the words : "Little Maria lies by the side of her fond mother." I had read about the missionaries, and my sister had told me respecting them ; I knew, therefore, at once, that the letter was from Mr. Judson, and that his little daughter was dead. How I pitied his loneliness ! And then a new train of thought sprung up, and my mind expanded to a new kind of glory. No, thought I, though the Burmans should kill him, I will not pity him ; and I—yes, I will be a missionary. After this I had my romantic dreams of mission life ; but they were of a different cast—of suffering, and toil, and pain ; and though they, like the others, ended in death, somehow death in such an employment came pleasantly. I read the "Pilgrim's Progress," and thought of the golden city ; then I read the Bible more, and novels less.

November, 1829. Removed to a farm in the vicinity of Morrisville ; Walker entered a printing-office in the

village ; and Harriet returned from Courtland county,
where she had been spending half a year with some
cousins. We suffered a great deal from cold this winter, though we had plenty of plain food. Indeed, we
never were reduced to hunger. **But the house** was large
and unfinished, and the snow sometimes drifted into it
in heaps. We were unable to repair it, and the owner
was unwilling. Father was absent nearly all the time,
distributing newspapers ; and the severity of the winter
so affected his health that he could do but little when
he was at home. Mother, Harriet, and I, were frequently
compelled to go out into the fields, and dig broken wood
out of the snow, to keep ourselves from freezing. Catharine and I went to the district school as much as we
could.

January, 1830. There was a revival of religion among
the Methodists in the immediate neighborhood, and one
evening, at a meeting, those who wished the prayers of
Christians were requested to rise. It was something new
to me, and I trembled so that I shook the seat, and attracted considerable attention. A girl next me whispered
that I had better arise—she was sure she would if she
felt as I did ; and a class-leader came and took me by
the hand, so that I succeeded in getting upon my feet.
After this I attended all the class-meetings, and thought
it a great favor to get talked with and prayed for.

February, 1830. A "three days' meeting" was commenced by the Baptist church in Morrisville, and we
all attended. The revival among the Methodists had
previously prepared our minds, and Harriet, especially, was deeply affected. This meeting was followed
by a similar one in the Presbyterian church, not one
hour of which was lost to Harriet and myself. A

great many young persons were added to both churches,
among the most joyful of whom was my sister Harriet.
They baptized her, while I looked on almost broken-
hearted. We joined two weekly bible-classes at the
village (a mile distant), and attended all the meetings we could hear of, walking when father was away.
When he was at home, though ever so much fatigued
and ill, he was too happy to see us interested in religious things not to go with us. I recollect feeling myself very heart-heavy, because the revival had passed
without my being converted. I grew mopish and absent-
minded, but still I did not relax my efforts. Indeed, I
believe my solemn little face was almost ludicrously familiar to worshipers of every denomination, for I remember a Presbyterian once saying to me, as I was leaving
the chapel, after having, as usual, asked prayers :
"What! this little girl not converted yet! How do
you suppose we can waste any more time in praying
for you ?"

March, 1830. Benjamin came home (he had been for
five years in the employ of a farmer), and he and father
commenced building fences and other spring work. Our
house had always, especially after Lavinia's conversion,
been the resort of very pious people, and a favorite home
for Hamilton students. We had now a large house, and
they made it a place of frequent resort. I remember
several whose society was very improving. We were
also well supplied with choice books, a luxury which,
even in our deepest poverty, we never denied ourselves.
For we had been taught from our cradles to consider
knowledge, next after religion, the most desirable thing,
and were never allowed to associate with ignorant and
vulgar children.

April, 1830. Commenced taking lessons in rhetoric and natural philosophy of Miss L. W. F. C. F. also volunteered to train me in English composition, but she proved a dangerous teacher. She had read novels till her head was nearly turned, and had, moreover, imbibed infidel sentiments from a young man of better mind than morals, with whom she was too well pleased. She was, however, supposed to be a safe companion, and as my health was the principal thing that brought us to the farm, I was allowed to spend as much time with her as I pleased. She introduced me to Gibbon, and Hume, and Tom Paine ; but more especially to Voltaire and Rousseau, whose style pleased her better. She read the French writers in the originals, though she had access to translations. She was very insinuating, and I not only loved her most sincerely, but really believed her one of the wisest persons in the world. I did not embrace her sentiments, however, though I felt my confidence in the Bible weakened, and lost, to a great extent, my religious impressions. Still I was constant in my attendance upon divine worship, remained a member both of the Bible-class and Sabbath-school, and, I think, never neglected secret prayer. C. F. was a great admirer of the misanthropic school of poetry ; Byron, especially, she was always repeating, and used actually to rave over his Manfred. When she mounted her stilts I always trembled, for though fond of being with her, I still feared for her. She was seven or eight years older than I.

November, 1830. Father's attempt at farming proved, as might have been expected, an entire failure, and for want of a better place, he determined to remove to the village. He took a little old house on the outskirts, the poorest shelter we ever had, with only two rooms on the floor, and a loft, to which we ascended by means of a ladder. We were not discouraged, however, but managed to make the house a little genteel, as well as tidy. Harriet and I used a turn-up bedstead, surrounded by pretty chintz curtains, and we made a parlor and dining-room of the room by day. Harriet had a knack at twisting ribbons and fitting dresses, and she took in sewing ; Catharine and Wallace went to school ; and I got constant employment of a little Scotch weaver and thread-maker, at twisting thread. Benjamin returned to his old place, and Walker was still in the printing-office.

April, 1831. A new academy had been erected in the village, and it now opened with about a hundred pupils. I was one of the first to attend. As soon as I came home at night, I used to sit down to sew with Harriet ; and it was a rule never to lay the work aside, until, according to our estimation, I had earned enough to clear the expenses of the day—tuition, clothing, food, etc. I have since thought that I was any thing but a help to my poor sister, as she always gave me the lightest and easiest work.

June, 1831. Were surprised by a visit from a maiden sister of my mother, an elegant, dashing, gaily-dressed woman, who contrasted oddly enough with our homely house and furniture. Harriet and I estimated that the clothing and jewelry she carried in her two great trunks would purchase us as handsome a house as we wished. She was quite surprised to find us in such humble circumstances, and wondered that we could be so happy. She told me a great deal of my mother as she was in former days, and frequently wept at the contrast.

August, 1831. The first term of school closed, and I lost no time in going into the employ of the thread-maker. While standing alone in his house, turning my little crank all day, I had much time for reflection, and I now began to think more of the books C. F. had taught me to read. If I was to be a missionary, which vocation I had never lost sight of, I must understand how to refute all those infidel arguments, and I now set about it with great earnestness. When I was puzzled with any thing, I used to go to Harriet, or father, or some of our visitors; and sometimes I startled them with my questions, which showed any thing but an orthodox train of thought. I knew they were a little alarmed, but as I was constant in attending the meetings, and had begged to be admitted into the more advanced Bible-class, as well as that of the youth, they were somewhat appeased. About this time, Walker purchased a share in a town library, and gave me the privilege of drawing one book a week. The first thing I drew (for the library was a heterogeneous mass) was Paine's "Age of Reason." This I pored over carefully, then took some notes, and returned the book without any of the family's knowing that it had been in my possession. Father, however, discovered my notes, and I remember that he looked pale, and his hand trembled, when he showed them to me, though I afterward partly succeeded in reassuring him.

October, 1831. My parents concluded it would be impossible to spend the winter where we were without suffering, and so we removed to a nice house, in a pleasant part of the village, with the intention of taking academy boarders.

November, 1831. Aunt Jane, who left our house in June to visit another sister in Michigan, returned, and again spent a week with us. When she left for her home in New Hampshire, father and mother accom-

panied her about eighty miles, to visit a common friend.
They had been gone only two or three days, when Harriet remarked to me, one morning, "I am afraid I am
going to be ill; I never felt so strangely in my life."   As
she spoke, I observed that her eye glared wildly and her
cheeks were crimson.   I took her hand, and it felt like
fire.   She snatched it away, laughing, and said, "Now
don't be alarmed, child ; there is nothing the matter ;"
and then she went on talking in a strain perfectly deliri-
ous.   I was alone in the house, and dared not leave her
to call for help ; and for a few moments I was almost
stunned with terror.   At last I succeeded in inducing
her to put her feet into warm water, and drink some
bitter herb tea ; but before I got her into the bed I was
immensely relieved by a call from her most intimate
friend, M. G.   I immediately ran for the physician, who
pronounced it a case of violent inflammatory fever.   By
the time my parents returned the fever had taken the
typhoid form, but after a time it abated, and reasonable
hopes were entertained of her recovery.   She was thin,
but her fine face was never before so spiritually beautiful, and she conversed most brilliantly, using the choicest
language, and overflowing with poetical conceptions.

December 6.   Two or three days previous to this, the
doctor had pronounced poor Harriet on the verge of the
grave from pulmonary consumption ; and now we all
knew that she was dying.   Her reason was disturbed by
the disease, though occasionally she would rally and
speak a rational word.   M. G. had never left her side
from the morning when she called so opportunely, and
now Harriet exhorted her, in the most glowing language,
to remain steadfast and meet her in heaven.   She bade
us all farewell separately, but although her words breathed

of hope and trust, and she seemed full of Christ and heaven, she expressed herself, during most of the time, incoherently. At first she was in great agony, but gradually her sufferings abated, till we scarcely knew when she ceased to breathe. Her funeral sermon was preached from a text chosen by herself—Eccles. xii. 1.

January, 1832. We could not enjoy the privilege of quiet mourning, for a great number of boarders came in upon us ; so we took a maid, and I went to school. On Monday morning I used to arise at two o'clock, and do the washing for the family and boarders before nine ; on Thursday evening I did the ironing ; and Saturday, because there was but half a day of school, we made baking day. In this way, by Katy's help, we managed to get on with only one servant. I also took sewing of a mantua-maker close by, and so contrived to make good the time consumed in school. My class-mates had spent all their lives in school, and they now had plenty of leisure for study. They were also, all but one, older than myself, and I therefore found it a difficult task to keep up with them without robbing my sleeping hours. I seldom got any rest till one or two o'clock, and then I read French and solved mathematical problems in my sleep.

March, 1832. My health again failed under my accumulated labors, and the physician was consulted. He said study disagreed with me, and I must leave school.

April 1, 1832. Mother insisted on my giving up my studies, and hinted that I might make millinery a very lucrative business. I had considered it all very well to work in the factory, twist thread, and take in a little sewing now and then, as a means of help for the time being, because I could stop when I pleased. But to devote my life to making bonnets was not in accordance with my plans, and I rebelled most decidedly. "But what do you intend to do?" asked my mother; "here you are almost fifteen, and you can not go to school always." That was true enough, and I went away to *think.* At length I proposed attending school one year more, and preparing to be a teacher. But our boarders had proved less profitable than we anticipated; father had been underbid, and so lost one mail route; and then another year in school might kill me. I must think of something else.

April 5, 1832. Mother spoke to Miss B. about taking me into her shop, and as I was already expert with the needle, she was able to make very good terms. I cried all night.

April 6. Went to Mr. B——, my Academy teacher, and after some awkward hesitation, ventured to ask if he thought me capable of teaching school. "Yes," said he, "but you are not half big enough." He, however, gave me a recommendation, and promised to keep the matter secret.

April 7. Told mother I wanted to make the F——k's a visit, which she was pleased to hear, as they lived on a farm, and she thought a little change would do me good.

April 8. Father carried me to the F——k's before breakfast, a drive of about two miles. As soon as he had left me, I inquired if their school was engaged. It was; but the J. district had not yet obtained a teacher, they thought. I took a short cut across the lots, and soon stood trembling in the presence of Mr. J. He was a raw-boned, red-headed, sharp-looking man, in cow-hide shoes, and red flannel shirt. "Is your school engaged?"

I timidly inquired. He turned his keen gray eye upon
me, measuring me deliberately from head to foot, while
I *stood as tall* as possible. I saw at once that it was
not engaged, and that I stood a very poor chance of getting it. He asked several questions; whistled when I
told him my age; said the school was a very difficult
one, and finally promised to consult the other trustees
and let me know in a week or two. I saw what it all
meant, and went away mortified and heavy hearted. As
soon as I gained the woods, I sat down and sobbed out-
right. This relieved me, and after a little while I stood
upon my feet again, with dry eyes, and a tolerably
courageous heart. I went back, though with great
shame-facedness, to Mr. J., and inquired the way across
the woods to Mr. F.'s, which I reached soon after sunset.
Here I found my old friend, C. F., and others of the
family, very glad to welcome me; and without stating
my errand, I went to bed, too tired and anxious to be
companionable.

April 9. Told C. F. my errand, and she at once volunteered to go to the trustees with me and do what she
could in my behalf. When we arrived at Mr. D.'s, she
spoke of the Morrisville Academy, inquired if they knew
the principal, Mr. B——, and then presented my recommendation, which I had not ventured to show the day before. Mr. D. was pleased, said he had heard of me, and
did not know of any one whom he should like so well for
a teacher. He hoped his colleagues had engaged no one,
but did not know, as Mr. B. was the acting trustee. To
Mr. B.'s we went, a frank, happy-looking young farmer,
with a troop of children about him, and made known
our errand. "Why, the scholars will be bigger than
their teacher," was his first remark. " Here, An't, stand

up by the schoolma'am, and see which is the tallest ;
An't is the blackest, at any rate," he added, laughing.
He would not make any definite engagement with me, but
said I stood as fair a chance as anybody, and he would
come to the village next week and settle the matter.
" You have got it," said C., as soon as we were out of
the house. I was not so sanguine, but I was too far
from home to think of going further, and so I had
nothing to do but to wait.

April 10. Left the F.'s, and without seeing the
F——k's again, walked home, a distance of three miles
and a half.

April 14. Mr. B. made his appearance, and announced to mother (much to her surprise and a little to
her embarrassment), that he had come to engage her
daughter to teach school. We were told that they never
paid over six shillings (seventy-five cents) a week, besides
boarding ; and though I could earn as much with the
milliner, and far more at twisting thread, we were all
very happy in the arrangement. Mother had intended
putting me with Miss B. only for want of something
better, and now she was highly pleased, particularly
with the ability I had shown to help myself.

May. On the first Monday in May father took me in
his wagon to Nelson Corners. The school-house was a
little brown building on the corner, all newly cleaned,
and in good repair. About twenty children came, some
clean, some pretty, some ugly, and all shy and noisy. I
got through the day tolerably well, and after school went
to Mr. B.'s. I was to "board round," and so took my
first week with the leading trustee.

The first evening at Mr. B.'s passed off tolerably well ;
but I was very timid, and not very fond of visiting, and

I had neglected to provide myself with either work or books. The B.'s were not a reading people ; their whole library comprised only a Bible and Methodist hymn book, and there was not a newspaper about the house. I had been trained in habits of the severest industry, and before the end of the week was completely miserable. I had no congenial society, nothing to do, and I had intended, when I left home, to be absent six weeks. I was downright home-sick, and after the third day could neither eat nor sleep. On Saturday I closed my school at noon, and without taking leave of the B.'s, hurried away over the hills to Morrisville. I think there was no happier being on earth than I when I bounded into the old dining-room ; and I wept and laughed together all the evening. On Monday morning father carried me back in his wagon, and after that he came for me regularly every Saturday night, and left me at the schoolhouse Monday morning.

August, 1832. Closed my school and returned home. I had been much less industrious this summer than during any three months of my life heretofore ; had not been very conscientious in the discharge of religious duties, and began to like attention and praise. I had been partly under the influence of C. F., and there were two other families of gay young people with whom I had been on terms of intimacy. I was happy, however, to be at home again, and none of the family seemed to remark any change in me.

November, 1832. Entered the Academy again, sewing out of school hours as before. I began to think more of my personal appearance, and of intercourse with my fellow-students ; hence I advanced less rapidly in my studies than formerly, though I still made very respectable proficiency.

January, 1833. A dancing-school was set up in the village, and I became very anxious to attend. Walker volunteered to break the matter to my father and mother, and solicit their permission for me ; but without success. They maintained that dancing was in no way essential to the most accomplished education ; and that this step, if not the first in a course of ruin, would, in all probability, exert a determining and permanent influence on my character and habits. I could not understand their reasoning, and I had set my heart on attending the school, not because I cared in the least for dancing, but because the other village girls went, and I wanted to be like them. I believed what I had often heard and read about the usefulness of this accomplishment, and I knew that a pleasing personal presence, and elegance of manner were invaluable to a woman; I therefore used all my powers of persuasion, and harped upon the subject so continually, that father lost all patience, and commanded me never to allude to it again in his presence. I now considered myself very ill-used, and thought that my father's obstinacy stood directly in the way of my advancement. Fixing my eye on a single point, and thinking of nothing else, I behaved with more foolishness than would have been believed possible. I told mother that I thought I had better get a boarding-place in the village ; for, as I had my own fortune to look after, I ought to be allowed to follow my own plans. She was exceedingly distressed, and said she would much rather have me attend the dancing-school than do so wild a thing. I suppose she talked with father ; for he came to my room one evening, and said he thought he had been unwise in laying his commands upon me. He spoke most feelingly of having been able to do so little for his children, and of his strong desire to see them virtuous and respected ; and said I would one day learn that the village girls whom I wished to imitate were by no means the lady-like models that I supposed. He then removed every obstacle to my attending the dancing-school, and said that though he and my mother disapproved of it in their hearts, I should be subjected to no annoyance. I said but little, though I inwardly resolved that I would *never* learn to dance, and never, while I lived, grieve my father and mother again. I think I have kept both of these resolutions—the first certainly.

CHAPTER III.

"I looked to the west, and the beautiful sky,
   Which morning had clouded, was clouded no more;
Even thus, I exclaimed, can a Heavenly Eye
   Shed light on the soul that was darkened before."

MRS. JUDSON's manuscript here abruptly closes, and my readers will regret with me its brevity, and that we have not the guidance of her pen, so simply, truthfully fascinating, amidst the deepening interest of her advancing years. A sketch like this impresses us profoundly with the unsatisfactoriness of those second-hand details from which the essence of biography—the interior life of its subject, has escaped. Each human heart, could its deepest workings be unvailed, is a microcosm which encompasses the whole essential life of humanity. The sketch does its own philosophizing, yet we may spend a moment in gathering up its impressions. We detect here already the germs of Emily's matured character, and we see under what influences it took its form and pressure. She was the child of adversity. Kind, affectionate, intelligent, watchfully solicitous for the welfare of their children, her parents were not able to shield them from the ills of poverty. The light that surrounded them was literally "all from within," for little of external sunshine fell upon their pathway. Emily can

2*

scarcely be said to have had a childhood—an experience
of that happy season, exempt from forecasting thought
and care, which, bird-like, carols away the passing hour,
before the "shades of the prison-house begin to close"
upon the maturing spirit. Life early shut in upon her
sternly, darkly, inexorably real. The brief inquiry in one
of her letters, "How *did* I live?" has a depth of meaning which the above little sketch abundantly illustrates.

Yet, if she knew the bitterness of poverty, she was no
stranger, in her early home, to the richer wealth of the
intellect and the heart. The domestic affections and the
domestic virtues—grace, sweetness, intelligence, piety,
culture—clustered around that lowly fireside, and lent it
attractions such as mere wealth could not shed over a
palace. And amidst the hardships of her lot, we find in
the youthful Emily essentially the same traits that
marked her maturer years—thoughtfulness for those
about her, an unselfish, almost prodigal generosity, and
a shrinking sensitiveness united with a self-reliant will,
and an almost masculine energy of action. Her expend-
ing all her slowly treasured earnings in giving a drive
to her invalid sister but anticipates the devotion which
led her, in advance of the calculations of prudence, to
provide for another sister's education, and to purchase
a home for her parents ; and the spirit with which, when
not yet fifteen, she planned and executed her purpose of
obtaining a school, shows the romance of her character
already deeply impregnated with that "sterner stuff"
which fitted her for the high resolves and the patient
sufferings of her later destiny. Already is foreshadowed
the character in which genius and good sense, the imaginative and the practical elements, were so harmoniously
blended.

And finally, her sketch shows us how scanty were her opportunities of education; against how adverse influences she struggled up to literary eminence. Few indeed of our successful literary aspirants have been so little indebted to the moulding hand of culture. She snatched its elements from chance acquaintances; from very imperfect schools; from the scanty remains of a day spent in exhausting labor. But her perceptions were quick, her powers of acquisition rapid, and her tastes instinctively delicate. A fuller education would have increased the range and depth of her mental action, but it may be almost doubted whether it would have improved its quality. Her mind was of that ethereal element, that delicacy of organization, that scarcely needed the refinement of culture. This might have given depth and body, but could scarcely have added grace and beauty to her mental movements.

Mrs. Judson's sketch terminates with her fifteenth year. The course which the little girl had marked out for herself she prosecuted with energy. In the summer of 1833 she opened a school in her native village, Morrisville, which she continued until autumn. The following winter she spent at home, and in April, 1834, she commenced teaching in Smithfield, a town lying immediately north of Morrisville. Her school continued until September. This summer constituted an eventful epoch in her life.

The religious impressions which, as related in her sketch, she had so long and deeply cherished, but which had been partially effaced, were revived and deepened, resulting in a joyful religious hope, and a purpose to consecrate her life to the service of her Redeemer. Whether she dated her religious life from this period,

or regarded her present experience as but the upspring-
ing of a germ of faith previously implanted, is not entirely clear, nor perhaps material. In a little collection
of memoranda, she refers the origin of her hope in Christ
to the year 1825, when she was but eight years old, and
I think that in later life she inclined to regard herself as
thus early the subject of a spiritual renewal. This, however, does not appear in her sketch, nor is it intimated in
a letter at this time stating her religious change. But
her education had been thoroughly Christian; pious
parents and sisters had watched over her youthful development; her religious sensibilities had ever been tender,
and it must not surprise us, therefore, that it should be
difficult to distinguish the precise period at which the
latent seed was quickened into spiritual life. At all
events, she now first ventured on a religious profession,
and a letter dated May 2, 1834, announces, with all the
glowing zeal of a convert, her new-found joy, and her
purpose of holy living. The letter, addressed to an
intimate friend, Miss M. L. Dawson, is written in a
cramped and immature hand, and does not rise above
the common-places of religious diction, but its glow of
pious feeling and earnestness of spirit are unmistakeable.

Perhaps you have heard, she writes, that I have learned, as
I trust, to love my God. O would that I could have your
company! Would that you, too, could know the peace there
is in believing! Would that you would engage in this glorious cause in which my every feeling is enlisted, and for the
promotion of which my every future effort, I *hope*, will be
made. I have loved you, Maria, as I never loved another
human being who was not bound to me by the ties of relation-
ship, and I shall never cease to love you till "the silver cord
be loosed, and the golden bowl broken." But the purpose of

my life is changed. Hitherto I have lived for myself, and now
I mean to live for God.

Then, in a strain of passionate earnestness, she ex-
horts her youthful companion to forsake the path of sin,
and become her partner in the joys of the Christian life.

In July following she was baptized by the Rev.
William Dean, himself a native of Morrisville, and
then under appointment as missionary to China, and
became a member of the Baptist church in Morrisville.
The following extract of a letter from Dr. Dean gives an
account of her baptism, and some brief earlier reminiscences.

You are quite welcome to my memories of Emily Chubbuck,
so far as I am able to record them. Soon after I rose to the
dignity of school-teaching, and "boarded round," I was employed in her father's district for the winter of 1827, and was
often in her father's family, and saw much of the timid little
pale-faced Emily, both in the family and in the school-room.
She ever appeared dutiful to her parents, cheerful in her home
duties, and diligent and successful in getting her lessons. I
recollect to have been especially interested in finding one of
her slender frame and sensitive temperament so successful in
arithmetic. Accuracy characterized all her lessons, and propriety all her deportment.

In the spring of 1834, before leaving the country, I had occasion to baptize some dozen or fifteen young persons in my
native town, and Emily Chubbuck was among the number. In
conversation, during her serious impressions, she was not com-
municative, but in answer to questions gave clear views of sin,
and her sole trust in the atoning sacrifice of Christ for salvation.
In relating her Christian experience before the church, she discovered her accustomed coy manner, but gave satisfactory proof
that she had been renewed by the spirit of God.

Not long before this event she had witnessed the death-bed triumphs of an elder sister, who had in her person presented a lovely example of piety. This sister had cherished a warm sympathy for a suffering world, and expressed a desire to go in person to teach the heathen.

A new and nobler element was now wrought into Emily's character. A principle was implanted in the depths of her nature, which, though unobtrusive, shrinking, sometimes almost disowning itself, yet never lost its power over her, nor ceased to act as a controlling element in her subsequent career. Her religious character was indeed slow in maturing, and its development was retarded, perhaps, by her peculiarities of temperament and constitution. Thoroughly sincere in her religious profession—as in all her professions—she shrunk with almost morbid aversion from any parading of her feelings, and chose rather to bury her convictions in the depths of her own bosom, than to hold out any appearances of piety which were not sustained by her conscious experience. Her progress in piety was also checked by some peculiar internal struggles. From the first an inexplicable conviction dwelt upon her mind, that she was destined to a missionary life. "I have felt," she said, in conversation with an intimate pious friend, in 1838, "ever since I read the memoir of Mrs. Ann H. Judson when I was a small child, that I must become a missionary. I fear it is but a childish fancy, and am making every effort to banish it from my mind ; yet the more I seek to divert my thoughts from it, the more unhappy I am." She never, she said at another time, heard a sermon preached, or opened her Bible to read, without feeling condemned, conscious that her Saviour's requirements were in direct antagonism to her cherished

purposes—not so much of personal ease or ambition, as
of ministering to the comfort of her parents, and securing an education to her younger brother and sister.
Thus her bosom was the seat of a constant struggle—
the heavenly and the earthly duty coming into seeming collision—while her will and purposes were con-
sciously not disciplined into harmony with her heavenly
calling.

From causes like these, she declined from the fervor
of her first love and the entireness of her early consecration, and lived for a time without the deep spiritual communion and the inspiring hopes which are
the privilege of the believer. Yet, if she shrunk timidly
from the utterance of Christian emotion, if her joys
were low, and her heavenward aspirations less intense,
her life, in its larger compass and higher aims, rested
on a firm foundation of religious principle. Her chosen
home was with the people of God ; her daily walk was
consistent and unimpeachable ; her occasional literary
effusions, and her first formal efforts in authorship,
drew their chief inspiration from the Bible. Even her
"Fanny Forester" sketches stood broadly distinguished,
by their pure and exalted moral tone, from much of the
lighter literature with which they were accidentally
associated ; and when, at length, "the hour and the
man" appeared that drew her forth to the realization of
her early missionary yearnings, the readiness with which
her spirit expanded to the sublime enterprise, the enthusiasm with which she entered into that great work of
redeeming the nations, which had absorbed her husband's
energies, prove how deep had been the work of moral
preparation.

CHAPTER IV.

THE SCHOOL-TEACHER.

"I have made a changeful journey
  Up the hill of life since morn ;
I have gathered flowers and blossoms,
  I've been pierced by many a thorn.
But from out the core of sorrow
  I have plucked a jewel rare ;
The strength which mortals gather
  In their ceaseless strife with care."

EMILY was now fairly inducted into the mysteries of the "birch." The beauties of "boarding round," of training regiments of literary aspirants, of all possible youthful sizes and ages, in the small, ill-constructed, ill-warmed, ill-ventilated school-houses of our rural and sparsely populated districts, I leave to the knowledge and fancy of my readers. But she pursued her employment "with a will," and consequently with success.

She closed her school in Smithfield in September. Allowing herself but a slight respite, she went in November to Nelson (the scene of her *début* as a teacher) to instruct in a private family. But the severity of the winter, and the feebleness of her health, compelled her to cut short her engagement, and she returned home in February. She continued ill during the summer, and though her pen was not idle, she was unequal to any steady employment. In January her health had improved, and she entered again the academy at Morrisville. After remaining one quarter as a pupil, she was transferred to the post of teacher, which she occupied until April of the year following. The integrity of the family was now broken in upon by the removal of her brother Walker to Milwaukee, in Wisconsin, where he still resides, editing a paper, and a respected member of the Presbyterian church. His conversion stood connected, I think, with a letter addressed to him by Dr. Judson a short time before Emily's marriage. This year also witnessed the marriage of her brother Benjamin.

During the summer of 1837, Emily had charge of a school in Brookfield, where she presided over about an hundred pupils. Repairing thence almost immediately to Syracuse, she taught in this place until the following April. There seems to have been need of her utmost exertions. "Many family troubles during this winter"—thus runs her brief record—"failure in stage-coach business; the family removed to Hamilton, but returned in the spring; home lost; horses, coaches, etc., seized and sold at auction." Such emergencies proved the genuine gold in Emily's character. When all seemed crashing round her, she stood and struggled with unabated courage, cheered the desponding spirits of her parents, aided with hand and counsel at home when aid was possible, and by her constant labors in school-teaching did all in her power to relieve the heavy burdens of the family. Her self-sacrificing generosity overlooked entirely her individual comfort. Her unrelaxed effort was expended upon those to whom she owed her life, and whose failing health and partially broken spirit caused them to lean largely upon her. Meantime her acknowledged ability as a teacher was securing an increased demand for her services.

On closing her school in Syracuse, Emily went almost immediately to take charge of the public school in Hamilton. She, as usual, divided her time between teaching, studying, and writing. Her active temperament scarcely allowed her a moment's rest from some form of literary labor. Her evenings she now devoted to the study of Greek under the tuition of a student in the Theological Seminary, and her occasional hours were occupied in some little graceful effusions in prose and verse, which adorned the columns of the village journal. She was now about twenty-one, and though ill health and care, and the irksome labor of teaching the rudiments of knowledge to children, stood much in the way of her literary development, still she scattered about many gems of beautiful thought, though without having more than the faintest conception of the depth and the richness of the mine whence they were drawn. From a series of contributions to the Hamilton village paper I select the following :

The midnight air is filled
With rich-toned music, and its deep wild gush
Sweeps strongly forth, and bids the earth to hush
Its din—and it is stilled.

Then with low whispering tone,
Like the last sigh of a departed one
That, all unmurmuring that his task is done,
Breathes out his life alone,

The soft sound floats along;
Or like a harp with one unbroken string,
Which still its plaintive notes around may fling,
Breathes forth this spirit song.

Now fainter than the sigh
Of the last faded rose-leaf when it falls,
As its departed sister softly calls,
The low sweet strains move by.

And then again they burst
In rich, deep strains of melody untaught,
Stirring the spirit's depths, and kindling thought
Pure as in Eden erst.

I may not read the spell
Flung on my soul, but I may feel its power,
And twine bright thoughts around this hallowed hour,
On which alone to dwell.

During Emily's residence at Hamilton, I believe, certainly during this year, her missionary impulses gained such strength that she addressed a letter to Rev. Nathaniel Kendrick, Pastor of the Baptist Church in Eaton (and theological professor in the institution at Hamilton), on the subject of devoting herself to a missionary life. The letter is unfortunately lost, and we are deprived of its aid in estimating her religious life at this time. But the fact that though bound by so strong attachments to her home, she should have cherished this desire strongly enough to make it the subject of a formal communication, shows that her childish dream was passing into a sober reality, and that she had not proved faithless to her early vow of consecration. Dr. Kendrick sympathizing entirely in her missionary zeal, yet advised her to await the openings of Providence. He, no doubt, saw objections to sending forth a girl so young and delicate into the rude struggles and privations of a missionary's life. Doubtless he judged wisely ; yet little did he or any one dream what "stuff for a heroine" tempered that fragile organism.

Her visit home was saddened by painful remembrances —remembrances of the early dead—of the recently removed. "How can I write," she says, as she sits down on Saturday evening to her solitary self-communings, "when those voices which have a kind of magic in them strike on my ear, while all the visions of other days dance before my eyes ? And then come thoughts of the absent. My brother, my own dear brother, why art thou away ? Come back and we will again be happy."

"And I again am home"—she continues, as the gushing tenderness of her spirit melts her prose into verse which gives an inkling of her heart history, and opens glimpses of the depths from which, under the inspiration of sanctified sorrow, welled up in later times strains of such soul-subduing pathos as "Sweet Mother" and "Angel Charlie." We, of course, claim for this piece no *such* poetical merit :—

STANZAS.

AUGUST 7, 1838.

And I again am home ;—again I hear
  The thrilling tone of voices early loved ;
And all I love on earth, but *he*, are near,
  All whom I have so long and deeply proved :
But *he* is absent—ah ! that he should roam ;
It must not, must not be—*Brother*, come home.

Come to the hearts that love thee—come and bless
  The fleeting moments of a *mother's* life ;
To her fond love what is the world's caress ?
  What its ambitious hopes ? its maddening strife ?
What seek'st thou there that thou alone shouldst roam
From those that love thee ? Brother, come, come home.

Come, for thy *sire* awaits thee—though he's shrunk
   From the proud world since Heaven has bowed his head,
Of sorrow's bitter cup has deeply drunk,
   And looks upon this life with almost dread,
Yet even there, brother, *thou* art not forgot;
Though *hope*, though peace be gone, yet *love* is not.

Come to a *sister's* arms—thou'rt almost all
   Her heart may cling to in this sunless day;
O let thy hand remove this fearful pall,
   Which wraps her heart while thou dost thus delay.
O gaze no longer on Fame's rainbow dome;
Cheat not thyself with meteors—come, come home.

We've naught but hearts to offer—but there's there
   A depth of richness thou hast long since proved;
Our web of life is darkly dyed with care;
   But shrink thou not, thou'rt e'en more deeply loved
Than when the stream of life unruffled flowed,
And hope our pathway with bright visions strewed.

Then come to us, 'tis but a little hour
   That we may spend in this dark world of woe;
Let us together cling—a sister's dower
   Is but her brother's heart—and thine, we know,
Is all our own—then why, why dost thou roam?
We wait thee, deeming thou wilt soon *come home.*

During all these years nothing could repress the
buoyant activity of Emily's intellect, nor keep her from
constant exercises in composition. To write was a necessity of her nature, and she lavished her effusions upon
the village journals and upon her port-folio with a prodi-
gality which might well justify high anticipations of her

future ; and this especially as these effusions were not the products of school training, but the spontaneous outgushings which the want of such a training could not repress. Their defects sprung from the necessary super-ficialness of youth, from the fact that time and experience had not yet developed the deeper elements of her character.

On leaving Hamilton, she opened a school in the academy building at Morrisville, to which her reputation attracted many pupils. While teaching, she still strove to supply the deficiencies of her education, and now took private lessons in mathematics with Rev. Mr. Reed, for a short time resident in Morrisville. With one of his sisters she formed a very close intimacy ; and several letters to Miss Reed, while not otherwise remarkable, display an intensity of affection such as belongs not to an ordinary character. Her timid, and even cold exterior, vailed a keen sensibility, and a passionate, almost morbid craving for sympathy and love. The tendency to bury her whole nature in a single absorbing friendship, of course diminished with her maturing character and experience ; but though taking a more subdued form, her attachments were always ardent and engrossing.

In March of 1839 the troubles of the family reached their crisis. To crown all, her mother fell dangerously ill of a brain fever, followed by inflammation of the lungs. Emily was compelled to close her school for a few weeks, and her own health was so sadly shattered that she was scarcely adequate to its duties. But temporal afflictions were compensated by spiritual mercies. Her only remaining sister, Catharine, was baptized into the fellowship of the Morrisville church, thus making two sisters rejoicing with the church triumphant, and two still struggling in Christian hope with the burden of the flesh.

She now renewed her long slumbering correspondence with her early friend Miss Dawson. Her letters to her (afterward Mrs. Bates) are marked less by intensity of passion, by the surrender of the whole soul to an engrossing attachment, than her earlier ones; and, on the other hand, are tinged with a slightly sentimentalizing tendency, of which nearly every vestige was swept from her later correspondence. She was in a transition period. Childhood was passed; the woman was not yet developed. The following, from her reply to Miss Dawson, shows her estimate of the discipline she was undergoing, and of the sterner elements which had been wrought into her character. Doubtless her mental analysis partially missed its mark. There was more of " the poetry of life" about her now than formerly, though for the moment latent. The exquisite nonsense of the poet, that

> Heaven lies about us in our infancy,

was no more true of her than of others. A rich, warm, golden nature—tender, energetic, passionate, romantic—full of the susceptibilities of love and the capacities of heroism, was gathering its unconscious elements within her. But hers was still the chrysalis state, and the winged being of light and beauty had not fully emerged. We need, however, make but slight allowance, either in her poetry or prose, for that affectation of sorrow, that merely sentimentalizing grief, in which youthful poets and letter-writers are so liable to indulge. She had little occasion to frame visions of imaginary suffering. Life had been with her too intensely real—care, often deepening into sorrow, too close a companion, to leave much leisure or occasion for the luxury of fictitious woe.

TO MISS M. L. DAWSON.

MOERISVILLE, September 5th, 1839.

MY DEAR MARIA,—

I am alone to-day—all, all alone, for the first hour since I received your dear, kind letter; so I hasten to improve the precious moment. I am exceedingly happy just now. Maria has not forgotten me. We are friends again—old, tried friends; we will meet and kiss, and the past with its years of alienation shall be buried in oblivion.

Maria, I will tell you the truth; Emily is *changed*. You would not recognize, I presume, either her face or her character. But her *heart* remains the same. Years could not change that, save, perhaps, to call up some deeper feeling, to unseal some hitherto undiscovered fountain. I have said that I am changed. You could hardly suppose that years would make no alteration, and I think that I should even look for some changes in your own dear self. I am not diffident and shrinking as I used to be, but perhaps approaching too much the other extreme. The world has given me some heavy · brushes; disappointment has cast a shadow over my path; expectation has been often marred and hope withered; the trials of life have distilled their bitterness; care spread out its perplexities; and all this has served to nerve up my spirits to greater strength, and add iron to my nature. There is but little of the poetry of life about me now; little of the bright, rich coloring of a warm imagination. In short, I am a plain matter of fact little body, somewhat stern and "quite too positive for a maiden," as the quaker said. The neighborhood calls me proud; my mother, rough; my sister, coarse; my brother, old maidish, and my dear good father, *rather too decided for a girl.* I have said this much of myself that you may know what it means, and that it is really I that write, should you happen to find something in my letters that does not fully coincide with your former ideas of Emily. What an egotist I am! But then I have nothing else to talk about; you, of course, do not care to hear the news. . . . .

In October declining health compelled her to close her school. In a congratulatory letter to Miss Dawson (Mrs. Bates) on her marriage, she writes thus :—

Although, I believe, somewhat my junior, Maria, yet your *heart* is older, and has learned a lesson in which mine can not sympathize ; yet be assured I shall ever be interested in your welfare, and should the "dark hour" ever come, in Emily you will find a faithful friend, and, Maria, *then* she will know how to sympathize. She is well instructed in the lore of care and trouble, for the hand of the world has touched not lightly. Sometimes in the hour of trouble and anxiety, when obliged to wear a smile to cheer my mother and sister, I have longed for some loved bosom on which to rest my aching head, and pour out the pent up anguish of my heart. . . . .

Talking of "rhyme," I will give you a little, if you will excuse the "reason." I profess no proficiency in that :

TO MARIA ON HER MARRIAGE.

'Tis past, that thoughtlessness of care—
   Bright girlhood's gift is thine no more ;
And though a smile thy lips yet wear,
   It seems not gladsome, as of yore.

Thou may'st not be a girl again,
   That fascinating, foolish thing ;
Restless and joyous, light and vain,
   Free as the wild bird on the wing.

Thine is a new and holy tie,
   Bound with a sacred, solemn trust,

3

To live, and live all lovingly ;
   To die, and mingle dust with dust.

Yet say not, dearest, we must part ;
   For, while new ties with old ones blend,
Though other loved ones claim thy heart,
   Thou'lt not forget thine *early friend.*

. . . Come and visit me, Maria, come. I have four rose-
buds, and you must see them ere they blossom ; for they are
like your own hopes in this wilderness of life, flinging a glad
promise over the darkness of the coming winter.

In January, Emily again took charge of a school in
Prattsville. This seems to have been a place to her of
some literary significance. In its factory "Grace Linden" was probably born ; its school-house, if we may
judge from the following fragment of a letter to Mrs.
Bates, gave birth to "Lilias Fane" :—

The evening I saw you at C——, safely landed us at Morrisville, at a not very late hour. The next day I received an
invitation to take a school in Pratt's Hollow, and accepted it
without hesitation. Behold me then the Monday morning
after, at the head of a little regiment of wild cats. Oh, don't
mention it, don't. I am as sick of my bargain as—(pardon the
comparison, but it will out)—any Benedict in Christendom.
I am duly constituted sovereign of a company of fifty wild
horses "which may not be tamed." Oh, Maria, Maria, pity
me. But the half has not yet been told you. Immediately
after coming here, I caught a severe cold, and have ever since
been afflicted with something like inflammation in the eyes, so
that I have been obliged to keep them bandaged, save in
school hours. This evening is the first time I have ventured
to take the bandage off, and I may rue it. My school is almost ungovernable. They have dismissed their former teacher—

an experienced one—a married man, and it seems a hopeless task to attempt a reformation among them. I receive three dollars per week, and board.

As might be expected from the above, her winter labors proved again too severe for her, and she closed her school in March in a miserable state of health, from which she did not rally through the summer. In September, however, she contemplated returning to her destiny. Cazenovia, Syracuse, and other places were under deliberation; meanwhile in a letter to her friend she thus unbosoms herself :—

O this is a sad world, where we must hope and weep, then hope again, and find even that in vain. I have spent the day alone, and I have almost felt as though I was alone in the world. And now, Maria dear, my heart as it is. I love my friends, and am grateful to them for regarding me; but I would have them *altogether mine*. O there is a fearful sense of loneliness comes over me when I think that none among my numerous friends love me as I would be loved; that I love no one with all the strength and capability of my nature. I would lay down my heart at a mortal shrine, and be, next to God, the supreme object of affection. . . .

Wednesday, September 9, P. M. I have been making embroidered butterflies and needle-books until I begin to think it small business for such a "big girl;" so I have taken my pen to tell you how much happier I am to-day than I was yesterday—happier, because I *will* be.

> Happy, happy! Earth is gay;
> Life is but a sunny day.
> Lightly, lightly flit along,
> Child of sunshine and of song;
> Happy, happy, earth is gay,
> Life is but a sunny day.

If perchance a cloud arise,
Darkly shadowing o'er thy skies,
Heed it not 'twill soon depart;
Bar all sadness from thy heart.
Happy, happy, earth is gay,
Life is but a sunny day.

Drink the cup and wear the chain,
But let them weave their spell in vain;
Lightly, lightly let them press
On thy heart of happiness.
Happy, happy, earth is gay,
Life is but a sunny day.

CHAPTER V.

"Thine every fancy seems to borrow
    A sunlight from thy childish years,
Making a golden cloud of sorrow,
    A hope-lit rainbow out of tears."

PROVIDENCE, meantime, was ordering an unlooked-for and grateful change in Miss Chubbuck's destiny. Toward the close of the summer term of the Utica Female Seminary, Miss Allen of Morrisville, one of its best pupils, and a warm friend of Emily, laid before the principal, Miss Urania E. Sheldon, the subject of her admission to its privileges. The proposition was, that she should be allowed to spend two or three years in pursuing higher studies in the school, and subsequently make payment when she should become established as a teacher. Similar favors had been already extended by Miss Sheldon, acting conjointly with her sister, Miss Cynthia, to many young ladies, who were now filling important posts as teachers in different sections of the country. The application was successful. Interested in what they were told of Emily's talents and energy, they invited her to the Seminary, with the assurance that, if circumstances favored, she should complete her education there without present charge, and otherwise

should receive gratuitous instruction for a single term.
The proposal was gladly accepted, and the next term
found her an inmate of the institution, pursuing French,
mathematics, drawing, etc.

How grateful the change the reader will readily anticipate. Hitherto, as far as domestic obligations and a
state of health ever trembling on the verge of illness
allowed, she had been struggling to eke out her scanty
means, and those of the family, by officiating as the mis-
tress of a country school. Whatever the benefits of this
employment—and its discipline was, in many respects,
salutary—yet she had to submit to much that sorely
tried her sensitive spirit, while the drudgery was often
well nigh greater than she could bear. Pegasus in the
harness of the boor was a fitting symbol of her delicate, ethereal nature in the rude companionship which
she often encountered. From all this she was now freed,
and the change, though it did not exempt her from the
need of strenuous exertion (for it was not to be strictly
a lucrative one), brought her into a congenial atmosphere,
and gave her a permanent place with sympathizing companions. The Seminary, pleasantly situated in the handsome city of Utica, had attained a high reputation under
the management of the Misses Sheldon, Miss Urania being
the principal, and Miss Cynthia having charge of the executive and financial departments. Their venerable parents, whom to know was to love and reverence as patterns
of every natural and Christian virtue, were at the head of
the household. With them, besides the Misses Sheldon,
resided an elder, widowed daughter, Mrs. Anable, with
her son, Courtland, and several daughters. One of these,
Anna Maria, near Emily's own age, was yet to become
her bosom companion. They were a family of rare ex-

cellence, and eminently qualified for the high charge which
they had undertaken—well fitted to meet the demands
of a nature like Emily's; able to appreciate her endowments of mind and character; to detect the rare gem
concealed beneath her shrinking exterior; and, though
not wealthy, endowed with a large-hearted benevolence
which evinced itself in the most affectionate interest in
all her concerns. Counsel, sympathy, encouragement to
that career of letters for which she soon displayed her
capacity, were all hers. They took her into their inmost
circle, and gave a home to her heart as well as to her
person. To the elder members of the family she ever
afterward looked up with the grateful reverence of a
child; to the younger ones she became as a sister; and
the unfaltering affection of all followed her through her
years of exile and of widowhood down to the gates of the
grave.

The following extract of a letter from Miss Anable to
Dr. R. W. Griswold, gives a glimpse of her appearance
at this time:

"I remember well her first appearance in Utica as a pupil.
She was a frail, slender creature, shrinking with nervous timidity from observation; yet her quiet demeanor, noiseless step,
low voice, earnest and observant glance of the eye, awakened at
once interest and attention. Her mind soon began to exert a
quiet but powerful influence in the school, as might be seen from
the little coterie of young admirers and friends who would often
assemble in her room to discuss the literature of the day, or,
full as often, the occurrences of passing interest in the institution. Miss Chubbuck had a heart full of sympathy, and no
grief was too causeless, no source of annoyance too slight, for
her not to endeavor to remove them. She therefore soon became a favorite with the younger, as with the older and more

appreciative scholars. Her advice was asked, her opinions sought, and her taste consulted. Many things illustrative of her influence over the young at this time crowd upon my memory, but I have no leisure at present to write them more fully.

Emily thus fully justified her friend's commendation and the anticipations with which she had been admitted into the Seminary. As a scholar she at once put herself into the very first rank, mastering with ease the most difficult studies. Indeed, her masculine intellect always delighted in grappling with abstruse problems. As a writer she distinguished herself even more, both by the easy elegance of her prose style, and her graceful facility in versification. True, the depths of her nature had not been yet sufficiently stirred to reach the deeper fountains of her poetic power. Larger experiences, richer joys, keener sorrows, were to evoke from her spirit its noblest harmonies. The following to Mrs. Bates gives an inkling of her situation :—

UTICA, December 8, 1840.

MY OWN MARIA DEAR,—

I wrote you last week, but as the letter remains in hand yet, and upon a review I find a very strong tinge of sadness about it, I have concluded to write again, lest you should think me *très-misérable*, when, on the contrary, I am *très-heureuse*. O, Maria, this is a happy, happy place, and Miss Sheldon I love dearly.

In my other letter, dear Maria, I talked to you a great deal about our childhood's days, when you were such a bright, busy " humming-bird," and I your shadow ; but as I feel now I can not mourn over them. I have been with Miss Sheldon to-night, and she is the dearest comforter in the world, and makes me believe that all will be right with me yet. My health is

much better than it was last summer, and my spirits rise in proportion, except when—*n' importe.* I shall not talk of that now.
But, O, when I sit down alone, and in my selfishness think
there is no woe like mine, then, Maria, I want you by.

Maria, I have half a mind to consult you concerning a scheme
which I broached to Miss Sheldon the other day. I have always shrunk from doing any thing in a public capacity, and
that has added a great deal to my school-teaching troubles.
But O, necessity! necessity! Did you ever think of such a
thing as selling brains for money? And then, such brains as
mine! Do you think I could prepare for the press a small
volume of poems that would produce the desired—I must speak
it—cash?

I wish, Maria, you could see Miss Sheldon, you would so love
her. My love for her I sometimes think is almost idolatry.
She makes every one happy about her, and the school is more
like a happy family than any thing else. Perhaps you already
know that her father's family are here, and they are all so good
and kind to us girls that we look upon them as parents and
elder sisters. I sometimes think of home, and then I want to
be with my parents and dear Kate; I sometimes think, too, of
the past—a few past years. O Maria, how *did* I live?

Yours truly,

E. E. CHUBBUCK.

The term closed in December. The experiment had
been tried, and of course with the only result possible
for one of her capacity. She returned in January with
assurances of support, so far as her board and instruction were concerned, and with brightening hopes. At
the suggestion, or rather urgent advice of Miss Sheldon
she began to employ her intervals from school duties in
writing for the press, the prospect of publishing a volume of poems hinted at in the preceding letter, being
abandoned. Her articles scattered through the newspa-

3*

pers had been mostly anonymous, and all without a
thought of remuneration. She shrunk now from appearing before the public; and the first suggestion of making
the Muses venal, of transmuting Helicon into Pactolus,
struck her almost as desecrating the gift of genius, much
as the contemplation of "Apollo's venal son" horrified the
youthful enthusiasm of Lord Byron. But Emily, like
Byron, got over this virgin weakness, as she ought, finding that romance and sensibility, though a beautiful
fringe for life, will not answer for its web. Genius must
eat as well as dream; and they who enrich the world
with their high spiritual creations, must not disdain
its vulgar material returns. And ordinarily they do
not. Experience and necessity are stern teachers, and
tread ruthlessly on sensitive nerves. In their school
Emily had learned many a bitter lesson. Taking counsel of necessity and of her excellent friends, the Misses
Sheldon, she commenced writing a small book for children. "Charles Linn, or how to observe the Golden
Rule," was begun in January and finished in March following. Through the kindness of Mr. Hawley, member
of a book-selling firm in Utica, it was accepted and put
to press by Messrs. Dayton & Saxton of New York city.
It was issued in July, and Emily was bodily—spiritually
rather, before the public.

Written as was "Charles Linn" within the space of
three months, in hours abstracted from heavy school duties, and frequent attacks of illness, it showed no slight
facility in composition. It has the faults of inexperience. The story is not very skillfully planned; characters are transformed with unnatural rapidity; and the
language of vulgar life is, perhaps, used a little too freely.
But its moral is excellent; it sparkles with many flashes

of genius ; it is not for a moment dull ; and it displays
much of that grace of style, and descriptive and dramatic
power which afterward won for her so brilliant a reputation. It was favorably and even flatteringly received by
the circle whom so unpretending a book would naturally
reach, and authorized sanguine hopes of yet higher success.

In April Emily was appointed assistant instructor in
the department of English composition. For this service
she was well fitted. The creative and the critical faculty
differ so widely that the power to write well does not
always argue a corresponding capacity to judge the productions of others. Some have much constructive, but
little analytical talent ; they can put together, but can
not take apart ; can create, but can not criticize. The
emotional and imaginative elements predominate over
the intellectual. This is likely to be eminently true of
woman, partly from her more sensitive organization,
partly from the prevailing character of her culture.
Emily combined with her highly enthusiastic and poetic
temperament, a clear eye and a keen analytical judgment. With a woman's quickness and delicacy of feeling she united a robust and masculine understanding.
She early learned to study the principles of the effects
which she produced, and hence the fervor of fancy rarely
betrayed her beyond the bounds of a regulated self-con-
sciousness. Thus she became a good critic of the productions of others, and ultimately of her own. But her
health now became miserable. Study, teaching, and authorship combined were too much for her slender constitution : her disordered nerves reënacted the caprices of
childhood, and forced her to abandon all her severer studies. The following letters give glimpses of her struggles

physical, mental, and pecuniary. The details of the
straits to which she was driven, and of the rigorous
economy which she was forced to employ to meet her
most necessary incidental expenses, if proper to be made
public, could not but enlist for her the liveliest sympathy. But we draw the vail over them, leaving the
reader to judge from two or three specimens.

I remark here that in giving Miss Chubbuck's letters,
I do not always indicate unimportant omissions. Real
letters must always contain much which should not
meet the public eye ; and Emily's were real letters,
dashed off hastily amidst pressing cares and duties.
Written also after the exhausting labors of the day,
they by no means do uniform justice to her epistolary
powers.

TO HER SISTER.

UTICA, June 16, 1841.

MA CHÈRE KIT,—

I am not in the best possible humor for letter-writing to-
day, but knowing that you will be obliged to pay the fee before
you examine the contents, here is at ye for a scribble. This
morning I had a mammoth tooth extracted, and the rest are
now dancing right merrily in commemoration of the event; so
you must not wonder if my ideas dance in unison. Kate, you
may be sick for aught I know—"dreadful sick;" but scarce a
particle of pity will selfishness allow me for you, for know that
I too am an invalid. I am growing rich "mighty fast," I can
assure you ; rich alike in purse and brain, by—doing nothing.
Do you not envy me? I wrote you that I could pay my way
this term, study French, draw, and be allowed the use of the
oil-paints. Well, first I dropped oil-painting ; it was too hard
for me. Then I threw aside drawing to save my nerves, and at
last French was found quite too much. Afterwards I wrote a

little, but have of late been obliged to abandon the pen entirely.
What is to become of me I do not know.   Here I am doing
enough to pay my board, and attending to *one* class, by which
I shall earn six dollars; thus wasting, absolutely throwing away
my time.   Miss Sheldon says, if I never pay her she shall not
trouble herself; but she intends, she says, to keep me here as
composition teacher, which will be as profitable as any other
teaching, and for me, rather easier.   I can attend to the compositions when I feel like it, and not at particular hours.   Miss
Cynthia has not returned yet, but Miss U. is very kind to me,
and although I am merely working for my board, I feel it my
duty to stay.

Now pray, do not think, by what I have written, that I
am really ill.   I am only "fidgety"—*i. e.*, *nervous*—as I used
to be in the days of babyhood.   To be sure, I do not see
" kittens " dance; but then sometimes the whole table full of
young ladies seem in tumultuous motion.   I can walk better
than I could last spring; but I can not endure the least mental
excitement, and the slight noise that I now make with my pen
produces a horrid sensation, as if every scratch went deep into
my brain.   I sometimes almost fear that I shall be crazy, but
that is nonsense.

Why do you not send the money for your dress?   I have not
had a new waist to my chalé, for I have not a cent of money on
earth, and Miss C., you know, is gone.   I had my brown bonnet
repaired, and it looks as simple as a cottage-girl's; but *I have
not paid for it*.   My white bonnet I have pulled to pieces and
laid by.   If I had any money to pay for the coloring, I would
take it to the dyer's, and exchange it with you when I come
home.   Miss S. has given me some slips of geranium, but I am
afraid they will die, because I can not get any jars to put them
in.   If they live I will bring them to you.   I could get pretty
flower-pots for eighteen pence apiece.   O poverty, how vexa-
tious thou art! ....

This is a wondrously *loving* letter, I must say.   But never mind; if I do not write the love I shall have the more for you when I get home. Seven weeks! Whew! They will go like a whiz! I would like to have you burn this, for I have something of an idea that it would not look well *saved*.

ELOISE.

TO MRS. BATES.

UTICA FEMALE SEMINARY, June 23, 1841.

VERY DEAR MARIA,—

I have to commence in a very letter-like manner, viz., by asking pardon for delays, at the same time, however, hoping that your attention has been so much engrossed by your pleasant cares, that my silence has been scarcely noticed. How is the little one, and your own dear self, and Mr. B.? I hope the spring brought back more color to his face than it wore when I was with you.

O, you do not know how much I want to see you; and, Maria, forgive me, but I can but wish that you were a schoolgirl again, and here. How can I help thinking of you when I look out on the sun-lighted hills, and the flowing Mohawk; on the waving shrubbery, and the dark, dense foliage of the distant forests? How can I help wishing you were by me, when I visit, with some uncaring friend, the thousand and one romantic spots that cluster in this delightful valley? You do not know how I like the scenery around Utica! The "slop-bowl of the Union" is likely to make itself very attractive to me. I have a most delightful view from my window, and often when my brain has ached with exertion, I have sat for hours and watched the waves of light as they chased each other over the brow of the far-off hills, or sparkled on the waters of the Mohawk.

Shall I tell you what I am about, dear Maria? Well, silencing all the poetic aspirations I may have ever had, and chaining down my thoughts and feelings to—what think you?—stories for children. *You* ought to thank me, for who knows but they may be the means of making your little Edward Francis (by the way, I *do* like the name) "moral, good, and wise." Seriously, Maria, I am engaged in the very thing that you would least of all expect, and for which, if I am any judge of my own talents, I am least qualified. I have a little volume now in the press of Dayton & Saxton (New York), entitled "Charles Linn, or How to Observe the Golden Rule," and am preparing another for the same publishers. They settle with me once in six months, allowing me ten per cent. on the net price of the books. A number of wise heads have together concocted this plan for me, and I think it, on the whole, the best that could be devised. Poetry, unless of a superior kind, is not saleable, and my present duties forbid my attempting any thing of a higher order. I do not study this term—my health is not good enough; but I have charge of a composition class consisting of an hundred and twelve young ladies. Is not that enough?

Now, Marie, I have *I'd* my way through two whole pages, and I suppose you can dispense with any more egotism; but I shall not promise not to talk of *I* any more. Have you seen the new work by Washington Irving, "Memoirs of Margaret Davidson?" I have just finished reading it, and know not which to admire most, the fond mother, the frail, but gifted daughter, or the justly celebrated biographer.

You ask if Miss Sheldon is all that she was. Aye, more. She is all the world to me now—my guide, my director in every thing. She takes a mother's care of me. If I ever succeed, I shall owe it all to her; and if I fail, I shall care more on her account than that of any being living. Four years ago the encouragements now held out to me, the bright hopes of literary distinction which sometimes I almost feel I am entitled to indulge, would have quite bewildered me. But now I have lost my ambition. Were I certain of the most unparelleled success, without any other inducement than fame, I should lay down my pen for ever, or take it up only for my own amuse-

ment.   Necessity at present urges me to this exertion, and
when the necessity is past, then is the work past also.

Excuse this letter, Marie, dear, for I am an invalid to-day;
and to-morrow, if well enough, I must resume my work of story-
telling.   I am anxious now to complete the volume on which
I am engaged before the vacation, which will occur in six
weeks.

Yours devotedly,

EMILY E. CHUBBUCK.

Write me often; please do, for I have but few correspondents
now; and when I am sad and lonely, a letter is, as the French-
man said, "like to von oasis in the desert," or, with the penny-
a-liner, "balm to the wounded spirit."

TO HER SISTER.

UTICA FEMALE SEMINARY, July 6, 1841.

DEAR KIT,—

Not a word do I hear from you, notwithstanding all my
trying and coaxing, and I suppose you would be much obliged
if I would follow your example; but that is out of the question.
I will write if it is only to plague you.   And why shouldn't I?
If you will not tell any news, why, I must make up for the deficiency.   Well, then, first, the July number of the *Lady's
Book* has come, but, terrible to relate! my poor "Old Man"
has not the expected place in its columns.   If I had not the
magnanimity of a—a—oh, dear! I can not think of a suitable
comparison; but I do think there is a wondrous deal of goodness in me not to sting the undiscriminating editors most
scientifically with my powerful pen!   But then I lay it to their
ignorance; what a soothing unction!   Secondly, the July number of the *Knickerbocker* has brought out with flattering haste
my "Where are the Dead?" for it has been in their possession not yet a month; and consider, Kate, the *Knickerbocker* is, perhaps, the most popular periodical in the United
States.   Thirdly, my "Charles Linn" has come—a beautiful

little volume of 112 pages. It will be worth about five shillings. I have no copies now in my possession, but suppose I can get some before long; at least I will try to bring home as many as *two* (you know I am obliged to pay as much for them as any body). I am very much encouraged about the sale of the thing. The publishers could not send me the proof-sheets, so there are some mistakes in the volume. My next book is about half written, but not copied at all. I shall not get it done this term, but mean to bring it home to finish. There is an article of mine in the *Mother's Journal* of this month.

My health is somewhat better than when I last wrote, and I do hope that it will continue. Miss Cynthia, Miss Urania, and ever so many other good folks here are as glad about my success as you will be. Oh, I love to write when people are interested for me; it makes the labor ten times lighter; and I have succeeded beyond what I ever expected, or even hoped. "Yet all this," as Haman said, "avails me nothing," so long as I see my empty wallet lying useless in my trunk, and my bills accumulating. But hope, hope. The publishers settle with me in six months, and next January brings, if not "golden opinions" exactly, silver ones. . . .

Do, if you care one cent for me, write immediately; for I have imagined that all sorts of things had happened to you till I became half crazy, and have then turned the scale by getting desperately angry. Now write, and make up friends speedily, or prepare for the everlasting hatred of

AMY SCRIBBLETON.

In September, Emily was duly installed head of the composition department, with a salary of one hundred and fifty dollars and her board. The duties were arduous, but to her taste, and the salary, with the proceeds of her newly-begun authorship, might justify some enlargement of her plans. The most urgent pressure of self-support taken off, she reverted to her cherished plan of sharing her privileges with her younger sister. She sent for her in October, although compelled by this added draft on her purse both to practice herself and enjoin on her sister the severest economy, and then, after all, throw herself back on the irrepressible trustfulness of youth. After mentioning a variety of little necessary things which she *must* procure for her sister and herself, she felicitates herself that she shall still be in funds by the amount of fifty cents.

In October, she received from her publishers fifty-one dollars for the first edition of " Charles Linn," which consisted of fifteen hundred copies, and was sold in eleven weeks. This was an auspicious opening. She began to feel the inspiring conviction that she had a mine of wealth within her which might be worked with unlimited returns, that " though the body might be dragged about with difficulty," she possessed in her intellect " unfailing resources." But, alas ! that " dragging about" of the body was no joke ; and every author knows how close is the sympathy between mind and body ; how heavily hang the fetters of the suffering flesh on the wings of the soaring spirit. Emily's whole path of authorship was, physically considered, an uphill and toilsome one. With throbbing head and tingling nerves, and an aching heart, she sat down to her papers, and it was only by sending her thoughts away to the humble roof which sheltered those who were dearer to her than life, and reflecting on the sweetness of ministering to their wants, that she could spur her flagging energies to their work. This was her fountain of inspiration ; and hence the deepening night often witnessed, sometimes those gushes of inspiration to which its stillness was so congenial, and sometimes the ineffectual struggles of her spirit with the weariness of the flesh. A single incident will stand for many. As Miss Sheldon was at one time passing near midnight through the halls, a light streaming from Emily's apartment attracted her attention, and, softly opening the door, she stole in upon her vigils. Emily sat in her night-dress, her papers lying outspread before her, grasping with both hands her throbbing temples, and pale as a marble statue. Miss Sheldon went to her, whispered words of sympathy, and gently chided her for robbing her system of its needed repose. Emily's heart was already full, and now the fountain of feeling overflowed in uncontrollable weeping. "Oh, Miss Sheldon," she exclaimed, "I *must* write, I *must* write ; I must do what I can to aid my poor parents."

In November Emily completed "The Great Secret, or How to be Happy." It was published in July following by Dayton & Newman, successors to Dayton & Saxton. She writes thus

TO MRS. BATES.

UTICA, January 11, 1842.

VERY DEAR MARIE,—

When I received your very kind letter dated—tell it not in Gath!—October 3d, I did not think two days would pass ere an answer would be on the way to you. But O the vanity of human expectations, in more instances than one! That very day there came a heavy disappointment. Before I left home I had laid a a plan for having Catharine come here if my "Monthly Rose" should meet with success, when lo! a failure. Now you must not tell of this ; for we would-be authors are rather sore on such points, and care not to have the world witness our mortification. You will recollect that our hopes of the "Monthly Rose" were rather sanguine, and Mr. Hawley wrote from New

York that the publishers were delighted, and intended bringing it out with some eight or ten engravings. Judge, then, of my disappointment when I found it returned upon my hands, fit for nothing but waste paper. It seems that the publishers employ a manuscript reader whose decree upon every work is law, and said critic decided that my humble effort should be laid upon the table, or subjected to the dissecting knife of the poor author! Who would dissect his own bantling? Not I—not I. My heart has "too much of tenderness." Well, after finding fault with the title, the plan, the style of the prose, the poetry *en masse*, and, in short, every thing but three or four stories, which he deigned to compliment, he sent it back to me for revision. Revision! As well pour water into a sieve, and try *to save what is left.* I stubbornly declared against the alteration of a single word—even "Alma Mater" which, said critic thought, sounds pedantic—and folded up my manuscript to await a more auspicious moment for introducing it to the world. I laughed and pretended not to care; but it was a disappointment nevertheless, and a severe one; for what now was to become of Kate? My spirit rose in proportion to the difficulties, and having received fifty-one dollars for the first edition of "Charles Linn," I wrote to her to come, and then sat down to scribble another book. In less than a fortnight I had written about one hundred and fifty pages, besides attending to my duties as composition teacher, and then all at once I failed and poor Kate, instead of studying, was obliged to take care of me. I recovered slowly, but not so as to be able to accomplish much, and so did not finish the work I had commenced *à la Jehu*, until the close of the term. I spent the vacation at home, but was not able to go out while there, and returned to school last Saturday, expecting to do just "nothing at all." Now I have given you a history of the past, and I suspect that you will more readily pardon me for not writing before than for telling this "long yarn" which has filled up so much of my letter. But a word more of these affairs. My new book is entitled "The

Great Secret, or How to be Happy," and I am not at all confident that it will be successful. Kate is with me and will remain until spring. She takes the guitar, flower painting, and drawing.

Now, how is your health, and how have you been since I saw you at Morrisville? Well, and happy? I doubt it not for why should you not be?

> The flowers around the ingle side
>   May not the proudest be,
> But they the richest fragrance shed;
>   And these unfold for thee.

Now do not criticize this doggerel; I am sure I do not call it poetry.

Marie, I thank you and Mr. Bates also for your praise of "Charles Linn," and your encouragement. Think how opportunely they arrived! Just when my New York critic had administered his bitter dose. It does not speak very highly for my ambition—(and, after all, I doubt if I was ever formed for such a rough-and-tumble, soap-bubble chase)—that I was very glad that the partial friends approved, and that the impartial stranger was the critic. I would rather receive the approbation of the few I love, than of the whole world and " England into the bargain." Tell Mr. Bates I thank him for his piece of a letter, and should be glad to see as much in all of yours, and the number of yours "multiplied by twelve." I remain, dear Marie,

Yours truly,   Emily E. Chubbuck.

CHAPTER VI.

LIGHTS AND SHADES.

" Whither is fled the visionary gleam?
Where is it now, the glory and the dream?"

"In the dim and distant ether
The first star is shining through,
And another, and another,
Trembles softly in the blue."

HAVING rallied from the illness mentioned above, during the winter, while the "Great Secret" was awaiting publication, Miss Chubbuck wrote a long poem in the Spencerian stanza, called "Astonroga, or the Maid of the Rock." "Astonroga"* is the Indian name of Little Falls, a place on the Mohawk River, about twenty miles east of Utica, familiar to the traveler as one whose picturesque and even savage scenery was worthy to have been commemorated by the author of the "Pioneers" and "The Last of the Mohicans." In the autumn an excursion had been made by the young ladies of the Seminary to this beautiful and romantic spot. Emily was deeply interested. She wandered thoughtful and almost enchanted amidst those scenes of primeval wildness and grandeur, where the pent up torrent foams and thunders down its precipitous and hardly won channel, while around,

Rocks piled on rocks, confusedly hurled,
Seem fragments of an earlier world;

---

* A note in Emily's MS. explains it as "Rock of Thunder."

and fancy bore her back to the time when only the roar of the torrent, the howling of the wolf, and the yell of the savage broke the awful solitude. The report of an Indian legend connected with a particular locality, drew her off with a single companion, and oblivious of time, she yielded herself to the wild interest of the scene. The time arriving for the return of the party, Emily was missing. Echo alone answered to their calls, and she had to expiate her enthusiasm by a late and solitary return. But if she came back outwardly unattended, the airy beings of the imagination flitted around her. The wild legend lived in her memory, and at length shaped itself into a poem of four cantos, and about one hundred and fifty stanzas. It is executed with much ability. The story, founded on the contact of a self-outlawed son of civilization with the rude children of the forest, is conducted with no little interest and skill; the descriptions are vivid and natural; and the difficult Spencerian stanza is managed with an ease and vigor worthy of a practiced hand—the fruit, in part of her early familiarity with "Childe Harold." A selection from the poem commences on page ninety-seven of "The Olio."

Emily's first use of the poem was, doubtless, to inflict the reading of it judicially on the runaway companions of her autumnal expedition. Her next—to lock it up snugly in her drawer; for she speaks of it in her letter as not designed for publication. But when was an author's resolution against printing not matter of legitimate suspicion? Here, as elsewhere, *c'est le premier pas qui coûte;* and abstinence from publication by one who has got a taste of printer's ink and snuffed the breeze of popular favor, may be counted on just as certainly as the forbearance of the wolf who has whetted his appetite with a single victim from the fold—and no more. "Astonroga" was sent to the *Knickerbocker* (to which she had contributed a few pieces), but that was its present end. It slumbered tranquilly on or under the editor's table, until the dawn of her Fanny Forester reputation drew it forth to grace under that popular soubriquet the pages of which, while unauthenticated by a name, it had been counted unworthy. It is, doubtless, a rightful prerogative of acknowledged literary reputation that its productions find an instant and unquestioning reception, while the unknown candidates for favor must await the slow processes of trial. But this *may* be carried too far, and sterling merit forced to too long a waiting.

In May, "Effie Maurice," a favorite Sunday school book was published by the American Baptist Sunday-School Union in Philadelphia.

TO MRS. BATES.

UTICA FEMALE SEMINARY, May 20, 1842.

MY DEAR MARIE,—

I ought to commence this letter with an apology, but if I should apologize to the end of it, I could not convince either you or myself that I had not been unpardonably negligent in allowing your valued letter of—I dare not mention the date—to remain so long unanswered. The truth is, Marie, writing has become such a matter-of-fact, dollar-and-cent business with me, that I have as complete a horror of the pen as a sweep of his chimney on a holiday. Oh, there is nothing like coining one's brains into gold—no, bread—to make the heart grow sick. But enough of this; only I beg of you just to take notice that though writing, from a pleasure, has become an intolerable bore, *reading has not;* so do not, pray, do not withhold your letters.

Kate went home in March, and I am lonely enough without her; but so is mother, and I must be content. Did you know that our people have removed to Hamilton, and Wallace is boarding with them? I suppose they are only too happy; why can not I join them? This is a delightful place; both of the Misses Sheldon are extremely kind to me, and I love the teachers very much; but *mother is not here.*

My affairs in the business line are not very prosperous—the hard times having put a great check on book-publishing. "The Great Secret" (Newman & Dayton, publishers) went to press some five or six weeks ago, and I am expecting it very soon. Appleton offers to take my "Monthly Rose" under the new name of "Buds and Blossoms;" but the price he would allow is too small to pay for copying, so I prefer keeping it. I have a manuscript of about fifty pages in the hands of a publishing committee in Philadelphia, but its fate I can conjecture only from a consciousness of its deserts.

Last term I perpetrated a sort of a poem called "Astonroga, or, the Maid of the Rock." It consisted of about one hundred and fifty Spencerian stanzas, and was divided into four cantos. It was not intended for publication. Now, I believe you have a full account of my past literary labors; and as you may wish to know what I have done this term (four weeks of it have passed), I will tell you. I have written one letter home, covering almost one page; written three lines of a temperance song, which jingle most beautifully; and written thus much of a letter to you, which latter effort I am sure you will pronounce *comme il faut.* Yet I have not been very idle. My composition class (consisting of all the young ladies in the school), toe the mark admirably, and of course I *claim* the credit. I have read "Tecumseh," a new poem, by George Colton; it has many faults, but is, after all, a fine thing. "Cranmer and his Times," by Miss Lee, I have read with the greatest pleasure; also the life of Aaron Burr, and find it vastly interesting. I have on the table before me an "American Eclectic," with a splendid article from the *Edinburgh Review*, written by Macaulay—a sketch of the life of Warren Hastings. So you see I have "plenty enough" to keep me busy, and as the *hard times* make writing of little or no pecuniary avail, I mean to do what I please. . . .

Your affectionate

E. E. CHUBBUCK.

In July, the "Great Secret" appeared from the press of Dayton & Newman. Both in its plan and execution it is superior to "Charles Linn," and shows that capability of progress which is one of the surest marks of genius. Genius sometimes begins nearly on the level of mediocrity, but it does not end there. New vistas of thought, new depths of spirit life open before it, and the wing which it at first unfolded timidly and feebly, soon mounts with conscious strength to a loftier region. An hundred young gentlemen of England could have written better poems than the "Hours of Idleness," but a few years later the author of "Childe Harold" had not his poetical peer. In the "Great Secret," the author moves with a firmer tread than in the preceding work ; her sketches are drawn with a freer hand, and the story is more artistically developed. The moral tone is pure and noble, and shows that while writing for a livelihood, she had at heart the interests of virtue and religion.

She performed mean time, with equal zeal and assiduity, her duties as teacher. She was not only skillful in imparting instruction, but, apart from lessons, had great power over her pupils. Though unobtrusive and retiring, she was a shrewd and accurate judge of character—quick to discern in her pupils the latent germs of promise, and assiduous and skillful in their development. Hence many were indebted to her for first awaking them to the consciousness, and then aiding in the direction of their powers. In judging her pupils she was at once discriminating and kind ; quick to discern their faults; still more prompt to recognize their virtues. Strong as were her personal likes and dislikes—and such belong to a temperament like hers—she rarely allowed herself in a prejudice which prevented her from doing complete justice to all.

It was Miss Sheldon's custom to hold a weekly meeting of the teachers for the purpose of receiving reports regarding their respective pupils, as the basis of any needful action. Emily sat at these meetings a timid but deeply interested listener, until her own report was called for. She would then characterize all of whom she had occasion to speak with such clearness and discrimination that her judgment commanded implicit deference, and all felt that her powers of imaginative delineation were fully equaled by those of the practical observer. The Misses Sheldon came to rely on Miss Chubbuck more and more, both in the instruction and discipline of the school. She could not be anywhere without being a power. A character at once positive and gentle, at once spirited and amiable, at once poetic and practical, at once energetic and even tenderly feminine, made a combination, not perhaps very unusual, but exhibited in her certainly in a very rare degree.

A change, however, was approaching of much importance to the institution, and of deep interest to Emily. The happy household of which she was a member was about to be invaded by that Foe that is the more formidable as he finds a sure coöperator within the citadel. The accomplished head of the institution was to pass from the post of the principal of a flourishing female school, to that of assistant principal of

a more celebrated—if not more interesting—institution. Miss Urania Sheldon was about to become the
wife of Rev. Dr. Nott, the venerable president of
Union College. Emily could not but anticipate the removal with deep regret. One of her most affectionate
friends, and judicious and faithful counselors was about
to be withdrawn from her, and she half trembled as to
what might be the consequences to her own connection
with the Seminary in the changes which would ensue, especially as her "health," she says, "is becoming a source
of so much trouble that she thinks of parting with it
entirely." Her fears were groundless. Her position was
too important for the trustees to wish to disturb it,
and in Miss Cynthia Sheldon, who remained as the man-
ager of the school, she had a friend whose sterling worth,
whose unwearied and efficient goodness every year of
Emily's life only more fully developed.

In August the contemplated marriage took place, and
Miss Sheldon took the position which she has since so
gracefully adorned as the wife of Dr. Nott. Miss Chubbuck spent the summer vacation with her parents in
Hamilton, and while there performed an act which
showed her readiness, in meeting the claims of duty,
to go to the utmost limit warranted by prudence.
She purchased for her parents the house and garden
occupied by them in the village for four hundred dollars, the debt to be discharged in four annual pay-
ments. It was an humble home; but as the precious
fruit of a daughter's love, it was to them more than a
palace; and small as seems the sum to the eye of wide-
grasping wealth, who shall say that the favor of Him who
blessed the widow's mite did not rest upon the offering?
She subsequently increased her indebtedness by nearly

one-half of the original sum, in repairing and enlarging the premises. Emily felt that she was taking a step of some hazard, and calculating largely on the "coinable" capacities of her brain; but filial love could not take counsel of cold-blooded prudence in such a case; and having indulged in about the only kind of luxury in which she ever allowed herself, and furnished her aged parents with a *home*, she went back to Utica with fresh incentives to intellectual toil.

Near the close of the previous term the establishment of a lady's monthly magazine, with Miss Chubbuck for its editor, had been agitated in the Seminary, though with a diversity of opinion as to its success. Some believed that it might at once stimulate and draw forth the talent of the young ladies, and prove a source of pecuniary profit. Miss Sheldon had discouraged it, judging correctly of the numerous and inevitable difficulties of such an enterprise. Emily, though not sanguine, inclined to the more favorable judgment, and "Young America" prevailed. The magazine was now established, with Emily duly installed as its editor, and accomplished probably all that its judicious friends could anticipate. While it drew forth much talent from the school, Miss Chubbuck, of course, under every variety of disguise, figured largely in its columns. Now a Greek "maiden"—Kore—now a Latin "nobody"—Nemo—now a reluctantly accepted country contributor—now in all the dignity of the editorial "we," she played off both her heavier and lighter artillery on the public. Essays, stories, songs, and sonnets, now grave, now gay, were thrown off from her facile and fertile pen. The magazine ran gracefully through its single year of existence, and then quietly resigned its breath, having delighted its friends, edified,

it is to be hoped, the public, contained much sound instruction, sparkled with many bright gems of genius,
and contributed much to the reputation, and not a cent
probably to the purse of the editor.   But the dramatic
genius of Fanny Forester flashes through its vivacious
sketches.

In November "Allen Lucas, or The Self-made Man,"
was published by Messrs. Bennet, Backus & Hawley, of
Utica.   This, like the preceding, a story for children, is
somewhat more elaborate in plan and execution than
either of them.   The descriptive power is greater ; it
has more depth of coloring, more power in delineating
character.   It shows her advancing with rapid though
unconscious step toward the point where she was to
dazzle and delight the public with those sketches which,
with their feminine grace and depth of sentiment, should
at once satisfy the mind and captivate the fancy.   Like
the others, also, "Allen Lucas," though not formally religious, was pervaded by the pure morality of the Gospel.   In February following, "John Frink" was published by the American Baptist Sunday School Union.

Regarded simply as literary efforts, the success of
Emily's small and unpretending books had greatly surpassed her humble expectations.   Though scarcely of a
character to attract the notice of the public, yet, within
the limited circle which they would naturally reach, they
were warmly and most flatteringly appreciated.   The
gifted young lady of Miss Sheldon's school was becoming known to many as a writer of rare and versatile capacity, who might yet contribute a star to the galaxy of
female authorship.   But though ample in their harvest
of praise, her books brought but slight returns of that
commodity which had given the chief impulse to her

pen : she was getting *not* rich with great rapidity. Their first flattering reception and rapid sale had induced a reasonable hope of handsome pecuniary returns. She had struck a vein which it required no dazzled and credulous vision to behold yielding a more than sufficient income for her more pressing wants. Prompted by this hope she had sent for her sister to the Seminary, and subsequently made the large purchase of a dwelling for her parents. From a variety of causes her expectations were not realized. Partly from general convulsions in the business of the country, partly from the remissness of her publishers, her books yielded but a meager profit, and some of them were for a considerable time entirely out of print. We need not enter minutely into these perplexing matters. The following letters to Mrs. Nott and to her sister, will show the nature of the difficulties with which she struggled, and shed other side lights on this stage of her history :—

TO MRS. NOTT.

UTICA, October 10, 1842.

DEAR MISS URANIA,—

I have just received your kind note by Dr. James, and although I wrote you last evening, find there are a few questions which I neglected to answer.

Mr. Hawley seemed to hesitate about the propriety of trying to get the copyright out of D. & N.'s hands, and I shall not have an opportunity to see him again before Mr. S. goes. I heartily wish somebody else had it, but do not know who. It would make a great deal of trouble, and involve some risk, for me to hold the copyright; and I should think it would be difficult, now that the chance of the first edition is lost, to dispose of it to any bookseller.

Dayton & Newman took the MSS., secured a copyright, and

agreed to pay me ten per cent. on all that were sold. The percentage is not increased for a new edition, and they are under no obligation to get out a new one at all unless they choose. The first edition of "Charles Linn" was only 1500 copies, and my receipts $51. I do not know how large an edition of "Life as It Is"* they have issued, but the volume being larger than the other, if the edition is equally large, I shall receive about $70. Mr. H. says these sell well, but he does not know how many are sold, and, of course, he does not know how many remain on hand : the first is out of print. The reason of their acting so strangely about the business ever since last fall I can not guess. I wish I had time to write something purposely for the district-school library ; but I am afraid I shall not.

Many thanks to you and your kind friends for the interest you take in the affairs of a simple girl, without money, without influence, and almost without friends.

I rejoice to find that you do not dislike the Miscellany. It is just the kind of labor that suits me, and gains a great many compliments ; yet I am by no means sanguine concerning its success. The number of subscribers is constantly increasing ; yet they come one by one, and it seems to me rather slow work. Only think of this child's being compared with Miss Sedgwick and Miss Mitford ! Dew-drops are diamonds, and pinchbeck may well be taken for gold. I wish—but no, I will take what I can get thankfully, though the best compliment I ever received was my father's sitting up till midnight to finish "Life as It Is." I have a magazine, containing a notice of this last, which I will send you.

I am very much ashamed of this careless note, but I have written to-day till my shoulder aches and my hand cramps. As for good pens, you know *Lydia*† *has gone.* Please write after Dr. Potter has seen the books, and advise me what to do about

---

* The same as the "Great Secret."

† Miss Lillybridge, then a pupil in the Seminary, and subsequently one of the companions of her voyage to India.

them; for I do not think —— is altogether disinterested (I may be wrong there), and you well know how little I am qualified to judge. Yours truly, EMILY.

TO MRS. NOTT.

UTICA FEMALE SEMINARY, October, 1842.

MY DEAR M——

There it is again! I can not write to "Miss Sheldon," and I am sure such a bashful body as I could not be expected to address so dignified a personage as Mrs. Nott. So what shall I do? I am very lonely just now, and feel inclined to be somewhat sentimental; for I have been up the hall, and found a certain corner room, looking—not desolate—O no, it is wondrous cozy and comfortable—but as though it *ought* to be desolate. Yet I will spare you all the things I *could* say, and turn to some other subject.. F—— and I are exceedingly quiet and happy together, and as for the rest of the house, things seem to go about right; at least when I put my head out into the hall I see nothing to the contrary. One new boarder has come to-day, and I hope the number will increase. I find the much dreaded task of giving out composition subjects not so bad after all, though I should not like a spectator any better than formerly.

I am very grateful for the interest you took in my affairs when in New York, and should of course be but too ready to avail myself of any thing that Dr. Potter was willing to do in my behalf. I think D. & N. act very strangely; for Mr. H. says they told him that the second edition of "Charles Linn" was in press several weeks ago. It has been out of print for a long time, and Mr. H. says he has had a great many calls for it. I was obliged to take the copy belonging to the library to send to you, for I could get no other. It can be replaced if the second edition ever appears. I have marred both books by corrections; but that is the fault of the most careless of all proof-readers. The publishers own the copy-right, and if it

4*

could be obtained I do not think it would pay for the trouble. Placing the books in the district-school library might, by creating a demand for them, induce the publishers to bring out a new edition; but I suspect that they have about had their day, and am content to let them pass. There is but one thing that would induce me ever to see another line of mine in print, and that is, the necessity which is the mother not only of invention, but of many follies. If I were in other circumstances I should undoubtedly be a scribbler, but not a professed one.

I have not told you what (perhaps unwise) thing I did during vacation. My poor old father and mother have had no home for about five years, and they have felt their lack of one severely. I hesitated, measured my own resources, that is, my head and hands, and made a very humble purchase for which I am allowed four years to pay. I am sure you would not think the act unwarranted if you could see how happy it made them; and if I fail to pay, it is but to fail. Kate is at home, quite well and happy.

I have not heard from Philadelphia since I wrote that I could not prepare that short Sunday-school series. I suspect that they can not publish for lack of funds. As soon as I get time I mean to commence a new book; but I hardly know whether to write one of the same character as the others, or something different; for I do not know how it could be published. However, I shall not waste much time in deciding.

I know this is a very tiresome sheet, and brimfull of selfishness; but you will know how to pass that over, for you have looked away into the writer's heart and will expect the fruit to resemble the tree.

F. sits studying close by; somebody is thumping Miss F.'s piano over our head tremendously; M. B. is passing the door—there! the bell rings—study-hour is over; there is a general increase of sound in the house, and I know by the voices in the hall that many a door has been flung open within the last half minute. How I wish—but no, there is no use in wishing! I will go to bed and dream (I have few day-dreams now) of pleasant things, and wake in the morning and see every thing pleasant; for this *is* a happy world in spite of its perplexities. Fine dreams to you too, both waking and sleeping; yet now and then intermingling may there come a little (though it were the least in the world) thought of

Your truly affectionate   EMILY.

TO MRS. NOTT.

UTICA, November, 1842.

MY DEAR MRS. NOTT,—

It is a splendid morning, and if I had not my bed to make and my floor to sweep, and all this sea of papers which escaped from my portfolio last night when I was so sleepy, to pick up, I should undoubtedly write some poetry about the golden clouds hovering above the Deerfield hills, and the broad sheets of silver—(*i. e.*, thinly scattered snow just a little bit tipped with sun-light)—now and then peering out through the openings. But beds and floors are very arbitrary things, and never would think of stopping getting tumbled or dirty, though the poetical world should suffer ever so much thereby.

I should have written you before about Mr. Hawley's negotiations in New York, but I have been expecting every day that Miss Cynthia would write and tell you all about it. Dayton & Newman will let me have the copy-right of the two books for a hundred dollars, fifty dollars apiece. Now as I could have had it for a mere trifle a year ago when the manuscript was in my own hands, and as they have had the advantage of a whole edition, of course making the right less valuable, I do not feel inclined to accept the offer. Besides, it would not be a very pleasant thing, even if I were sure of making money by it, to hold the copy-right myself, and have the books printed; and disposing of it otherwise is in the present case out of the question. They say that they can sell it for more than fifty dollars to publishers in New York. So, assuming that I could dispose of it for ten or twenty dollars more, it would be of little use, as I should cut myself off from the percentage which I am now to receive. They promise to republish "Charles Linn" before January; but I shall not depend much upon any profit from either of the books.

According to your suggestions I have commenced a new book designed exclusively for district schools, but I have written as yet only about a dozen pages. My time seems completely occupied, and though I have prepared and laid aside copy enough for two numbers of the Miscellany, yet there are little hinderances constantly arising to prevent me from accomplishing any thing. However, I shall do what I can, and hope to finish something by the middle of next term.

The very flattering compliments which I received from Schenectady a few days ago encouraged me not a little. You can not imagine how they lightened my heavy foot, and straightened my bent shoulders. I need not say, my dear Mrs. Nott, how grateful I feel for all the interest you take in my little affairs, for you must know it all, must know that I could not feel otherwise. And now—and now for a little more motherly counsel—but I have no room, and "there is time enough yet."

Yours truly,

EMILY.

TO HER SISTER.

UTICA, Monday morning, November, 1843.

DEAR KITTY,—

A letter which I supposed had reached you more than a week ago has just returned on my hands, and I suppose, therefore, you must by this time be wanting to hear from me. . .

Tell father there is but little hope of getting any money just now toward my payment on the place, but he must not be discouraged. I expect a windfall of some sort or other, though I can not for the life of me tell what, or where it is to come from.

" The darkest day,
(Live till to-morrow), will have passed away!"

I have received the first proof-sheets of " Allen Lucas :" they are doing it handsomely, and intend to have it out by Christmas. I wish I could strike upon some plan for money-making to help us out of this difficulty ; but *n' importe*, " every dog *must* have his day," and ours will come by-and-by. I hope you are well, and behaving well. I do not know, Kitty, what has got into me lately. I dream of home every night, and awake in the morning—and *so* disappointed and lonely. But every thing is pleasant here, and we are all like sisters to each other—we teachers, I mean. It *does* seem too bad, though, that poor I must always be away. There are so few of us, too—how comfortable and happy a few hundreds would make us !—the hundreds which some are spending so carelessly. Write me every thing, *do !*

Your homesick sister,

EMILY.

UTICA FEMALE SEMINARY, January 4, 1843.

MY DEAR MRS. NOTT,—

The "blind harper" has been entertaining us this evening, and those simple airs are of all things the "open sesame" to the heart. While listening I have been back, not many years, it is true, but in the review singularly long, over the whole ground of my past life, visited every nook, sat down awhile by every friend, and acted over again what distance has robbed of almost all its bitterness.

Tuesday, January 7. I was interrupted on Saturday evening ; so you are relieved of the "association of ideas" which brought me up to the time of my first landing in Utica, not quite "friendless and homeless," but certainly very forlorn. Well, you can judge from that of whom I last thought, but not how pleasant were those thoughts ; for even you can not comprehend all you have done for me, nor how unwilling I should be to be able to say, "I owe her nothing." But let that pass ; however much the subject may be in my thoughts, I know you will not care to hear it talked of, so I will turn to other topics.

The school this term is very pleasant. There is no one to head mischief among the young ladies, so they are all remarkably correct. True, we feel a lack of something; but that can not be helped, and I believe in all cases the true philosophy is to " take it easy."

And now for myself;—egotism is pardonable in a letter. I am doing just nothing this term, and am as busy about it as though I was servant-general to the whole world. You know I never had much time to read; I have taken the matter in hand now, and hope I shall make something of that, if nothing else. I have not written a line of poetry this term; for, saith the poet Sands,

> "Thou who with the eagle's wing,
> Being a goose, wouldst fly, dream not of such a thing;"

a caution worth observing. My district school book stands right where I left it last term, and I have not the courage to touch it. I can not write as I could before people expected me to succeed; and when I now take up the pen I feel the same embarrassment that I do before company. I do not *say* this, for people would consider it affectation; but I feel it none the less, while making other excuses. You may tell me that it is foolish to feel so about those simple little books that nobody but children reads, and sometimes I try to laugh myself out of it in the same way. But I care more for my small circle of friends than for a hundred critics, and they, if nobody else, read them. I heartily wish I had never touched a pen but to write letters; may be then I should have been more expert in this line. Mary comes to say that a man wishes to see me in the hall. It is the printer after copy, no doubt; so my letter must have another beginning.

Saturday morning. Mr. and Mrs. Sheldon are going this morning, and I have concluded to send this by them, if you will excuse its age. I heard from home yesterday; I am afraid my poor old father is failing, and will be before long confined entirely to the house. The rest of the family are in usual health. . . . .

The little Sabbath school book that I sent to Philadelphia last summer is in print. There are sixty pages, for which they have paid me thirty dollars. Do please write to me at your first leisure, and believe me, with the greatest affection and respect,

Yours truly,

EMILY E. CHUBBUCK.

The allusion in the following letter is to Mr. William Miller, formerly of Hampton, Washington county, the celebrated lecturer on the millennium, and originator of the "heresy," known as "Millerism." The sensation which he produced will be remembered by many. Had Miss Chubbuck heard more of his lectures, her sound judgment must have confirmed her estimate of the visionary character of his views.

TO HER SISTER.

UTICA, January 13, 1843.

DEAR KIT,—

The Miscellany is very late this month, but I expect it out to-morrow. Have not yet heard from New York. There is an article on neurology in the *Democratic Review* which I wish Wallace to read. I begin to believe in it; it is no more mysterious than our breathing and thinking. All is mystery, and if we believe in nothing which we can not comprehend, we may as well go back to the scholastic philosophy, or disbelieve the existence of matter. Dr. and Mrs. Nott were here when I came back, and we had a delightful visit. Did Wallace write the notice of Dr. N.'s lecture in the *Whig?* It was capital.

I understand that Mr. Miller (he left town yesterday morning) has created quite a sensation in the city. One merchant has dismissed his clerks, and shut up his shop. We do not know much about it in the Seminary, but I learn that some families are nearly crazy. I went to hear him once, and must own that I was a good deal disappointed. He was more visionary than I expected to find him. However, they *say* that his lectures are characterized by sound reasoning and good common sense, and that positions in which I thought him visionary he had previously established. He is evidently sincere and very pious, and—deluded or not—I would rather be in his place than in that of those who sneer at him. I do not wonder that wicked men do it, but I think it awful in ministers.

My plants thrive beautifully. I have commenced an article, "Our Village," for Wallace, but do not know that I can finish it; I get so little time. Can't write his story, "no how." Don't expect ever to get my book done.

Monday morning. Have been sick, but am a good deal better. I am pretty much discouraged about earning any thing, but don't care much. What is the use of money when one has enough to eat, drink, and wear, as I am sure I have? The commercial article in the *Democratic Review* predicts a change of times in the spring—hope it will be verified. Write, *do*, immemediately to

Your very loving sister,

EMILY.

TO MRS. NOTT.

UTICA, November, 1843.

DEAR MRS. NOTT,—

The girls are about starting, so I have only time to say, How do you do? and good-bye. We closed up last night, and to-day are feeling exceedingly free. To-morrow I leave for home. Delightful thing—a stage-coach ride in this mud! "The Self-Made Man" made his appearance yesterday, and I inclose you a copy. You must wink as you read, but I shall not trouble myself about that; you have seen the like a time or two before, and would not undertake to read with your eyes open. I should feel complimented by some of the little newspaper puffs if I did not happen to know that the writers of them could not have read the book. So if you see them, estimate them at their proper worth. Please remember me to the doctor, if he would recollect me, and believe me,

Yours ever and truly,

EMILY.

Miss Sheldon's marriage had made no change in Miss Chubbuck's relations to the Seminary. Her sister, Miss Cynthia, whose energy of character was equaled only by her benevolence, remained its executive and financial head, hiring the teachers and superintending the departments. From the first she had been Emily's zealous and efficient friend, and she continued those offices of affection which, never intermitted, were repaid by Emily with answering gratitude and love. During about two years after Miss Sheldon's marriage, the post of literary principal was held by Mr. and Mrs. James Nichols, Mrs. Nichols having, previously to her marriage, been a valuable associate teacher in the school. Mrs. Nichols' health requiring their withdrawal, in February, 1844, Miss Jane Kelly was appointed to this office. She was seized, however, with a violent illness, and new duties were now devolved upon Emily. Her literary avocations were suspended, and besides taking some extra classes, she " tried her hand at government and peace-making." On Miss Kelly's recovery, she gladly laid down her honors, and returned to her manuscripts. But her manuscripts, it is seen by the above letters, had but illy requited her toil, and her first hopes had been sadly dashed. Difficulties crowded upon her. The debts which she had incurred hung upon her as a heavy weight ; and the expedients to which the desperate state of her affairs drove her proved mostly failures.   Her articles sent to different journals were returned, or thrown silently, and probably unread, under the editor's table.   Nothing but the irrepressible buoyancy of a most elastic nature prevented her heart from utterly sinking within her, and it needed all the encouragements of sympathizing friendship, and all the stimulus of necessity to prevent her from renouncing for ever the baffling pursuits of authorship.   Her hour, however, was coming, and, as a prelude, she at this time was engaged as a contributor to the *Columbian Magazine*, then under the editorial care of John Inman, at four dollars per page. Yet this was little, and other means were imperatively demanded to meet her pressing wants.

In April she made a trip to New York with Miss Anna Maria Anable, with whom she had been gradually forming a closer intimacy.   The origin of their friendship was characteristic of her loving nature.   Of a larger worldly experience, and more at home in general society, Miss Anable had regarded indeed with interest her character and genius, but scarcely thought of opening to her the inner sanctuary of her affections.   As they chanced, one day, to be sitting together on the sofa, and the conversation drifted toward some matters of personal interest, Emily, turning her dark eye upon her friend, said half-playfully, half-beseechingly : "I wish you would let me love you."   The words struck a responsive chord in the heart of her young companion.   She *did* let her love her, and drew her into an embrace which, in spite of time and distance, grew closer and closer through all the checkered and eventful future.   They became fast friends, with likeness enough to give sympathy, with diversity enough give zest to their companionship. Highly gifted, yet not addicted to authorship herself, Miss Anable, her name curtailed of—all but—its *fair* proportions, was obliged, as " Cousin 'Bel," to esquire her friend's literary knight-errantry. They now went together to New York. It was Miss Chubbuck's first visit to the metropolis ; all about her was stamped with novelty, and the fresh glow of youth and conscious genius and half dawning fame, which shed its delicious light upon her heart, invested the scenes of the great city with a magic charm.

Whether Emily really saw in Broadway the "balza-rines" and " neapolitans" which figure in the next scene of our narrative we need not curiously inquire, since a young lady author's playful epistle is no more than the poems of Homer, to be held to the rigorous verities of history. Be that as it may, this scene forcibly re-minds us on how slender and casual a thread may hang the weightiest destinies—with how unconscious and un-divining a step we may enter a path which shall direct the whole future of our lives. A playful word often issues in serious earnest ; the comedy of to-day deepens into the tragedy of to-morrow ; a thread, light as a spider's web, carried across a chasm, initiates the pro-cess which will span it with a bridge that shall abide the shock of centuries.

CHAPTER VII.

"FANNY FORESTER."

"Her every tone is music's own,
    Like those of morning birds;
And something more than melody
    Dwells ever in her words.
The coinage of her heart are they;
    And from her lips each flows,
As one may see the burdened bee,
    Forth issuing from the rose."

THE *Evening Mirror* was at this time flourishing in New York, under the editorial conduct of Messrs. Geo. P. Morris and N. P. Willis. In June, after her return, while the splendors of the metropolis were still fresh in her fancy, with her own timid figure stealing along Broadway beside that of her more world-experienced friend, Emily, in an hour of frolic sportiveness, addressed a letter, half-playful, half-serious, to these gentlemen, intimating her great desire to become the possessor of one of those balzarines and neapolitans which the shops of Broadway paraded in tempting luxuriousness, and delicately hinting that she would like to make the columns of the *Mirror* the means of procuring the funds which the shopkeepers were impertinent enough to ask in exchange for their commodities. The letter purported to come from a country maiden making a brief sojourn in the city, and bore the suggestive signature of Fanny

Forester. Its elegant playfulness attracted the attention of the editors of the *Mirror*. "The dip of their
divining rod," as Mr. Willis felicitously expressed it,
"detected the neighborhood of genius." They saw under
its light and sportive garb indications of a vigor and
force of intellect that might raise their possessor to a
high place in the walks of literature. They were indeed
a little mystified by the letter, and at a loss to determine
whether the writer was really the naïve and unsophis-
ticated child of nature that she gave herself out for,
wantoning in the creations of a genius that was just re-
vealing itself to her virgin consciousness, or a veteran
and wily spinster, a practiced magazinist, who had
trained herself to that last perfection of art which shows
as perfect artlessness. The correspondence forms so important a turning-point in Emily's career, and so strikingly illustrates her peculiar talents, that although familiar
to many readers, I shall make no apology for inserting it
here, along with Mr. Willis' graceful introduction :

New Mirror, June 8, 1844.

"We are fortunate in a troop of admirable contributors, who
write for love, not money—love being the only commodity in
which we can freely acknowledge ourselves rich. We receive,
however, all manner of tempting propositions from those who
wish to write for the other thing—money—and it pains us
grievously to say, 'No;' though, truth to say, love gets for us
as good things as money could buy—our readers will cheerfully
agree. But yesterday, on opening at the office a most dainty
epistle, and reading it fairly through, we confess our pocket
stirred within us! More at first than afterward—for, upon reflection, we became doubtful whether the writer were not old
and 'blue,' it was so exceedingly well done. We have half a

suspicion now that it is some **sharp old maid in** spectacles— some regular contributor to Godey and Graham, who has tried to inveigle us through our weak point—possibly some varlet of a man scribbler—but no; it is undeniably feminine. Let us show you the letter—the latter part of it at least, as it opens too honiedly for print :—"

You know the shops in Broadway are **very** tempting this spring. *Such* beautiful things! Well, you know (no, you don't know that, but you can guess) what a delightful thing it would be to appear in one of those charming, head-adorning complexion-softening, hard-feature-subduing neapolitans; with a little gossamer vail dropping daintily on the shoulder of one of those exquisite *balzarines*, to be seen any day at Stewart's and elsewhere. Well, you know, (this you *must* know,) that shopkeepers have the impertinence to demand a trifling exchange for these things even of a lady; and also that some people have a remarkably small purse, and a remarkably small portion of the yellow "root" in that. And now, to bring the matter home, *I* am one of that class. I have the most beautiful little purse in the world, but it is only kept for show; I even find myself under the necessity of counterfeiting—that is, filling the void with tissue paper in lieu of bank notes, preparatory to a shopping expedition.

Well, now to the point. As Bel and I snuggled down on the sofa this morning to read the *New Mirror* (by the way, Cousin Bel is never obliged to put tissue paper in her purse), it struck us that you would be a friend in need, and give good counsel in this emergency. Bel, however, insisted on my not telling what I wanted the money for. She even thought that I had better intimate orphanage, extreme suffering from the bursting of some speculative bubble, illness, etc., etc.; but did not I know you better? Have I **read** the *New Mirror* so much (to say nothing of the graceful things coined "under a bridge," and a thousand other pages flung from the inner heart), and not learned who has an eye for every thing pretty? Not so stupid, Cousin Bel; no, no!

However, this is not quite the point, after all; but here it is. I have a pen—not a gold one, I don't think I could write with that, but a nice, little, feather-tipped pen, that rests in the curve of my finger as contentedly as in its former pillow of down. (Shocking! how that line did run down hill! and this almost as crooked! dear me!) Then I have little messengers racing "like mad" through the galleries of my head; spinning long yarns, and wearing fabrics rich and soft as the balzarine which I so much covet, until I shut my eyes and stop my ears and whisk away, with the 'wonderful lamp' safely hidden in my own brown braids. Then I have Dr. Johnson's Dictionary—capital London edition, etc., etc.; and after I use up all the words in that, I will supply myself with Webster's wondrous quarto, appendix and all. Thus prepared, think you not I should be able to put something in the shops of the literary caterers? something that, for once in my life would give me a real errand into Broadway? May be you of the *New Mirror* PAY for acceptable articles—may be not. *Comprenez-vous?*

O I *do* hope that beautiful balzarine like Bel's will not be gone before another Saturday! You will not forget to answer me in the next *Mirror*; but pray, my dear Editor, let it be done very cautiously, for Bel would pout all day if she should know what I have written. Till Saturday,

Your anxiously-waiting friend,
FANNY FORESTER.

"Well, we give in! On *condition* that you are under twenty-five, and that you will wear a rose (recognizably) in your bodice the first time you appear in Broadway with the hat and balzarine, we will pay the bills. Write us thereafter a sketch of Bel and yourself, as cleverly done as this letter, and you may 'snuggle down' on the sofa, and consider us paid, and the public charmed with you."

Miss " Forester's" reply to this appeared in the *New Mirror* of June 29th, prefaced by the editor as follows : "Our readers will remember in the *Mirror* of two weeks ago, a very clever letter, written to us by an anonymous lady who wished to conjure a new bonnet and dress out of her inkstand. The inveiglement upon ourselves (to induce us to be her banker) was so adroit and fanciful, that we suspected the writer of being no novice at rhetorical trap—one indeed, of the numerous sisterhood who scatter their burdensome ammunition of contrivance and resource upon periodical literature. We 'gave in,' however—walking willingly into the lady's noose, on condition that she should wear a rose recognizably in Broadway the day she first sported the balzarine and neapolitan, and afterward send us a sketch of herself and her cousin. The 'sketch' we have received, and shall give it next week, and when we have seen the rose, we shall not hesitate to acknowledge the debt. . . . In the following parts of her letter which accompanied the sketch, the reader will see that the authoress feels (or feigns marvelously well) some resentment at our suspicions as to her age and quality."

REPLY

To the Speculations of the Mirror as to who and what the Author might be.

. . . Have you never heard, my de—(pardon—I fear it is a habit of mine to write too 'honiedly')—but have you not heard that " suspicion is a heavy armor, which, with its own weight, impedes more than it protects?" Suspicion is most assuredly a beggarly virtue. It may, now and then, prevent your being " taken in," but it nips you in the costs most unmercifully. Oh ! sharpsightedness is the most extravagantly *dear* *whistle* which poor humans ever purchased! That you should suspect *me*, too, when I was opening my heart away down to the core! How *could* you? "Inveigle!" No inveigling about it! I wanted a bonnet and dress, and said so, frankly and honestly. Moreover, I never wrote a line for Graham in my life—no! nor for Godey either. As for *couleur des bas*, your keen-eyed hawk pounced on less than a phantom *there*. From the day that I stood two mortal hours with my fingers poked into my eyes, and a fool's-cap on my head, because I persisted in spelling "b-a-g, baker," to the notable morning of christening my cousin by her profession,* I have been voted innocent of all leaning toward the hue celestial. Indeed, it is more than suspected by my friends (cousin Bel excepted) that I affect dame Nature's carpet, rather than her canopy.

May be I am "some varlet of a man scribbler"—Oh! you are *such* a Yankee at guessing!

Old! ah, that is the unkindest cut of all! You an editor, and the son of an editor, and not know that "old maids" are a class extinct at the present day, save in the sewing societies, etc., of some western village, subject only to the exploring expeditions of the indefatigable "Mary Clavers!" Have you never heard of five-and-twenty's being a *turning point*, and ken ye not its meaning? Why, *faire maydens* then reverse the hour-glass of old gray-beard; and, one by one, drop back the golden sands that he has scattered, till, in five years, they are twenty again. Of course, then, I *must* be "under twenty-five;" but as a punishment for your lack of gallantry, you shall not know whether the sands are dropping in or out of my glass. One thing, however, is indisputable; I am not "sharp"—my face has not a single *sharp* feature, nor my temper (it is I, you know, that say it) a *sharp* corner, nor my voice a *sharp* tone. So much in self-justification, and now to the little package which you hold in the other hand.

* The cousin's name was spelled in the first letter *Belle*, and corrected by the editor.

I send my sketch in advance, because I am afraid cousin Bel and I might not interest you and the public so much as we do ourselves; and then how are we to "consider you paid?" In truth I can not write *clever* things. Bel might, but she never tries. Sometimes she plans for me; but, somehow, I never find the right words for her thoughts. They come into my head like fixed up visitors, and play "tea-party" with their baby neighbors, until I am almost as much puzzled by their strange performances as the old woman of the nursery rhyme, who was obliged to call on her "little dog at home" to establish her identity. No, no! I can not write *clever* things; and particularly on the subject to which I am restricted; but if it is the true sketch that you would have for the sake of the information, why here now it is. You will perceive that I have been very particular to tell you all.

Pray, do you allow us *carte blanche* as far as the hat and dress are concerned? You had better not; for Bel never limits herself. How soon may we have them? The summer is advancing rapidly, and my old muslin and straw are unco shabby.　　　　Yours, with all *due* affection,

FANNY FORESTER.

The next number of the *Mirror* contained the required sketch, which, under the guise of a substitute for it, was in fact a most spirited and dramatic delineation of the assumed character and relation of the two cousins. The name she had thus sportively assumed clung to her, and thanks to the generous praises of her new friends, and her own merits, Fanny Forester at once arose on the literary horizon a star of unwonted brilliancy. Authenticated by the journal which led all others in the walks of strictly elegant literature, she found for every production of her pen a listening and admiring public. To the quick appreciation and timely aid of Mr.

Willis (through whom the correspondence was mainly
conducted) she felt ever under the deepest obligation,
and the sentiment of gratitude and literary admiration
naturally blended itself with a warm personal friendship.
He soon succeeded in unmasking the pretended aspirant
after balzarines and neapolitans, and finding behind the
light laughing face a warm woman's heart, a frail physical organization, a nature quivering with the quick susceptibilities of genius, and all struggling under a heavy
outward pressure, he devoted himself to the cultivation
of her talents and fame with a generous ardor, which she
repaid with a profound sense of indebtedness as to the
" foster-father" of her intellect. Their intercourse was
indeed almost wholly impersonal. They never met except on the occasion, nearly a year later, of Emily's passing a few days in Brooklyn on her return from Philadelphia. Otherwise their sole communication was by letter
from the beginning of their friendship to its close.

How potent as well as timely was the aid of her new
friends the reader will readily imagine. General Morris,
already a veteran in literary journalism, was one of the
most popular song-writers in the country. To Mr.
Willis we do but simple justice in saying that, beyond
most writers of our country, he adorns whatever he
touches ; that without claiming to fathom the depths of
philosophy, or yielding often to the tide of passion, he
possesses a certain subtle alchemy of genius, resting on
a basis of acute and just observation, which transmutes
the most commonplace topic, and invests it with grace
and beauty. His keen vision detects its most hidden essence and most curious analogies, and his mastery of language enables him to embody them in words as daintily
delicious, as magically beautiful, as tersely vigorous as

the thought which they portray. And this subtle play
of fancy, this sorcery of expression, which condenses into
a word the essence of a paragraph, characterizes his familiar letters, thrown off amidst the hurry and press of
business, no less than his more elaborate productions, as
will be evident from the few selections from his correspondence with Emily, which adorn the pages of this
memoir. The eminent services which he rendered her
at this time, (when she was in distress and needed it),
together with the light which they throw upon his estimate of her character, and the warmth and steadiness
of his praises and friendship up to the time of her leaving the country, will be my apology for giving a few extracts from his inimitably graceful letters.

Emily's period of discouraged waiting at the door of
the great audience-chamber of the public was over. She
was at once in the full flush of her literary career. She
almost literally "awoke one morning and found herself
famous." The path to competence and fame opened itself attractively before her. Ere she was aware of it,
ere she began to dream of it, the name of Fanny Forester was echoed through the country, and her praises
were on every tongue. The timid, trembling girl, who
had shrunk, like the sensitive plant, from the breath of
public notice, dreading the very applause which she
courted, was now the cynosure of all eyes—the admired
of all admirers. Applications soon came in from the
publishers of the popular magazines for the aid of her
attractive pen and the prestige of her name, at the highest
current prices in this department of literature. Most of
them she was compelled to decline. In October she engaged to contribute to Graham—then, perhaps, the leading journal of its class—at five dollars per page, and

renewed her connection with the *Columbian* on the same terms. Between these two and the *New Mirror* (which about this time passed into a daily) she mainly divided her contributions. The following letters will need little explanation :

TO HER SISTER.

DEAR KATY,—   UTICA, June 27, 1844.

I have made an arrangement for you to come on and take lessons of Sarah Bell just as soon as you can get ready. School closes five weeks from to-morrow, and I think you need to be here certainly four weeks. Can you get ready so soon? . . . I have made the arrangement now, because there never will be a better time—Wallace being at home with mother, and things here being in a proper train. Come the last of next week, or, if you can not possibly get ready, the week after; but a week is invaluable to you. Do not think another time will do as well. I may not be here another time; another time you may not be able to leave home. You *must* take lessons to run a race with S——.

The *New Mirror* has just come, and you will see what a splendid compliment N. P. Willis has paid me. I shall not get any money, however, now—that is, from him; but it will put me in a way of making money like smoke. All well. Write soon. In haste,   NEM.

TO MISS ANABLE.

HAMILTON, August 7, 1844.

O Anna Maria! If you *did* know how I want to ride! Why, I am actually suffocating for the want of a breath of air. The house is stuck away down, down, down, and here I am burrowed up in it without the possibility of seeing out. Walk, did you say? O innocent! little do you understand your suggestion! Where shall I go? To be sure, the streets are like a dozen ribbons knotted in the middle; but which to go off

on! That is the query. One way you encounter innumerable
perils in the shape of students, another, of bogs, another, of
barn-yards; *all* have their peculiarities, and Kate has put a veto
on each proposal of mine. Besides, I do not want to walk; I
want to ride. "Spring-halt" has made me aristocratic. Have
I ridden so many times after him to foot it now? (That blot is
a tear-drop of the pitying ink.) Tell Miss Cynthia, if she has
a spark of love for me, if any bowels of compassion, she will
either send out Spring-halt, or a portion of the needful. And
now, mother-in-law, what more shall I say? It is above sixty
miles from here to Cooperstown, and fifty to Cherry Valley. I
have given up the thought of going anywhere this vacation, but
I *do* want to stir here. When are you coming? Do come, if
you do not wish me to turn into a pillar of salt. Kitty, you
know, is like her bulk in lead as far as concerns any project for
going out, and I have not the spirit to keep myself from moping
alone.

Thursday, 8. Blessings on ye, Anna Maria, for that *New
Mirror*. I thought of you all day yesterday while reading it,
though I did not expect such a nice bit for myself. We had a
delightful time on Saturday part of the way. The air was deliciously fresh, and the scenery magnificent; but as evening came
on it grew "damp, moist, and unwholesome;" the roads were
rough and poor; and Kate was sick. I made her up a bed on
the back seat (my dictionary and shawls for a pillow), and on
we came in some tribulation. It was amusing enough to see
the men gather around for news at every place where we
stopped. At Boukville (a little cluster of houses about as big
as your fist) the portico of the inn was swarming with men,
and as we drew up a dozen voices shouted, "What news?"
"Bag full," said the driver, throwing the stuffed mail-bag to a
little man waiting for it. "Hurrah for Polk!" broke in a pert
feminine voice from one end of the portico. "Hurrah for Polk!"
echoed a bull-frog at the other. Another, very deliberately,
"Hurrah for Harry Clay!" A tall, lean man, rather sheepishly,

"Hurrah for Birney!" Then a general shout, with but the variation of a name, broke from bar-room and portico, and all scrambled off for the mail, now assorted. The whole country seems up in arms about politics. We reached home about ten o'clock. Monday, made mother a cap, and read Hallam's "Middle Ages." Tuesday, made two collars, and read the same —had nothing else to do. Wednesday, too impatient to do much, but in the afternoon coaxed Kate off into the swamp, where we had a very nice time, and got an abundant supply of flowers. To-day I have been reading the *New Mirror*, and afterward made Kate a bracelet of pearls. Wallace has gone to Morrisville, and what do you guess I have been making for us against his return in the evening? A set of chess-men. I have checked off a paper for a board, and made all my large men of poppy heads. The difference in the length of the stems distinguishes between king and queen; the castles are made of two heads fastened together; the bishops have split stems for mitres, and the knights are decorated with plumes in the absence of their horses. My pawns are marigold heads, which, set on the flat side with the little stems sticking up, are as perfect pawns as you ever saw. O they are a capital set of men; you would be charmed with them. The two parties are distinguished by a a streak of red paint on one. To-morrow we can have father's donkey—a miserable beast, not half as good as Spring-halt, and mother, Kate, and I are bent on a ride. It is the only day in the week when we can have him, and so I presume it will rain.

Friday. No, it did not rain; but I managed to get up a nervous head-ache, and have been hugging the pillow all day. So we must wait for another Friday. I can not sit up yet; my head goes like a spindle; so no more at present. I have got up again, and carry myself a little more respectably. The mail leaves at nine, and I carry myself a little mo—bless me! I am copying from the line above. I believe I am growing daft; but *n' importe*, I am determined to send off this blotted sheet to-night. . . . I think you may well consider yourself among the favored (*alias* the bored) ones; you know I do not write such long letters every day. If you can not find out who this is from, send it back and I will find a place to sign it.

FROM N. P. WILLIS.

DEAR LADY FANNY,—   AUGUST 20, 1844.

The lost letter was directed to "Utica Female Academy," and either "Cousin Bel" is a bad mouser, or my man Tummus mis-boxed the letter. But no matter. It was merely a letter of warm thanks for what you had done for us, and an assurance that though we could not pay you, we could make your name so *coinable* by praises that you could sell high to others. Every line your clever pen indites should bring you an equivalent *besides* praise, and we will bring that about speedily. You have remarkable talent at writing the *readable*, and if you are not over forty you have a career before you. I esteem you, authorly, very much, and should be delighted to know you, pretty or plain. A lady tells me to-day that you are *not* pretty, or you would not have so much wit and leisure to throw away! Woman's sagacity! Please tell me what you are like, and I beg you to write for us as long as you can afford to. How can we send you the *Mirror* and our extras—one and all? How can we serve or please you?

Yours admiringly,
N. P. WILLIS.

FROM N. P. WILLIS.

NEW YORK, September, Sat., 1844.

Your beautiful story, kindest of Fannies, is already in type, and it is time my thanks were on the way to you. The *Mirror* reflects most pleasurably from and about you, and "we" plume ourselves not a little on having been selected by you as your literary god-father. As to *my* "making a world," I could never have made it except out of your genius, and to that same fire within you I beg to acknowledge no inconsiderable debt.

I think, by the way, that you had better be looking forward to an enlarged reputation, and while you put an extra drop of Macassar on your organ of *hope*, put two on your organ of painstaking and caution. The time is not very far off when you will "have a call" to collect these tales into a volume, and it will save trouble to polish while the iron is hot. You are very much more gifted than you think, dear Fanny, (I may "dear" your *nom de guerre*) and pray, bind yourself to nothing, not even to a husband, if there be hinderance in it. I was talking to Mrs. Ellett about you a day or two ago, and she quite glorifies you.

Give my kindest remembrance to our common friend, Mrs. Kirkland, when you return to Utica, and believe me,

Yours as faithfully as admiringly,

N. P. WILLIS.

FROM N. P. WILLIS.

NEW YORK, September 27th, 1844.

Your womanly and natural letter is full of charm for me, my friend, and I assure you, I see, through its simple earnestness and modesty, a heart worth treating with respect and delicacy. I wish I could talk with you an hour, instead of writing; for writing letters to me is like the postman's walking for pleasure. It is the drop too much. Briefly let me offer you my friendship, and a vow to serve you and your reputation to the best of my means and ability. Mrs. Willis, who sits by me, offers you her admiring friendship also, and now to business.

The *Mirror* of this week will explain to you why, with all our success, we are under the necessity of starting a new paper, requiring great outlay, and impoverishing us, for a year at least, most uncomfortably. Therefore, and *therefore only*, we do not employ you at once, and give you more than any other writer could get from us; for you are more readable than any female writer in this country. We consider ourselves your debtor, however, and shall, with our first emergence from this new

5*

plunge, give some signs to that effect. Thus much, though you claim no money, it was necessary for me to say.

As to your *one vein* of writing, you are under a very natural delusion. The fog clears up as you go along, and you will go on writing charmingly for twenty years. No need either of painting the dark side. The world is full of beauty. Dismiss the attempt to weigh your to-morrows, and believe this, *with me*, that you have a fame before you. If I were "in the market," I would marry you on speculation to-morrow, as a girl with an unquestionable dowry—let alone your "black eyes."

I shall go on glorifying you in our new daily paper, until the magazine people give you fifty dollars an article, and meantime if you have any thing you can not sell (particularly a short story, or essay, or sketch of character), let us have it for the *Evening Mirror*, and we will give you its value in some shape. Do not waste time or labor, however, even upon *us*, but write a novel little by little. You *can*. . . .

I have no more time (for less than twelve thousand pair of eyes), and must stop writing to one pair only—black though they be.

Yours, with very sincere friendship,

N. P. WILLIS.

FROM N. P. WILLIS.

ON THE SKETCH ENTITLED "DORA."

NEW YORK, November 16, 1844.

I have just read the proof of your exquisitely beautiful outline story, my dear Miss Chubbuck, and my heart is in my throat with its pathos, and with my interest in your genius. I see the *inner iris* of the story, of course. I could talk, talk to you *days* of what is in your brain and heart at this moment; for I read it with my own recollections of first fame, and with the eye God has given me to see hearts with. You are gifted far beyond your own belief, but your heart is more gifted than your head. Your affections are in more need of room and wings than your imagination. I should bless God for your sake to hear that a poet and man-angel had taken you to a dell in the wilderness, never to be heard of more.

With nothing but your writings to guide me, I have begun with gaily rejoicing over a new found star, and ended with a tearful interest in your destiny, and a respect for your truth and purity which makes me repent of ever having spoken of you triflingly. You will forgive this. Hereafter you will see no word touching yourself that does not pass through the fountain of reverence you have called up in my heart.

I am writing while "proofs" are coming—interruptedly and carelessly of course. I was pleased and displeased at ——'s changing her opinion of me; displeased at the suspicion that my *inner-self* had ever committed its purity to the world, or had ever been on trial in a pure mind. My dear friend, you know, though you have never perilled your *outer* mind by laying it open to all comers, that there is an inner sanctuary of God's lighting which brightens as the world is shut out, and which would never suffer profanation. It is in this chamber of my better nature that you are thought of—but I have no time to explain.

The pain that you are suffering from the *exposure of fame* is a chrysalis of thought. You will be brighter for it, though the accustomed shroud of seclusion comes off painfully. The opinion of the "Uticanians" as to any thing but your amiableness and respectability, is not worth one straw—though a straw stuck in your eye is as formidable as a house-beam. By an effort of mind you can throw Utica to the distance of Rochester or Buffalo, and then every thing you hear will have just the value which the same thing would have if said in Buffalo. Still, perhaps you have yet to learn that genius burns darkest nearest the wick, never, *never* appreciated by those who eat, drink, and walk with it. You are a hundred times more admired in New York than you ever could be in Utica, and it is the charm of city life that the "solitude of a crowd" throws even your near-

est neighbor to the proper perspective distance.   Keep making
an effort to *shed neighborhood.*   .   .   .

Yours, with sincere respect and affection,

N. P. WILLIS.

NEW YORK, November 24, 1844.

MY DEAR FRIEND,—

At the close of five hours of mental labor, I can scarce
undertake to do more than make *mems.* of what I would say
to you, and you must write me long letters for these scraps
of sentences. Your last was delightful, because it was frank
and sisterly. Your bump of caution must be very large, however, since you supposed that the public might see the "inner
bow" as I did, and dreaded the interpretation, "parading your
feelings," etc. Nobody could ever read a line of yours and see
any thing but merit over-modest, as far as that goes; and there
is no writing well without coloring from one's own heart—particularly in first beginnings. I was exceedingly interested in
the fact that there was a touch of Dora in your own history,
though I did not and do not seek the least intrusion upon your
confidence in such matters. My interest in you is a shadow of
your intellect, and followed, of course, when your intellect
went into your heart as a comforter. There are two worlds,
my dear Dora—one imaginative and the other real life—and
people of genius have separate existences in both. . . . .

I had a call, a few days ago, from a very able artist, who was
so struck with a descriptive passage in your story of Dora that
he wished to paint it. I commissioned him to do it, and shall
send you the picture.

In another letter, Mr. Willis says, in regard to the
picture :

I am glad the idea of the picture pleases you. It is likely to
be an interesting matter, for the artist, Flagg, whose mother

relies on me as her son's guardian angel, told me to-day that he should take the opportunity to put his mother's head and mine on the same canvass! I am to be the "stranger," his mother the motherly guardian of Dora, and Dora imaginative. If you were here he should paint your head for Dora. The subject is the putting the question to Dora, as she sits in the window. Your imagination will easily see how it will look; but you must prepare to be disappointed, and it will show you one very curious thing—how other people conceive of the scenes you describe. Mr. Flagg's mother, by the way, was the sister of Washington Allston, and is a woman of admirable qualities. Flagg himself is a most beautiful youth, and of an eccentric character that I love, but sadly dissipated. I do my best to cultivate his virtuous side. He is about twenty-five, and a capital artist. He has promised the picture for next Saturday, and I will send it to you the week following.

I regret that I am unable to furnish any thing from Emily's side of the correspondence between herself and Mr. Willis. In answer to a note respecting the correspondence, Mr. Willis very kindly replies : " I think it most probable that Mrs. Judson's literary novitiate might form an exceedingly interesting chapter of her biography, and I need not assure you that I shall be most willing to furnish any material for it which either my documents or my memory may retain. Of my own letters to her you are quite at liberty to make a discretionary use, though I can only judge of their tone by my remembrance of her most truthful and sweet nature, and the impossibility that there could be a word which would not breathe of respect and homage, in any letters addressed to her. Of her letters to me I think I could find the greater number, but they are buried in a wilderness of correspondence stowed away, and I should require time and leisure for the task." On subsequently exploring the "wilderness," Mr. Willis found that nearly all the letters had disappeared, only two or three being left, which contained nothing of sufficient importance to justify their publication.

In December he writes to Fanny again :

MY DEAR FRIEND,—

I have been intending to write you a long letter, and have wasted odds and ends of time in the hope of an hour of leisure. But I must now simply advise you of the boxing up of the picture of Dora, and assure you how large a slice of the kindest side of my heart goes with it. I do not know when I shall be able to write to you, for I am so overdone with cares and work that my doctor has ordered me out of town, and I must confine myself to the most needful pen-work. . . . The picture has been visited by thousands, and is much admired. Hang it with a *side light*, and be careful in having it unpacked.

Your " bald composer,"

N. P. W.

How diligently Emily must have labored under the fresh stimulants now applied to her will be seen when we observe within how brief a period her magazine authorship was compressed. She wrote to Mr. Willis in June, 1844. In December, 1845, a year and a half afterward, she formed that acquaintance with Dr. Judson which changed the whole current of her destiny. And the eighteen months which thus embraced her entire "Fanny Forester" career, were largely occupied with her school duties, and even still more largely broken in upon by repeated and prolonged illness. While her sketches were rapidly succeeding each other in the magazines, she relaxed none of her assiduity in her daily and more quiet duties in the Seminary. These were her

calling ; the rest but filled her hours of relaxation.
Congenial as was the employment of writing, and stim-
ulating as were the praises of the public, the approval
of friends, and still more, the Hope which was rising
like a glad star of promise on her night of perplexity
and embarrassment, she still regarded this as but a side-
labor, which was not to interfere with her life profession.
This may well be borne in mind by those who look upon
her magazine labors with a suspicious eye. These were
not her leading pursuit. They were indulged in chiefly
when her companions were buried in slumber, or enjoying
the recreations of society—and this under an overmaster-
ing sense of filial obligation. She was straining every
nerve to support herself, and to *pay her debts*—debts
contracted in procuring for her aged parents the comforts
of a home. Emily's disposition was not demonstrative ;
she made no parade of her benevolence or her exertions.
She silently resolved, and then resolutely—almost dog-
gedly—worked, scarcely half aware, herself, either of the
depth of her sensibility, or of the extent and sternness
of her toils and sacrifices. The only true heroism is unconscious heroism—that which performs prodigies of love
under the simple impulse of duty—and this was hers.
Let now the majority of those calling themselves Christians, bearing in mind the above facts, read over her
sketches, and observe the spirit which they breathe, and
the lessons which they inculcate, and then ask themselves
if *they* can give as good an account of their hours of relaxation from the sterner purposes of life. Dress, party-
going, frivolous conversation, even the most of lighter
reading—place over against these the truth and purity
of Emily's delightful sketches ! She was exhausting
the springs of youth in behalf of the sinking energies of

age, but never by a moment's compromise of moral principle.

And equally should *they* bear in mind the checkered brevity of Emily's literary career, who would judge fairly that literary reputation which rested so largely on her "Fanny Forester" sketches. Within little more than one short year—a year of engrossing duty and of the frailest health—she achieved nearly all by which she was known to the literary public before she went abroad. How much, then, might have been anticipated as the ripened fruit of time, and health, and leisure! For that hers were no precocious and hot-bed productions—that they were but the first fruits of what might have expanded into a rich and noble harvest, her after life in which, while her frame was wasting under deadly disease, her mind displayed still increasing vigor, abundantly evinced.

The sensation days of Fanny Forester are of course forever gone by. In this on-rushing age even the most brilliant intellects can rivet the public gaze but for a moment; then, yielding to some new brilliancy, they withdraw into their permanent shining place in the clustering firmament of genius. But there they are, unextinguished and immortal. "A thing of beauty is a joy forever," and passes from being the transient excitement of the age, into a lasting inheritance of the ages. And those who now turn over the stories of Alderbrook will, I think, be at no loss to explain the popularity which they attained. They will find in them a truth to nature—a freshness and raciness of thought and diction —a freedom from the hackneyed conventionalisms of ordinary story-telling, a descriptive and dramatic power, which lend to them an unfailing charm. The language is ever plain and simple. They never affect "big" words, nor deck themselves out in fripperies of expression. If there are occasional conceits of thought—and such are almost inevitable in a young woman's first converse with the public—the style is almost wholly free from them. It delights in that plain Anglo-Saxon that comes freighted with home associations to every heart ; and yet this simple style, under her delicate handling, has all the grace of ornament.

Another source of the popularity of her sketches is found in the spirit and vivacity of her descriptions— showing a clear and close eye for the observation of nature—and in the life-like truthfulness of her character drawing. Her personages are not mere pegs on which to hang a story—a train of external incidents : they are themselves the story. They are not mere labeled embodiments of the virtues and vices of the decalogue, but actual men and women, brought by a few simple but effective touches livingly before the eye, and, even in her lightest sketches, sharply individualized. Thus the interest of her stories is emphatically a human interest. It is not what the actors *do*, but what they *are*, that rivets our attention, and chains us to her fascinating pages. As might be inferred from this, she possesses extraordinary dramatic power. The *dramatis personœ* live and breathe and move through the story. The author transports herself into the scene ; identifies herself with her characters ; and instead of conducting her narration by cold, second-hand details, makes it gush warmly and livingly from the lips of the speakers. Not unfrequently nearly the whole story is unfolded by dialogue, natural, racy, and spirited, and that which in its mere outward details would be but a trivial incident, under this warm, dramatic handling, and imbedded in human passion, is impregnated with life and interest. Equally happy, too, is Emily in the conduct of her narrative—in the management of the plot—in so seizing upon the hinging-points, the *nodes* and crises of the story, and so coloring, and grouping, and contrasting them, as to give them their utmost effect. With the instinctive eye of genius, she separates the incidental from the essential, and strikes to the inmost core of her subject.

And finally—and here perhaps was preëminently the secret of Emily's power—she was drawing from her own life, "coloring from her own heart." With every stroke of her pen she daguerreotyped herself upon the page before her. The trials of her youth—her own harsh experiences—quivered through her bright and glittering fancies, and compelled many a tear from hearts unknowing of the cause. She was unconsciously obeying the dictum of the great master ; she moved others because she had first been moved herself. The tear that trembled in their eye answered to that which had first glistened in her own. The emotion that swelled their bosoms was responsive to that which had throbbed in her own breast. True to herself, she was true to the universal elements of humanity.

And yet she was far from being the mere recorder ; she dealt not in the mere statistics of experience. Her power of fancy was equal to her power of feeling. The germ of her conception sprung from the actual, but it developed itself in the realm of the ideal. When fancy supplied the ground-work, her feelings insensibly blended themselves with it, giving it genuineness and vitality. When she started from experience, fancy instantly stood as its servitor, ready to invest the creation with her bright and glittering hues. Thus her heart and life-experiences were so transfigured and idealized that she did not obtrude herself indelicately or painfully before the public. "Grace Linden," "Lilias Fane," "Dora," "Nora Maylie," "Ida Ravelin" even, were all born in the depths of her own nature, all embodied a certain portion of her spiritual essence ; yet all were so wrought and moulded, so blended with imaginative elements, that she for whom they really stood "passed in music out of sight." So amidst the deeper emotions of later life her power of imagination kept pace with her power of passionate emotion. "My Bird," "Watching," "My Angel Guide," are beautifully idealized, and it is only perhaps in "Sweet Mother" that the bleeding, agonizing heart of the stricken wife and daughter comes nakedly before the public. And with all this, there breathes through all her pages a tenderness and delicacy of sentiment which impart to them a nameless charm.

In this slight analysis, I am not claiming for "Fanny Forester's" sketches the highest order of genius. They are a woman's production, and are thoroughly womanly. They aspire to no heights of masculine eloquence, no depths of philosophical teaching. They deal with the heart, the fancy, and the imagination. Nor in mere vigor and grasp of intellect is she, perhaps, to be classed with Joanna Bailie, Mrs. Browning, and Miss Brontë ; although looking at *all* which she did, I am satisfied that she approaches much nearer to them in intellectual vigor than they do to her in womanly delicacy and softness. It is one of her high excellencies that she never compromises her womanhood ; and yet to her who could write the "Madness of the Missionary Enterprise," and render such contributions as she did to the memoir of her husband, is to be assigned no mean rank among the intellects of the world. Mr. Willis, Dr. Griswold, and Mr. H. B. Wallace, than whom our country has produced no more competent literary critics, estimated her genius as of a very high order, and regarded her true sphere as that not of popularity, but of fame.

CHAPTER VIII.

THE INVALID.

"For I mind me that the gifted
Are the stricken ones of earth."

"O Saviour! whose mercy, severe in its kindness,
Has chastened my wanderings and guided my way;
Adored be the power that illumined my blindness,
And weaned me from phantoms that lured to betray."

BUT the sword was wearing out the sheath. Emily's slender frame was not equal to the drafts made upon it, and on her visit home in December she was seized with a fever which prostrated her for several weeks, and left her when able to return to Utica, extremely feeble.

The picture of "Dora" spoken of above arrived with the New Year. It is a beautiful picture, worthy of the taste of the donor, and the capacity of the artist, as well as an elegant tribute to the genius which had inspired it.

TO MRS. BATES.

HAMILTON, January 14, 1845.

MY DEAR MARIE,—

I was much disappointed at not seeing you here; but I could not have gone with you if you had come, for I have not yet stepped my foot upon the ground. I thank you for your kind offer of sending for me; but I am now needed at Utica every day, and must return as soon as I am able to ride at all.

I shall hide myself in a cloak and hood, on Saturday or Monday I think, if it is pleasant, and put myself into Wallace's hands to take back as he would any other baggage. This is absolutely necessary, and mother consents to it with a better grace that I promise her that I will do nothing more than oversee my affairs until I am quite well. I am very sorry that I could not have made the visit at your house—it would have been charming— but I promise myself the pleasure at some future time.—Really, you ought to have been here and seen my picture; it is exquisitely beautiful, and charms everybody. There is an artist in town who spent the last winter in New York; he says he never saw so fine a painting of the kind. It came to hand on the 1st; so my Christmas gift was turned into a New Year's one. They were intending to notice it in the paper; but I begged them not—(it would be telling everybody who Fanny Forester is, you know)—and the article was suppressed. They, however, copy the notice from the *Mirror*.

I received last night a letter from Graham, asking for stories which I can not write—is it not provoking? "The Chief's Daughter" and "Katie Holland" in the February number are mine.

I am glad your sister is so well, and above all happy. I should like exceedingly to know her, and will write if I can. But pen-work is no play with me, you know. I shall try to make a compromise with my friends, and write them one poor letter for half a dozen good ones. Will *you* accede to such terms? Here begin I. . . .

Shall I say to you, Maria dear, that I am more annoyed than pleased with the sensation I am making just now? If people talk of me, I, of course, prefer good to ill; but I would much rather they would not talk at all. There has been a New York "lion" to Utica, on purpose to see me; he would have followed me out here, but they told him I was too ill to see company. Now I do not like to be an object of curiosity like the Siamese Twins or Tom Thumb. You appreciate the matter.

It is getting quite dark, and they will not allow me to write by candle-light; so I must close my shabby apology for a letter while I can see to sign my name. My very kindest regards to your dear, good husband, and every body else that you love, and believe me,

Your warmly attached friend,

EMILY E. CHUBBUCK.

Emily returned to Utica the last of January, how feeble the following will show:

TO HER SISTER.

UTICA, February 8, 1845.

DEAR KITTY,—

I have been looking and looking for a letter from home, but as I do not get it, I suppose I may as well write myself. I do not think I am any better than when I left home; though I am a good deal better than on the week following, for it threw me back wonderfully. The teachers help me correct compositions, and I do nothing else; fear that I shall not write any this winter. As for eating, I do not go to the table, and do not make a glutton of myself exactly. I have lived nearly all the time on the beef, and it is not more than half gone. I am expecting my breakfast of gruel to be brought up every minute. I have four kinds of pills to take—three kinds of the largest size imaginable; the others I have to take after dinner to sweeten the meal. Then I have other doses besides. Dr. J. is in for it, and he seems to think that if he cures Fanny Forester it will be the making of him. Anna Maria went to Schenectady yesterday to spend a week, and I miss her sadly. . . . I had a letter from Mr. Willis yesterday week; he says he lets the daily go to Hamilton still for you people. Have received a letter from Graham, but there was no particular news in it, except that "Nickie Ben" was too late for the March number; but he has a little tit-bit of a story of about two pages which he intends to insert in it. Do write. I have no news, and do not feel well enough to stretch out a long letter.   E.

But Miss Chubbuck's health was deemed too feeble to endure safely the rigors of the spring climate of Utica. Miss Sheldon's thoughtful kindness, sustained by the advice of the physician, suggested a temporary retreat to the milder region of Philadelphia. Emily writes thus to her sister :

March 17, 1845.

I was sorry to hear that you were ill; I believe it is the fate of the family, for I am not quite so well as I should like to be. . . . Dr. James and Miss C. think it best for me to go to a warmer place until summer comes, and so Miss C. has concluded to go next week with me to Philadelphia. She will put me under the care of the Rev. Mr. Gillette, a Baptist clergyman, find me a nice boarding-house and then leave me for four, five, or six weeks as I think best. It will cost some money, but it seems absolutely necessary. This spring weather almost kills me. I shall get the money for my payment, and send it home before I go. . . Did you read the poetry addressed to Fanny Forester in the *Mirror* ? And do you not think it beautiful? It is by Jane Wright. You will find my " Weaver " in Friday's paper. . . " Nickie Ben " is in the April number of Graham, but I have not seen it yet. I have written another story entitled " Blanche de Monville," and that is all I have done this winter. The Columbian people pretend to think all the world of me ; Graham is as good as the bank, and Willis fifty times better. . .

The following are the lines referred to in the preceding letter. Miss Wright was a member of the Seminary.

LINES TO FANNNY FORESTER.

BY MISS MARY FLORENCE NOBLE.

Saw you ever a purer light,
  More still and fair than the harvest moon,
When day has died in a shadowless night,
  And the air is still as a summer noon?
No? Ah, sweet one, your eyelids shrine
A light far purer and more divine.

Heard you ever the silvery gush
  Of a brook far down in its rocky dell,
And stilled your breath with a trembling hush,
  As its mystic murmurs rose and fell?
'Tis thus I list to the liquid flow
Of your silvery accents soft and low.

Yes, sweet Fanny, the light that gleams
  'Neath the sweeping fringe of your radiant eyes,
Too purely chaste and too heavenly seems
  To dwell in the glare of our earthly skies;
And too soft and low your tones have birth
To linger long 'mid the din of earth.

The sweet brow shrined in your clustering hair
  Has gathered a shadow wan and deep;
And the veins a darker violet wear,
  Which over your hollow temples creep;
And your fairy foot falls faint and low
As the feathery flakes of the drifting snow.

'Tis said the gods send swift decay
  To the bright ones they love of mortal birth;
And your angel Dora passed away,
  In her youth's sweet spring time, from the earth;
Yet stay, sweet Fanny, your pinions fold,
Till the hearts that love you now are cold.

The little poem, "The Weaver," mentioned in her letter, Emily had sent to the *Mirror* in February. It is a beautifully imaginative piece, but much less finely finished than as it subsequently appeared in Alderbrook. Mr. Willis writes to her: "Your 'Weaver' is a pure and perfect chrysalis of a thought lacking finish," and in a subsequent letter recurs thus to the subject :

"I am waiting for a moment of *fresh-minded* leisure (the other I could more easily find) to take a sunny impression of your poem, and see just where the blemish was that first struck me. I am determined you shall not slight any thing you write simply from over-toil in your other duties. You are too precious a commodity, and as your trumpeter, I will not blow my blast till I know you are ready for the attention it draws to you."

It was by such services, by friendly and just criticism, as well as by his praises, that Mr. Willis rendered her at this period valuable aid. He taught her to appreciate herself, inspired her with self-confidence, and yet gave her the advantage of his larger experience and fine taste in detecting and removing her faults. This was the fidelity of true friendship ; and the excellence which Emily reached in her later poems, while in part the product of her riper experiences, was, in no small measure, the result of assiduous labor and severe criticism.

CHAPTER IX.

THE CONVALESCENT.

"A thousand sweet ties bind her here;
  Oh friend, thy fears are vain!
The blessed angels will not break
  So soon the golden chain;
And God, our God, who loveth her,
  Shall breath on her again.

"The languor of her step shall yet
  With winter snows depart;
Her foot shall spring on carpets wrought
  By Flora's loving art,
And keep time to the joyous beat
  Of her exulting heart!"

THUS, in response to the lines of Miss Wright, sang, in the *Mirror*, Mrs. Sarah J. Clark (Grace Greenwood that was to be), giving utterance to her interest in the fate of our fair and gifted authoress. I add the three closing stanzas of her sweet little poem:

Our souls' arms are around her thrown,
  She *must not* pass away
Now, when too humble for the proud,
  Too lonely for the gay,
The altar of sweet poesy
  Is falling to decay.

> O, there we may behold her yet
>   In her young beauty bow;
> There may we hear her glad lip breathe
>   Her consecration vow;
> Earth's warm life lighting up her eye—
>   Its glory on her brow!
>
> There, there a priestess may she serve,
>   With vestments pure and fair;
> There offer up her winged dreams,
>   Young doves from heaven's own air,
> And pour the rich wine of her soul
>   As a libation there!

In accordance with the purpose intimated in her last letter, Emily, with her faithful friend and guardian, Miss Sheldon, was soon *en route* for the city which, to an extent then undreamed of, was to be linked with her future fortunes. Instead of allowing them to carry out their purpose of procuring a private boarding-house, Rev. Mr. Gillette and his wife—acquaintances of Miss Sheldon's, but strangers to Emily—tendered to her their hospitalities, and so cordially that Emily could not decline them. In their house and society she found a comfortable and delightful home. April 1st, she writes thus to Miss Anable:

They (Mr. and Mrs. Gillette) received me as if they had known me always, Mrs. Gillette not even waiting for an introduction. It will not be particularly convenient to them to have me here, but they will not listen to my going away. I am growing better and better every day, and promise myself a delightful time. I think I shall like the city better than I do New York—all but the white blinds; them I can not endure. It seems all the time as though somebody was poking white sticks in my eyes. When I am in walkable order, and little Jemmy Gillette gets well, Mrs. G. and I will measure the pavements at a great rate. The weather yesterday and to-day is like June. You will be able to judge something about it, when I tell you that (such a cold body as I am) I sit all the time at the open window.

Emily's literary reputation had preceded her to Philadelphia, and drew about her some literary friends, whose attentions added to the pleasure of her stay. Her patron, Mr. Graham, early called upon her, and after some little playing at cross purposes, they met. She was new to the presence of literary lions, or those whom she took to be such, and although she could make very free with them on paper, when shielded by several hundred intervening miles of post route, she found meeting them face to face a more formidable matter. She had written some spirited letters to Mr. Graham about his publishing articles under the signature of Fanny Forester, which he had previously suffered to lie unnoticed, yet now her heart went pit-a-pat at the prospect of a personal meeting. The following, from the same letter, details their first interview :

The meeting was very stiff. He was surrounded by little boys (he brought one with him—a nephew ; he has no children). I walked in shaking from head to foot. He inquired if I was Miss Chubbuck, and gave me the tips of his fingers. I expressed regret for being out this morning—then a long pause. Afterwards we talked about the *Columbian*, Mr. Willis, and finally about our last quarrel and money matters. Sometimes I trembled, and blundered, and stumbled against big words, and then I talked on for a few minutes quite straight. On the whole, I guess he thinks I am very sensible girl, though not

quite so pretty, and poetical, and easy, etc., as he expected. He
has a mighty positive way of saying things, but you can not
help believing every thing he says. He talks beautifully, and
with perfect ease, when he gets a-going; but he makes very
long pauses.

Among others who early called on Emily were Dr.
Rufus W. Griswold, the distinguished historian and
critic of American literature, and Mr. Joseph C. Neal,
the witty author of the Charcoal Sketches, and editor of
the *Saturday Evening Gazette*. With all these gentlemen she became intimately acquainted. Dr. Griswold
and Mr. Graham entered warmly into her literary plans,
and urged her to a more exclusive and aspiring literary
career. The time thus glided rapidly by, her health
was improved by her long drives in and about the city
of "Brotherly Love," and in May she bade her many
friends a reluctant adieu, and turned her steps homeward. She spent a fortnight in Brooklyn on the way,
and made the personal acquaintance of her friend and
patron, Mr. Willis. The death of his wife just then
occurring had prevented him from seeing her when she
passed through on her way to Philadelphia. While in
Philadelphia she had received a letter from him in reply
to one from her of sympathy for his recent loss. In
it, after paying a beautiful tribute to his deceased wife,
he adds : "I have once or twice tried to loosen the lock-
jaw of my bosom, and write to you as I could talk to
you, but I must abandon the idea. I am compelled to
wall in my heart, so as to go on amusing the world
without braiding in threads that belong only to myself,
and it requires a *habit of reserve* to do this. When you

come to New York we shall meet, and my tongue is not used in my trade as my pen is.

"I am made happy by hearing of your brightening under the bright weather. Continue to *idle*, and do not write one line for the *Mirror ; I positively forbid it.*"

Mr. Willis and Emily now met for the first and last time, and their personal interviews strengthened her gratitude for his services and her admiration of his genius. He was much interested in her health, and urged her removal from what he deemed the ungenial climate of Utica—perhaps a trip to the West Indies or to Italy. He proffered any services in his power, but Emily was unwilling to incur the added obligation of accepting them, and they parted not to meet again on earth. Emily returned to Utica, and Mr. Willis a few weeks after, set sail for Europe for the purpose of conveying his orphaned daughter Imogen to her relatives in England.

On returning to Utica Emily took her wonted place in the Seminary, bringing to her duties invigorated health and spirits. Her visit had been serviceable to her in other respects. It had brought her into society under circumstances calculated to banish her timidity, and inspire her with self-confidence. The shy, timid, silent girl, whose nervous frame quivered with emotion at the prospect of an introduction to strangers at all distinguished, would hardly be recognized in the genial, joyous, animated, and often brilliant young lady of a little later date. Few, probably, have suffered more keenly than she from timidity—a timidity almost inseparable from her slender frame and delicate organization, and which no amount of familiarity with the world could ever entirely overcome. There was always a little fluttering of spirits in the company of strangers ; she always rather glided into a room as if unwilling to attract observation, than entered it with the easy self-possession of the thorough-bred woman of the world.   In a little poem written at Utica, the one boon which she craves of the Muse is— not beauty, not genius, not the laurel wreath of fame— but physical courage.   As the painful timidity of her earlier years passed away, the constitutional reserve that remained, betokening the most genuine womanhood, rather heightened than detracted from her personal at-tractiveness.

The following long letter written in reply to a note of gentle caution from her faithful friend Mrs. Nott, will show how rightly and soberly, amidst the rush of her popularity, she estimated her literary position :

TO MRS. NOTT.

MY VERY DEAR FRIEND,—   UTICA, June 6, 1845.

Your note to Anna Maria and myself was most gratefully received (on my part at least), because it gives evidence of your kind interest.   Do you know what a strong light it throws on your opinion of myself, my weakness, etc.?   I really thought that I stood higher with you; but I find it is one of the most difficult things in the world to find out precisely how " others see us."   Now if I write you very frankly, and even egotisti-cally, I know you will forgive me; because this is a subject that my friends *must* understand, if they would not make me very uncomfortable.

You are afraid that I will grow vain—or rather you think I am so; for people never caution without supposed cause.   I have a great deal of *pride ;*—more than you ever thought, be-cause you have always been so very kind to me that it has never been called out in your presence.   I have some *vanity ;* but unless I am seriously mistaken in my estimate of my own char-

acter (and I have scrutinized it more severely than you could),
I have less, rather than more, than the generality of women.
Now what cause have I given you to believe that I was puffed
up by praises? Do I look pleased with a compliment? I am
pleased particularly when I am conscious of deserving it, and so
willing to share my gratification with others that I act as I feel.
This (the pleasure) is human nature, and if I pretended to rise
above it I should be a hypocrite.

My life, from my cradle, has been full of changes. Without
one of my own kindred to assist me, I have struggled with almost every kind of difficulty up to the present moment. Even
you can not dream of half that I have borne. Heaven knows,
enough to make me humble. Within the last year—one short
year—I have gained for myself a position which others have
been all their lives in attaining, and I have a right to be proud
of it. You may tell me it is a small thing to be a magazine
writer. So it is. But it is *not* a small thing for a woman,
thrown upon her own resources, and standing entirely alone, to
be able to command respect from every body, rising by her own
individual efforts above the accidents of fortune. Does all this
sound like boasting? I only want to prove to you that I understand my ground, and take too comprehensive a view of it to
have my heart set a fluttering by every swing of Mr. Nobody's
censer. I know precisely what my reputation is worth to me,
for I have measured it carefully; and I know, too, what all
these silly compliments are worth. If such a man as Bryant
praises me (I believe he has had the bad taste to set me before
Miss S——), I suppose that he thinks what he says; still it is
only *the opinion of one man.* If a hundred other people echo
the praise, I know that they take it on trust; so the compliment
is in reality to Bryant, not to me. These newspaper puffs are
accidental and ephemeral things, and while I will not despise
them, because in their way they are an advantage to me, do not,
I beg of you, think that I am such a simpleton as to be "spoiled"
by them. As to the attentions I have received since I have

6*

been gone, they have certainly put me a little more at ease with
myself, but I do not believe that you will say they have been
disadvantageous. In sober truth, Heaven has blessed me (as a
balance for the romance which I am not going to disclaim)
with a sort of mathematical genius, a dollar-and-cent way of
estimating things, which, when necessary, takes the poetry out
of them in a twinkling. Will you not give me credit for some
common sense at bottom ? Think of all the things that I have
to occupy my mind : the serious duties of life ; the cares which
nobody can share with me, and which I think about none the
less for not always talking of them. Think of these, and
see if I have any *time* to spare to vanity. Have I ever, my
dear Mrs. Nott, managed my own affairs indiscreetly, that you
should fear that, with more experience to guide me, I will do it
now ? Do I look or act like a vain woman ? Do I try to make
a great show and attract attention to myself? Do I put myself forward in society ? I intend to take a little different position from what I have, for I see that people expect it of me,
and my diffidence and disposition to keep out of sight have obtained for me the reputation of being cold-hearted and indifferent. Indeed, I am not a little child, to go into ecstacies at
every pretty thing that is said to me, and as for romance, I have
not half so much as when you first knew me. It is my *trade*
now, and much less in my *heart* than then. As for talking, I
must talk to my room-mates of the things that I think about,
and with others I will try to use all needful discretion. If you
hear of any thing unwisely said or done on my part, please sus-
pend judgment until you know the wherefore. Things always
have two sides. I have been treated by some persons most
generously, and it would be the height of ingratitude in me to
refuse them the slight tribute of a kind word. It is not in my
nature to do it, and I do not believe that even the coldest kind
of policy requires it. Trust me, my dear Mrs. Nott, I can be
discreet, and will. .   .   .   .   I am governed by *a sense of
right* in these things, though I seem to have lost the confidence

of some of my friends to such a degree, that I should hardly get credit for any thing better than vanity—or, at least, fancy.

I should like much to have a long talk with you, for there are, of course, many things which I can not put into a letter. Indeed, it seems to me that I have said nothing as I meant to say it; but I hope to see you before long. Let me entreat you, however, once for all, never to be for a moment troubled about all this fol-de-rol stuff's turning my brain. Were you in my place, you would see it with different eyes from what you do. Things very pretty to look at become smoke when you touch them. Now, *I am touching* them, and I laugh to find what painted bits of butterflies' wings might have seemed wondrously attractive, if, half a dozen years ago, I could have foreseen that it was to be my lot to catch them. "Distance," you know, "lends enchantment." One thing more I wish to say. I beg of you not to be annoyed on my account, if you hear my literary merits spoken of lightly. It is what I ought to expect, and I am fully prepared for it. I hope those who take an interest in me will be prepared too, for, of course, I can not please every body.

I more than half suspect that I have spoiled my own case by telling you so frankly my opinion of myself while disclaiming undue vanity; but, surely, a sober consciousness of one's own capabilities is the surest safeguard against all vagaries of fancy. Forgive my long, tedious letter. Forgive me, also, if I have written too seriously and earnestly, for really I could not bear to be so misunderstood by you. I do not expect to be appreciated by the multitude, and do not care to be; but if I lose the confidence of my friends, I shall be a forlorn thing indeed. Please write me a line to say that my plainness has not offended you, and believe me, my dear Mrs. Nott, your truly attached friend, now and ever,   EMILY.

P. S. Anna Maria and I "chum" it together beautifully, and the room is as pleasant as pleasant as can be. It lacks only its old occupant to make it as agreeable as in its palmiest days. When can you come and see it? Dear Mrs. Nott, do not think, from what I have written, that I am ungrateful for your generous interest, or impatient under your advice. If you did not advise me, I should think that you did not love me any more; and what I have written has been from a sense of justice to you as well as to myself. You ought to know me, for I owe to you a great deal of care and kindness.

TO MRS. GILLETTE.

UTICA, July 2d, 1845.

MY DEAR MRS. GILLETTE,—

I should have written you before, but I really did not believe my letter would be worth eighteen pence; and so I have waited to "patronize" the new postage law. I hope you will follow this most laudable example far enough to write me on the day that you receive this. Will you? May I hear from you very, very soon? . . .

I had a delightful time at Brooklyn. Spent two weeks there, and saw my good friend W—— nearly every day. I like him even better than I anticipated; he is, however, any thing but happy. He sailed for Europe just a week after I left. I wish you had been along, for there were a thousand little things happening every day, very pleasant to enjoy, but scarce worth detailing, or at least writing down. . . .

I shall claim your promise to let me come and live with you next winter, provided I do not go where it is still warmer. I have some anticipation of going where the oranges grow, and they have roses in winter time. Seriously, I talk somewhat of a trip to Italy this fall. Mr. L., our consul to Genoa, is now here and will return in a few months with his family, and I entertain the idea of accompanying them. Would it not be quite an expedition for me? The matter, however, is quite doubtful yet, though I certainly shall not remain in this cold climate. . . .

The pleasant time that I spent with you I shall not soon forget. I only wish that the whole could be repeated. Is my little husband married again, or does he remain constant? Tell him that when I come back from Italy I think we shall be about big enough to commence house-keeping. Kiss all the little fellows for me, and tell them that Cousin Emily would cry her two eyes out if they should forget her. . . . All unite in sending love, and please accept for yourself an extra share from

Yours very sincerely and affectionately,

E. E. C.

TO HER SISTER.

Utica, July 9, 1845.

DEAR KITTY,—

I was glad enough to get your letter I can assure you, for I had got almost crazy about mother. . . . I am not able to write any yet, and think I shall not attempt it again until I come home in vacation. Then I intend to "put in." I have been making arrangements about getting my book published, or rather have written to Gen. Morris about procuring a publisher for me, and I shall want some of the stories that are in your hands as I am too stingy to buy the magazines over again. I want "The Bank Note," "The Peep within Doors," "Nickie Ben," "Two Nights in New Niederlands," and "Grace Linden." I believe I have all the rest. I want you to cut them from the magazines and send them by the first opportunity.

I have an invitation from Mrs. Nott to attend commencement, and shall go down week after next, if I am well enough. I anticipate a rare time. . . .

Emily spent a part of the summer vacation in a little excursion through some parts of Central New York, visiting Cooperstown, the romantic home of the novelist Cooper, and subject to the doubtful pleasure of being "annoyingly lionized." The remainder of the vacation she spent in her quiet home in Hamilton.

The follwing is an extract from a letter of Mr. Willis, written at this time. It is alike just in its sentiments, and shows his estimate of one phase of her character.

FROM N. P. WILLIS.

September 27, 1845.

. . . You ask me whether you shall marry for convenience. Most decidedly, no! What convenience would pay you for passing eighteen hours out of every twenty-four for the rest of your life, within four walls, in company with a person not to your taste? I judge of you by myself. I would not pass one year thus for any fortune on earth. The private hours of one single month are too precious for any price but love. Think how little of the day poverty can touch after all. Only the hours when you are out of your chamber. But the moment your chamber door is shut on you alone, all comparison between you and the richest is at an end. Let the majority of women marry for convenience, if they will; but *you* are brim-full of romance, and delicacy, and tenderness, and a marriage without love, for you, would be sealing up a volcano with a cob-web. You must love—you *must* and *will* love passionately and over-poweringly. You have as yet turned but one leaf in a volume of your heart's life. Your bosom is an altar on which there is a fire newly lit—lit by the late and sudden awakening of your genius. Your peculiarity is that your genius has its altar on your heart, and not like other people's, in the brain. Take care how you throw away the entire music and beauty of a life for only a home that will grow hateful to you. I warn you that you *must* love sooner or later.

In reading over the last page I find that I have advised you to a course that will keep you at work for the present. But let it be so. You are lifting yourself up through a stratum of valuation at every struggle, and leave off when you will, it will be better than having left off before. . . .

On Emily's return to Utica, her health being still delicate, she was obliged to commit to other hands the duties
of her department, reserving to herself merely its general
superintendence. Her complaints continued so obstinate,
and her system so frail, that it was again deemed advisable for her to soften the rigors of the winter by seeking
during the few weeks of the later autumn her former
asylum, Philadelphia, the way not being opened for realizing her conception of spending the winter "where
the oranges grow, and they have myrtles in winter time."
A tropical winter was indeed soon to come, but in a way
of which she had not as yet the remotest dream.

The arrangements alluded to in her letter to her sister
had meanwhile been consummated, and a volume containing her principal magazine sketches, was brought out
by Paine & Burgess, of New York, under the title of
"Trippings in Author Land." I need not repeat my
estimate of its merits, and the public verdict upon it had
been given in advance.

In October Emily proceeded to Philadelphia, spending,
on the way, a few days in New York, where her friends,
both literary and personal, were lavish of their attentions. In Philadelphia, her former hosts, the Gillettes,
again threw open to her their hospitable doors, and received her as if she had been a friend of years. Those
also who had contributed so largely to her enjoyment in
the spring, Dr. R. W. Griswold, Mr. and Mrs. Graham,
Joseph C. Neal, and many other friends, both literary
and religious, welcomed her return to their circle.

Among other gentlemen who were attracted to her
society was Mr. Horace Binney Wallace, with whom she
formed an acquaintance equally delightful and improving. Mr. Wallace belonged to one of the highest families

of Philadelphia. His polished and gentlemanly bearing, his broad culture and sound judgment, his ripened knowledge of the world, his taste at once enthusiastic and discriminating, made a profound impression on her fresh and susceptible intellect, while he in turn perceived all the delicate beauty, and as yet half-latent capacities of her opening genius. She writes thus of Mr. Wallace in one of her letters:

"He is a man of talent, a scholar, and a perfect gentleman; refined, high-bred, delicate, and manly. He is not handsome; that is, there is nothing striking in his appearance; but he has a very intellectual look, and a peculiarly sweet expression. He is about as large as ——; has an easy, gentlemanly carriage, and never does any thing awkward. . . . He is an excellent critic, not only of books, but of painting, sculpture, etc. His conversation is more improving and interesting (combining the two beautifully) than any man's I ever met."

Mr. Wallace deserved even more than these encomiums. The few products of his genius which he has left behind, distinguished alike by originality, depth, and acuteness, by a fine command of language, and the genial catholicity of taste which marks the true scholar, prove him capable of reaching the very highest walks of literary criticism, and show that his sad and untimely end snatched from his country's annals one of their brightest prospective ornaments. Mr. Wallace admired exceedingly the "fascinating delicacy" of Emily's character, and the freshness and originality of her genius. The following paragraphs, taken from a notice of "Fanny Forester," in his "Literary Criticisms," will show his estimate of her powers:

"She possesses many talents; and an assemblage of lesser accomplishments, which in her seem to be so genuine and instinctive, that they might almost be mistaken for natural talents. The movements of her mind have a quiet, soft brightness that seems to shine for itself rather than for others, and to be spontaneous more than exerted; glowing, apparently, without design, and almost in despite of consciousness. Her powers of reasoning are strong; her feelings prompt and abounding; her sense of humor quick and various—but these and other faculties are subordinated in their exercise to a *delicacy* of character and taste, ethereal almost in sensibility, and timorous, even painfully, of every offense against refinement,—the deepest, surest fascination that can belong to a woman; beautiful in the errors it may lead to, and most enchanting perhaps when it is most in excess; whose power is as enduring as the pleasure which it imparts is pure and exquisite. But there are secondary qualities, going rather to the manner, than to the nature or degree of that capacity which we desire to define as constituting a great and splendid faculty in this gentle and modest person. We regard her as possessing talents for *narrative* of a very high and rare order—talents which place her in the front rank of writers of dramatic fiction on either side of the water." . . .

"We are desirous to see the fine and varied faculties which this lady unquestionably possesses exerted upon some extensive and sustained work of fiction upon which all her powers may be fully concentrated and tested. She lingers below her destiny in being contented with even the greatest popularity; the native and true atmosphere of her renown is in the regions of fame."

With such encouragements, and under the unrelenting spur of necessity, Emily devoted herself afresh, so far as her delicate health allowed, to composition; and she might well feel justified in looking forward to a brilliant future. The "glittering bow" of promise, fame, arched

the heaven of our literary neophyte, and who can say
what "visions of splendor that bloomed but to fade"
were weaving their enchantments round her heart? But
Providence had in store for her a different destiny—a
harder ascent to a sublimer eminence. *Via lucis, via
crucis*—her way of light was to be the way of the cross.

> "I dreamed of celestial rewards and renown;
>   I grasped at the triumph that blesses the brave;
> I asked for the palm-branch, the robe, and the crown;
>   I asked—and thou show'dst me a cross and a grave."

Mild as was the climate of Philadelphia, the cold
weather still affected Emily so seriously, inducing cold
and cough upon the slightest exposure, that she at length
yielded to the persuasions of her friends, and determined
to pass the winter in that city. The Gillettes, though
at the expense of considerable domestic inconvenience,
proffered warmly the comforts of their home, and others
were urgent for a portion of her time. The following
note to Mrs. Nott gives a glimpse of her employments:

                                December 23, 1845.

MY DEAR MRS. NOTT,—

I meant to have written you a long time ago, and really
commenced a letter; but I have been O, *so* busy! Did you
receive the magazine which I sent you, containing the story of
Willard Lawson? Well, I have been requested to re-write it
for a Sunday-school book, and have been engaged in that and
some magazine things, hardly giving myself thinking time. I
am very agreeably situated in Mr. Gillette's family, rooming
with F——. They are dear, good people, amiable, kind, and
warm-hearted, and we could not have a pleasanter place to stay.
I had intended to leave them and stay with another family, but
they would not hear to it at all. . . . Mr. Gillette has been to

Boston, and we are expecting him back to-morrow with Dr. Judson. We are promising ourselves a rare treat in the company of the good missionary. . . . My health is very good indeed, though not quite equal to what it was when I left Utica. The cold weather is rather hard upon me, and, indeed, I don't know what I *should* have done there, away among the snows. It has been severely cold here for a few days past, and it quite shrivels me up.

Mrs. Gillette and F—— both send love, and more kind wishes than they seem to know exactly how to put into words. Please remember me kindly to your good Doctor, and believe me, my dear Mrs. Nott,

Ever sincerely and affectionately yours,

E. CHUBBUCK.

P. S. They were talking to me while I was writing, and so I have written your letter not only upside down, but wrongside out and backside before. I hope you will be able to find your way.

This letter foreshadows the approaching change in her destiny—a change whose first realization startled alike herself, her friends, and the public, both literary and religious, that had watched with interest the rising star of her genius and fame. Her literary friends were planning for her abundant occupation, and urging her to some work of larger pretension and higher flight than mere magazine stories. Her reputation in her own department of literature was established ; her conversation, freed from the shackles of that timidity which embarrassed her first entrance into society, was becoming scarcely less racy than her writings, and doing justice to her fine practical sense and brilliant imagination ; and her genius and personal accomplishments were becoming a passport to the most intelligent and refined circles. Never before, probably, had life looked so bright ; never

had a career of honorable and not unuseful distinction
shaped itself into so definite certainty ; never had the
world presented so much to attract ; never, perhaps,
during her Christian career, had heaven receded into so
dim a distance, and "the powers of the world to come"
held so feeble possession of her soul.

But she was led by ways that she knew not. Her
visions of literary fame were to be exchanged for prospects on which lowered the darkest and sternest realities.
The thorns that had strewn her earlier pathway were but
to anticipate the hardships of her later lot—a lot softened
only by the sweets of devoted love—brightened only by
the radiance from an unseen world. How seductive
would have proved the lures of worldly fame : how far
its illusory splendor might have eclipsed to her vision
the brightness that rests on the heavenly hills, we may
not know. From the dreams of first fame she would
ere long have awakened ; her "dissatisfied spirit" would
have broken the spell of its enchantment, and spiritual
things have reasserted their supremacy in her soul ; for
that soul had been touched and transformed by a rod
more potent than that of any earthly enchanter. But
from the perils of the trial Providence mercifully deliv-
ered her. It brought upon the stage a new actor, whose
gentle but powerful attractions, whose commanding intellect and fine culture, harmonized and exalted by a
fervid piety, proved mightier than literary ambition, or
the claims of merely earthly usefulness, and drew her
away from a career of growing worldliness to a path

"All rugged with rock, and all tangled with thorn,"

but on whose difficult ascent was shed the deepening
brightness of immortality.

CHAPTER X.

"Ask me no more, thy fate and mine are sealed;
I strove against the stream, and all in vain;
Let the great river take me to the main.
No more, dear love, for at a touch I yield;
Ask me no more!"

IN the spring preceding, Rev. Dr. Judson had been obliged to leave India by the alarming illness of his wife, the lovely widow of the sainted missionary, Boardman. The flattering hopes excited by the commencement of the voyage were soon dissipated, and instead of parting upon the "green islet," as anticipated in her precious little gem of song, he "for the eastern main," they bent their united way toward "the setting sun." But she died upon the passage, and the vessel reached St. Helena just in season to enable the veteran hero of the cross to deposit his precious treasure in that "rock of the sea," which had been the prison and the grave of the great hero of the sword. Having rendered to the dear remains the last obsequies, he proceeded on his voyage, and in October, 1845, landed, after an absence of nearly thirty-four years, on his native shores. We need not follow his movements up to the point where his history links itself with that of Miss Chubbuck. A rapturous enthusiasm every where greeted his coming, and upon his whispered words of consecrated eloquence listening thousands hung as upon the accents of an angel.

In December, being in Boston, he was requested to attend a series of missionary meetings in Philadelphia, and Rev. Mr. Gillette, Emily's host, went on to Boston to secure his presence. On their way between New York and Philadelphia, a slight railroad accident detained them two or three hours, and to relieve the tedium of the delay, Mr. Gillette, seeing a volume of the newly published "Trippings" in the hands of a friend, borrowed it, and handed it to Dr. Judson. He hesitatingly took it, the title not promising a work specially to his taste ; but carelessly opening it, he soon found his attention riveted by the grace of the style, and the truth and sprightliness of the narrative. On Mr. Gillette's returning to him, he inquired who was the author of the book, adding that it was written with great beauty and power—reiterating emphatically, with great beauty and power. He asked if the lady was a Christian, and being informed that she was, said : "I should be glad to know her. A lady who writes so well ought to write better. It is a pity that such fine talents should be employed upon such subjects." Mr. Gillette replied that he would soon be able to make her acquaintance, as she was then an inmate of his own house. "Is she a Baptist ?" asked Dr. Judson ; and being answered affirmatively, he renewedly expressed his desire to see and converse with her, as it was a pity that talents so brilliant should not be more worthily employed. They arrived in (or out of) due time at Philadelphia, and Dr. Judson was welcomed to the house of Mr. and Mrs. W. S. Robarts, who became warm personal friends, as they were already active friends of the mission cause.

Promptly on the next day he came over to Mr. Gillette's. Emily (in her morning-dress) was submitting to the not very poetical process of vaccination. As soon as it was over, Dr. Judson conducted her to the sofa, saying that he wished to talk with her. She replied half playfully that she should be delighted and honored by having him talk to her. With characteristic impetuosity he immediately inquired how she could reconcile it with her conscience to employ talents so noble in a species of writing so little useful or spiritual as the sketches which he had read. Emily's heart melted ; she replied with seriousness and candor, and explained the circumstances which had drawn her into this field of authorship. Indigent parents, largely dependent on her efforts—years of laborious teaching—books published with but little profit, had driven her to still new and untried paths, in which at last success unexpectedly opened upon her. Making this employment purely secondary, and carefully avoiding every thing of doubtful tendency, she could not regard her course as open to serious strictures. It was now Dr. Judson's turn to be softened. He admitted the force of her reasons, and that even his own strict standard could not severely censure the direction given to filial love. He opened another subject. He wished to secure a person to prepare a memoir of his recently deceased wife, and it was partly, in fact, with this purpose that he had sought Emily's acquaintance. She entertained the proposition, and the discussion of this matter naturally threw them much together during the ensuing few days. The consequences of the coming together of two persons respectively so fascinating, were what has often occurred since the days of Adam and Eve. They became mutually in-

terested.   Dr. Judson discovered in her not only rare intellectual powers, but a warm heart, an enthusiastic and
richly endowed nature that throbbed in sympathetic
unison with his own.   That she was not in the exercise
of that living piety—those high spiritual graces so essential in the missionary, and scarcely less in the missionary's wife, he saw with pain ; but detecting in her experiences the undoubted germs of genuine faith, he soon
conceived the idea of her not only writing the life, but
taking the place of the sainted deceased.   Having reached
this conclusion, he pressed the subject upon her with al.
the energy of his impassioned and most truthful character.   He painted to her the glories and the deformities
of the Orient ; its moral desert in a wilderness of luxuriant beauty.   He set forth the toils and privations of
the missionary's lot, and over against this, the privilege
of being a reaper in the great moral harvest of the world ;
the blessedness of those who turn many to righteousness ;
the glory of that coming world whence faith already
draws many a presaging token of bliss.

It was not in Emily's nature to be insensible to the
force of such arguments from such a pleader—falling
from "lips wet with Castalian dews," as well as with the
dews that descend upon the mountains of Zion—coming
from one whose tastes were as cultivated as his faith was
lofty, and who could appreciate equally the fascinations
which he asked her to resign, and the glories to which
he asked her to aspire.   Yet a revolution in her destiny so sudden and total, so complete a reversal of her
plans, filled her with perplexity and almost alarm.   Her
family friends—her literary friends—her religious friends,
and above all that ubiquitous, myriad-headed, myriad-
tongued personage called the World—what would they

say upon hearing that Fanny Forester, the popular
magazinist was about to turn her back on her newly
commenced career, and quench her rising fame in the
night of heathenism ? Above all—and here was the
stress of the conflict—she weighed her spiritual deficiencies—her want of that deep consecration so imperatively
demanded in one who lays hands on the sacred ark of
the missionary cause. She had declined from her earlier
consecration, and the path which she once sought the
privilege of treading, it now, as she afterwards declared,
" seemed like death for her to enter." She urged these
objections upon Dr. Judson ; but he overruled them with
the impetuous logic which characterized his energetic
career, and laid upon her the spell of a nature that combined what is holiest in the saint with what is most attractive in the man. Time, too, with him was pressing :
he longed to be back to the scene of his life-labors ; the
children that he had left behind pleaded eloquently for a
mother ; and in the gifted young lady whom he at first
intended merely to secure as the biographer of his lamented Sarah, he saw one well fitted to take her place as a
mother, as well as to meet the yearnings of his intellect
and heart. The rapid decision to which they arrived
sprang from a conscious congeniality of temper and endowments. The ripe experience, the mellow wisdom,
the ardent piety of Dr. Judson were combined, amidst
all the severities of his missionary consecration, with an
inextinguishable warmth of heart, a delicacy of taste, and
a breadth of culture which recognized in Emily answering qualities, and drew him to her with all the warmth
of his singularly gifted and susceptible nature, while they
in turn stirred her deepest fountains of reverence and love.

Dr. Judson was now fifty-seven. But one needed only

to look into his dark eye beaming with benignity, and flashing with intelligence, and to listen to him, when, in his moments of unreserve, he poured forth the exuberance of his joyous spirit, to see that age had passed lightly over him, and that the dew of youth was yet fresh upon his soul.   That Dr. Judson at this age could love with the ardor, and almost with the romance of a first affection, instead of being just matter of skepticism or reproach, is in fact a beautiful tribute alike to the native largeness of his soul, and to the power of that piety which keeps the heart green and youthful ; which, by husbanding and purifying, preserves unspent that fountain of affection which libertinism recklessly squanders, and keeps undimmed and beautiful that "pearl of the soul" which is soon melted away "in the lavishing cup of desire."   Love to God is the true parent and preservative of love to man—and to woman.   In this the sweetest blossoms of affection live and shed their fragrance long after they lie withered and dead in the bosom of the sensualist and the worldling.   Byron, at the early age of thirty-six, wrote with terrible and most instructive truth :

> My days are in the yellow leaf;
>   The flowers and fruits of love are gone ;
> The worm, the canker, and the grief
>   Are mine alone.

Compare this desolate utterance of a palled and sated spirit with the unaffectedly warm and tender letters of Dr. Judson down to his latest years: with that death-bed utterance of his sixty-second year, "O, no man ever left this world with more inviting prospects, with brighter hopes or warmer feelings."   This is the genius of Christianity—such the power of that religion which

pours heavenly oil on the flame of earthly affection, and
keeps the lamp burning undimmed down to the very
verge of the sepulchre. It is beautiful to see Dr. Judson ever linking in memory his third wife with his former
ones, and even in his first avowal of affection blending
the three in sacred association. Nor did Emily feel that
love for her demanded any restraint upon his expressions
of affectionate remembrance of them. His unforgetting
regard for them was her surest guaranty of her own permanent place in his heart, and she writes with equal
truth and beauty:

> For death but lays his mystic spell
>   Upon affection's earthliness ;
> I know that though thou lov'st me well,
>   Thou lov'st thy sainted none the less.

The following little note contains Dr. Judson's formal
avowal of attachment. It seems half like sacrilege to
lift the veil upon a thing so sacred as a marriage proposal ; but this interweaves so ingenious and graceful a
memorial of his former wives, and in its delicate playfulness illustrates so admirably a large element in his character which found little scope in his ordinary correspondence, that the reader will pardon its publication.

January 20, 1846.

I hand you, dearest one, a charmed watch. It always comes
back to me, and brings its wearer with it. I gave it to Ann
when a hemisphere divided us, and it brought her safely and
surely to my arms. I gave it to Sarah during her husband's
life-time (not then aware of the secret), and the charm, though
slow in its operation, was true at last.

Were it not for the sweet sympathies you have kindly extended to me, and the blessed understanding that "love has taught us to guess at," I should not venture to pray you to accept my present with such a note. Should you cease to "guess" and toss back the article, saying, "Your watch has lost its charm; it comes back to you, *but brings not its wearer with it*" —O first dash it to pieces, that it may be an emblem of what will remain of the heart of

Your devoted,   A. JUDSON.

Miss Emily Chubbuck.

Emily's reply to this letter we know only by the result. They were affianced, and on the 23d she writes thus to her faithful friend Miss Sheldon:

TO MISS SHELDON.

January 24, 1846.

I am *so* thankful to you, dear Miss C. for favoring this wild-looking project of mine. My good doctor has now gone away, and I have just said to him the irrevocable *yes*, though I must acknowledge that I have acted it slightly before. It was most kind and thoughtful in you to write to mother; it will soften the matter to her greatly, and even then I fear the result. You think there is a mysterious Providence in this singular proceeding, and so does Mr. Gillette. As for the doctor, he finds in it a combination of circumstances which mark clearly supernatural agency. He is a blessed man; you can not begin to dream how good he is, and I suppose that I have a good share of it yet to learn. Well, I shall have years of at least partial loneliness to learn in. Dear Aunt C., I have not taken this step without a great, *great deal* of thought, and I would not take it but that I believe the blessing of God is in it. I must acknowledge indeed that I have little of the proper missionary spirit. Perhaps it will increase; I hope so. I would gladly be useful, and this has influenced me very much in my decision. Still I do not wish to make any professions, and you will find me the same as ever. But one thing it may be well to say to you now. Whatever may happen—if I should die on the passage—I should not be sorry that I went. In regard to preparations I shall not concern myself, for I know there are kind and good friends enough to attend to that. Mr. G. will, as he says, "beg the privilege," and I shall leave the matter to you and to him; but I have several debts at Utica, and I am anxious to get back and see about them. I do not know exactly my resources; but I know they are in a pretty bad state. For this reason I have declined going on to Washington, and am very anxious to return to Utica. I do not even know just how much is due on my place. I shall have enough to make out my April payment, but beyond that I am very destitute. I shall collect all my "Fanny Forester" stories, and make as good a bargain as I can. . . .

My good doctor is as attentive to my comfort as though he had been accustomed to luxuries instead of self-denial and suffering; and he proposes to me to take out a servant or humble companion, if I wish it. The native servants are not to be depended upon, and I should, of course, manage a house very poorly. One thing the doctor says, if I take out a pretty girl I must make her agree to pay back the passage-money in case of getting married; for one of the provincial officers will take her in spite of herself. Please look about you a little, and help me to somebody. If you can contrive any way to get me home, please do it, for I am in great haste to be among you. Tell grandpa he would have been burned for his prophecy if he had lived in Salem. Take warning from my case, and do not let any more of your girls go away to spend the winter. Love to all, especially yourself.

EMILY.

On the 24th, Dr. Judson left Philadelphia for Washington, Richmond, etc. From Washington he thus writes:

WASHINGTON, January 25, 1846.

MY DEAREST LOVE,—

Since closing my last I have attended an evening meeting, and had a most interesting time. There was a crowded house, and young Samson is a truly eloquent preacher. All passed off well, except that the most appalling praises were poured out on me; so that I felt obliged to get up and disclaim the praise, confess my sins, and beg the people to join me in praying for pardon. But they will not understand me; they will take every thing the wrong way, and I can not help it. As to *you*, I am afraid you will find me out too soon, and understand me too well. And perhaps you will go to the other extreme, as is frequently the case; and—though it would be no more than just retribution—how could I bear to see your scanty sources of happiness in distant Burmah so grievously curtailed? I can only promise to try to alleviate your disappointment by being as kind to you as my poor nature will permit. But I beg you will endeavor to rest your happiness on a better foundation than my love. There is, you know, One that loves you infinitely more than I do. His love is unchanging and endless; for with Him is no variableness, nor shadow of turning. And when He has once set His love upon a soul, He will ever draw that soul to Himself. Have you not found this to be true from the day you first loved the Saviour, though your love may have been low and dim, and subject to occasional fluctuations and eclipses? Yet have you not found that the magnetic influence would never leave you, and that you can truly say,

> "As, true to the star of its worship, though clouded,
>   The compass points steadily o'er the dim sea,
> So, dark as I rove through this wintry world shrouded,
>   The hope of my spirit turns trembling to Thee—
>   True, fond, trembling to Thee."

. . . I have been praying for every blessing to rest on you that I think you need; especially that your mind may be gradually drawn from every thing that is dubious, or barely good, to the *better* and the *best*, and that, in pursuing "the more excellent way" you may not be repelled or deterred by the company you may occasionally meet on that way. Christ went about doing good. May it be our glory to imitate His example; and in order to this, we must do good to the evil and the unthankful. Herein is true glory, as the light of eternity will show.

Thine ever,

A. Judson.

TO DR. JUDSON.

January 25, 1846.

My Very Dear Friend,—

. . . I do not know what to say to you about going home. Miss Sheldon says in a letter received to-day that the thermometer ranges from six to sixteen below zero, and she dare not have me come. I shall wait a little and be governed by the weather. In the meantime I am very, very lonely. . . . If you were only with me, I should be happier than I have been in years. I dare not look at my future much more than at first, but I trust myself to my God and you—the Heavenly Friend who is all powerful, and the earthly one who would not deceive me, who loves me, I know, most unselfishly— and I feel perfectly secure. I thank God for sending you to Philadelphia, and for giving me your priceless affection. I can not become worthy of it, but dear, dear doctor, you shall teach and guide me, and I will do the best I can; I can love you at least, and will.

Heaven guard you! so prays your

Emily.

TO DR. JUDSON.

January 31.

... It was not this which brought about "a low state of religious feeling." The declension in religion came first; and I believe,

as I now look back, that it was occasioned by the wish to show
people that I was not the saint they supposed. You know I carry
something of a serious face. I had written a little for the *Register*, and some of my books for children brought me credit for
qualities that I did not possess. When I was a pupil in Miss
Sheldon's school, I was nick-named (affectionately, of course,)
"the little saint," and when I found people thought I had so
much religion, I came to the conclusion that I had none at all,
and so went about to convince others of it. I know it was
wrong; but however agreeable flattery may be, it is painful to
be praised for such things. You must watch over me now, and
not let me take the first step in wrong; and may God in heaven
watch over you, my dearest friend.

TO DR. JUDSON.

January 31.

Mr. W. writes, in one of his last letters, " If you should ever
be placed in circumstances to call it forth, the world will find that
there is stuff for a heroine hidden behind your partial development
by literature." I fancy he will think me playing the heroine
sooner than he expected. That Burmah is a great bug-bear.
Mr. W——e continues to be "alarmed." He wonders, if people
will be missionaries that they do not "select some decent place."

TO DR. JUDSON.

Philadelphia, February 7, 1846.

"But art thou sure of all the future turnings of thy heart ?"
No, dearest friend of mine, not entirely sure, for it is a very
mysterious thing; but I suppose that I have seen the brightest,
or rather, the most attractive side of " gay and fashionable life."
I have seen it softened down, with its most beautiful features
on—nothing to shock or startle; seen it in its most poetical
dress. You know this has failed to gain my entire heart, and
so you need not fear the glitter for me. What have you seen
in me that could lead you to suppose for one moment that the

parade of fashionable life would be agreeable to me—that it would not be annoying? Here I have refused three invitations to-day: two to dinner (one with one of the most fashionable families in the city), and the other two to a dashing party made expressly for me. I know it is the general impression that I like gay society—an impression which I have taken some pleasure in heightening rather than correcting—but I thought you knew my tastes better.

With (not boasting, but for truth's sake, I write it) a very wide power of choice—much more extensive than would generally be supposed a woman in my position, poor, and without high connections, could have—I have voluntarily, and with but a single condition, founded on regard for you, said "all, all your own." . . . Is it such a very light thing to adopt an entirely new course of life—new in feelings, thoughts, associations, every thing—is it such a very light thing to do, that I can take it all back to-morrow, as I could undo a ribbon that I had knotted? The future certainly looks very dark to me, but with my hand in yours, if you will only clasp it close, and the certainty of a place in your heart, I can look upon it courageously. Dear Doctor, only love me, do not see too many faults, censure gently, lead me "to the enjoyment of higher religion, and to more extensive usefulness," *trust* me, and no place on earth is half so pleasant as "grim Burmah." I shut my eyes on all you tell me about it, because I know that all my conceptions must be very imperfect, and *you* can make gloom or sunshine for me. The *place* is not what constitutes my home—it is your presence.

Emily now remained in Philadelphia, impatiently awaiting the earliest relaxing of the rigors of winter, that she might proceed homeward as soon as possible. On the 17th of February she went to New York, and reached Utica on the 20th. Her intention had been to stop and visit her friend Mrs. Nott, in Schenectady, but the stormy weather forbade. She met a cordial welcome from her friends in the Seminary, who entered heartily into her new arrangements, and proposed to take upon themselves (her Philadelphia friends joining in it) the main responsibility of her outfit. She remained in Utica until the first week in March, when she proceeded to Hamilton, whither it was arranged that Dr. Judson should follow her for a few days' quiet visiting with her parents and family. He came on the 12th, and spent a few days in making the acquaintance of his future relatives.

In giving a few extracts from his and Miss Chubbuck's correspondence at this time, I have no wish to minister to a prurient curiosity, nor to violate that principle which would generally place letters written during the period of an "engagement" under the shelter of inviolate secresy. The case, however, is a peculiar one ; and, on the one hand, a few extracts from Emily's letters will best illustrate the state of mind in which she entered upon her new career, and on the other, the public will be grateful for any thing from Dr. Judson's private correspondence that may with propriety be published—especially as so little of it has escaped destruction. Dr. Judson was unquestionably one of the finest epistolary writers in our language—chaste, simple, elegant, every word selected with felicitous yet unconscious precision, and passing spontaneously from delicate playfulness into those regions of sacred thought in which he habitually dwelt. The selections from the present correspondence, made, of course, with reference, not to their literary merit, but to their fitness for publication, can do but slight justice to his versatile epistolary powers.

The world will never appreciate, until the revelations

of the judgment, the sacrifices of this remarkable man—what a wealth of endowments and susceptibilties—what exquisite tenderness—what exuberant vivacity and humor—what capabilities and aspirations after every form of worldly excellence he cheerfully offered upon the altar of the world's evangelization. Not that his case is peculiar, except in degree. The intellectually halt, and blind, and feeble, have not been the church's chief sacrifices at the shrine of missionary zeal. Those who have led the van in the assaults on the gigantic systems of Paganism, have been generally fully as rich in all the elements of culture, fully as susceptible to the refinements and comforts on which they turned their backs, as those who have stayed at home.

TO DR. JUDSON.

NEW YORK, Feb. 18, 1846.

MY OWN DEAR " HOME,"—

I carried a sad heart with me in the cars yesterday, notwithstanding I was on my way to old friends. The disappearance of Philadelphia seemed like the dissolving of a dream, and I could not make myself believe that my relation to you, my prospects, or even my own feelings, were real. How I longed to have you with me! I reached here about two o'clock, my brain half muddled with thinking, and half disposed to wish for drowning, and found Col. G. waiting for me. We proceeded here forthwith (to the Colgates'), where I met an old school-mate. Col. G. leaves for Albany to-morrow morning, so I hope to reach Utica Friday afternoon. I find myself very well this morning, but think I shall not go out to-day.

I told you I was troubled yesterday. There is something so unreal (sometimes) in the position in which I find myself that reflection becomes absolutely painful; and I am half tempted to doubt my own identity. But like the old woman of the nursery rhyme, I hope home will dissipate the mist. They will make it all real when I get to Utica, for they seem to think it a very proper thing for me to become a missionary. I thought it a very nice thing, too, when I went to my room last night and laid my head upon my pillow, perfectly happy. Things were reversed. The bug-bears haunted me in the day-time, and at night they fled. I seemed to feel that you had been praying for me, and thought there was a double guard of angels set for me. Oh, I thank God constantly for the sweet way in which He has chidden my follies, and pointed out a better path for me to walk in. I have been (and am still) a great world-lover, and He might have sent severe punishment—might have led me on to find pain and sorrow in the things I valued. But instead of that He has made the way *so* attractive! He has sent you, dearest, to love and care for, to guide and strengthen me. I believe what you have so often said that God delights in the happiness of his creatures ; and I know that Burmah will be a happier palace for me than any place on earth. Shall I not have your own arm there to lean upon, and your own wisdom to guide me? Mr. Hoffman remarked when in Philadelphia that the reason why literary women are so universally unhappy is, they marry men who can not appreciate them. He said they needed cherishing and guidance more than any other class— that their husbands at first thought them little less than goddesses ; but, looking for equality of excellencies, a well-balanced character, and discovering striking defects, weaknesses, and eccentricities, they soon come to think them little better than fools. So, dear, pray do not think me a *goddess*, for I must have you to think and act for me ; but woe be to the day when, for that, you call me *fool*. Then, just to show you that I am not a fool, I shall set up for myself, and such a house as we shall have! . . .

EMILY.

TO MRS. NOTT.

UTICA FEMALE SEMINARY, February, 1846.

MY VERY DEAR FRIEND,—

. . . I received a letter from my good doctor on Saturday, and shall expect him in Hamilton about the middle of next week. I think of going myself on Thursday. Kate advises me not to come so soon, as she fears it will become known that I am there; but I am anxious to see my mother. We shall manage to pay you the proposed visit, if possible. If you will only see him as I do! I am not afraid but that you will like him; every body likes him. But it is not the wonder, the lion that I care to have you see; it is the refined, generous, high-souled, strong-minded, true-hearted *man*, and the humble, devoted, unostentatious Christian. I fancy that you will be pretty sure that no common man could have made a missionary of me; and no common man would have had the independence to choose me. I will endeavor to behave as well as I can; but I must own that I have been twice surprised—at seeing the tear in the eye of the careless worldling, and receiving the God-speed from his lips, and at seeing those from whom I had a right to expect encouragement looking askance and doubtful. I have resolved, however, not to see any of the latter things, and I hope they will not be forced on my attention.

I must close my letter, or Mary will be gone. Please remember me always kindly, and drop me a line when you have time. I shall try hard to return to those who need it most all the kindness which you have shown to me; and however lightly I may speak sometimes, believe me, if God spares my health, I *will* do good. I know I can. I have always felt that I had unappropriated energies, and, however wild the notion may seem, I think my whole life has had a tendency to prepare me for this very thing. I can see it from the very beginning to this present winter, which I commenced so gayly in P.

It has been, you know, a peculiar training, and had I but more religion ! Give me your prayers, and God help me !

Ever yours affectionately,

EMILY.

TO HORACE B. WALLACE, ESQ.

UTICA, February 23, 1846.

MY VERY EXCELLENT FRIEND,—

I regret exceedingly the *malapropos* illness which prevented me from seeing you again before I took my final leave of Philadelphia, particularly as I wished to have a good, cozy, confidential *talk* with you, which, for reasons that you will understand and appreciate, I deferred till a good-bye meeting.

What induced you to suspect that I was going to Burmah ? Did you see any thing missionary-like in Fanny Forester ? You don't know how your suspicion pleased and encouraged me ; for I expected that the first thought of my friends would be a lunatic asylum and straight jacket. You were right. I expect to sail about the first of July, and under the protection of Dr. Judson. I am a great admirer of greatness—real, genuine greatness ; and goodness has an influence which I have not the power to resist. I believe the reason that I have never loved before (for I think that I have a somewhat loving nature) is, that I never saw the two so beautifully combined in one person. My good Doctor's hair is as black as the raven's wing yet ; but if it were not, if he were many years older, it would be all the same : I would go with him the world over. There is a noble structure within, singularly combining delicacy and strength, which will afford me protection and shelter in this world—a place where my own weak nature may rest itself securely—a thing that never will grow old, and that I shall love in eternity. So you see that, in going to Burmah, I make no sacrifices ; for the things that I resign, though more showy, are not half as dear to me as those which I gain. I believe that you know women well enough, and know this one woman well enough, to see clearly how that can be.

What I have told you is, perhaps, enough to make you understand that I would not object to Siberia, or Patagonia, or *Burmah*, since my heart-home goes with me; but will you believe me when I tell you that I find actual pleasure in the thought of going? Did you ever feel as though all the things that you were engaged in were so trivial, so aimless, that you fairly sickened of them, and longed to do something more worthy of your origin and destiny? I can not describe the feeling entirely; but it has haunted me for the last six months, sleeping and waking—in the crowd and in solitude—till, from being the most contented of humans, I have been growing dissatisfied with every thing. True, I had the power to amuse, and make some people momentarily happy. I tried to weave some little moral into all I wrote; and while doing so, endeavored to persuade myself that this was sufficient. But, though I seemed to convince myself, I was not convinced nor satisfied. Now it is different. I shall really have an opportunity of spending my short life in the way which would make me most happy—in doing real, permanent good. Here, there are so many others better and more influential than myself, that what little influence I now and then find myself capable of exerting, seems entirely lost—is like one leaf on the tree which shelters you from the sun—of some worth as part of a great mass, but comparatively useless. There, every word and act will have a very important bearing. The consciousness of this will make me more watchful of myself, more careful to be governed by the very highest of principles and motives; and so a double good will result. It is the same with my pen. With all the wise heads in the country plotting a literary inundation, what can the brain of poor, simple Fanny Forester effect? *There* is a great nation on whose future character every pen-stroke will have a bearing. Doctor Judson has given them the entire Scriptures, written several small books in the Burmese, and has nearly completed a dictionary of the language. He will be the founder of a national literature, give its tone (a pure and holy influence he exerts) to the character of a mighty people; and I must own that I feel rather inclined to thrust in my own little finger. Do you wonder? Do you think that I am carried away by a foolish enthusiasm—a false zeal? or do you think that I have made a sober, common-sense estimate of things, and decided wisely? As to my way of living there, I shall be obliged to deny myself many luxuries and elegancies which I know I shall miss very much at first, for the salary of a missionary is small; but I shall try to make every thing as tasteful and home-like as possible, and then accommodate myself to circumstances.

I will promise you not to *write a journal,* for I have no greater fancy for holding up a heart-thermometer before the world than you; and I don't think that I shall be any "wiser," or any more in love with wisdom than ever. I confidently expect, however, to be very, very happy; and to make a dear, little home, which, if you ever "go to the Indies to make your fortune," you shall not think it a very great bore to visit. And hereby, Mr. Wallace, consider yourself invited to Maulmain. When may we expect to see you?

Please keep my secret for me until it becomes public; and let me know that I have your earnest and hearty God-speed. The approbation of my friends will make the painful parting from them and the home which I love, oh, so dearly! much easier. Probably I never shall see you again; but whether I do or not, I shall think of you, and the kind interest you have shown in me, often; and shall always be your most sincere friend,

EMILY CHUBBUCK.

Breaking in slightly on the order of dates, I here subjoin Mr. Wallace's beautiful reply. It is a tribute equally honorable to him who wrote, and to her who called it forth :

I have read your beautiful letter, dearest lady, with deep interest, and the liveliest gratification. If anything could have given increased enthusiasm to the perfect respect with which I have regarded the pure and exquisite nature that was evidently revealed to my admiration when I had the happiness to become acquainted with you, it would be such new evidences of goodness, and high principle, and noble sentiment as are implied in the intelligence which your letter communicates. So faithful a picture of a refined, and elevated, and generous heart, must touch and charm the feelings of every one who has any sensibility to excellence, or any preception of what is honorable and great. I beg you to permit the warmest congratulations and the most earnest good wishes of one who loves you as a brother, and feels in all that concerns your welfare the concern of a devoted friend.

Your choice is worthy of you. It commends itself to my highest sympathy and admiration. You always seemed to me to be too exalted and heaven-like for the mere affection of ordinary persons; and not to be waited upon by them with any feelings but such as are blended with something of worship. You may recollect that I said to you, at the time when I could not be suspected of a design to flatter, that Dr. Judson was one of my *heroes ;* that goodness, such as his, was the highest type of greatness—far surpassing all such ambition as is founded on views that are limited by this world, and beating down the rivalry of such fame as has in it any admixture of vanity. It produces no wonder in me, but the highest interest and delight, to know that your spirit is so finely sensitive to the lofty attractions that belong to a character and career so disinterested—so sublime. That which first engaged my regard and curiosity in relation to you, was the fascinating delicacy of thought and feeling which your writings displayed: what struck me most, in approaching you more nearly, and placed my respect upon a higher and surer basis, was the superiority which your nature insensibly always displayed to the interests and excitements of literary reputation. That "pettiness of fame" which is the glory of so many, seemed to excite your aversion ; and that which, in other cases, is the coveted result of authorship, seemed to be to you the only annoying and painful part of it. These traits and evidences of a lofty and noble nature, I appreciated thoroughly, and understood. That your feelings, unsusceptible to all that addresses that portion of our being which is earthly and transitory, should respond so fully to that which appealed to those great sentiments of duty and goodness which partake of the eternal, and bring us into union with what is permanent and changeless, shows me that I had not mistaken my gentle friend ; but that she whom I had valued so highly, "deserved to be dearest of all.'

You must acknowledge that I possess some discernment, since, from the moment in which I first heard the name of this eminent and honored person pronounced by your lips, I saw and predicted the result. The purest streams are the most transparent ; and it seems to me that I can read your feelings and their operations, with great distinctness. I hope that this will be a tie of friendship between us, or at least that you will suffer me always to indulge those sentiments of proud and tender interest in your welfare, which, perhaps, I may express more strongly than you will approve, but which are inseparable from my recollection of you.

You speak of the probability of my not seeing you again. I shall surely see you before you take your leave of shores where your name will long flourish with added honors and new distinction. I shall come to mingle my best and brightest omens with the "might of the whole world's good wishes," that will attend your going. You will not be separated entirely from me in seeking the realities of that Burmah which I prophesied would be your destiny; for my constant thoughts, and earnest interest will accompany you, and, even if your remembrance should never visit me, will deprive you of the power to escape from me entirely.

I feel highly honored by the confidence which you reposed in me ; and you may rely upon the secret being faithfully kept, until it suits your convenience to permit it to become known.

May all your hopes be realized! May all of kind and good that you intend for others, be fulfilled on them and on you! May you be happy!—"a wish that came—but it hath passed into a prayer."

H. B. WALLACE.

TO DR. JUDSON.

UTICA, February 25.

. . . I must own to you, dearest, now that I am away from you, misgivings will trouble me. I believe that you love me with the whole of your noble heart; but I am afraid, when the whole storm of wonderment bursts upon us, you will—perhaps you will not doubt your having acted wisely—but I am afraid you will be very much troubled. I know that there will be a great deal said—a great many unpleasant things—and should I not feel badly to see you made sad for a single moment by having taken such an unworthy creature to your heart? I can not make-believe good when I am not; but I pray God daily to make me better and wiser, to fit me for the future, and make me a blessing instead of a curse to you who have loved me with all my follies. I will try to be all to you that I can, and to do all the good that I can, but I feel that it would be wicked cant in me to sit down and talk in the way that the multitude will expect. . . . My thoughts are not for one moment away from you; but I think too little of my Saviour. I do desire to love Him better, but I have a dull eye for the invisible. Still, pray for me, my beloved guide—pray for faith, spirituality, and all the good things that I need. I still think more of earth than heaven, "for I am frail;" but I find some pleasure in the contemplation of higher things; and a heaven with you, dearest! That is the *visible* link, my love for you. I am not afraid of loving you too much, for that love is closely connected with all my better feelings. You freed me from a glittering coil which was growing irksome to me, and you are to be my spiritual teacher. God will lead us both, but my hand will be in yours. It is His own work: He sent you, and I shall not displease Him by clinging to you with all the affection He has blessed my heart with. And you will not disappoint me when I have none but you; I am sure you will not. It is a long way to Burmah, and I have a great many friends to leave.

FROM DR. JUDSON.

March 2.

Your dear, precious letter has just came in and what a load is removed from my heart. Thanks be to God. But I know not when I shall reach Utica or Hamilton. I took a very severe cold on my way from Baltimore, and it has left the worst cough I have had since arriving in the country. The weather is dreadfully cold, and it is snowing here to the terror of the Philadelphians. And all say that it is infinitely worse at the north, and the delay of the mails shows that the roads must be blocked up with snow. I intended to leave to day, as I think I mentioned in my last, but it is out of the question. I may get to New York day after to-morrow if the roads are opened. There I shall hope to get another letter from you, and thence I shall write you again. Don't think, however, that I am ill. The cough is merely the result of a common cold—is much better to-day, and will, I doubt not, with proper care be removed in a few days. I am only unwilling, for your sake, to plunge into too great exposure, and get it settled on my lungs. I shall be able to reach New York without much exposure, and I am sure of a warm house at Mr. Newton's.

Do, dearest—most dear from every letter, and every recollection—do erase that word "misgivings" from the vocabulary of your heart. "Storm of wonderment"—I shall only exult in it. "A great many unpleasant things"—my love would not be worth your accepting, if it could be affected by such things. I have some confidence in my love for you, because I began at the bottom of the ladder. I loved you not as a goddess, but as a very sinful creature—more sinful than myself. Now I have discovered my mistake, and can I love you less?

FROM HER REPLY.

February 28, 1846.

I do not have "misgivings" except on my own account. When I think of my own utter uselessness—my unfitness for any thing except to write stories, I can not help being sad; and when I look away over to Burmah, and see you in your study, and me engaged in things that have never interested me and that I do not know how to do, spending day after day *alone*, my very heart retreats in utter consternation. I do not know how I shall get along with it. But the Heavenly Friend who I believe has directed all this, will be still a better friend than any one on earth; and you, dearest, will be considerate and patient —I know you will. You don't expect me to be very good or very sensible; but I shall take no advantage of that. I will be as good and wise as I can. God in heaven help me!

CHAPTER XI.

THE CONSECRATION.

"I waste no more in idle dreams my life, my soul away,
I wake to know my better self—I wake to watch and pray;
Thought, feeling, time, on idols vain I've lavished all too long;
Henceforth to holier purposes I pledge myself, my song!"

I DESIGNATE this chapter "The Consecration," not as indicating any sharp separating line in Miss Chubbuck's Christian life. She had not previously wasted her "life in idle dreams," nor did she now rise at once to the due level of missionary consecration. Personal regard for Dr. Judson was doubtless her first tie to the missionary life; but it would be strange that, in a Christian heart, connection with such a man, and the prospect of such a destiny, should not stir powerfully its slumbering elements and wake intenser religious aspirations. Such was the fact. Emily deeply felt the importance of rising from the "barely good to the better and the best;" of so training her spirit that she could enter with her full soul into the glorious work which lay in near view.

Emily reached home—"the loggery," as she playfully styled her father's humble but very comfortable dwelling—the first week in March. Dr. Judson came a few days later. The news of their engagement had of course preceded them, and as matrimonial arrangements are everybody's property for comment and strictures, theirs could scarcely prove an exception. That it should take the world by surprise—should startle many and grieve some—is not marvelous. The regret would naturally take two very different directions. The worshipers of the newly risen star could not sufficiently wonder at her stopping short in the very outset of her career, and sacrificing her brilliant prospects on the altar of a fanatical philanthropy. They had no adequate words for the infatuation which could bury talents, virtues, fame, life itself in the sepulchral glooms of heathenism ; and could hardly stigmatize severely enough the sorceries by which Dr. Judson had wrought upon that youthful heart, and lured it to so wanton a sacrifice. The dark-skinned inveigler of the affections of Desdemona was of angel whiteness compared with the Asiatic prowler who had decoyed " Fanny Forester" into the homes of the barbarians.

The religious public, with whom the missionary enterprise stood in moral dignity incomparably above every other—to whom the perishing laurels of literary fame were worthless beside the amaranthine wreath of piety, would feel very differently. To them the surprise was that he who, from his distant home, was looked upon as superior to the weaknesses, and almost the vulgar virtues of humanity—who had been the husband of Ann Hasseltine and Sarah Boardman, should take as the successor to that sainted pair a young woman—slightly known to the religious world, and figuring in the magazines as the most popular female writer of polite literature. Little was known of her personal character ; next to nothing of her domestic history. Her struggles for long years to support herself and family by teaching ; her ill success with her strictly religious books ; the

purely accidental character of her association with the
magazines, and the pressing pecuniary engagements which
compelled her to continue it ; and, above all, the fact
that light, elastic, playful, and exceedingly readable as
were her sketches, they never proved false to the principles of virtue, and often cogently enforced some profound
and solemn truth—all this was generally unknown or
overlooked by the censurers. Yet Dr. Judson knew it
all ; to him her magazine reputation was a mere adventitious thing which he could not take into account for
a moment in estimating her fitness to become his wife,
except so far as it might shed light on her moral or intellectual character. Nor could it be a serious crime in
his eyes that she was writing under an assumed name—
that the papers were echoing the praises of "Fanny
Forester;" and that God had given her a genius to write
well and brilliantly, so as really to have become a literary
celebrity. All this might be, as it really was, somewhat
annoying to his sensitive shrinking from notoriety. He
would doubtless have much preferred to have found her,
as she was a year and a half before, amidst the unobtrusive duties of the Seminary, and in the comparative ob-
scurity of her Christian authorship. But inasmuch as
she had happened to be brilliant, and if he took her at
all he had got to take her with the drawback of a reputation which was growing into fame, he may be pardoned
if he took the authoress for the sake of obtaining the
woman—if he endured genius and reputation for the
sake of uncommon loveliness of mind and character.
In short, whatever may be in a name—and there *is* a
good deal in it—it would have been hard to deprive Dr.
Judson of a good wife, and the world of a good missionary, and send him back, his mind all teeming with rich

fancies and richer affections, to his desolate exile, because Emily was a woman of so much humor and so much genius—so playful and so brilliant—*so exactly like himself*, all running over with buoyant and irrepressible enthusiasm, that she had first laughingly masked herself under a *nominal* disguise, and then unexpectedly made herself famous in it.

I should be greatly misunderstood if these remarks, on which I have hesitatingly ventured, should be construed into any thing like a defense or apology for Dr. Judson's course in this matter. Marriage is a sacred thing, with which the stranger intermeddleth not, except impertinently and injuriously. The question, who shall be our other self, our bosom companion, the repository of our dearest confidences, the sharer of our inmost joys—is too sacred, too intensely and entirely individual, to be pronounced on even by our best friends, much more by a necessarily ignorant public. Even parental love and guardianship can only decide negatively, and shield its objects from the consequences of gross inexperience or infatuation ; when it takes the positive position, and dictates to the heart in what heart it shall find its answering life-throb, it asserts an unwarrantable privilege ; it tramples on the fundamental law of wedlock. There lives not the man or woman on earth, high or low, in any position, private or public, secular or sacred, who has a *right* to sink this into a mere question of convenience or of duty, and overlook the elements of love and mutual sympathy, from which alone a happy marriage can spring. Assuming no gross violation of outward propriety, the question must be left to the decision of the parties themselves ; and they who can not give in a verdict of approval must be content to hold their

8

peace—remembering that they themselves either may
yet be or may have been in a situation to require the
like forbearance.   Dr. Judson's relations with Emily
were strictly a matter between himself and her—a matter with which, public man as he was, and treading in
the shadow of a world-wide reputation, the world had
nothing more to do, in the way of public comment and
criticism, than if he had been a boor dwelling in the
obscurest nook in the Rocky Mountains.   Perfectly
suitable as his marriage was, had it been ever so unsuit-
able—I mean, no external proprieties being violated—
it was no legitimate matter of public comment.   Eminently happy as it proved—happy beyond the most of
even happy marriages—had it been ever so unhappy, it
was nobody's business but their own ; and the busy
tongues, and, still more, the busy pens that indulged
their strictures upon it, were not only invading the peace
of two spirits as sensitive as they were noble, but out-
raging the universally recognized principle on which the
institution *must* rest, viz., that in this sacred alliance of
the heart the parties to it who behave decently shall be
let alone.

That Emily should deeply feel such comments can not
be wondered at.   She felt that in forsaking friends and
home for the untried duties of a missionary she had
enough to bear, without meeting the publicly-expressed
doubts of those to whom she naturally looked for sympathy and support.   She entered on her course with hesi-
tancy and trembling, and often it seemed one of such
desperate rashness that she was ready, at all events, to
turn back.   But if she knew her weakness, she knew
her strength.   She had a heart alive to all the lofty
graces of her future husband's character ; a spirit to

kindle at the noble career which he placed before her, and that high, though humble consciousness, which true merit always feels, of ability to meet, with divine help, the exigencies of her position. Hence she went forward with steady foot and unfailing heart amidst the dark waters which flowed around her. Hence she bore with lofty courage, though with bitter distress, the various forms of censure that assailed her—the censures of an unsympathizing world—the much more keenly-felt suspicions of the religious public. From the latter she shrank and bled in silent anguish ; against the former she threw herself back on the transcendent intrinsic nobleness of her new vocation. To the inquiry of the *National Press,* "Does she deem that stern duty calls her to resign the home and friends of her heart—the fame which she has so gloriously won, nay, perhaps, even life itself, for the far-off heathen ? Methinks the ' orphans of the heart' are gathered in crowds about our very doors "—she responded in a strain of noble eloquence, which needs but the revision of a few harsh lines to place it among her finest pieces :

REPLY.

"Stern duty ?" Why rest on the breast of thy mother ?
Why follow in joy the proud steps of thy brother ?
Why flutters thy heart at the voice of that other
   Who calls thee from mother and brother away ?
When the lip clings to thine, why so fondly dost press it ?
When the loved arm encircles, why smile and caress it ?
That eye's gentle glancing—why doth thy heart bless it ?
   Why love, trust, or labor for loved ones, I pray ?

There 's a Dearer than mother, whose heart is my pillow,
A Truer than brother's foot guides o'er the billow

There 's a Voice I shall hear at the grave-guarding willow
  When they leave me to sleep in my turf-covered bed;
There 's a lip with soft love-words forever o'er flowing,
An eye in which love-thoughts forever are glowing,
A hand never weary of guarding, bestowing,
  A heart which for me has in agony bled.

"Stern duty?"   No; love is my ready foot winging;
On duty's straight path love her roses is flinging;
In love to the FRIEND of my heart I am clinging;
  My "home" is His smile—my "far-off" is His frown.
He shaped the frail goblet which Death waits to shiver,
He casts every sun-ray on life's gloomy river,
They 're safest when guarded by Maker and Giver—
  My laurels and life at His feet I lay down.

"Stern duty?"   Came death to thy door a prey-seeker,
Markedst thou the eye glazing, the pulse growing weaker,
And clasped in thy hand were a life brimming beaker,
  In duty, "stern duty," the draught wouldst thou bring?
Sawest thou a rich crown to thy brother's brow bending,
At his feet a black pit, its death-vapors upsending,
As thou sprangst to his side, thy voice, eye, and hand lending,
  Is it only "stern duty" thy footsteps would wing?

Away to my brother, the orphaned of heaven!
Away, with the life-draught my Saviour has given!
Away, till the web time is weaving be riven!
  Then my wings, and my harp, and my crown evermore!
But back this one prayer my full spirit is throwing,—
By these warm gushing tears that I leave thee in going,
By all that thou lov'st, by thy hopes ever glowing,
  Cheer *thou* the "heart-orphans" that throng at thy door!

Dr. Judson left Hamilton on the 24th, Emily accompanying him to Utica, and thence she and Miss Anable

went to pay a visit with him to **Mrs. Nott in** Schenectady. Dr. Judson then left for the East, **and Emily, with** Miss Anable, returned soon to Utica—**now to commence** in earnest her preparations for her approaching departure. I continue my extracts from their letters. Dr. **Judson writes first from Albany,** where he shared a second time **the elegant hospitalities of Mr. and Mrs. John N. Wilder.**

ALBANY, March 28.

I hope there is no harm, dear love, in writing you a short line, though at so early a date since leaving you. At any rate there is no great cause for apprehension; for I have but a short time before breakfast and getting off in the cars. I am writing in the chamber of Mr. Wilder, which I occupied the early part of last November, when I had my dear children with me, going and returning—when I had never so much as a thought of Fanny Forester, and was ever pouring out my griefs and my tears at the tomb of St. Helena. What strange changes take place in outward things and in the inner heart! And what greater changes are just at hand, when we shall tread the untrodden path, and look for the first time into the unknown world! Let them that have wives be as though they had none, and those that weep as though they wept not—*for the fashion of this world passeth away.* There is true wisdom communicated by the light of inspiration to guide man in his passage through this dark and dangerous world. I wish not that I had loved you less, but that I had preached to you more—and you to me. Dearest, we *must* be blessings to one another. We must *so* love and *so* live, that we shall love the more, and live the happier through endless ages. If we truly love, what greater desire can we have than to brighten up each other's eternal crown? We can and shall exert a greater influence on each other than all the world beside. *O let it be of the best kind.*

We can not be too good. O let us be good and appear good,
avoiding even the appearance of evil.   .   .   .

Thine ever,　　　　　　　A. JUDSON.

FROM DR. JUDSON.

Plymouth, April 2, 1846.

How I wish, my dearest love, that you were here! I arrived
last night, and found my sister and three children, and this is
the last visit, in all probability, which we shall all enjoy together
in this world. I shall stay here three days more, and then we
shall be all scattered again. I have not yet received a line
from you, nor shall I now until I get back to Boston, for I
have not directed letters to be sent on, lest they should pass
me on the way. The children are mightily amused at their
papa's marrying Emily Chubbuck. Abby Ann had found
out from some of the neighbors that it was Fanny Forester:
but she is quite sure that Fanny Forester must be very
good, since she wrote "Effie Maurice," one of her favorite
books. Our affair, I find, has been, not the town-talk, but the
country-talk, for a fortnight or month past. The Philadelphia
announcement, that "marriage was intended between the Rev.
etc., and the dear, delightful Fanny Forester," opened people's
eyes a bit. Even that slow, deliberating —— committed it to
memory, and was able to repeat it verbatim, which I made him
do. He did not know, not he, but I had found a jewel, but
timidly inquired whether you would be arrayed in other jewels
and finery!—evidently fearing that you would come dancing
through the country, like other Fannies, in the style laid down
in Isaiah, chap. iii. I replied that, from considerable acquaintance, I was satisfied that you enjoyed a tolerable modicum of
common sense. How astonished they will be when they see
you, and become a little acquainted with you. . . The truth is,
it is not strange that there should be a great wonderment; we
calculated on it. But we need not care for it. We can both
of us, perhaps, afford to be pretty independent of it. And we

know it will soon pass away, and still more, that a reaction will probably take place. We feel that God has directed us in this affair, and we may hope that He will grant His rich blessing; and if He bless us, we shall be blessed indeed.

April 3. Where are you now, and what are you doing? It is a week to-day since we parted. I have almost forgotten how you look. Let me consider—but you have such a Protean face that it is impossible to fix you. There is Kitty Coleman's mischievous face, full of fun and frolic—"catch her, catch her, if you can!" And then there is the philosophic or poetic development—pen in hand—form bending—upper lip full of thought. "O, fair and fanciful Fan Forester." Or is it Jeane Marie Guion?

> " Ye who know my heavenly fire,
>   Softly speak, and soon retire."

Pass on, ye fair, fascinating fantasies—what comes next? O, I see, I feel, it is the face of love, not hidden in the hands—upturned, beaming, glowing, in the sympathetic mesmerism of commingling spirits. And must this face ever become settled, cold, lifeless, like those other faces that I once feasted on? And must I again press down the stiffening eye-lids on the extinguished orbs of love?

> " Are hope, and love, and beauty's bloom,
>   But blossoms gathered for the tomb,
>   And nothing bright but heaven ?"

Well, be it so; for heaven is in full prospect, and immortal life, and love, and joy. . . .

"Clinging to Earth" is too good to be lost. Suppose you should, some time when you have nothing else to do, write a counterpart—"Aspiring to Heaven," or the like—and let them stand together. . . .

Thine ever,
A. Judson.

TO DR. JUDSON.

April 3, 1846.

I am distressed to death with the thousand things which I am called to endure, and I can not help letting you know it. I wonder if men—Christians or infidels—have any human feeling about them, that they should think their fellows made of stone. I carefully kept my name from the public eye, assumed a *nom de plume* for the sake of privacy, and now every one that can pen a clumsy paragraph, must needs drag it before the public and make his senseless comment. I don't care whether they praise or censure me ; of the two, perhaps the praise is the most provoking. I wish they would just let me alone. Give me some place to be quiet in, if it be only a hovel, and I will be grateful. I am heart-sick now, and if the feeling be not wicked, would rather die than live. It is not enough that I have resolved on a step which is almost death—forgive me, dearest—I am troubled, and do not consider what I write. I shall be happy with you, I know ; but now I am most miserable. It seems that all New York is alive about the affair. It is the common subject of conversation on steamboat and in hotel, in parlor and in grog-shop. H. Anable, who has just returned from New York, says there is no place nor circle where my name is not heard. There is even talk of preventing such an insane proceeding as F. F.'s "throwing herself away." They say such a senseless sacrifice is unparalleled. . . .

TO DR. JUDSON.

April 4.

. . . . Then I am worried—in a constant state of excitement —so nervous that the slightest thing startles and alarms me. I am not afraid you will cast me off; but sometimes I fear that you will almost wish you could do it; and the wish would be equivalent to the act. Does the wish ever creep into your mind? Is it unjust in me even to think of it? I suppose it is ; but if you could only be in my place for a little while, this strange, terrible position, you would not wonder that I have a dread of things indefinable. That poor I should be set up in a pillory! Please write me a little (a *very* little if you should chance to be busy) every day, and put down all your thoughts and feelings. . . It does not agree with my mental or moral constitution to occupy such a conspicuous position. I grow unamiable every day, and shall be a perfect Xantippe before we get to heathendom. Seriously, pray for me, dearest; I never felt in so much danger of turning to the world as at this time, when I should be all for the Saviour. I find much among Christians which is called religion, and which is just its antipode; and there is so much in the world (particularly the refined, poetical part of the world, which, perhaps, has too much of my sympathy) like the purest religion, that it attracts me in spite of myself. I know it is to Jesus Christ alone that I should look, and dearest—my truest, best friend—my all in this world—pray for me; help me in every way, that I may not be a hinderance to you; that I may do all I can to make the autumn of your days brighter than their summer has been, that their winter may be glorious. Pray for me constantly, dearest, for I am exposed to severe temptations, and I am very weak. The God we both love watch over you, and bring us again together in love and happiness. How kind of Him to make us capable of loving each other. Do not forget me, and believe, my best beloved, that you are ever in the heart of your affectionate EMILY.

FROM DR. JUDSON.

BOSTON, April 7, 1846.

MY DEAREST LOVE,—

I have just been having a good cry here alone, in Mr. Colby's chamber, about my poor dear children. I left the two boys yesterday crying as they set off in the cars for Worcester. Abbey Ann I took on to Bradford, and this morning I left her crying at the Hasseltines'. And thoughts of the children bear my mind to their departed mother, and I review the scenes on

8*

board the Sophia Walker and at St. Helena. And then I stretch
away to my two little forsaken orphans in Burmah; and then I
turn to you whom I love not less, though but a recent acquaintance.   What a strange thing is the human heart!   O if all
our severe trials, and our sweet enjoyments are but sanctified to
us, it will be well.   All my children are now settled for the
present.   George Boardman will enter Brown University next
fall.   My pecuniary arrangements are such that we shall have
an ample sufficiency for all our purposes, and enough to furnish
your parents with what you may think necessary; so that you
can write as much or as little as you choose, and if you take
any remuneration, you can have the pleasure of presenting it,
through the mission treasury, as an expression of gratitude to
Him who gave His life for you, and is now preparing your seat
and your crown.   This is the course I have taken myself, and I
am more and more convinced that it is the best, the most excellent course.   You thought so at once when we first conversed
on these matters, and it was I that proposed another course and
have been trying to ascertain whether it was consistent and
practicable.   But I rather think that it is neither.   The rules
of the Board, which some consider too rigid, I made myself
when I viewed the subject impartially, and consulted the general and the ultimate good.   I sent them home to the Board,
and they were adopted without even a verbal alteration, and
have been acted on ever since.

In regard to yourself you say, "My impression has been that
you, considering all the circumstances of the case, thought I
had done right, though the publication of a few letters might
not have been wise."   Your impression is perfectly correct.
That is just my sentiment.   But you know I always thought
that you had not been for a year or two in *the most excellent
way*, and that it was exceedingly desirable that you should
henceforth pledge yourself and vows to holier purposes.   And
this was the aim of my first plain and rather ungallant exhorta-
tion.   And I shall always think that your own sense and love

of right essentially aided me in my adventurous attempt on your heart. But by whatever means it was effected, it is the joy of my life that I have secured a little lodgment in that dear, dear heart. Do not, darling, turn me out because —— distorts what I have said. You know how a thing can be almost honestly misrepresented by being repeated and re-repeated. I don't recollect what I said, but certainly not what is imputed to me. . . . As to who shall marry us, and the time and place, have it all in your own way. Only give me the root *marry*, and you may vary it by any inflections, and conjugate it in any mood or tense you please.

"I dread the coming of something that may separate us, or make us less happy in each other." I wonder if you think that I divide my heart between you and my friends here in Boston or elsewhere; and whether you think that any thing I hear or can hear will ever make me regret the blessed Providence that carried me to Delaware 12th, or feel ungrateful for your kind love which has allowed my spirit to mingle with yours in a union which neither time nor death can ever dissolve.

As to what the newspapers and the public say, can you not receive it with that cool, quiet composure which best becomes you, nor let any one but me know that it disturbs you? In fact, be not disturbed. There is nothing that ought to disturb one of your pure and high purpose. Before God we are indeed full of sin; but we may still feel that the path we are treading is one which the common people have neither capacity to investigate, nor right to judge. The opinion of one such man as President W. is worth that of ten thousand, and here it is under March 26th: "I know not where you are, but hear you are tripping in author-land under the guidance of a fair Forester. I am pleased to hear of your engagement, as far as I know of it. Miss C. is every where spoken of as a pious, sensible, cultivated, and engaging person. I pray God it may prove a great and mutual blessing. I write at a venture, to say that our house is at your service whenever you will come and occupy it. Should you bring any one with you both will be equally welcome." Would you like to have the "Dissatisfied Spirit" put into a Boston paper? And will you alter the last sentence, or let it remain as it is?

April 8th. I have received three letters from Utica—thank you, darling. The last contained the extract from the New York *Express*. That surely does not trouble you. True it is unpleasant to have our private affairs before the public; but after all it is a small matter. Let us rest in one another's love, but chiefly in the love of Jesus, and in the consoling consciousness that we are endeavoring to serve Him, and that He will forgive all our follies and sins, and send forth judgment into victory. I have been so cried down at different periods of my life—especially when I became a Baptist and lost all, all but Ann—that I suppose I am a little hardened. But I feel for you, for it is your first field. Whatever of strength or shield is mine, or I can draw down from heaven, is yours.

Thine with my whole heart,
A. JUDSON.

FROM MISS CHUBBUCK'S REPLY TO THE FOREGOING.

UTICA, April 10.

Thanks for your beautiful letter. You do take all the trouble away so sweetly! I don't know why you should be so good and kind to me when I get out of patience. Yes, I do know that you will never repent the step you have taken, though the entire world should disapprove of it, and with full faith in that I will not be disturbed by trifles. I know these are all trifles—things that I shall laugh at when I get away from them; but sometimes they seem terrible now. They shall not any more, though; I will rest in your love, and in a holier. . . .

Would that I could have charmed away the tears for your children, poor things! . . . I am longing to see the little darlings. And, dearest, my own dearest, best friend, God helping me, they shall never feel the loss of the sainted one. Do not call them " orphans" any more. I will love them and watch over them, and when I fail in any thing, you will point out the faults and teach me better. Oh, we will have a happy little home—thankful that God allows us to care for some of the beloved ones, and leaving the others to Him who can do it much better than we can.

I hope I have not troubled you by any thing that I have written you about the strict rules of the Board. I don't like to be a burden to you, who have already too much on your hand; and then I suppose that I have a little woman's pride in the matter. It is quite enough for you to have the care of *me*. But I know that you will do the best for me that you can, and whatever you do will be right. If they can not vary the rule in our favor, why we must trust more to God, and less to ourselves. If we give ourselves *all* to Him, He will care for us, and for those whom we love.

Do whatever you please with the "Dissatisfied Spirit." Mr. Beebee has my copy, and is to publish it in the *Register* next week. I did not make the alteration at the end of the "Dissatisfied Spirit," for it does not read quite as smoothly, and I do not care to help people in making a personal application. I must stop without filling my sheet, or doing justice to my heart.

Your loving

NEMMY.

FROM DR. JUDSON.

BOSTON, April 10, 1846.

I seize a little time, early this morning, for I am so driven with business and company through the day and evening that I have scarcely time to write, though I do now and then think of you. "Does the wish ever creep into your mind" that you could get rid of me? Suppose it did. Doesn't Mr. —— say that " now the name of the one is seldom separated from that of the other." Why, we are as good as married. I don't

see how I can help myself now, whatever my wishes may be.
I couldn't discard you without incurring universal execration ;
and that would be worse than the other alternative even. But
there is one way—you can discard me, and I can tell you
how to do it, so as rather to rise than fall in public estimation. But I wont, though ; and what is more, I am sure
you don't want to know. No. —— says that our *names* are
seldom separated; our *hearts* are *never ;* and may the time
soon come when our *persons* shall be never separated. But
that wish is linked to another thought, that a separation, a
dread separation, must finally come. And that will be the more
bitter the longer we live together and the more we love.
Nothing can temper that bitterness but the assurance of an eternal reunion. Let us so live that we shall have this full assurance. I must confess that with you I am disgusted with
much I see in the religious world, and am sometimes pleased,
too much pleased, with what I see in the irreligious. But this
I ascribe to my lowness in religion ; for we ought to love the
Saviour so entirely as to be unable to find pleasure in any thing
which does not accord with His mind. But I have not the
most distant desire of "turning to the world," nor ever have
had since I first entertained a hope in Christ. Nor do I understand you to say that you have, though you feel exposed to
danger. I know no other way than to make up one's own
mind in regard to the right course, and then to pursue it steadily, always pressing to the right side, and keeping as far as
possible from the wrong, whatever may be our own secret in-
clinations; and thus, with the divine blessing, habits of virtue
will be formed, and our inclination, at first wavering, will become coincident with the Saviour's. We shall love what He
loves, and hate what He hates. Do not the late circumstances
of your life, ordained of God, unsought by you, call on you as
with a voice from heaven to become a devoted, holy missionary
—to love not the world, nor the things of the world ; to set
your affections on things above ? Pray turn away your ear

from the censure and the commendation you may hear. Remember that the eye of Christ is especially observing you, and that your whole future life will take its coloring from the manner in which you now consecrate yourself to God. . . .

I shall leave this afternoon for Maine, and be absent a week or more. The probability is that we must be ready to embark by the middle of June. "Do not forget me," you say. Forget thee!

"If prayers in absence breathed for thee to heaven's propitious power,
If winged thoughts that flit to thee, a thousand in an hour,
If busy fancy, blending thee with all my future lot—
If this thou call'st forgetting, then indeed thou art forgot."

Though I am not the author of these beautiful lines, they express my very thoughts and feelings toward you, dearest.

. . . Live near the throne of grace, and pray for me that I may be more deserving of your precious love.

Entirely and for ever thine,

A. JUDSON.

TO DR. JUDSON.

UTICA, April 13, 1846.

My blessed one! God make me grateful to Him for sending you to love me, to teach and guide me—make me more and more grateful, for I am very much so now. Your letter received last evening shows that I have worried you by my murmurings. Forgive me, I will try not to give way to such feelings again. I know it is wrong—I know it is the very height of ingratitude; for I am really happier in your love, and in the consciousness of doing right, than when my praises were sounded from one end of the country to the other. Yet sometimes this *does* seem a severe ordeal. My health has not been quite as good, and the loss of sleep and appetite together may have made me a little more excitable. Pray for me, dearest; God help me, and I will try to consecrate myself to Him entirely. I do love His cause more than any thing else, and am happy in the thought of being permitted to do some good; but I need your constant, unremitting prayers. I do not know how far I am influenced in this important step by love to you, and how far by love to God; the two seem to be pointing so entirely in the same way, and He has made it so sweet to do right. I am sure I can not love you too much; pray for me that I may love the blessed Saviour more. . . .

O how entirely I must belong to you—you whom four months ago I had never seen. Now all my hopes for this life cluster around you—all my earthly interests are bound up in yours; all my other feelings are but air balanced against my love for you; my thoughts, wishes, and sentiments are under your control—your wish is my law, your smile my happiness, and your frown my misery. Ah, well, there is something so sweet about this *heart* slavery! Take the hand I place upon your lips, and lead your "unuseful" one through life up to heaven—thine through life, thine in death, thine when we shall both awake in our blessed Saviour's image.

Yours lovingly,

EMILY.

P. S. I have succeeded at last in getting some medicine from Dr. James which I hope will do me good. I have scarce eaten a meal since my return from Schenectady. I have taken my third singing lesson, and Mr. E—— speaks quite encouragingly. The singing is all for you; so if I sometimes make your ears ache you can not find fault.

TO DR. JUDSON.

UTICA, April 17.

Shall I send another letter to Boston? There will be three or four awaiting you, but perhaps you would like something of a later date. Yours from Boston was received last evening; it takes letters such a long time to come!

Pray, don't make arrangements for sailing the middle of June, if you can help it—don't. It is so, *so* soon. I have been through with a terrible scene to-day. I was induced to go into the school-room for an hour, and such sobbings! I haven't got the tears out of my eyes yet. O it is hard to leave these dear little creatures who love me so much, and over whom I have so much influence. Do you wonder that I doubt whether I can ever do as much good elsewhere? Have you ever thought that teaching in this school has been my *business?* and that I have incurred censure because I have employed my *leisure hours* in the way which I considered the most useful? My writing time was made up of the stray hours which I saved from society, etc. Yet everybody looks upon the writer and forgets the teacher entirely—everybody out of the house. They forget, too, that what they call my better sort of writing (I do not think it so) balances the other in quantity, fully; and seize upon the innocent doings of lighter moments as though these things had been the business of life. I believe nobody ever lisped a word against my usefulness as a teacher. . . .

Evening, eight o'clock. What a dull, statistical letter I have written you! The truth is, I was fatigued into utter stupidity this afternoon, and am very little better now. I fancy that I am nearly as much thronged with company as you are; having been away so long, all my friends come now to see me, and it is fatiguing and exciting. My precious guide and teacher! God keep me humble that your instructions may be always dear to me—your kind censure sweet. Do I seem to lack the proper degree of meekness when I try to defend myself from what seems to me undeserved blame? I know that God sees a very wicked heart in me. I know that you and other intimate friends must be aware of faults; and I love you better for telling me of them; but the censure which I receive just now is unjust. Perhaps, though, I ought to take it just as patiently. Pray for me that I may have wisdom to guide me through all difficulties.

Early in May, Dr. Judson returned from his eastern trip to Utica, and he and Emily made a visit together to Hamilton, and she had the privilege of spending yet a few days with her parents before the final coming which was to separate her from them forever. It was now the advancing spring, and nature was putting on her beautiful livery, and beaming with a gladness in harmony with the tempered yet buoyant happiness of their spirits. She now paid off the debt due on the house which she had purchased for her parents, by a loan from Dr. Judson (to be repaid from the sale of her books), and was thus able to leave them an unincumbered home.

She received also from Philadelphia the engraving of that picture of her which forms the frontispiece to Alderbrook. The following letter to Rev. Mr. Gillette gives her strictures upon it :

HAMILTON, May 8, 1846.

My Dear Mr. Gillette,—

I received yours, together with the engraving and newspaper, this morning. You are so very kind that I do not know how to thank you enough. I like your suggestion about curving the neck more. There is also too much of a dimple in the chin, though perhaps not more than in the painting. The nose, as I have often said before, is too pointed, a little too long, perhaps, at the tip, and, where it joins the face, a little bit too narrow. It gives the whole face a sharp look. Yet I do not know as it would be best to touch it. I wish, however, that something could be done to subdue and soften down the expression of the whole thing. It is quite too spirited—not so meek-looking as I fancy myself to be. The amount of the whole is, the picture is a grand one—beautifully painted and very beautifully engraved —but precious little, if at all, like me, except in the outline— not the least particle in expression. However, I do not care; it is as like, I suppose, as engravings usually are, and I would

rather be flattered than caricatured, as Dr. **J.** is.   Please have
no name attached to it; neither my old true **name, nor** my intended new one.   I have concluded not to have any loose engravings out (at least until I leave the country), but reserve the
picture for my " **Fanny** Forester" sketches.   For the same reason
I do not wish it to appear in any magazine.

I thank you for your warm, kind interest; but I am not
troubled now by what people say.   Indeed, I never in my life
before was so perfectly indifferent to any thing relating to myself.   I am very happy in my new prospects—though there are
terrible sacrifices close at hand—and in my happiness I can
afford to hear the wind blowing around me.   It is all wind—
" only that and nothing more."   Do not be troubled for me.
" If God be for us, who can be against us?"   I feel in my very
soul that I have the approbation of God in this step; and
really the approval or disapproval of men, who are incapable
of understanding or appreciating the matter, is an exceedingly
small thing.   Let it pass.   .   .   .

Yours sincerely,

E. C.

Dr. Judson and Emily visited together her early home
in Eaton.   Dr. Judson had read her description of Underhill Cottage in the "Trippings," and he remembered the
invitation there given to the reader to come and survey
its beauties, with herself for his cicerone, when it was
surrounded by the laughing beauty of spring.   This invi-
tion he now felt irresistibly inclined to accept, and Emily
probably was not disposed to recall it.   They visited the
hallowed spot together ; took tea in Underhill Cottage ;
and wandered at leisure by the stream which, fringed
with alders, gave to the subsequent collection of her
sketches its graceful and appropriate name.   Fancy may
be excused for lingering a moment on the scene in which

two such spirits—the one full of the warm affections, the fresh hopes, the bright fancies of youth and youthful genius—the other that of one who had filled a hemisphere and a half century with his deeds of sublime Christian devotion, but whose genial character time had but touched with a mellow grace—in which they together visited the spot which had witnessed the early joys and sorrows of the fair and gifted being who was soon to lay her hand in his, and share his fortunes on the other side of the globe. What memories of the past, what visions, chastened yet joyful, of the future, throng upon those spirits both of which have drunk deep of the cup of sorrow, and know well the stern realities of life, and yet both of which possess within a permanent well-spring of joy and hope such as God bestows only on the favored few! With what touching pathos did Emily recount the childish memories with which each scene was associated—the memories of joys—O how sweet! and of griefs—O how bitter! And how eloquent were the words in which he pointed forward to their future of enjoyment and of trial, and then to that scarcely remoter future of blessed and boundless reward which, in near prospect, stood open to the vision of his faith! Dr. Judson's spirit was intensely, unconquerably youthful. He seemed to have quaffed the elixir that keeps the heart always young—to have drawn his very life-blood from that "deep heart of existence" which "beats forever like a boy's." How exquisitely touching that scene upon his death-bed in which, in reply to his wife's remark that it was the opinion of the members of the mission that he would not recover, he said, "I know it is, and I suppose they think me an old man, and imagine it is nothing for one like me to resign a life so full of trials.

But I am not old—at least in that sense ; you know I am not. O no man ever left the world with more inviting prospects, with brighter hopes, or warmer feelings—warmer feelings," he repeated, and burst into tears.*

And his were no ordinary fascinations—a character of the rarest quality, in which the hero of practical life and the hero of romance blended their seemingly incongruous elements ; in which, by a rare felicity of temperament, the energetic will of the man of action, and the almost ascetic devotion of the saint, were blended with the playfulness of the child, the tenderness of the woman, the enthusiasm of the poet, and the clear vision of the sage. And now he was wandering—amidst the home and the scenes of her childhood—with the one whom his heart and his judgment had selected to be the successor of his former wives, and the companion of his future fortunes. Few men, who have been so deeply afflicted, have been so highly favored as he. Few have found a trio of so highly gifted spirits to share their path of toil and self-denial. The gentle being who now stood beside him was a worthy partner of the lovely ones whom he had laid beneath the hopia tree of Amherst, and in the rock of St. Helena. She had not, indeed, the deep religious experience which had impelled those two sainted ones to

---

* I would gladly quote the entire paragraph. Let me beg the reader to turn to the memoir of Dr. Wayland (vol. ii. p. 345, '6) and read it; for there is nothing, outside of inspiration, more touchingly and sublimely beautiful; nothing which, in its blending of the gushing tenderness of the man with the hallowed raptures of the saint, gives a juster conception of the real elements of heaven. "A few years would not be missed from my eternity of bliss, and I can well afford to spare them, both for your sake and for the sake of the poor Burmans. . . . *So strong in Christ:* He has not led me so tenderly thus far to forsake me at the very gate of heaven."

their place of earthly exile. But his discerning eye saw the slumbering traits of a noble missionary character, while her delicate and beautiful genius ran, perhaps, through a larger compass of correspondences to his versatile and many-sided nature than that of either of her predecessors. Ann Hasseltine more than met all the demands of his earlier years of youthful and heroic action ; Sarah Boardman shed the light of one of the most exquisite of womanly natures over the calmer scenes of his manhood ; Emily, with a heroism not less devoted, with a womanliness not less pure and gentle, met his ripe culture, his keen intellectuality, his imaginative and poetic temperament, with a richness and variety of endowments which belonged to neither of those admirably endowed women.

Linger then yet a little, ye gifted ones, in this home of the heart, on the banks of this fairy rivulet, and let the gentle influences of the scene and the season steal into your souls ! Spring waves her amber wing, and breathes her delicious breath around you ; the birds pour their melodies upon your ear ; the mellow sunlight rests on hill and valley, and bathes in beauty the enchanting landscape. Dream for one brief moment the delicious dream of youth and love ! Whisper the vows of affection, whose truth is to be tested by many a stern and bitter trial ! Thou, veteran soldier of the cross, revel for a moment in those delightful fancies which thine unworn spirit knows so well how to conjure up, before thou replungest into the stern battle of life ! And thou, gentle child of genius and of sorrow, on whose heart love has laid its holy spell, pause and dream a moment by this brooklet of thy childhood, ere thou embarkest on the stream whose rushing tide shall sweep thee with arrowy rapidity toward thy destiny ! The ocean, Burmah, toil, solitude, sickness, bereavement, widowhood, an early grave—these, unseen, are in the distance ; but beyond, the blissful reunion, the unfading crown, the everlasting reward ! One sweet hour, gilded with the fairy visions of romance, and then away to the reality of life and toil !

CHAPTER XII.

THE MARRIAGE.

"Like the swell of some sweet tune,
    Morning rises into noon,
    May glides onward into June."

THEY spent a Sabbath with the churches in Morrisville and Eaton; the one, before her residence in Utica, her own religious home; the other for many years that of her parents. In Morrisville occurred the little scene mentioned in Emily's reminiscences of her husband, in which he disappointed the congregation who anticipated some story of missionary adventure, by dwelling with great pathos on the love of the Saviour, declaring that he knew no more interesting story than this.

They returned to Hamilton and thence to Utica—she to complete her preparations for her departure; he to go on and attend some religious meetings in New York and Philadelphia. Emily wished before leaving the country to make a final and revised collection of her tales and sketches, embracing those written subsequently to the publication of "Trippings." Dr. Judson entered heartily into her plan, and aided in its accomplishment. A careful perusal of her writings had satisfied him, not only of their genuine literary beauty, but of the prevailing healthfulness of their moral tone. Although he did not regard her *as in the best way*, and desired to lead her out into higher usefulness, yet he still felt that these writings might influence favorably many hearts, and prepare the way for higher spiritual truths. Soon after his leaving for New York, Miss Chubbuck was annoyed by a surreptitious edition of some of her pieces under the title of "Lilias Fane and other Tales." In her letter to Dr. Judson she spoke of having consulted a lawyer about the matter, who, however, informed her that, though she might sue the publishers for a breach of copyright, it would subject her to much trouble, and to an annoying publicity. The cover of the book contained a picture, designed by the artist for the likeness of the fair authoress, but, as ordinarily in the case of such catch-penny publications, too hideous to reach even the dignity of a caricature. Dr. Judson happened to see a copy of the work in a bookstore in New York, and he wrote to Emily, congratulating her that her health had not suffered from her recent trip southward as was "evident from the ruddy complexion on the cover of 'Lilias Fane and other Tales.'" He then proceeds:

And now, darling, don't you think you cut a pretty figure on the cover of the book from which you extracted "The Dissatisfied Spirit?" That was the reason why you were in such a "pet" and sent off for a lawyer. And you did not like to tell me, or let me see the picture, naughty, distrustful one! And did you think that my heart's love would be ruffled by seeing the caricature of my bride-elect by the side of Fanny Elsler, and the Fair Bandit, and other demireps, in the low book-stalls through the country? And did you think that my courage would quail, and that I should wish to "take it all back," though, alas, too late? Let us rather be glad, dearest and best, if your beautiful sketches, which can never be tainted or depreciated by any contact or association, may, through the low artifice of the publisher, reach even the dirty hand, and tearless eye, and hard-crusted heart, and soften and cleanse and prepare, it may be, for higher and more spiritual influences. . . .

May God preserve your health and life, and may the Holy Spirit so direct your thoughts, and sanctify your mind in view of the missionary life, and service also, that we shall be blessings to one another in time and in eternity.

FROM MISS CHUBBUCK'S REPLY.

No, my own best friend, I never was alarmed or afraid to have you learn all about me, the worst and the best, otherwise I should have not been so happy in your precious love. If I had the shadow of a concealment on my conscience, I should be made miserable by your arms opening to me so trustingly.

Had I supposed the red picture on the cover intended for me, I should, of course, have been much more mortified than I was, by having my sketches appear in such low company. But I deemed it a kind of gratuitous embellishment. Mr. —— remarked that he wondered whether it was intended for Fanny Forester or Lilias Fane; but I did not suppose him in earnest. Why are you so good to me? Talk of sacrifices! There is nothing which I would not cheerfully resign, no place to which I would not willingly, gladly go. Take me to your heart, and fashion me entirely. There is a blessing, a deep, sacred blessing even in the humiliating position which I now occupy. A year ago nobody could equal Fanny Forester; nobody so praised and petted by the public. Now I bring disgrace, where I would give the world to bring just a little honor. But it is sweet to know how much love it requires to cover all this! . . .

I had a letter from Carey & Hart yesterday. They offer me twelve and a half per cent. on the retail price of my book, but object to republishing any thing in " Trippings," and to including the poetry. They say that republished articles injure the sale of a book, and that poetry is a drug. I shall not, of course, make an imperfect collection, and so am again without a publisher. Will you try to make a bargain for me with Lippincott? Mr. Gillette consulted him about an illustrated edition, but I think the one which I propose making far preferable. In truth, I don't care so much about making a good bargain as about having the book brought out for other reasons. It is unjust to myself to rest my literary reputation on the "Trippings."

I have been out all the day shopping, and am too tired to write any more. I think of you now and then between exclamations concerning pretty frocks. Oh, that is a charming blue! and that purple, how exquisite! You don't know what absorbing things new frocks are, for you, poor man, never had any; so I must not look for sympathy. Mrs. Quin, however, is in ecstacies; so adieu, that I may join her.

Yours (all that remains from the frock),

NEMMIE.

The following extract from a letter to Dr. Judson contains her proposal that Abby Ann should return with them to Burmah. It is creditable alike to her heart and her judgment, and points incidentally to a feature in her character—her strong, personal influence over youthful minds—which was likely to be overlooked in the general reserve and almost timidity of her manner. The portion of her observations on the training of the youthful character needs no comment:

UTICA, May 17.

. . . The mention of the ship sends my heart down into my shoes. How nice could we but sleep a half year, and then awake in our own dear home. That home is very dear to me already, and the children I am longing to see. By the way, I have been seriously thinking of asking you to take Abby back.

She is your only daughter, you love her so much, and it will be so hard for the little creature to stay behind. And you may be assured that she shall not lack for any good which I am capable of exerting. I know the point where I should be most likely to fail; but I would pray most earnestly to exert a healthful, religious influence. And how I should love to have the training of her active little mind! I would pursue a regular system of instruction: give daily book-lessons, besides the other lessons which we could extract from things about us. It would be something of a task, certainly, but a very agreeable one, and one which doubtless would contribute to my own improvement. Then to have her with you, developing under your own eye—can you think of any thing pleasanter? Her having been in this country, though but for a little time, will be an advantage to her; and, if it is best, I dare say she will have the opportunity of coming again at some future day. . . . The truth is, I plead half for my own sake; for I begin to feel that I shall be out of my proper element when I miss my accustomed employment. For more than eight years I have had almost constantly some young girl, in whom I was more especially interested than others, under my eye; and I suppose that I have (partly from peculiar taste, and partly from favoring circumstances) had more influence in the formation of individual character in our school, than all the rest of the teachers together. The interest which I feel in some of those young ladies is peculiarly strong, and their love and gratitude very dear. Dare not trust Abby with me, eh? Ah! you don't know how wise and dignified I can be when occasion requires it. Not one of my *pupils* was surprised at the news of my purpose to become missionary. Please think the matter over seriously, and if there are not insuperable objections, let your heart decide. She would grow dearer and more interesting to you every day, and—perhaps you will charge me with vanity, but I must out with it—I am afraid she will not (if she is like her papa) be understood and appreciated, and trained accordingly. I am afraid her peculiarities will be curbed, instead of cultivated; her warm impulses checked, instead of directed. Do my fears smack of vanity? It is natural, doubtless, for us to think we can manage some such things better than anybody else; and I have seen many lamentable instances of bad training from mere misapprehension of character among sensible, cultivated, and pious people.

I fully expected a letter from you last night. If it should fail to-night I should be quite alarmed. You were not well when you went away. Write often—not *long*, but very often. It is strange how you have weaned my heart from those whom I have formerly loved better than myself. I think it is very naughty of you, but somehow—somehow I can't help being reconciled. Adieu. Thine lovingly,

EMILY.

I have been very much alarmed, since you went away, about my side, being afraid of a liver complaint; but I have quite recovered from that fear now. I have found an outward application which helps it, and it is much better to-day. I dare say I shall be able to go out to-morrow. I presume I took a cold, which settled there.

Dr. Judson made further efforts, in New York and Philadelphia, to arrange for her proposed new publication. The copy-right of "Trippings" having been purchased from Paine & Burgess, the new work was subsequently brought out, in two handsome volumes, under the title of "Alderbrook," by Ticknor, Read & Fields, of Boston. After her arrival in India, she made some revisions and additions for a subsequent issue.

The following extracts from their letters reach down to the time of their marriage:

NEW YORK, May 19.

.   .   .   So happy that you have got rid of the pain in your side, and are better in health. But you don't mention the tooth. I found your dear letter of the 17th on my return home last evening at eleven o'clock. Out all day at Brooklyn ; such crowds, and shaking of hands, and exclamations of congratulation, and frequent inquiries from old acquaintances whether Miss C—— was present and could be seen. In the evening it came my turn to address the assembly, which I did in a small speech—a dead one—but Brother Stow galvanized it. The missionary spirit is certainly very high, but well regulated. Prospects were never brighter. We all feel that God is blessing us, and will bless us more and more. All my intelligent friends say that *our affair* will turn out well; that it is honorable to both parties, and that the more you are known the better you will be loved and the match approved. But I shall love you no better for that.

> " All thine own 'mid gladness, love ;
>   Fonder still 'mid sadness, love."

May we love one another well, but Christ better.

We will talk about Abby Ann when we meet. There are serious objections to your proposal, but after stating them all, I shall be inclined to leave the matter to your decision.

Yours (a little bit),

A. JUDSON.

HAMILTON, May 24.

I received yours of the 18th last evening, darling, together with one dated the 22d. I am kept at home another Sabbath by illness, although much better than when I wrote last. The jaunt in the stage-coach made my side worse, and I find this

no place to recruit in. My last days at home! Every thing—
every word, every look—brings this to mind constantly, and
although I am always cheerful, it wears from day to day upon
health and spirits. O, it is a dreadful thing to live—a thing
for many reasons more to be dreaded than death. And this
new life, on which I am about to enter—in every respect new
and crowded with responsibilities! It is too heavy for me; all
the future is shut away by heavy clouds that I can not look
beyond. How do I even know that you will continue to love
me, except from habit, when you know me still better, and the
knowledge has become "an old story?" And then, who can
imagine a more miserable creature? "As thy day is, so
shall thy strength be," is a glorious promise sometimes, and
sometimes it seems to be utterly without meaning. Now, my
faith in it is so low, and my dread of the future is so great, that
I would entreat God to let me die here, and be buried away
from all this tumult, this jarring, these trials, duties, and cares,
but for leaving you again alone. It is impossible that I shall
ever be any thing but a weight upon your hands and heart.
Why has all this been suffered to come about, dearest? Doubtless for good, but it is a good which is hidden. I was making
myself indirectly useful—improving the peculiar talent which
God had given me—perhaps not always with judgment, but my
judgment was improving. Now I have placed myself in a position to be canvassed, and have the little influence which I was
exerting destroyed. You were a demi-god, and I have brought
you down. That is the worst. Do you recollect the evening of
our last arrival here? The same feeling comes back to me every
time I go into the parlor, and then (forgive me; you know I love
you with all my heart and soul) I am sorry that we ever met.
I believe that some regret *must* come over you sometimes. Indeed, though no clairvoyant, I am sometimes quite sure that I
feel it shaping itself in your mind among the strangers whom
you meet in New York and Philadelphia. . . .

I understand what you mean by exalting genius too highly,

and in looking over the articles will try to express myself more clearly. I believe genius to be a peculiar gift from God, requiring great simplicity of character, purity, and innocence for its proper development. When this gift is desecrated its possessor is rendered miserable in proportion to his superiority to other men, and proportionally depraved. The angels that sinned and fell became devils. There is something in the inspiration of genius partaking of religion—a hallowing influence; but men possessing this gift are exposed to peculiar temptations, and frequently fall; perhaps not more frequently than others, but the fall is more obvious because the descent is greater. . . Yet, wherever you find it (even in Byron), it has some touches to show its origin; like Milton's Fallen One, you can still see in it the angel; otherwise it were less dangerous. Christians do not do well to eschew the aid of genius. Some of the inspired writers had also this inspiration, as David, Isaiah, and John of Patmos. . . .

FROM N. P. WILLIS.

NEW YORK, May 26.

MY DEAR FRIEND,—

I have delayed replying to your letter till I could make some further inquiries touching your book. And, after all, I have no news to give, for the best reception I had was from a publisher who said that the news of you from India would give an impetus to the curiosity about you that might make it advisable to publish the revised edition; but that the first edition was still in possession of the field. Apropos of *Field*—send for him and talk to him about it. He is the partner of Ticknor of Boston, and will be delighted to render any service to Fanny Forester. He will do all that is possible. I am myself a wretched bargain-maker, though I have done my best.

I should have understood Dr. Judson by a single look at his face. It is a physiognomy of great sensibility and enthusiasm, and natural moral elevation. He looks refined and very gentle-

manlike, and I am sure is what the English call a "fine fellow."
I am very sure, since I have seen him, that you are to be very
happy.

I shall be in Boston the first of next week, and shall hope to
find you there. God bless you.

Ever affectionately yours,

N. P. W.

FROM DR. JUDSON.

NEW YORK, May 26.

I send you a copy of the improved engraving, and one of
the old, that you may see the difference. I think the improve-
ments are very considerable. If you have any farther altera-
tions to suggest, write immediately to Sartain through Mr.
Gillette. I had an idea of a closer sleeve, more like what you
wear; but it would probably not have been in good keeping
with the rest of the costume, and perhaps not easily done, as
you will perceive he has made the new sleeve out of the old. I
got your letter of Monday on arriving here last night. This
morning I wrote to Lippincott through Mr. Gillette, and may
get an answer before I send this. I have also been to the Harpers, and shall have definite proposals from them to morrow.
But they talk of "8 or 10 per cent." only, and they wish to
have the matter all clear with Paine & Burgess, before they can
think of engaging. This, I suspect, was the real reason why
Carey & Hart objected to including any part of the "Trippings."
I then went to Paine & Burgess. They are very gentlemanly,
but they say that all they ever intended to decline publishing
was a revised and enlarged edition, such as you proposed.
They never thought of giving up the "Trippings," nor could
they when they had paid $190 for the stereotype plates; and
they intended to proceed and publish another edition as soon as
the first is out. I then requested them to make out their bill,
and prepare to give me a quit-claim to-morrow. All say that
there is no other way in which we can suppress indefinite edi-

9*

tions of that work, and it is really altogether reasonable. So
don't be worried about it. I will get all these matters arranged
before I leave these parts, or see them in a fair way.

Don't you think that if I had foreseen some things, I should
never have put my foot into a certain puddle, and that it is
great forbearance and condescension that I do not pull it out
now? Do, dear, think so with all your might, and perhaps you
will love me more, and your precious love I value beyond all
money. . . In great haste to reach the mail.

Yours ever,

A. JUDSON.

FROM DR. JUDSON.

NEW YORK, May 27.

I have got the stereotype plates out of the hands of Paine
& Burgess, and had them packed up, ordered to be sent,
and deposited at Lewis Colby's. They cost $190. P. & B,
have also paid me $70 for you, being the percentage on the
whole edition, beside what they have already paid you. So
that your business with them is closed. The $70 I will send
you, and take a receipt, dear, to avoid mistakes. The Harpers
decline "publishing the proposed volume of miscellanies by
Fanny Forester partly on account of the pressure of preëngage-
ments, and also from the present inauspicious aspect of political
affairs for all kinds of literary enterprise." Wiley & Putnam
ditto—with the additional remark that there has been a glut
of light writing for a year or two past, and the reading public
is satiated. I see no chance of finding a publisher in New
York; perhaps I shall hear something favorable from Philadelphia. The Harpers say that next fall they may be induced
to undertake, but can not give any definite encouragement. I
guess we will not indulge the spoiled public at present. . . .
The truth is that the present is a most unfavorable time for any
literary speculation. People's minds are full of the Mexican
war, and probable rupture with England and all the world. Too

much stern reality to allow time for fiction ; too close engagement with Mars, to allow time for flirting with Venus and the Muses. You can arrange for the purchase of the additional lot, if you please, for $300, before I come, and for the fence at $50. I shall be able to let you have as much of the sum appropriated for your outfit, that is $200, as you may wish. The $300 for myself I have declined. . . .

Is not this a beautiful letter, full of gold and pearls, and costly array? Do not wear it in your hair. It will be contrary to Scripture. . . .

I have just had another interview with Mrs. ——. I am afraid a shall get to dislike her. She is a woman whom I could make some use of. She has a sharp, strong intellect—is a good writer in the rough, but not in the nice. No heart—no amiability—and what is worse, glaringly envious. . . .

May 28th. Your letters, the one misdirected to Anna Maria, and that of the 24th have come to my hand and heart. I feel thankful to God that He has given us such congeniality of taste, that we like and dislike the same persons and things. I allude to what you said of Mrs ——. I presume our sentiments and feelings regarding her are just the same. Still it is best to cherish no strong prejudices, but to try to love all and be loved by all.

FROM DR. JUDSON.

Utica, May 29, 1846.

. . . Just before leaving New York last night, I received a line from Lippincott, saying that he " accepts the proposition of publishing Fanny Forester's works with pleasure, provided the volume contains enough new matter to prevent it from being termed a reprint." He says nothing about terms, but I mentioned twelve and a half per cent. to Mr. Gillette, and I suppose that that is understood. I have also opened a correspondence with a house in Boston on the same subject. Lewis Colby of New York is strongly inclined to undertake the publishing of the three Utica works, partly encouraged by the hope of getting the memoir of the late Mrs. Judson.

I arrived here at two o'clock, much disappointed in finding that Anna Maria had gone. I should have answered her very interesting and excellent letter, which I received in New York, but expected to see her in a day or two and talk over the matter.* And that is my present expectation. I have seen her good, appropriate letter to Mr. Wiley, and I have no doubt the whole affair will be arranged satisfactorily.

I have got a nice time this evening and to-morrow morning to bring up my arrears of correspondence, which I intend to do as soon as I have dispatched this letter—the last letter, I hope, that I shall ever be pestered to write to Emily Chubbuck. What oceans of ink I have expended on that girl!

I inclose you a line from Mrs. Stevens, the only one that I have lately received from Maulmain.

Notwithstanding the nonsense I write you, I am full and overflowing with most serious, joyful thoughts. The past, the present, and the future are before me. If I should attempt to write, I should not know where to begin or to end. May we meet "in love and happiness." May God crown our union with His blessing, that we may be blessings to one another through life and to all eternity!

I love you "a little bit," but I have never loved you so much as you deserve.

Ever thine,

A. JUDSON.

Emily was now in Hamilton, awaiting the coming of him who was to take her beyond the ocean. As she moved among her parents and relatives, conscious that it was "the last time," that her farewell was soon to be uttered, and an ocean to roll between her and all she had

* Referring to her baptism.

before loved, no wonder that her heart sometimes sunk within her, and it required even more than her all of faith to banish the gloom that rested upon her spirit. From her heart's fountain gushed forth the following lines :

TO MY FATHER.

A welcome for thy child, father,
   A welcome give to-day ;
Although she may not come to thee
   As when she went away ;
Though never in her olden nest
   Is she to fold her wing,
And live again the days when first
   She learned to fly and sing.

Oh, happy were those days, father,
   When gathering round thy knee,
Seven sons and daughters called thee sire—
   We come again but three ;
The grave has claimed thy loveliest ones,
   And sterner things than death
Have left a shadow on thy brow,
   A sigh upon thy breath.

And one—one of the three, father,
   Now comes to thee to claim
Thy blessing on another lot,
   Upon another name.
Where tropic suns for ever burn,
   Far over land and wave,
The child, whom thou hast loved, would make
   Her hearth-stone and her grave.

Thou'lt never wait again, father,
   Thy daughter's coming tread ;
She ne'er will see thy face on earth—
   So count her with thy dead ;
But in the land of life and love,
   Not sorrowing as now,
She'll come to thee, and come, perchance,
   With jewels on her brow.

Perchance ;—I do not know, father,
   If any part be given
My erring hand, among the guides,
   Who point the way to heaven ;
But it would be a joy untold
   Some erring foot to stay ;
Remember this, when, gathering round,
   Ye for the exile pray.

Let nothing here be changed, father,
   I would remember all,
Where every ray of sunshine rests,
   And where the shadows fall.
And now I go ; with faltering foot
   I pass the threshhold o'er,
And gaze, through tears, on that dear roof,
   My shelter nevermore.

On the 2d of June they were married, the Rev. Dr. Nathaniel Kendrick officiating. It was in the early part of that long and agonizing illness in which Dr. Kendrick traveled by inches of indescribable torture toward the grave. He had already betaken himself to his bed under the assurance from the physician that his case was past relief, but with more than the calmness

> " Of him who wraps the drapery of his couch
> About him, and lies down to pleasant dreams ;"

for his was "the morning dream of life's eternal day."
This was the last, or nearly the last occasion on which
he quitted his house.   Pale and feeble, he arose from his
couch, and walked the few rods which separated his house
from the home of Emily, to pronounce the words which
gave the pride and ornament of our village into the arms
of her noble suitor.   The wedding was strictly private,
there being present but the family and her especial friends,
Miss Sheldon and Miss Anable from Utica.   With what
tearful gratitude did Miss Sheldon look back to the agency
which she and her sister had had in preparing Emily for
so hallowed a destiny; with what admiring wonder must
she have regarded the mystery of that Providence that
directs our paths !   How little had they thought when
the timid, trembling girl first glided into their presence,
poor in all but the abounding wealth of heart and genius,
that she was yet to stand before the world the partner of
the first missionary of the age, the successor of his two
admirable wives, and to prove herself worthy of so hallowed a companionship !   And it must have been with
no superficial emotions that Dr. Kendrick saw before
him that noble missionary, and by his side the girl who
many years before had addressed him a letter proposing
to devote herself to the missionary work, and whom he
had characteristically advised " to await the openings of
Providence."   What an unanticipated opening of Providence was this !

Dr. Judson and his bride spent three or four days with
her parents, exchanging greetings with their numerous
friends, and accepting their hospitalities.   It was to many
a memorable occasion.   Mrs. Judson's quiet dignity and

simplicity of manner, the joy of satisfied and happy
love sparkling in her eye, yet tempered by the shadow
of her near and final parting from those whom she
loved, lent to her an added charm ; while Dr. Judson,
with renovated health and buoyant spirits, casting off
all reserve, gave loose to his matchless powers of capti-
vation, and made himself the life and soul of many
delighted circles.

They spent the following Sabbath in Utica. Here Dr.
Judson immersed Miss Anna Maria Anable, who had been
previously a member of the Presbyterian church, but for
some time a Baptist in her religious convictions. The
day was one deeply interesting to Mrs. Judson. She
could not wholly forego the hope that her most intimate
and sympathizing friend, now united with her in a more
perfect Christian fellowship, she might yet have the
privilege of welcoming as a co-laborer on the far-off
shores of heathenism. It was not to be. Rather, that
friend was to receive her back when returning, a few
years later, "weary and desolate" to the parent roof, to
join parents and sister in shedding around her bereaved
spirit and dying-bed the sweets of sisterly and Christian
sympathy, and to spread a wing of motherly shelter over
the "bird" that had sought her Indian nest.

They proceeded on the following week to New York,
thence to Boston, Plymouth, Bradford, etc., to pay a final
visit to Dr. Judson's sister and to his daughter Abby
Ann (then at Bradford), thence to Boston, whence they
had anticipated sailing on the 1st of July. The vessel,
however, was delayed until the 11th. On the 30th of
June a large missionary meeting was held, at which Dr.
Judson made a few oral remarks. He had prepared
a written speech, which was read by Rev. Dr. Hague,

beautifully characteristic in its literary finish, and its glowing Christian sentiments. "Where," he asks, "are those who moved among the dark scenes of Rangoon, and Ava, and Tavoy? And where are the gentle yet firm spirits which tenanted forms delicate in structure, but careless of the storm—now broken and scattered, and strewn like the leaves of autumn, under the shadow of overhanging trees, and on remote islands of the sea?"

The following letters written and received about this time closed her correspondence with her friends Messrs. Wallace and Willis:

TO HORACE B. WALLACE, ESQ.

BOSTON, June 19, 1846.

MY DEAR MR. WALLACE,—

I received your kind, *very* kind letter, in due time; and you may be assured that it was highly valued. It is said that "blessings brighten as they take their flight;" and although such heart-blessings as are furnished us by social intercourse, were always very dear to me, I do not know but I must acknowledge that the poet has told truth. As the time for sailing draws near, and I am doing up my last work on this side the globe, cords begin to tighten around me so closely that it seems almost death to dissever them. And yet I am cheerful and strangely happy. There is a great object before me—my hand is about to be *filled*, and so I shall not waste my time on follies. Do not think now that I am anticipating perfect happiness, or any thing perfect. I know something of the disappointments incident to life, and something of my own weakness and inefficiency. I am only better satisfied to have an object before me—a great one, which does not begin and end with this life.

I should not venture to ask you to come to Boston, but that you promised it; but it would afford me great satisfaction to see you here. We sail in the *Faneuil Hall* on the first day of July; if there should be any delay, you would probably learn it by the papers—though I presume there will not.

Now, God in heaven guide, guard, and bless you, my friend! I hope to meet you again; but if I do not, there is a shadow-less world where angels dwell; and I believe that the redeemed are furnished with their wings, and their harps, and their hearts of love. May we both be among the redeemed. Till then, adieu!

EMILY C. JUDSON.

No. 12 Pemberton Square.

FROM N. P. WILLIS.

WASHINGTON, June 26, 1846.

Your letter enclosing the money for books I received only yesterday from Boston, with two forwardings, and to-day comes this, written as you left Utica. I reënclose the money, for the books can be had without it. I spoke to Secretary Bancroft at a party last night, and he was, of course, proud of the opportunity to present you with his books, and so will be Prescott and Longfellow—and myself. I shall make you up a box of books from my own stores to take with you, and I shall be in Boston when you sail, and see you, with a tearful God-speed, off the shore. Will you write me at what time precisely you will be in Boston, directing your letter here.

The more I think of your marriage, the more I think you are doing the best for your happiness. Your husband has a prodigal largeness of nature, and the kindest and most affectionate of hearts; and you required a trying and unusual destiny to fill the capabilities of which late years have seen the dangerous formation. Both for your heart and your peculiar mind, therefore, Providence has sent you the needful scope, and you will be happy. Dr. Judson's errand abroad will soon draw on your volcanic enthusiasm, and the vent will be healthful to soul and body. With love satisfied and talents employed, change of climate and improved health, you will bless God for a merciful direction of your destiny. . . .

Ever yours affectionately,

N. P. WILLIS.

NEW YORK, July 6, 1846.

DEAREST FRIEND,—

I had intended to be in Boston during the last week of your stay, and to be present at your embarkation. A little closer approach to the scene which that embarkation would probably be—with the number of Mr. Judson's friends and the enthusiasm felt for him—made me shrink from compelling you to reserve for me any of the attention which those friends will expect from you at the parting hour, and still more to shrink from adding to the emotion of that troubled hour the pain of parting with one who must be dear to you as the foster-father of your genius. I see that it is better that we exchange our farewells, as we have exchanged all other feelings, on paper. You must not think hardly of me for this.

I had another intention, which I had not matured, but which I can do after you are gone. I heard that Prescott was away from Boston, and I thought I would make up the parcel of books for you and send them by the next ship. Will you leave word, and let me leave them with Mr. Colby, to be forwarded?

Write me a word of farewell before you sail. Give my warmest remembrance and every possible kind wish to your husband. May God preserve and restore you to us. Write to me from India. Command me freely in all that you wish me to do. Farewell.

Yours, ever most faithfully,

N. P. WILLIS.

Many personal friends and friends of missions had been drawn together from different quarters of the country to witness the embarkation. Overwhelmed with kind attentions, Mrs. Judson could but drop hasty adieus to her distant friends. The following note was in acknowledgment of a present received from some of her pupils in Utica :

TO THE MISSIONARY SOCIETY, UTICA FEMALE ACADEMY.

Boston, July 7, 1846.

My Very, Very Dear Friends,—

I have postponed writing you till the present moment, hoping that I should find at least one half hour of leisure. But my time is constantly occupied, so you must excuse the hand-work in consideration of the heart's still lingering with you. I have received many presents since I left Utica, both from societies and individuals; but the work done in that dear school-room has a peculiar charm to me, bearing, as it does, the traces of loved fingers. May the kind interest you have exhibited in me awaken a yet deeper interest in those among whom my future lot is cast; and those of you who pray (do not *all* of you?) pray for the Burmese and for me.

Remember me when I am gone; speak of me sometimes kindly; forgive and forget my thousand faults and follies; *serve God truly*, and may He bless you ever !

Affectionately and gratefully,

EMILY C. JUDSON.

A WORD OF FAREWELL TO THE CHRISTIAN CHURCHES WITH WHICH I HAVE BEEN CONNECTED.

Boston, July 6, 1846.

In dissevering the various ties which bind me to the land of my birth, I find one of peculiar strength and interest. It is not easy to say farewell, when father and mother, brother and sister, and those scarcely less dear, are left behind us at the word; it is not easy to break away from the sweet, simple attractions of social life, or the increasing fascinations of a world but too bright and beautiful; but there are other ties to break, other sorrowful farewells to be spoken. The parents and friends, brothers and sisters, whom Christ has given us, and who for His sake have loved us, occupy no remote corner of our hearts. Such friends of mine are, I trust, scattered over various parts of the country; those whose prayers are at this very moment strengthening both hand and heart. Oh, I know you have prayed for me, ye whose prayers "avail much;" for, casting away my broken reed, and trusting in God only, I have been made strong.

We do not always feel the deepest love for those with whom we are visibly connected; so, though the beloved church in the village of Hamilton has never been my home, the strongest tie binding me to it is not that the names of those to whom God first gave me, are enrolled among its members. I have often worshiped there; there a resolution, a consecration of self which cost—the Omniscient only knows how great an effort—received ready encouragement and sympathy; there prayers were offered, tears wept, and blessings spoken, which I shall bear upon my heart—a precious burden; and thither I shall turn for future prayers, future encouragement, and future sympathy. Oh, my eyes grow dim when I think of the loved ones, friends of Jesus, in my own dear home—the beautiful village of Hamilton.

There is another church with whom I have a more intimate connection—the one whose commendation I bear to a strange people in a strange land, but worshiping no strange God. There are to me no dearer ones on earth, than a little circle at UTICA, with whom I have hoped and feared, rejoiced, and wept, and prayed. God grant that I may join that same circle above! that the tremulous voice which thousands of times has borne a confession of our sins and follies up to our Intercessor, I may hear again in songs of praise; that when the thin gray hairs are brightened, and the heavy foot made swift and light, I may return heavenly love for the counsels to which I have so often listened. I do not *ask* to be remembered there, for I know that parting in person can not mar the union of spirit; and when my hand is strong, and my heart light, when Christ confers upon me any peculiar blessing, I shall think that Deacon SHELDON and those who love him and me, are praying for me.

There is another little church worshiping God quietly away in an obscure village; and with that church before all others, I claim my home. All the associations of childhood cluster there; and there still sparkle the bright waters where the revered Chinese missionary, now on his way back to the scene of his labors, administered the initiatory rite of the church, when she consented to receive the trembling, doubting child into her bosom. Oh, the church at Morrisville, the sober, prayerful ones who were my first Christian guides, must let my heart have a home among them still. There are my Christian fathers and mothers, my teachers in the Sabbath school, and those whom I have taught; the dearest, sweetest associations of my life cluster around the little missionary society, the evening Bible class, the prayer circle, in which I first mingled; and the little plans for doing good, in which I was allowed to participate, when I first loved my Saviour, are as fresh in memory as though formed yesterday.

Dear friends of Jesus at Morrisville, ye whose prayers first drew me to the protection of your church, whose prayers sustained me through the many years that I remained with you, whose prayers, I trust, have followed me during the little time that we have been separated, will you pray for me still? When dangers and difficulties are about me, will you plead earnestly, "God help her?" Will you pray for me, now that we are to see each other's faces no more in this world? Ah, I know you will; so let me ask the same for those among who I go to labor, those who know not Christ and His salvation, and yet, "are without excuse." Pray for them, and for me, that I may do them good.

EMILY JUDSON.

On the 9th she writes to her sister, " I meant to have written you before, but if you *could* know what a siege I have had ! I have been crowded almost to death with company. Sometimes my hand has been so swollen with constant shaking that I have not been able to get on a glove, and I have been obliged to use my left hand." She had been to see her cabin in the *Fanueil Hall* and found all things to her mind. The prospect before her was solemn but not saddening. She speaks of having made the acquaintance of many delightful people, and mentions with especial gratitude the family of Mr. Gardner Colby by whom they had been entertained with a most unwearied and munificent hospitality. On Saturday, July 11th, amidst the tearful adieus of hundreds, they went on board the *Fanueil Hall.* Miss. Lydia Lillybridge, Mrs. Judson's associate in teaching at Utica, was now also an associate in her devotion to the missionary work. From the ship Emily addressed the following lines to her mother :

We have just said good-bye to thousands and are fairly off. The land is a small speck in the distance—all strange, strange ! I have an opportunity to send back by the pilot, and I thought you would like to know how very, very well I am. Notwithstanding all my fatigues, I have not been nearly so well this spring. The ship is beautiful and comfortable. . . You must not have a single sad thought about me, for I am very happy, and God is with us on the sea as on the land. Pray for me often, for that is now your only means of keeping harm from me."

Emily has thus bid her "native land good night," and strong in love and trust in her husband, and still more in her husband's God, turns her face joyfully toward that mysterious Orient that had visited the visions of her childhood. Dr. Judson probably has never breathed so freely in America as now, that, on his favorite element, his impatient heart leaps forward to its eastern home. The gallant vessel speeds her on her way ; the "fair white cloud of snowy sail" soon blends with the blue of the horizon, and only fancy, and the invisible messengers of light, can accompany the wanderers over the trackless path of the deep. A happy voyage to that noble band ! We turn tearfully away ; the reader may close the book, and when he resumes his reading, Emily will be sitting under a palm tree, or riding on an elephant, on the other side of the globe.

CHAPTER XIII.

OUTWARD BOUND.

" And o'er the hills, and far away
　　Beyond their utmost purple rim;
　　Beyond the night, across the day,
　　Through all the world she followed him."

" Pass we the long, unvarying course; the track
　　Oft trod, that never leaves a trace behind;
　　Pass we the calm, the gale, the change, the tack,
　　And each well known caprice of wave and wind;
　　Pass we the joys and sorrows sailors find,
　　Cooped in their wingéd, sea-girt citadel;
　　The foul, the fair, the contrary, the kind,
　　As breezes rise and fall, and billows swell,
Till on some jocund morn—lo, land! and all is well."

Our last sentence was a little over-hasty. It is a long
way from the gates of the sunset to the gates of the
morning. When the curtain next rises on our heroine,
she has overpassed the dark and stormy waters of the
Atlantic, encountered the hurricanes that sweep round
the southern cape of Africa, and is beginning to catch
the golden sunshine and the balmy breath of the Indian
seas. She has caught glimpses of the strange and
gigantic forms of tropical life, and has gazed on those
mysterious constellations which never rise upon our
northern vision. The voyage has been in the main

10

prosperous and delightful—hope urging forward the one, hope and memory the other, toward their destination. At length the hills that line the eastern coast of the Bay of Bengal break upon their view; then the pagoda which crowns the promontory of Amherst; then the hopia tree, beneath which rest the ashes of the first Mrs. Judson; and amidst the strange costumes of the East, and enthusiastic welcomes from swarthy faces, they come to anchor, on the 30th of November, in the harbor of Amherst. We leave to Mrs. Judson the story of the voyage.

TO MISS JANE E. KELLY.

Off Cape Good Hope, Sept. 25, 1846.

My Dear Jenny,—

We have been lying by for the last three days under nearly bare poles, a strong gale dead ahead, and we all the time drifting landward "willy-nilly." There is a deal of fun in a heavy gale like this during the first day, but it becomes a rack after a while. Why, all my joints are stretched and my bones aching, as though I had been pulled by wild horses and cudgeled to a jelly. I can not sleep o' nights for the fear of being tossed out of bed, which I most assuredly should be but for the board at the foreside of my *bunk*. But the gale has at length subsided, the canvas is out, and we are stretching off southward with rather precipitate haste, considering that the bosom of the sea is still swelling and heaving like that of a passionate child whose anger is subsiding into involuntary sobs. But we have reason for haste. This morning a peculiar tinge in the water, warning us of the vicinity of land, startled the captain somewhat, as he had not been able to "take his observations" during the gale; and he soon ascertained that we were within thirty miles of the latitude of the Cape. A most dangerous proximity I learn this to be, and we are now putting off with the utmost speed. This gale has probably been the grandest sight that we shall have the pleasure of beholding. The sea lashed into perfect fury, rising and sinking in strange contortions, wresting our little floating nut-shell from the hands of the crew, to leap, and plunge, and wrestle, as though born of the mad billows which bellow as they rise, and, bursting, cover it with their foam. The water is of inky blackness in the hollows ; but each billow, as it bounds upward, becomes green and half transparent, and bursts at the summit, the long wreaths of foam curling over and over each other, tumbling to the bottom, and disappearing like immense piles of down, with which your weary bones would sympathize, were there not more safety in the hard mattress. The air is thick with spray, at first tossed to an incredible height, and then every foam-bead shattered into ten thousand fragments, each invisible of itself, but helping the general mistiness, and making itself felt in chilling dampness through cloak and shawl. And still we go on rearing and plunging, reeling and tumbling, as though the centre of gravity were surely lost, and our frail tea-saucer capsizing itself, and then pausing on the top of a billow, quivering in every spar before venturing another plunge, which it seems must be fatal. Last night I dreamt that I could see the centre of gravity, in the shape of a *bull's-eye*, slide sideward and dip to the water at every plunge, each time approaching within a hair's-breadth of the water-base of the ship. I watched every plunge with trembling breathlessness—a kind of night-mare feeling—a little more, just a little more, and we were lost for ever ! At length it came. I bounded from my berth, staggered, and tumbled headlong, grazing my shins most beautifully. It was an immense billow bursting over the quarter-deck with a roar like the report of a cannon—no unusual thing, and exceedingly lucky just then, as I am no friend to the night-mare.

Now, I know I have made a ridiculous affair of my fine gale, and you can have no idea of the sublime grandeur of such a scene at sea. Indeed it is indescribable, and should I attempt a formal description, I should inevitably fail. We lack nothing but sunshine to make it glorious. The old monarch of the upper regions has muffled his face in clouds, or even now the swell of the sea might give our fancies fine picking. I should like to observe the effect of a brilliant sunlight upon the angry face of brave old Neptune. But I am tired, Jenny, dear, and so a kiss, and more chit-chat on a stiller day.

Nov. 14, Lat. 5 N., Long. 93 E.

I find, dear Jane, that I have told you above that we should scarce be likely to welcome so fine a gale as that first one off the Cape. But I was mistaken. We have had another, which beat it all out and out. The wind blew a perfect hurricane, but it was astern, and so swept us on our way at a furious rate. A Dutch bark came within a few rods of us, and I assure you my heart went pit-a-pat when I saw it reeling and tumbling, though I was told that it went on quite as sedately as we did. At one minute it seemed leaping to the clouds, and at the next not even the top of a mast was visible, so low had it sunk behind the mountain billows. But the beauty of the scene was the showers of rainbows, for the sun was gloriously bright. This was off the Cape, where we may always expect gales ; but a few days ago we had a succession of squalls, which were more dangerous than a continued gale. They come on without a moment's warning ; and then to see the tarpaulins scramble, racing after each other up the rigging like so many rats, and shouting a chorus something in the tone of a bellowing bull, is, as Mark Tapley would say, " reg'lar fun." But we have now reached the simoom, and may expect to see Maulmain in a fortnight, or perhaps ten days. To-day we heard the chirp of a land-bird, probably from Sumatra, and the long, brown wreaths of sea-weed go drifting past us, as we have not seen them since we left the Bermudas. It is eighteen weeks to-day since we left Boston; so imagine, if you can, how the vicinity of land must affect us. . .. .

Last night we had a supper of dolphins, which, but for their being fried in rancid lard, would have been delicious. As it was, I only tasted them. In truth we have been reduced to pretty scanty fare, and I shall be quite willing to stick my teeth into an orange when we get ashore. The dolphin is very beautiful: rich brown on the back, and blue, and green, and gold, shaded into each other along the side to the belly, which becomes of a deep salmon hue, then pale rose, and then white. While dying, the color changes in rapid flashes, now deepening into almost blackness, and now the white extending to the streak of brown upon the back. One of those caught yesterday had several small fish in its stomach. The most curious of these was the toad-fish, about the size and shape of a full-grown dace, with a round bag on the under side three times as large as itself, which it can contract and expand at pleasure. A flying-fish was also taken out, and another creature a little larger than a silver dollar, and very nearly as flat and round. This would be a grand place for a naturalist like you. The captain has promised to try to get me a "Portuguese man of war," which, if I can preserve in spirits, I will send you. You will find a description in the books, but you can not imagine how beautiful it is. The sail is of ribbed silver, fringed with pink and purple; the body seems silver, and then the long strings of purple beads. I assure you he is a rare little fellow.

My letter will be scarcely readable, but they say I must use this good-for-nothing thin paper. Good bye, Jenny dear; God bless you, and may you be happy.

Affectionately,

EMILY C. JUDSON.

The following is from the *Columbian Magazine*, August, 1847:

OUTWARD BOUND.

And so, it is all over! The hurry, the bustle, the thousand cares attendant on departure are at an end, and the unusual excitement is about to give place to the dull monotony of a long sea voyage. It is all over, and here we stand, a lonely little company, looking into each other's face in something like bewilderment, as effectually severed from friends and country as though those kind beings had a moment since waited at our funerals. The last sob has had its answering sobbings; the last farewell has trembled upon lips that I had fain hoped would breathe it above my death-couch; the last touch of the loved hand, the last glance of the eye—ah me, it is well that life seldom darkens into days like this.

Still do I see those dear, dear faces thronging the wharf; still my eye peers eagerly among them for those best loved; those by whose side I have stood in joy and sorrow, whose slightest whisper long since forgotten now comes back flinging upon me the weight of a new heart-ache; those who bent fondly above me when my cheek paled and my eye grew dim, and, winning me back from the grave, rejoiced to see my foot once more firm. O but for one more *last word* with these! As my eye wanders in search of the friends of other days, it falls upon those of later date, but still beloved as truly if not as tenderly. Again and again the vision rises to my confused sense and passes and repasses before my eye, face after face bearing familiar features standing out from the mass with the distinctness of reality. Again handkerchiefs are waved in thrice repeated adieu, and kisses are flung from fingers that have often, O *so* often twined with mine, but which I may never, never clasp again. Then come like a death signal the shrill cry of the boatswain, the quick rattling of ropes, and slowly we wheel away, striving for yet one more glance and yet one more, till wharf and carriage, new friends and old, are left behind together.

And this close, narrow cabin, with its small window and low ceiling, is to be my home, not merely for days and weeks, but for long, weary months, without the possibility of change. Not one spot of green earth to set my foot upon, not a forest leaf to soothe my ear with the familiar sound of its rustlings, but a few planks for my promenade, and this incessant dashing, dashing, for daily and nightly music. I, who have never loved glittering spires and proud monuments, still strain my eyes for a last look at the tall shaft of granite rising from yonder battle hill and now but a shadowy line against the sky, turning them away only to look upon the burnished dome of the State House, made visible by its glitter in the dim distance. Now both are lost, and I have looked my last upon the land of the robin and the violet, the land of kind hearts and free hands, the land of Sabbath bells and prayerful voices—my bright, my beautiful, my own beloved land. There, even the wild flower shooting from the split rock in the neglected forest, and the humble wild bird nestling in the green knoll by the wayside, are dearer to me than all the gold of the South or the treasures of Eastern India. I was cradled amid its rugged simplicity, lulled to my earliest slumber by the music of its rills, and fanned in my hours of play by the green boughs ever waving in its fair forests. Its mossy knolls have been my altars, its groves my temples, and its birds, and flowers, and pebbles, the beautiful books in which, side by side with the pages of inspiration, I have studied the character of Him who placed both them and me in this strange lovely world. It was the home of my infancy, the home of my childhood, the home of my youth, and thrice ten thousand times the home of my heart. "If there were no other world," O who would thus turn to voluntary exile? Father in heaven, fling Thy sunlight upon our trackless way, else are we indeed in darkness.

Hurra, hurra, how gayly we ride! How the ship careers! How she leaps! How gracefully she bends! How fair her white wings! How trim her hull! How slim her tall taper

masts! What a beautiful dancing fairy! Up from my narrow
shelf in the close cabin have I crept for the first time since we
loosed cable and swung out upon the tide, and every drop of
blood in my veins jostles its neighbor drop exultingly, for here
is sublimity unrivaled. The wild, shifting, restless sea, with its
playful waves chasing one another laughingly, ever and anon
leaping up, shivering themselves by the force of their own mad
impulse, and descending again in a shower of pearls; the soft
azure curvature of the sky shutting down upon its outer rim as
though we were fairly caged between blue and blue; and the
ship, the gallant ship, plowing her own path in the midst, bearing human souls upon her tremulous breast, with her white wings
high in air and her feet in the grave. And then the tumult, the
creaking of cordage, the dash of waters and the howling of
winds—"the wind and the sea roaring!" I have felt my heart
swell and my blood tingle in my veins when I stood in the
silent forests of Alderbrook, and I have looked up at the solemn
old trees in awe mingled with strange delight; the awe and delight have both deepened at the blaze of the lightning and bellowing of the thunder amid the wild echoing rocks of Astonroga;
and now, in this strange uproar, they come upon my heart and
make it bound like the arrow from the bended bow. The trees
were the temples built by the Almighty for His worship, and
there is something awfully beautiful in their shadows; the light-
nings "go and say unto Him, here we are!" and "He shut up
the sea with doors and made the cloud the garment thereof, and
thick darkness the swaddling band for it." And here as I stand
poised upon the wild elements I feel myself near, very near to
the only Protector who has a hand to save, and in the hollow
of that all-powerful hand I rest in perfect security. God, my
God, I go forth at Thy bidding, and, in the words of Thine own
inspired poet, "Thou art my buckler, the horn of my salvation,
and my high tower." The sea can not separate Thee from me,
the darkness of midnight can not hide Thy face, nor can the

raging of the storm drown Thy still small voice. My heart
leaps joyfully as I trust in Thee.

On, brave little wrestler with the elements! On, right gallantly! I love the bounding, the dashing, and the roaring, and
my heart shall know no faltering while "my Father is at the
helm."

Hurra, hurra! Here we are upon a sea of fire! How
the waves leap and sparkle, while, curling backward from their
tops down their black sides, roll long wreaths of flame! The
stars are quenched, and the heavy clouds go hurrying by in
dismay as though they feared the fearful mandate had gone
forth, the taper been lighted, and the hour was at hand when
the "heavens should be rolled together as a scroll." The scene
is wildly, startlingly beautiful. Those who look into such mysteries say that the fiery sea below us owes all its brilliancy to a
small insect floating upon the surface of the wave. In these
strange regions I can almost fancy them the torch-bearers of the
mighty sea king. If we are to credit the gentlemen of the
tarpaulin and pea-jacket, there is a coral palace just below us
now, where his majesty of the trident holds his imperial court,
but I have a suspicion that the deep might lay open to us greater
wonders than ever glittered in ancient mythology or modern
poetry. There is many a brave ship suspended fathoms deep,
still floating, floating, floating, with the blue waves for sail and
pennon, and rich treasures mouldering and rusting in he rbosom. .
There secrets, which have made thrones tremble, and crowns
bow, lie forever hid from the eyes of mankind. There knowledge slumbers with sealed eye; there wisdom folds her powerful
pinion and forgets how she moved a world; there the star of
beauty has set in utter darkness; there the tuneful finger of
love thrills never more the palsied heart strings; and there
goodness and purity, in their white vestments, wait the signal
to mount to heaven. Greater wonders! Why, this same deep
upon whose glittering breast we are now floating will at some

10*

future day fling back her locked portals, unfold her curtaining waves, while from her blue caverns will spring, strong in life and radiant in beauty, all whose hearts have said, "Thy will be done," when lying down to their strange rest. No monarch of mystic realms has reared his throne of "turkois and almondine" in those purple twilights, there treading pearl-strewed floors, listening to notes breathed from the crimson lips of silver shells, or winded on the pearly horns of water nymphs, and reclining within the bower formed by the branching jasper. No merry mermaid looses the golden fountain of her own enshrouding tresses, and bends her bright face to the mirroring wave; no fabulous naiad of the olden story laves her rosy limbs in the rainbow tide; and no pale Undine comes in shape of mortal maiden, to weep beneath the green bough in the starlight, or walk forth in gay vestments at noonday, with nodding plume and well-filled quiver, to lure the unwary to her cold, damp palaces. But greater than these lie beneath us, those who shall wear crowns beneath the stars—tread among the varying lights which, in the god-lighted atmosphere of the Eternal, flash from the sapphire, the emerald and jasper, the soft green chrysophrase, the blood-red hyacinth, and the purple amethyst, listen to the lays of angels, and recline on couches of transparent gold in the shadow of that tree whose "leaves are for the healing of the nations;" who shall plunge into all the wise mysteries of the universe, and dwell forever in the presence of Him whom no man can now see and live. Ah, there are richer treasures beneath us than ever found life in Grecian song or fable, or stirred the fingers of troubadours and minnesingers—the caskets which have held the precious purchase of the Son of God, and which shall be restored in glorified beauty when He takes them to the mansions which He is now preparing.

We are just "crossing the line"—that great brass rim which on Mr. B——'s globe used to "divide the earth into two parts called the Northern and Southern hemispheres." We mount the metallic ridge without any perceptible decrease of

motion, and off we bound away, away! stretching southward
into another world. Ha! How the wind blows! How the
canvas swells! How the waves dash!

Hurra! Gallantly ride we in this skeleton ship, while the
sunlight glints gayly on white bare mast and slender spar. Gallantly ride we over wave and hollow, over foam and rainbow;
now perched upon the white ridge, poising doubtfully and trembling like a frighted steed; now plunging down, down into the
measureless trough which seems yawning to engulph us forever.
Wildly blows the gale, more and more wildly bound the mighty
billows, with a roaring as though all the monsters of the deep
were swarming around us. But not so. Neither the wide
mouth of the shark, the brown back of the porpoise, nor the
spouting nostril of the whale is visible; the brilliant dolphin in
in his opal jacket has retreated to his own haunts below the
storm, and the little "Portuguese man-of-war" has drawn in
the pink and purple fringes of his silver sail, and rolls like a
cunning beetle from wave to wave, as light as the bubble from
which he can not be distinguished. Even the albatross flapped
his strong pinion and wheeled away when he saw the winds
gathering dark in the heavens; the cape pigeon lingered a little as though caring lightly for the ruffling of his mottled plumage, and then spread his butterfly-embroidered wings and hurried after; but the stormy petrel, though small and delicate as
the timid wren (I will take a lesson from thee, busy daring
little spirit that thou art, bright velvet-winged petrel), scorns to
seek safety but by breasting the gale. And here he remains,
carousing amid the foam as though those liquid pearls, leaping
high in air and scattering themselves upon the wind, had a
magic in them to shield him from danger. He dips his wing
in the angry tide as daintily as though it were stirred but in
silver ripples; then he darts upward, and then plunges and is
lost in the enshrouding foam. But no, he is again in air, whirl-
ing and balancing, wheeling and careering, up and down as

though stark mad with joyousness, and now he vaults upon the back of the nearest foam bank and disappears to rise again as before.   And still the billows roar and bound and lash the sides of the trembling ship, and sweep with strange force her decks; and still we reel and plunge, down, down, surely.   No, we are up again, leaping skyward; we pause a moment and—what a fearful pitch was that!   Ah, my brain grows giddy, but still I can not hide myself in my dark cabin.

And now careering and caracoling yonder, like an untamed steed that has freed himself from the trappings of civilization, comes a bark with sails close reefed like our own, and something that appears like the stripes of Holland flying at her stern. Ride we a race—the skeleton ship and bark—that we travel the waves so madly?   Are these two immense ribbed things that seem to revel in the storm really of this upper earth, or are they dark spirit-creatures that come to us from a phantom world below?   As the bark leaps from billow to billow I can almost fancy that I hear the voice of some poor Matthew Lee from her foam-shrouded deck—

"You know the spirit horse I ride;
    He'll let me on the sea with none beside!"

I have heard of a "flying Dutchman" off this rude coast, and I should well nigh believe that the mystic churl had drawn near to spy out our belongings, but that our own sober Bostonian "cradle of liberty" is every whit as full of antics.   But look, look!   How our suspicious neighbor reels, dipping up whole decks full of surf; see her spring from the white yeast and leap to the clouds; and now, as I live, not the tip of a mast is to be seen, and she but a brace or two of rods distant!   Still shines the sun and still the wind comes roaring from the clouds and howls among the rigging with a dismal tone, strangely contrasting with the glorious brilliance of the light.   A thick white mist scattered from rich heavy foam-wreaths spreads itself over the face of the waters and becomes at once an iris curtain.   Up curls the mist from every shivered billow—up, curl on curl, it winds in silvery beauty, and meeting the sun, falls back in gorgeous showers of million-colored rainbows. Beautiful, gloriously beautiful! The sea, even as "the earth, is full of thy riches."

Onward we trip buoyantly and blithely. Up from the chilling south come we to regions of perpetual warmth and sunshine. Up, hurrying on like the lithe roe-buck among his native hills, bounding and dancing, oh, so gayly! and here we are where sleep in purple mist the fair islands of Eastern India. Blithely, still blithely speed we onward, and still softer grow the breezes, while the light gushes warm and golden from the fleecy clouds, and far away by the verge of the horizon a slumbrous vail like silver gossamer is settling down on sky and wave. A piece of half-molten gold seems to have grazed the luxuriously sleepy blue from the south around to the west, leaving everywhere its traces rich and glowing, but with none of the harsh glare which is common to sterner skies. As it reaches the west it is entirely melted and circles around the setting sun, a girdle of glory but still subdued into a soothing softness. This is a rare East Indian scene, such as can not be copied where frosts have made the sun pale and set the clouds in a shiver. And now the sun nears the water, dips his lower disk in the tide, and drops down behind it with but little of the ceremony that marks his exit on land. And now for other beauties, since the store-house of creation is exhaustless. But look upon the surface of the water! One half is of a pale flickering orange, while the other displays fold on fold of crimson, lost in the blackness of approaching night; and far behind us we are dragging in the wake of the ship long lines of green and amber and purple, each rarer than ever robed a Tyrian princess. A still dimmer haze, though all of a dark rich purple, creeps over the face of the sea as twilight deepens, and one by one the stars open their bright eyes on the misty scene below. Sweet, mild

Maia Placidus, brilliant Canopus, and half of the southern cross are left behind; but we greet night-watchers better loved to-night, for lo, yonder, gleaming from its gray curtains, the polar star!

The polar star, ever the same in its unpretending, unobtrusive loneliness, has been made an emblem of faith and trust, a way-mark, a balancing point, and we feel lost when we look to the place it has occupied in the heavens and find it vacant. A welcome back, thou pale-eyed northern queen, lone pearl of the earth-arching heavens; and a blithe welcome too to thee, old shaggy monarch of the icy regions, ever unmoved even by the sight of the huntsmen upon thy track with their hounds in the leash, ready to rend thy tough hide at the slightest signal. And there shines the noble Arcturus, he of whom the son of Amram sang from the plains of Midia after he had cast aside the princely purple of Egypt; asking in the name of his God, the great mechanist of the stars, "canst thou bind the sweet influences of the Pleiades or loose the bands of Orion? Canst thou bring forth Mazzaroth in his season? or canst thou guide Arcturus with his sons?" How long has that silver lamp been shining up in heaven? and who are the beings that bask in its light? Angels, creatures bearing the form of man, or those framed to exhibit the versatility of the Contriver's power, whose very mode of existence is utterly inconceivable? Has it ever fallen under the ban of sin? Can sorrow and death visit it? Probably before our little earth or even our fair solar system sprang from the moulding hand of the Architect—it may be myriads on myriads of ages before "the stars sang together" at sight of the beautiful new creation—Arcturus moved in the midst of his sons, chaining them within their orbits by a subtle resistless power, and receiving from them the reflected light of his own smiles. The same large, mild eye, hundreds of centuries ago, looked down upon the sublime historian, the poet-chieftain of Israel, in his desert wanderings with his murmuring people; and the shepherds upon the star-lit plains of Chaldea gazed upon the beacon and braided with its rays strange mysteries. And yet that very orb, that proud, regal Arcturus, with his full unflickering blaze, may at this very moment be among the things which were and are not. The taper, whose rays may have been myriads of centuries traveling to us, could easily have been extinguished before the fires of our own system were lighted, and yet we stand wondering at the semblance. Ah, well, noble star! whether thou art or art not, I greet thy fair seeming right joyfully, for the light of other days is upon thee. The loved ones whose feet are now pointing to ours, with the diameter of the globe between, may look upon thy face even as we look.

And yonder is our own magnificent Jupiter, his large eye fully opened, and there is the northern crown, and there the heart of the royal Charles, and there bright Cassiopeia, and still beyond, the tiny sparklers forming the pale tresses of Berenice, and there—and there—and there—why they are old friends, every one. I am home again.

Land ho, land! A succession of dark rich purple festoons are turning their convex side to the sky in the far distance, telling us that not more than twenty-five miles lie between us and the southernmost islands of the Nicobar chain. And that is really land! Happy as we have been in our little floating bird's-nest, my foot aches to press it.

Land ho, land! Another purple island, regal in the morning light. It sits like a pyramid upon the water, and tapers until its soft, shadowy outline is nearly lost in the clouds. Nearer and nearer we come, and several peaks are now visible, covered with something which seems like foliage, while bald gray cliffs, streaked with chalky lines, descend perpendicularly to the water. On we go, and the rocky sugar loaf of Narconidam fades in the dim distance.

Land at last—the strange land that for us bears the fond

name of *home.* In a long chain, made up of irregular links, which it seems that a breath might dissever, stretches from the south far up to the head of the bay the shore of Burmah. The faint wind dallies about the deck, and creeps over brow and cheek with a soft, soothing deliciousness, but there is only a breath of it stirring, and that is "dead ahead." We have been beating landward with but little success during the past week, but patience! the goal is now in sight, and it matters little whether we reach it to-day or to-morrow, or the day after. Surely we will not murmur at a day more or less tacked to the end of a twenty weeks' voyage. Thank God, that He has spread the land before our eyes at last; that He has shielded us when wrath was stirring in the heavens and darkness was upon the waters; that He has pinioned the wings of the wind, and said to the waves, " thus far shalt thou go, and no farther."

Last night a poor, tired little land-bird, with a head like a blue violet in the spring-time, and a neck slender and most gracefully arched, entered at the window of the saloon, and nestled down on the cushions of the transom with the fond confidence of our own tuneful robin. It was a sweet harbinger, and most joyfully welcomed. Before the unsuspecting little sleeper opened its eyes this morning, it was seized and caged under a morah, where it still flutters, displaying through the bamboo bars its chameleon plumage in all the changeable shades which it has stolen from a tropical sun. It needs not the olive leaf to be a dove to us—the beautiful little stranger!

On—on—on—slowly—very slowly; but the land gradually becomes more distinct; the purple hue of the hills is changing to emerald; masses of trees appear like small clumps of shrubbery; the glass discovers to us the tiny sails of fishermen close in shore, and hark! the cry, "Amherst!" Ay, yonder point of land, with the badge of its degradation on its front, is Amherst, our first anchoring place. Nearer and nearer, tree by tree becomes visible as it appears in relief against the sky—the palm, the cocoa, and the tamarind; and, lo! on that green bank

sloping to the water, the hopia shading the ashes of the sainted.
From the highest point rises the taper spire of a pagoda, and
another is built on the rocky promontory that stretches into
the bay.   It must be a land of beauty—even at this distance
we can but feel sure of that—but how dark! how dark!   The
Burman is not like

> "The poor Indian whose untutored mind
>   Sees God in clouds and hears Him in the wind."

He has no God, not even the Great Spirit of the Indian's hunt-
ing ground, nor the frail deities of ancient mythology.   The
object of his worship is a man whose ashes are scattered to the
four winds of heaven, and whose soul has been for thousands
of years extinct.   His system is one of cause and effect, and he
believes that ages of suffering in the lowest hell will be the
unavoidable effect of the sins he is daily committing, while his
good deeds are only an offset to the evil.   His future life is a
long transmigratory round of toil and suffering ; and the most
glowing of his hopes, the acme of his promised bliss, is anni-
hilation.   And it is not merely one small nation that is hugging
such misery—groveling in this terrible darkness; Buddhism in
its various modifications is the religion of more than a third of
the population of the world.   To kindle the fire which shall
illuminate such a people, though it be at first but the faint, fitful
glimmer of a rush-light, how glorious!   To plant the seed of
one pure principle in natures so degraded, to place one bud of
hope in the core of such misery, and watch its beautiful and
beautifying expansion, to hold in hand the lever which after
hundreds of years shall elevate a mighty nation, as the barbarians of the British Isles have been elevated by that same instrument, has a glory in it which no truly wise man would barter
for the sceptre of an Alexander.   Good can be done every
where, and nothing is truer than that "missionaries are needed
at home ;" yet if I have but one morsel of bread, let me give it
to the famishing; if I have a single flower, let me take it to the

cell of the dying prisoner, on whose cheek the free air never plays, and who knows nothing of the pleasant sights and smells in which others are revelling.

We have approached as near the shore as safety will permit, and already the white sail of a pilot-boat is gliding across the water to meet us. It is preceded, however, by a boat-load of natives, with their broad muscular shoulders bared, and their gay *patsoes* spread over their heads, to protect them from the broiling sun. They bring fresh offerings of fruit, fish, and milk, for there is one of our number that is no stranger to them. What glad faces they bear! And how delicious the fruit tastes! Adieu to salt fish and sea biscuit. Ha! how every thing smells of land!

These men seem almost beautiful, coming from among the green trees, and certainly such an orange as this never grew before—never. For the land, for the land—away!

Ship Faneuil Hall, 1846.

CHAPTER XIV.

THE ORIENT.

"Or to burst all links of habit—there to wander far away,
    On from island unto island at the gateways of the day;
    Larger constellations burning, mellow moons and happy skies,
    Breadths of tropic shade and palms in cluster, knots of Paradise.
    Never comes the trader, never floats an European flag;
    Slides the bird o'er lustrous woodland, droops the trailer from the crag;
    Droops the heavy-blossomed bower, hangs the heavy-fruited tree,
    Summer isles of Eden lying in dark purple spheres of sea."

THE East—that East which to the occidental imagination lies

Under the opening eye-lids of the morn,

and is bathed in the rosiest light of the yet youthful day; that gorgeous East which

With richest hand
Showers on her kings barbaric pearls and gold;.

that romantic East, which had haunted Mrs. Judson's youthful imagination, has now greeted her vision, and become her home. Interesting, however, as may be the strange forms of oriental life to a European, and especially to one of her poetical temperament, it will require but a brief glance to disenchant her fancy, and disclose

the intrinsic poverty veiled by its glittering and picturesque exterior.

Amherst, at which Dr. and Mrs. Judson first landed,
lying at the mouth of the Salwen river, one of the large
streams which pour down from the north into the eastern side of the Bay of Bengal, was hallowed to Dr. Judson's mind by some peculiar associations. He had aided
Mr. Crawfurd, the British commissioner of the Governor-
General of India, in selecting it as the site of the capital of the provinces ceded by Burmah to England, after
the war of 1826. The ceremony of founding the new
town (named from the Governor-General) had been accompanied by a prayer from Dr. Judson so appropriately
eloquent as to receive a special notice in Mr. Crawfurd's
published journal. Dr. Judson assisted at the inaugu-
ration with views of far wider scope, doubtless, than
those of the official actors in the scene. He looked
upon the place as the prospective seat not merely of a
political and military dominion, but of a spiritual empire, which should rise on the ruins of idolatry. With
this hope he had brought hither Mrs. Judson, and was
commencing his labors when he was persuaded by the
British commissioner, with the concurrent advice of his
wife, to accompany him as interpreter in a mission to
Ava, in the hope of securing, along with the commercial
treaty, religious toleration in Burmah. The hope was
disappointed ; the stay of the embassy at Ava was vexa-
tiously protracted by Burman faithlessness and stupidity ; and to crown his distress, while he was wasting his
time in a distasteful and fruitless negotiation, his wife
sickened and died in loneliness, and her sorrowing husband came back not to her bosom, but to her grave.

His hopes regarding Amherst were also doomed to disappointment. The British commander had meantime fixed his cantonments about twenty-five miles up the Salwen, at Maulamyang, or Maulmain, and this determined the place of the capital against the official designation, and the more favorable locality of the sea-port. The Salwen was the dividing line between the Burman and the newly-acquired British territory, and Maulmain, picturesquely situated on its eastern side, naturally attracted the missionaries, and promised to realize what Dr. Judson had anticipated for Amherst. Here they gradually assembled, enjoying under the British flag entire freedom for their work, while the mixed population of the town, embracing Burmans, Chinese, Mohammedans, Armenians, gave scope to almost every department of missionary labor. Here Dr. Judson had been residing before his visit to America, engaged in his dictionary, and acting as pastor of the native church ; and thither he now returned. He returned here the more willingly as its proximity to the idolatrous empire for which he had so long labored enabled him to catch the first hint of an invitation from Providence to reënter it with his oft-rejected message of life, while it introduced Emily to the land of the heathen under the most favorable auspices. Maulmain, though the bulk of its population were idolaters, felt the breath of civilization. Cultivated English and several missionary families made a large circle of refined society.

A few hours brought them up the river in a boat to Maulmain ; his two little sons, Henry and Edward, were welcomed to his arms, and with them and their new " mamma," he was soon reëstablished temporarily in his old quarters. I leave details to the pen of Mrs. Judson.

AMHERST, November 28, 1846.

Well, Katie, here we are at last in queer, ridiculous, half-beautiful, half-frightful, exceedingly picturesque Burmah. We took in a pilot yesterday, and this morning came to anchor in full view of all the greenery of the odd little promontory named Amherst. The old weather-beaten wooden pagoda, stationed away out in the water, and fully visible only at low tide, is overlooked by a charming sister on the bluff above, clad in bridal whiteness, with gilded ornaments, and odd surroundings of various sorts, that I can hardly describe at this distance. How my heart bounded, and every nerve thrilled, as I yesterday watched the purple hills, gradually resolving themselves into the radiant flush of real life, until the green trees stood out in beautiful relief against the blue above them, and the brown roofs of cottages nestling among humbler greenery, became distinct enough to be guessed at. After a five months' surfeit of brackish ocean breezes, to drink in such an air as this!—actually freighted with the odor of fresh turf, and the delicate breath of fading grasses, and the perfume of delicious fruits and rich tropic blossoms.

We were visited last evening, before the pilot came off, by a boat load of nearly naked Madrasees—great athletic looking fellows, some of our party remarked; but as they mingled with our crew, their inferiority of stature could not but be noted, and their finely rounded limbs struck me as displaying more of the grace and beauty of a woman than the bold, muscular development of the athlete. They are erect, with their round bullets of heads finely, even royally balanced, a graceful carriage of body, a pliability of limb that would do no discredit to one of their own serpents, and, of course, great agility in their movements; but in a contest of mere strength, I should scarcely doubt that one of our sailors would be a match for a half dozen of them. The pilot is a Portuguese, fat, square, and heavy. Catch any stress of wind or weather disturbing *his* equilibrium.

He states with a very magisterial sort of an air the impossibility of taking the ship up to Maulmain, as the river is not navigable by so large a vessel at this season; so I suppose we shall go up in boats.

We were scarcely anchored this morning when a boat of six or seven men came bounding toward us, who, by the fluttering of gay silks, and the display of snowy jackets and turbans, were judged to be something above mere boatmen. As they drew sufficiently near to be distinguishable by their features, one of our number who had been for some time silently watching them from the side of the vessel, leaned far over for a moment gazing at them intently, and then sent forth a glad wild hail. In a moment the glancing of oars ceased, a half dozen men sprang to their feet to the imminent peril of the odd nut-shell in which they floated, and a wilder, longer, and if possible more joyous cry, showed that the voice of the salutation was recognized. Christian beckoned me to his side. "They are our Amherst friends," he said; "the dear, faithful fellows!" And these were some of the Christians of Burmah! the pioneers of a nation! Men born in idolatry, sought out by the Saviour, while yet buried in the black depths of heathenism, redeemed and marked for His crown in glory! What a sublime thing to be a missionary! In a few moments the men had brought the boat along side, and were scrambling up the sides of the vessel. How the black eyes danced beneath their grave brows, and the rough lips curled with smiles behind the bristling beards! Then came a quick grasping of hands, and half-choked words of salutation, in a strange, deep guttural, which he only to whom they were addressed could understand; while I, like the full-grown baby that I am, retreated to the nearest shadow, actually sobbing; for what, I am sure I do not know, unless I might have fancied myself a sort of flood-gate for the relief of other people's eyes and voices. However, though it had been pretty strongly intimated that "mamma" must not be out of sight, just at present, I do not think her madamship was missed until she had made herself tolerably presentable, and then she **was** again beckoned forward. The Burmans gave my hand a cordial American grip, but their dusky palms were so velvety that I do not think **even your fingers** would have complained under the pressure. Then a venerable old man, who, as I afterward learned, is a deacon in the church, came forward, and bending his turbaned head respectfully, commenced an animated address, waving his hand occasionally to the troop behind him, who bowed as in assent. I have no doubt it was a rare specimen of eloquence, but, of course, I could not understand a word of it, and could only curtesy and simper very foolishly in acknowledgment. You will laugh when I tell you I have seldom been so embarrassed in my life. I soon learned that the men had reserved nicely matted seats for us in the boat, and that several of their wives and daughters were waiting at the jetty, with cart and oxen, to take me up to the village. Off ran I for my bonnet, but somebody very peremptorily interfered, declaring that a certain pair of thin cheeks were quite thin enough already for their owner's good; and, moreover, that it was very foolish to waste life by keeping the heart all of a flutter, asserting that mine made a dozen trills and quavers, while that of a sensible person took but one moderate step.

Our visitors had brought us bottles of milk, eggs, fish, shrimps, yams, sweet potatoes, plantains, and oranges for our comfort, and while they were unloading their treasures, I borrowed the captain's glass, and took a long look at the jetty. I could see, now that I knew they were actually there, the women grouped along the beach, and another object, which I was told was the cart and a pair of cream colored oxen, standing farther back upon the greensward. My feet fairly ached to press that soft carpet of earth and vegetation, but even the strong men who came for me acknowledged that "mamma" was too small for the undertaking, and so went away alone.

Now, darling, you know I am not a Niobe; you know I always did try to steer clear of certain sentimental indulgences, because they were sure to bring on headache without leaving any mortal good in return. You know I say that I am not one of " earth's sorrowful weepers," but somehow I did get *overtaken* this time. Down into my cabin I went, every nerve in me quivering, and treated my pillow to a regular tear-bath. "Twice of a single morning?" you ask. Twice of a single morning, dear—or what is nearer the truth, the quarter deck operation continued. I was deep in the melting luxury, when the door was softly opened, and I knew that some person stood beside me. I did not move; but kept my face covered with the tolerably well wetted bit of linen, that had divided my favors with the pillow; fortifying meanwhile my voice in anticipation of a question.

Presently I heard words, but though spoken close to my ear, they were not addressed to me. How that low, mellow voice crept down into my heart, calming its foolish agitation, imparting the strength of faith, illuminating its tremulous, shadowy depths with hope, and elevating it to a still, serene reliance on Him who can be touched with the feeling of our infirmities, simply because His nature though sinless, has vibrated to every earthly emotion. ·

Then how strange to be so thoroughly comprehended! Any body else now would have thought that I was in a pet from the disappointment of not going on shore, or something else of the kind.

He knew, I can not tell how, but he told it all in that prayer as I never could have done—he knew just how a faint heart feels, suddenly pressed upon with a view of moral sublimity to which it is for the moment inadequate; he knows what it is to have the doors of time, all shut and barred, and the long vista of eternity stretching in solemn perspective before the shrinking soul, and he knows just what is needed at such a crisis.

I remember a soothing, balm-distilling influence, a feeling of perfect security and serenity, and then I went to sleep. When I awoke, the jolly boat with the officers and gentlemen passengers, Christian among them, had gone on shore, and with the exception of a half-hour devoted to the hopia tree, I have been writing to you ever since.

FROM A LETTER TO FRIENDS IN BOSTON.

. . . We had a long but most delightful voyage in the pleasant *Faneuil Hall*, with its fine accommodations, kind officers, and quiet, orderly crew; and between our internal resources, and the constantly varying character of the sea-scenery, we could find no time for *ennui*. Twenty weeks from the day on which we went abroad, we anchored off Amherst; and the next Monday morning, were lowered into a Burmese boat, to proceed up to Maulmain. I was most agreeably disappointed by my first view of the land of palms and mosquitoes. Our boat was very much like a long watering-trough, whittled to a point at each end, and we were all nestled like a parcel of caged fowls, under a low bamboo cover, from which it was not easy to look out. But the shore, along side which we were pushed up stream by the might of muscle, was brilliant with its unpruned luxuriance of verdure, and birds, and flowers.

Here some strange tree dropped its long trailers to the water, there the white rice-bird, or a gayer stranger, with chameleon neck and crimson wing, coquetted with its neighbor, and the wealth of green, bending below; and then followed rich blossoms of new shapes and hues, and bearing new names, some in clusters, and some in long amber wreaths, stained here and there with lemon and vermilion, and all bearing that air of slumbrous richness characteristic of the Indian climate. Our oarsmen were Amherst Christians, who seemed as wild with joy as the birds themselves (not that they were particularly bird-like in any other respect), and there was laughing and chattering enough to make any heart merry. The first, being a universal language, I had no difficulty in understanding, but the latter sounded to me even more outlandish than their gaudy patsoes, bare, brawny shoulders, and turbaned heads, appeared to the eye.

TO MRS. GILLETTE.

MAULMAIN, Dec. 20, 1846.

MY DEAR MRS. GILLETTE,—

A year ago I was sitting in your pleasant little parlor, never dreaming of such an overturn in life as this, and very happy; but no happier than I am now. Now I have measured half the world by ship-lengths, and stand here (or rather sit) one of the four legs of your bedstead while you sleep. These turn-abouts in life really tip one's brains over curiously. I never quite got my ideas straight after crossing the equator until I came in sight of the north star again; and now things are worse than ever. Nothing here, not even a bird or tree, is like the vegetable or winged things across the water; and the few articles that bear a slight resemblance to those seen before must needs have new names. Little boys' trowsers are *bombees*, their frocks *engees*, and people don't lunch, they take *tiffin*. . . .

I am delighted here with every thing so far as I have yet observed. To be sure there is little of what in America is considered comfort (what an outlandish oddity our house would be, set down in Delaware, 12th!) but there is a picturesque beauty—a mingling of awkward simplicity with magnificence quite as clumsy and awkward—a rich gorgeousness, a fantastic extravagance, a rudeness sometimes annoying, but oftener ludicrous—in short, the scenery, the works of art (there is no small degree of skill displayed in building a pagoda, and ornamenting the carriages that go up with offerings to Guadama), the manners of the people, the color of the sky, the atmosphere, are all in perfect keeping with each other, and all have an oriental air which is quite fascinating to me. The houses of the missionaries are the plainest possible, built of teak boards, and furnished with the same kind of wood, without varnish. The partitions between the rooms are mere screens, reaching a little above the head, so that a word spoken in one room is

heard all over the house. To my eye, however, even these
houses have an air of relative beauty about them which nicer
ones would not have. If I were fond of new things, I should
think it was because they were new and odd; but I think I
was made for an uncivilized land. . . .

Were we to settle down in this house with the comforts we
should be able to secure, the pleasant English and missionary
families about us, although in a very different condition from
a pastor's family at home, my taste would be gratified, and I
should, as far as the things of this world are concerned, be
perfectly happy. But that is not to be. My conscience will
not allow me to remain in delightful Maulmain while there is
the slightest hope of my husband's being able, by going to a
place of danger and privation, to do any thing for the miserable nation, at the door of which we are standing. I am not
myself made for great things, but when I see his heart turning that way, I can say "go," and when the trials come, I
know I can cheer and comfort him. As soon as I can get a few
words of the language—a couple of months, perhaps—we shall
put off to Rangoon, and there wait an opportunity to creep
into Ava. . . .

I have discovered since I left America that I am incapable of
the emotion of fear. I have been two or three times pretty
severely tried in that respect. I may meet with things at Rangoon, however, that will make my hair bristle. God only
knows, and quietly in my own closet I ask His direction and
assistance. You and your dear good man will, I trust, help
me ask, for none ever needed all the graces of godliness, combined with singular wisdom, more than I do just now. I love
the cause of Christ with my whole heart, and I love, too, these
poor wretches, who, in ignorance of the ways of life, are going
down to eternal misery. God make me useful to them. I do
not believe in practicing self-denial for self-denial's sake—I
think that a relic of popery—but I should not shrink from

suffering or even death in His cause. I pray that I may not be like Peter when I say *I never will.* . . .

Your affectionate friend,

EMILY C. JUDSON.

TO MRS. STEVENS.

January, 1847.

MY DEAR MRS. STEVENS,—

I have been all day divided between my desire to attend your meeting this afternoon (which I know will be interesting) and the awkwardness inseparable from my appearance in a company of matrons, where I feel as though I had no right to be.

I do love the dear children that a saint in heaven has left me. I love them for their own sakes; for sweeter, more lovely little creatures never breathed; brighter, more beautiful blossoms never expanded in the cold atmosphere of this world. I love them for the sake of one still dearer, who had the power to break all the ties which were twined with tenfold strength about my heart; and I love them because they are immortal beings, because for them a Saviour died, even as for me. I love them; I pray to God to help me train them up in His fear and love.

I shall be very thankful, my dear Mrs. Stevens, for any advice you or the loved sisters who will meet with you to-day, can give me; for I know that I am utterly unfitted for this sweet burden which God has laid upon my heart and hands. Please ask them for their prayers, first in behalf of the orphans afar off; next, in behalf of the little ones here, that they may never know the want of a fond mother's care and love; and next, in behalf of the new, inexperienced mother, that God may give the wisdom, patience, gentleness, humility, and entire dependence on Him, necessary to their proper management; so that at last I may be able to lead them up to her who loved them even more than I, and say, "here are thine own jewels, polished for thy crown."

Believe me, my dear Mrs. Stevens, it is only the bashfulness attendant on a strange situation, and which it seems impossible for me to surmount, which keeps me from your meeting. May Jesus Christ be in your midst.

Affectionately,

E. C. J.

I send the children. Will you or Mrs. Haswell be kind enough to take charge of them as formerly?

JOURNAL.

Maulmain, January 1, 1847.   Actually in Burmah! And is it really myself? Is the past year a reality, or am I still dreaming up there in Dominie Gillette's chamber, where I lay down (seemingly) a year ago? If it *be* a dream, I pray God that I may never wake, for I believe that it would break my heart to be other than I am. Thank God, it is a reality—a blessed reality ; and I am in the very spot I so longed to plant my foot upon, years and years gone by.

January 2.   I have got a teacher, and made a beginning in the language, but the children absorb so much of my time that I can not study much. They are dear little fellows, but *so* full of mischief! Precious gems they are ; may they not be spoiled by so inexperienced a polisher as I am.

January 5.   It seems to me as though I do nothing but get up, turn round, and then go to bed again! I believe there never was such a novice in housekeeping ; and then the children, and the language, and the thousand and one other botherations! I expected to make a rush at the language, take it by storm, then get a parcel of natives about me, and go to work in "true apostolic style." Not that I had the vanity to think myself very apostle-like, but I know, O my Heavenly Father, that Thou canst bless the very meanest of Thy children if they but look up to Thee. And I will continue to look ; for though my work is not what I expected, Thou canst bring great results from little causes. It is all of Thy ordering.

January 6. We are looking toward Rangoon, and I pray that we may succeed in going. God's "ways are not as our ways," and His time may be nearer than we suspect. But it is very, *very* pleasant here. Many think we are not wise in going to Rangoon, and perhaps we are not. But if God's time *should* be at hand, we might regret that we had held back. At any rate, it is good to stand in the way of His providences; and I do not wish to stay here until I become attached to the comforts of the place.

January 10. This taking care of teething babies, and teaching darkies to darn stockings, and talking English back end foremost to teetotum John, in order to get an eatable dinner, is really very odd sort of business for Fanny Forester. I wonder what my respectable friends of the anti-F. F. school would say, if they could see my madamly airs. But I begin to get reconciled to my minute cares. I believe women were made for such things; though when I get settled, I hope to put in a mixture of higher and better things, too. But the person who would do great things well, must practice daily on little ones; and she who would have the assistance of the Almighty in important acts, must be daily and hourly accustomed to consult His will in the minor affairs of life.

January 13. It is late, and we have spent the greater part of the evening in talking over old times. O, how I rejoice that I am out of the whirlpool! Too gay, too trifling for a missionary's wife! That may be, but after all, gayety is my lightest sin. It is my coldness of heart, my listlessness, my want of faith, my spiritual inefficiency and inertness, my love of self, the inherent and every day pampered sinfulness of my nature, that makes me such a mere infant in the cause of Christ—not the attractions of the world.

January 14. I did not think that I should feel so sad to be left alone only these few weeks; but the prospect actually makes my heart faint. We have been daily and hourly together ever since our marriage, and his presence is my very life. I hear his step now, as he goes from room to room, making all the arrangements in his power for my comfort. So thoughtful! so tender! so delicate! O, there are few on earth so blest as I! And how kind must be my heavenly Friend, to lead me in such a pleasant path, and make a place for me in such a heart!

January 16. Not well to-day. I slept but an hour or two last night, and that very brokenly. I suppose it is foolish in me to allow this matter to weigh so heavily upon my spirits; but it is a little solace to my wounded vanity that I am not the only foolish one. If men who have been through prisons and all perils weep at such separations, surely such a weakling as I should not be put in a strait-jacket. The truth is, we poor humans are utterly baffled in attempting to estimate each other's sufferings. I will venture to assert that it required a far greater effort in Ann H. Judson to leave her husband (*such* a husband!) in Rangoon, and go to America alone, than to play the heroic part in his presence, and for his sake, that she did at Ava.

But Dr. J.'s going to Rangoon for two or three weeks is not my going to America, and I must try not to be quite a fool. What would people in America, who believe that missionaries are or ought to be destitute of natural affection, say to this struggle? But they can not know of it, and I shall be the last to tell. Let them think, if they like, that I came on a literary speculation, and so made merchandise of myself for ambition, as some have done for the sake of religion. How little they know the hearts of either of us. And what a blessing that God is omniscient!

January 20. All alone, and so lonely! My life is one continued heartache, for I continually feel as though he was dead. My family worship is broken by tears, for it is *his* business; and when I attempt to bless the food at meals, my voice sometimes utterly fails. Alone with the children about me, and trying to fill *his* place, I feel widowed indeed. I have but one refuge, and this helps me to live. I know too that he is praying for me.

January 27. As I lay alone upon my pillow to-day, my head racked with nervous pain, and the children frolicking about the rooms, many strange thoughts passed through my mind. What are God's designs toward me, that my life from the very cradle has been such an uninterrupted chain of discipline? Has He been preparing me for any unheard of sufferings? Does He intend to make me an instrument in accomplishing some mighty good? Or is all this designed merely to fit my own soul for the inheritance of the saints? If the latter, how ought I to labor and strive to improve by His strange dispensations! I have not yet seen thirty years, and such changes!—such varieties of fortune! I seem to have lived a century. I have been tried both by adversity and prosperity, by undeserved praise and by censure equally undeserved. I have toiled both by night and by day, have been pinched by want and overwhelmed by plenty, and all for what purpose? O, my Heavenly Father, bless unto me all Thy past dispensations, and prepare me for whatever Thou hast marked out for me in future. Make me a good wife, a good mother, and a good teacher of the heathen— an example which the native converts may safely follow.

January 29. I am going on beautifully with the language; I do not believe it will be very hard for me.

January 30. Both children are quite ill to-day, and I am full of cares. O, my poor little motherless boys! I do pray that our Heavenly Father may give me a soft and pitying heart toward you. It is so sad for such mere babies to be torn from their homes and put into a stranger's hands, especially a stranger so inexperienced as I am. How much I need to pray!

11*

CHAPTER XV.

"THEN on, then on, where duty leads,
My course be onward still."

MRS. JUDSON is left alone. Right across the narrow
Gulf of Martaban lies Pegu, subject to Burman dominion, with its capital, Rangoon, the seat of Dr. Judson's
earliest missionary labors. Thither he has now determined again to repair, to try what hope there may be of
resuscitating its extinguished mission. On the 18th of
January he embarked in the ship *Cecilia*, and reached
Rangoon on the 23rd. He was received by the Governor
(or Woon-gyee) with great personal kindness and respect,
(for he had rendered important services to the Burmese
in bringing about a peace with England,) and was permitted and invited to come there as a preacher to the
resident foreigners, but not as a missionary or "propa-
gator of religion." The Burmese Government had receded even from its former partial religious tolerance, and
thrown itself back for the maintenance of the national
faith on the sure argument of power. But, doubtful
as was the experiment, Dr. Judson resolved to try it,
and stand ready, at least, for any possibilities of effort.
He engaged for his family the upper story of a large,

desolate brick building, in a street of Mussulmans, which figures in Mrs. Judson's correspondence sometimes as "Bat Castle," and sometimes as "Green Turban's den." Returning he reached Maulmain on the 6th of February.

FROM DR. JUDSON.

ON BOARD THE CECILIA, January 19, '47.

MY DEAREST LOVE—

I awoke this pleasant morning thinking of you, and imagining how you were sleeping, and how you were getting up, and how you were employing yourself about the children and the house. It seems as if I had been associated with you for many years; and hardly knew how to deport myself in your absence. When I came out of my cabin this morning, we were losing sight of Maulmain, and are now in sight of Amherst. I write this line to send back by Captain Crisp, Sen., who is now on board. I received letters and accounts yesterday from my agents in Calcutta, and put them under the cover containing the other valuable papers; you had better look them over. I only noticed that the balance due me at the close of last year was two thousand six hundred rupees, which is much larger than I expected.

I feel in excellently good spirits in regard to making the attempt at Rangoon, though I see no particular reason to hope for success. I intend to do all that lies in my power, and am quite willing to leave the event in the hands of God. "Trust in God and keep your powder dry," was Cromwell's word to his soldiers. Trust in God and love one another is, I think, a better watchword. Let us do the duties of religion and of love, and all will be well. Conjugal love stands first. Happy those who find that duty and pleasure coincide. Then comes parental love and filial love; then love to associates, and then love to all that come within our reach. I have been talking with Crisp this two hours, and you see I have become quite ethical.

Sweet love, I wish I could reason out the subject, and come to a satisfactory solution on your lips. Farewell for the present.

Ever thine,   A. JUDSON.

FROM DR. JUDSON.

ON BOARD THE CECILIA, Jan. 20, 1847.

MY DEAREST LOVE,—

We are just passing between the two buoys off Amherst, the pilot's boat is coming off, and he will leave us in an hour. I write a line by him, but it may not reach you immediately. Another beautiful morning. The hopia tree is just visible from the shore. I seem to have lived in several worlds; but you are the earthly sun that illuminates my present. My thoughts and affections revolve around you, and cling to your form, and face, and lips. Other luminaries have been extinguished in death. I think of them with mournful delight, and anticipate the time when we shall all shine together as the brightness of the firmament and as the stars for ever and ever.

I should be glad to get a line from you and the children before I lose sight of the coast, but it can not be. I trust I shall get something by the *Erwin*, in which Captain Antram is to take passage. Pray take care of yourself. . . . I left four books at the printing-office to be bound. Ask brother Ranney about them, and when you get them, I should be glad to have you read the memoir of Hester Ann Rogers. Once more farewell, dearest and best. "Think of me, sweet, when alone."

Yours ever,

A. JUDSON.

TO DR. JUDSON.

MAULMAIN, Jan. 20, Saturday Evening.

MY OWN BLESSED DARLING,—

I have been exceedingly distressed about writing to you, for I thought you would be worried about us, and have no opportunity of hearing until your return. Captain Antram has, however, just sent word that he leaves early to-morrow morning, and so I sit down in my night-dress to tell you that all is going on like clock-work. There has been a robbery in the printing-office, and so I have got two of Mrs. Howard's scholars to sleep with Moung Shway Kyo, and they *do* sleep! Captain A.'s servant made plenty of noise, and I walked fairly over them to the door, but they are snoring still. Little Edward is quite well again, though I was obliged to go to Mrs. S. about him again, being unwilling to call a physician, unless obliged to.

We have heard that the king is really assassinated. I am prepared for almost any thing strange, and I think that these various overturnings *must* turn up something favorable to our object. How good of you, darling, to write me those two sweet letters, when I didn't expect any! They made me cry, like the baby that I am, in gratitude. Oh, if we are ever safely together again, I will follow you wherever you go, in spite of difficulties. Not that every thing is not pleasant now, but these separations are not good. I look in my room and through my dressing-room window up to the chapel for you every day in vain. And you.—I think of you, darling, although I write about myself. I think of you on the sea, perhaps in danger; on the land, alone and exposed to—what? Oh, if I could only know precisely what!

I have no choice at all between Maulmain and Rangoon. Decide as you shall think best. I know you will not let this world's comforts weigh with you, and yet you will be prudent.

Farewell, my "home," my life, my all but God and heaven. Farewell for a little while, but come as soon as possible. May the best blessing of Heaven be about thee, my precious, precious husband (my heart bounds with pride and pleasure as my pen first addresses thee by this title, darling); may the blessing of

Heaven be upon thee, and all sad thoughts and remembrances be kept far away. So prays daily,

Thy loving wife,

EMILY.

I have not let the clock run down, nor neglected to feed the fowls ! !

FROM DR. JUDSON,

TO FANNY FORESTER JUDSON.

RANGOON, Jan. 29, 1847.

Tide ebbs and flows, day comes and goes,
　　The orbs inconstant shine ;
One vestal lamp for ever glows,
　　The thought that thou art mine.

Though now, an exile far remote,
　　In foreign lands I pine
To catch a glance of thy bright eyes,
　　I know those eyes are mine.

Though seas and mountains interpose,
　　And elements combine
To bar the mutual, melting kiss,
　　I know thy lips are mine.

And though around thy graceful form
　　In vain I long to twine
My arms, and feel thy beating heart,
　　I know that heart is mine.

And joy it gives my inmost soul
　　That, as thy love is mine,
Thou know'st, beyond a shade of doubt,
　　My constant heart is thine.

Nor death shall loose the bonds of love,
   Or cause me to resign
My claim upon thy lifeless form—
   In the grave thou shalt be mine.

And when before the Throne we stand,
   Arrayed in charms divine,
I shall be thine, and thou, my love,
   Be ever, ever mine.

MY DEAREST LOVE,—

The vessel by which I wrote you last night is, I believe, still in the river. She has had the blue Peter (the sailing flag) hoisted ever since we have been here. Such is the endless delay of the place. The *Gyne*, in which I have engaged my passage, will not sail till next Monday; to-day is Friday. I think she will sail then, because Antram and the rest will be anxious to return. No further news. I have made all my inquiries, and done all my business here, and want to be off.

Your precious letter by Rozario came in this morning. I fold you in my inmost heart.

I forgot to mention that for several days I have suffered from an ophthalmic affection of the left eye. It is now better; but I don't like to write by lamp-light, as I am now doing.

So farewell, dear, dear wife, and kiss Henry and Edward for papa, and Lydia too, and keep one eye open in the night.

Yours ever,

A. JUDSON.

TO REV. MR. COREY.

MAULMAIN, January 31, 1847.

MY DEAR MR. COREY,—

  . . . I am writing you, merely because I feel like doing

so—because I think of you as you used to sit when I went bounding down to Aunt Cynthia's room of a bright morning. I can not write a "missionary letter," and you will not disgrace me by letting any one see a "common letter" such as I would have written on American soil. So then—to you just as I would chat with you if you were to step in now, and sit down by the square hole which we dignify by calling window. We should be alone, for the Doctor has been gone to Rangoon a couple of weeks, and I have sent the children out, now that the sun is nearly down, to have a frolic upon the grass. The first thing you did probably, would be to remark the difference between our barn-like looking house, and the comfortable ones in Utica; and I should tell you that a Utica house here would be tipped into the river. And so it would; for though they are mere board shanties in comparison, nobody could live in it; then, perhaps, I should tell you that Edward cried in the night (last night), and as he is not well, I sprang up to go to him. As I stepped my foot upon the floor, it was like thrusting it into the fire. I immediately got a light, and found the floor black with ants—no uncommon thing. We are obliged to have our bedsteads stand constantly in water. I do not know whether or not I should tell you how the frogs hop from my sleeves when I put them on, and how the lizards drop from the ceiling to the table when we are eating. I do not think I should mention my feet; but you would see that I found it impossible to keep them still, and had them in immensely large shoes, and you would probably think of the ant-bites, especially as you would see several on the backs of my hands.

You would not need to be told that Maulmain is a beautiful place, for you would see it; still I think I should launch out somewhat in its praises. To my eye there is nothing in a land of frosts to compare with it. Our house, as it was built first, is much the poorest one in the mission, and the least pleasantly situated; but I would not exchange it for any thing belonging to a cold climate. Then the scenery around is perfectly charming. Just mount a little Burman pony, and come along with Mrs. Stevens, Mrs. Haswell and me, just as the mist is rising from the river in the morning. The hills are bristling with white and gilded pagodas ; the tiny bells attached to them are giving out faint music ; and at their base the mendicant priests wander about in their yellow dresses, looking the personification of the misery which they are dealing out to their fellows. You pity the poor wretches in spite of yourself. As you turn your back upon the hills, a scene unrivaled in picturesque beauty opens upon your view, and you involuntarily draw up in the middle of the street, and stand erect in your stirrups. The mist hangs like a silver vail above the river which is specked with very curious looking boats, and just before you lies, like a gem of emerald, the island of sacred water. On the right hand the land rises, in some parts precipitously, and here and there little houses like last year's hay-stacks, are stuck down in groves of various kinds of trees—the palm, cocoa, orange, lime, and jack, etc., etc. You are met all along the way by the turbaned heads of different nations ; for Maulmain seems to be a place of general conference. A portly, king-like Mogul rolls by in his lumbering gazzee ; a Jew in his own peculiar costume is wending his way to his merchandise, looking, poor fellow! little like a child of Abraham ; the Chinaman toddles along in his high-toed shoes and silken trowsers; the Indian from the other coast covers himself entirely with his white flowing drapery, making a very ghost-like appearance as he squats on the hill-side, or glides along the street; the ugly Portuguese, aping the ungraceful English style of dress, jogs on his way in clerk-like fashion; and the Burman with his chequered *patso* thrown over his shoulders and descending to his knees, to protect him from the chill air of morning, steps from the road, and stares admiringly, exclaiming meanwhile at the courage of the English ladies. I believe both Burmans and Hindoos think English *women* braver and more daring than any of the *men* of the East. And though they are, most of them, fine, muscular-looking fellows, I think I should scarce fear a half-dozen. A robbery took place in our compound at the printing office, since Dr. J.'s absence, and Miss Lillybridge and I have but a timid Burman boy to garrison our weak fort, who I know would run at the least rustling of danger. If we can put on a bold front and stand erect, I suppose there is no danger here; but I am told we have a different kind of men—more savage—in Burmah proper. If we go to Rangoon God only knows what lies before us. Maulmain to my taste is pleasanter than any thing in America; though to a person of less romance (I find that I have romance, although I supposed it entirely worn out before I left America), there must be a great many blots upon the picture. Articles to eat and wear are sadly circumscribed, but the eye has a feast. And then, while I lay no claim to much missionary spirit, it *is* a comfort to pick the poor wretches out of the mire and filth, and give them the hope of a crown in heaven. There is a "romance" in that which makes me deem a residence in a Maulmain barn or a Rangoon prison, preferable to the most splendid American mansion or European palace. . . .

I was just called to look at a *bŏng bŏng tantah,* as little Henry calls it—a Burman funeral. It is a very splendid affair, and the music has been within hearing for a couple of hours. The dead is borne in a magnificent car of gold and scarlet, with offerings of fruit and flowers before, and a priest in his yellow robes at the side. It is a strange sight. I have written two long letters already, or I would describe it more particularly. My love to Mrs. Corey, and believe me, my dear sir,

Yours most sincerely,
EMILY C. JUDSON.

February 2. I received a letter from Mr. Judson yesterday. He had not seen the governor but had found a house which he says is "as gloomy as a prison." He writes, "I turn from all this filth and wretchedness to you; and how *can* I think of taking you from the comforts of Maulmain into this den?" We shall go now unless the government absolutely forbids it, as soon as he returns. I am busy packing up again.

FROM DR. JUDSON.

Rangoon, February 2, 1847.

My Darling,

We move from the *Gyne* to the *Thistle*, and from the *Thistle* back to the *Gyne*, according to the whims of Antram & Co. I dutifully follow in their wake. Yesterday we got all our things on board the *Thistle ;* to-day we have changed our quarters to get more room. For a day or two I have had nothing about me but the clothes I have on. The *Thistle* drops down with this noon's tide, and I write this line to send by her. The *Gyne* says she will move with this evening's tide, but I guess not till to-morrow's. It is doubtful which will arrive first —both, probably, near the end of the week. I have received two precious letters from you, and have sent you several to which I am afraid that epithet can not be fairly applied. I have *some* desire to see your sweet face once more, and fold you in my arms. May we be blessed with a happy meeting! From all I hear, we shall be a fortnight, or three weeks or more, in Maulmain, before we get passage in the *City of London*. The longer I stay here the more tolerable a future residence appears. But it will be dull work, except so far as we find happiness in ourselves and in God. And there will be many external discomforts. I don't care so much for myself, but I hate to reward your kindness and love to me by dragging you into this forlorn, dreary place. They are pretending to put some polish on the upper story of " Green Turban's" den, against Madam's arrival. And they are taking some precautions against fire, according to my suggestions. Farewell, Ζωή μου, my life, my love, and dear Henry and Edward.

Yours ever,

A. Judson.

FROM DR. JUDSON.

ON BOARD THE GYNE, February 5, 1847.

MY DARLING LOVE,—

We sailed from Rangoon on the 3d, and must be near Amherst. In fact, the Martaban Hills are said to be in sight. I write a line to send up by some chance opportunity, in case we are detained a tide or so at Amherst. This little absence has taught me how much dearer you are now, my wife, than formerly, my—my ladye-love—is that the word? Ah, you have been doing the thing ever since we were married, though I have repeatedly told you not to do it, and you faithfully promised, before Dr. K——, to love, honor, and *obey;* you will not attend to the latter particular, but will keep going on making me love you in spite of myself. This is what you have done ever since we first met. However, I am determined to assert my right one of these days, and rise superior to all vain fascinations. Yes, when I get you into Burmah proper, we will see if you wont mind. Ah, darling love, what nonsense I am writing! Your last was the 24th of January. Twelve days have passed, and many things may have happened in that time affecting you seriously.

We have just anchored in full view of Amherst, and must wait six hours for the tide to turn. But it is impossible to write with all this chattering about me. What shall I say? It has been the plague of my life to be forced into the company of people whom I had no wish to see or hear. I hope the time will come when we shall be able to enjoy one another's society, and pursue our proper work, acquiring and using a heathen language for the dissemination of Gospel truth (the most glorious work that man can be engaged in), without the everlasting annoyance and din of company. But then, perhaps, you will get tired of me, and long for the society you formerly enjoyed. And I am sure I should not blame you, or think it at all strange. I only think it strange that you could make up your mind to follow "the fortunes of that lone missionary" so contentedly as you have. You say you love me because I am so good! Why don't you add—and so handsome? That would be equally appropriate. Ah, poor girl, you have been sadly taken in. Circumstances combined to make me a sort of lion at home, and I took advantage of my adventitious position to find my way to your heart. I almost condemn myself for a villain, and my only apology is that I could not help it. However, when I think of the affair in connection with religion and eternity, I feel that it has been my precious privilege to draw you from a situation of danger to one which, with the blessing of God, will conduce to your highest, your everlasting benefit. And to attain such an end, I should not value another voyage to America, dearest and best.

Here we lie, with Amherst in sight from our cabin window. Amherst, whither I brought Ann, and returned to find her grave; Amherst, whither I brought Sarah, on returning from my matrimonial tour to Tavoy, and whence I took her away in the *Paragon*, to return no more; Amherst, the terminus of my long voyage in the *Faneuil Hall* with Emily. The place seems like the centre of many radii of my past existence, though not a place where any of us have lived for any length of time. Ann never saw Maulmain; Sarah never saw Rangoon. If we should remove to the latter place, it would seem to me like beginning my life anew. May it be under more propitious auspices, and may the latter part of life make some atonement for the errors of the former. May you, my dearest, be happy, and useful, and blessed there! May we be luminaries to Burmah, and may our setting sun descend in a flood of light! Who shall paint the glories of the eternity before us? Eye hath not seen, nor ear heard, etc. I hope to get up to Maulmain some time to-morrow. So farewell once more, and believe me to be, with ever growing affection and esteem,

Your devoted husband,

A. JUDSON.

They immediately commenced their preparations for departure. Pleasant, picturesque, English Maulmain was to be exchanged for gloomy, idolatrous Burman Rangoon —the former with English society and under English safe-guards of life and liberty; the latter withdrawn from Christian influence, subject to a despotism absolute, capricious, and cruel, and with almost nothing to relieve the loathsome aspects of heathenism. The little Church once gathered here had been scattered to the winds, and all the Christian labor of years had not probably left the slightest perceptible influence on the general aspect of society. But Dr. Judson was not a man to balance comfort against usefulness. His early devotion on the altar of sacrifice had been absolute and irrevocable; and his delicate wife, if she possessed less of strictly missionary zeal, had a high, heroic heart, and a self-sacrificing temper, which responded to and sometimes almost outstripped the glowing ardor of her husband's. As she had turned with tearful joy from the refined endearments of her American home, she now abandoned no less readily the comforts and intelligence of Maulmain, and willingly plunged with her husband into the deepest night of heathenism, if with him she might scatter through it some rays of celestial light.

Rangoon, too, was far from being the Rangoon of the present. This was in 1847. Five years later the thunders of the British cannon were again heard in the Rangoon river, and a British army was compelled to vindicate the rights of British subjects against the outrages of a government equally stupid and ferocious. Again Burmah was dismembered, and the ancient province of Pegu was wrested from her and annexed to the English dominions, which now almost girdled with an unbroken chain the Bay

of Bengal from Cape Comorin to Malacca. Rangoon felt
the renovating power of English enterprise. Its harbor,
one of the finest in Eastern India, became the centre of
an active commerce. Its rows of native huts were plowed
through, like so many ant hills, by the streets of an English
city. The pledge of religious protection reinvited the
exiled missionaries ; and light and freedom began to
penetrate its dark and stagnant recesses. But as yet all
this was not—and was not to be until Dr. Judson slept
the sleep which shall know no waking till the sea gives
up its dead. It lay in the gripe of an unrelaxed despotism, and under the heavy cloud of an idolatry through
which scarcely shimmered some deceitful gleams of a
foully corrupted Christianity, when Dr. and Mrs. Judson
entered it, and, after innumerable vexations, were safely
lodged in their uncouth home.

CHAPTER XVI.

"BAT CASTLE."

"The heavy rain unceasing falls ;
　　Winds hurry to and fro ;
The damp mould gathers on the walls,
　　So dreary, dark, and low ;
Dull shadows throng my aching brow—
My *heart* is never shadowed now."

RANGOON! The cradle of American Indian missions!
The first missionary love of Dr. Judson and his last!
Where he first knocked with the message of life at the
gates of the Burman empire, and whence he finally
turned away, reluctantly and slowly, like Adam leaving
Paradise, as from the Eden of his missionary hopes!
We follow our hero and heroine to thee now with
trembling solicitude, fondly hoping that the set time to
favor thee has come, and that he who would so often
have gathered thy children beneath the wing of heavenly
mercy is about to realize his life-long aspirations. But
it is not to be! He comes to thee again, to be again
rejected. Again that inscrutable wisdom of Providence,
which mocks the short-sighted impatience of man, delays
the time when the light of the cross shall gild the spires
of thy pagodas, and the foul orgies of idolatry be exchanged for the blessed rites of Christian worship.

But while our party are domiciliating themselves in
"Green Turban's den ;" while Dr. Judson is spreading
out his books and papers in the room that is to be his
study, and Emily's tasteful and dexterous fingers are
"tricking" the dreary apartments into the show of civilization, let us lift up our eyes for a moment's general
survey.

The traveler who passes the Brahmaputra from the
west finds himself within that vast territory vaguely defined as India beyond the Ganges.   He has exchanged
the dominion of Brahma for that of Buddh, a form of faith
which, spreading over China, holds a wider sway than any
other religion on the globe. Of the immense region above
designated, stretching through more than a thousand
miles, from China to Siam, the chief provinces, when first
known to our missionaries, had become incorporated into
the powerful Kingdom of Burmah. Arracan, Pegu,
Martaban, Tenasserim (omitting lesser names) had all,
after many struggles and vicissitudes of fortune, yielded,
one by one, to the hardy valor of the people of Ava, and
rendered their tribute to the "Lord of the Golden City."
The vicinity of such an empire—haughty, jealous,
unscrupulous, and regardless alike of natural right
and international law—to the vast power of Britain
(with whose territory its own was through a long way
conterminous), made a collision between them, sooner or
later, inevitable. It came in 1826. After repeated demands for redress, insolently refused, a British army cap-
tured Rangoon, and proceeding slowly up the Irrawadi,
annihilating in its march the proudest forces of the empire, compelled Burmah to a humiliating peace. Arracan, the most of Martaban, Tenasserim, comprising its
entire sea coast except Pegu, were ceded to the British,

12

cutting down its territory to the still extensive districts of
Pegu and Ava. So matters stood until 1853, when Pegu
also, occupying the fertile delta of the Irrawadi, was
dismembered from Ava ; thus completing the chain of
British dominion around the Bay of Bengal.

Doubtless these fluctuations of Oriental conquest and
subjugation have but small significance for the history
of humanity. The varying fortunes of these semi-bar-
barous races are but the shifting of sand hills in the desert, all arid and fruitless of permanent result. King-
doms rise and vanish like the baseless fabric of a vision.
Cities fluctuate like empires. Capitals are as migratory
as the tents of an Arab Sheik. Like Birnam wood
coming to Dunsinane, a whole city will transport itself
almost bodily, and men take up their houses and walk,
almost as easily as the healed of Scripture did their beds.
The Burmese capital has fluctuated back and forward
between Amarapura and Ava, and has recently sought
an entirely new location. The most populous quarter
of Rangoon was burnt up in a few hours by the boiling
over of a pot of oil, and in a month was rebuilt and even
more populous than before ; and Rangoon itself has
superseded the "faded glories" of Pegu, the ancient seat
of royalty. The savage has no history ; semi-barbarism
next to none. Their movements fluctuate in an eternal
chaos of barren change. Their institutions crystalize around
no great moral truths which give them permanence and vitality. When civilization comes with its profound ideas ;
when agriculture turns deserts into gardens ; when commerce weaves over land and ocean her network of enterprise ; when science reveals nature as a vast repository of orderly and harmonious truths ; when art fills it
with creations of utility and beauty ; when religion per-

vades it with the presence of God and the radiance of immortality, then the records of man rise to the dignity of history.

Rangoon itself lies on one of the largest branches of the Irrawadi, about seventeen miles from its mouth. It stretches about a mile along the northern bank of the river, and presents little that is attractive in itself or its environs. It "bristles with pagodas," but there are no handsome dwelling houses; the narrow streets are wretchedly paved with brick, and intolerable to walk on. And here our party are, voluntary exiles. The gates of civilization have closed behind them. They can scarcely "feel the stir of the great Babel," much less "hear its din." Look northward, and four hundred miles up the Irrawadi lies Ava, the golden city. To the east, nearly a hundred miles across the Bay of Martaban, are gathered their brethren in Maulmain. Six hundred miles to the northwest is Calcutta, the capital of the Anglo-Indian empire; while far to the west—beyond a continent and an ocean—where "imagination faints to follow him," the sun, that here sows with Orient pearl the hills of the morning, sheds his descending beams on the homes and hearts of their native land.

We give place to Mrs. Judson :

TO MISS ANABLE.

RANGOON, Feb. 22, 1847.

Thank God, we are here at last, and able to *see* our way through to the end of present botherations, though we are by no means *through*. The poor Doctor escaped the fever which I dreaded, but is still quite ill with bowel complaint. He is, however, able to sit in the custom-house, unlocking his chests, etc., and waiting with exemplary patience the overhauling, and in some instances, *spoiling* of his goods. Amai! amai! You can have no idea of the impudence of these wretches. I have not seen our house yet; but they are beginning to get the goods which have passed the custom-house into it, and I shall go over to-morrow. We came ashore Saturday morning (it is Monday now), and on the invitation of an English captain of a schooner, took up our quarters at his house. He is married to a creole one of the better specimens of the class, and at least far superior to any thing else in Rangoon. Captain Crisp's father knew the Doctor before the war, and the son is very kind. His house is built in English style, and is the best but one in town. But such a house! How you would stare to see it set down in Genesee street! It is very large, and built of brick with massive walls. The partitions are of brick, and the floors, even of the second story, of brick, thick and ugly enough. This is to prevent fire, for which the bamboo houses of the natives furnish most charming tinder. The walls and floors are pretended to be plastered inside, but the plastering is thin and unlike any thing you see in America, and, with the bricks, is broken away in thousands of places. Madam Crisp has kindly assigned us a couple of rooms in which that part of our luggage and that of our servants, which we were able to get ashore on Saturday, lies in most glorious confusion. There are mats (Burmese mats, remember,) spread upon the uneven floors, which have probably lain for years, for they are rotted and mildewed; and one of them in our sleeping-room has entirely disappeared, except the four tattered corners, leaving the red bricks and gray and white plaster very prominent. Then the broken and mildewed furniture! It is quite dangerous to attempt sitting down on chair or couch till you have examined into its capabilities; for ten to one the chair has a broken leg, and the couch a hole through the bottom, deftly covered with a cushion.

You have no idea of the troubles we passed through in reaching the happy state recorded on the last page. The captain of the *City of London*, a regular bear, insisted on our goods being taken from the ship on Sunday, and it was in vain that the Doctor pleaded both his principles and his illness; the ship must be emptied at any rate. We had discovered while aboard the reckless character of the captain, and the half mutinous state of the crew. You may imagine, therefore, our feelings when we laid down our weary heads on Saturday night. The articles could be taken from the ship without the Doctor's presence, but thence they would be conveyed to the custom-house, and he *must* be there if ever so ill. He was in great pain and very weak; but at last he said, "Why need we be troubled? To-morrow is peculiarly God's own day, and He will take care of it." He seemed to receive from this a little comfort, and before morning had a refreshing sleep. About day-light the captain came in to say that the goods might remain in the ship. "But why? You said yesterday that they could not remain." "The truth is, sir, my boys are bad fellows; they say they have worked three Sundays and wont work to-day, and I can't make them." We suppose that the wretches, wicked as they are, yet had kind feeling enough to take this stand for our sakes; for though we could have no communication with them, we dispensed some smiles, and smiles are rare things among them, poor fellows. And now how do you think I spent the half hour before commencing this page? Why, in the very important business of teaching Master —— to put on and tie his own shoes. Not that he is so brave as already to have learned the lesson, but he has made a very respectable beginning. The children in this country are ruined by domineering over servants, and I am determined to save mine from such a curse. I will teach them to help themselves, and to treat servants properly, if it requires my whole time. My nurse has a little girl who is so accustomed to be knocked about that she never thinks of defending herself from a white child. I put a stop to all such proceedings for my children's sakes.

February 23. We had grand good luck yesterday. The Dr. dispensed presents right and left at the custom-house, and before dark his goods were all through. As soon as breakfast is over, I am going to help put things in proper trim. We shall sleep there to-night. I went to see the house last night, but reserve the description until we are settled in it. . . .

TO HER SISTER.

BAT CASTLE (Rangoon), March 15, 1847.

DEAR KITTY,—

I write you from walls as massive as any you read of in old stories and a great deal uglier—the very eye-ball and heart-core of an old white-bearded Mussulman. Think of me in an immense brick house with rooms as large as the entire "loggery," (our centre room is twice as large, and has *no* window), and only one small window apiece. When I speak of windows, do not think I make any allusion to glass—of course not. The windows (holes) are closed by means of heavy board or plank shutters, tinned over on the outside, as a preventive of fire. The bamboo houses of the natives here are like flax or tinder, and the foreigners, who have more than the one cloth which Burmans wrap about the body, and the mat they sleep on, dare live in nothing but brick. Imagine us, then, on the second floor of this immense den, with nine rooms at our command, the smallest of which (bathing-room and a kind of pantry) are, I think, quite as large as your dining-room, and the rest very much larger. Part of the floors are of brick, and part of boards; but old "Green Turban" white-washed them all, with the walls, before we came, because the Doctor told him, when he was over here, that he must "make the house shine for madam." He did make it shine with a vengeance, between white-washing and greasing. They oil furniture in this country, as Americans do mahogany; but all his doors and other wood-work were fairly dripping, and we have not got rid of the smell yet; nor, with all our rubbing, is it quite safe to hold too long on the door. The partitions

are all of brick, and very thick, and the door-sills are *built up*,
so that I go over them at three or four steps, Henry mounts
and falls off, and Edward gets on all-fours, and accomplishes
the pass with more safety. The floor overhead is quite low,
and the beams, which are frequent, afford shelter to thousands
and thousands of bats, that disturb us in the day-time only by
a little cricket-like music, but in the night—Oh, if you could
only hear them carouse! The mosquito curtains are our only
safe-guard; and getting up is horrible. The other night I
awoke faint, with a feeling of suffocation; and without waiting
to think, jumped out on the floor. You would have thought
"old Nick" himself had come after you, for, of course, you believe these firm friends of the *ladies of the broom-stick* incipient
imps. If there is nothing wickeder about them than about
the little sparrows that come in immense swarms to the same
beams, pray what do they do all through the hours of darkness,
and why do they circle and whizz about a poor mortal's head,
flap their villainous wings in one's face, and then whisk away,
as if *snickering* at the annoyance? We have had men at work
nearly a week trying to thin them out, and have killed a great
many hundreds, but I suppose their little demoniac souls come
back, each with an attendant, for I am sure there are twice as
many as at first.* Every thing, walls, tables, chairs, etc., are
stained by them. Besides the bats, we are blessed with our
full share of cockroaches, beetles, spiders, lizards, rats, ants, mosquitoes, and bed-bugs. With the last the wood-work is all
alive, and the ants troop over the house in great droves, though
there are scattering ones beside. Perhaps twenty have crossed

---

* The following, from a letter of March 2d, is Dr. Judson's amusing account of the state of matters between the different claimants of "Bat
Castle," and the opening operations in his war of extermination.

"We have had a grand bat hunt yesterday and to-day—bagged two
hundred and fifty, and calculate to make up a round thousand before we
have done. We find that in hiring the upper story of this den, we secured
the lower moiety only, the upper moiety thereof being preoccupied by a

my paper since I have been writing. Only one cockroach has
paid me a visit, but the neglect of these gentlemen has been
fully made up by a company of black bugs about the size of the
end of your little finger—nameless adventurers. . . .

EMILY.

Such was "Bat Castle," of which Mr. and Mrs. Judson
became temporary occupants ; and they now addressed
themselves to their respective labors. Forbidden to act
in his proper vocation as a missionary, and meeting the
few disciples who still lingered in the town, and the few
inquirers whom his presence attracted, only by stealth,
Dr. Judson addressed himself with characteristic energy
to the preparation of his dictionary, to which, after the
completed translation of the Bible, he now reluctantly
gave his chief labor. Mrs. Judson found ample employment in the care of the family, the learning of the language, and then in the preparation of the memoir of
Mrs. Sarah B. Judson, which she had been waiting the
favorable moment to commence. It proves strikingly her
power of literary execution, that while confined to the
bed much of the day from illness, and amidst the mani-
fold cares of house-keeping (which she never neglected),
she yet completed this work in six weeks after commencing
the examination of the papers; and equally her conscientious fidelity that she subsequently gave as much labor

thriving colony of vagabonds, who flare up through the night with a vengeance, and the sound of their wings is as the sound of many waters, yea,
as the sound of your boasted Yankee Niagara; so that sleep departs from
our eyes and slumber from our eyelids. But we are reading them some
lessons which we hope will be profitable to all parties concerned, and remain,

"Yours affectionately,

"A. JUDSON."

more to the preparation of one or two brief notes in the appendix. It was a labor of love—the sketch of a character eminently beautiful in itself, and rendered doubly interesting by its relation to two such men as Boardman and Judson. The work is written with great spirit and beauty. It is a worthy tribute paid by a woman of genius to another woman, not indeed her equal in genius, but her equal in womanly graces, and her superior in Christian consecration. It was regarded by some as marked too much by the sparkling manner of her magazine sketches, and wanting in the gravity which befits a record of Christian toil and self-denial. The adoption of this style, however, was matter of deliberate purpose on the part of the biographer. She hoped that her peculiar literary reputation might win for her a class of readers not hitherto interested in missionary literature ; and the style which could fascinate the world when employed on themes of fiction, might, she deemed, be equally legitimate and attractive in the scarcely less veritable romance of a missionary heroine's biography. Hence she diffused over her pages the vivacious features of her "Fanny Forester" sketches, and adorned its title page with that popular soubriquet. Her husband concurred in her view, and the wide sale of the work, of which edition after edition was rapidly exhausted, practically at least confirmed their judgment. March 27, Mrs. Judson writes thus to Miss Lillybridge :

"I wrote you a little while ago that I was going on with the language swimmingly, and now you will be surprised to hear that I study only between seven and eight in the morning, and that by no means every day. My plan was to study during the

12*

day (what time I could spare from family cares), and write in
the evening. Accordingly I began collecting my papers for the
memoir; but before I had fairly entered upon my course my
health failed from too close application. I must abandon either
the study or the memoir, and so the former is waiting, as the
latter, if delayed, would be too late. Writing always affected
my nervous system, and writing and study together I shall
never be able to practice."

I proceed with extracts from the letters of Mrs. Judson :

ro HER SISTER.

RANGOON, May 30, 1847.

MY DEAR KATY,—

   We are in a charming coil just now, and though it is Sabbath day, have had no worship in Burmese. Night before last
we had secret information that the Ray-Woon had ordered our
house to be watched; and but for that information, before this
time (for it is evening) our assembly of Christians would have
been shut up in prison, suffering the lash, the stocks, or even
worse torture. The Ray-Woon is a very cruel man, and it is
said that the screams of poor tortured wretches are heard almost
incessantly, night and day, to issue from his house. He is the
second in power, but the Governor is a weak man, over seventy
years of age—a regular old woman in " hose and doublet"—
patso and goung-boung, I mean. The man whom the Doctor
baptized came in with his father-in-law. One of our people
met them on the way and told them of the danger, but they
were anxious to come, and managed to provide against it. The
old man asked baptism for his son, a fine fellow about twenty,
and the young man made known his wish to go over to Maulmain and prepare to preach. The Doctor came to my room,
after they were gone, all animation; but he is sad again
now. . . .

   May 31. Last night, after trying in vain to comfort my

poor husband, as he walked with clouded face up and down my room, by saying that God would take care of His own cause, etc., all of which he of course understands and feels more than I do, I was obliged to give up and sit down in silence. At last I turned suddenly to him, and inquired, "Would you like to know the first couplet that I ever learned to repeat?" I suppose he thought I was trifling, for he only turned his head, and said nothing. "I learned it," continued I "before I could read, and I afterwards used to write it every where—sometimes, even, at the top of the page, when I was preparing the story on whose success more depended than its readers ever dreamed." I had gained his attention. "What was it?" he inquired.

"Beware of desperate steps; the darkest day,
   (Live till to-morrow,) will have passed away."

"I declare," said he with energy, and his whole face brightening, "if I could only believe in transmigration, I should have no doubt that we had spent ages together in some other sphere, we are so alike in every thing. Why, those two lines have been my motto; I used to repeat them over and over in prison, and I have them now, written on a slip of paper, for a book-mark." He stood a few moments, thinking and smiling, and then said, "Well, one thing you didn't do: you never wrote 'Pray without ceasing' on the cover of your wafer box." "No; but I wrote it on my looking-glass." This furnished one of our never-ending subjects, and we chatted away almost as cheerfully as if there had been no Vesuvius under our feet. . . .

June 2. Just one year to-day since I stood before good old Doctor Kendrick, and said the irrevocable "love, honor, and obey." It was on many accounts a day of darkness, but it has dragged three hundred and sixty-five *very* light ones at its heels. It has been far the happiest year of my life; and, what is in my eyes still more important, my husband says it has been among the happiest of his. We have been in circumstances to be almost constantly together; and I never met with any man who could talk so well, day after day, on every subject, religious, literary, scientific, political, and—and nice baby-talk. He has a mind which seems exhaustless, and so, even here in Rangoon, where all the English I hear, from week's end to week's end, is from him, I never think of wanting more society. I have been ill a great deal, but not in a way to hinder him ; and he treats me as gently and tenderly as though I were an infant. . . .

As for living, I must own that I am within an inch of starvation, and poor little Henry says, when he sits down to the table, "I don't want any dinner—I wish we could go back to Maulmain." His papa does better, for he never has a poor appetite. For a long time after we first came here, we could get no bread at all ; now we get a heavy, black, sour kind, for which we pay just three times as much as we did at Maulmain. You will say " Make it." What shall I make it of? or a biscuit, or pie, or any thing good? And when it is made of nothing, what shall I bake it in ?

Our milk is a mixture of buffaloes' milk, water, and something else which we cannot make out. We have changed our milk-woman several times, but it does no good. The butter we make from it is like lard with flakes of tallow. But it is useless to write about these things—you can get no idea. I must tell you, however, of the grand dinner we had one day. " You must contrive and get something that mamma can eat," the doctor said to our Burmese purveyor; " she will starve to death." "What shall I get?" "Anything." "Anything?" "Anything." Well, we did have a capital dinner, though we tried in vain to find out by the bones what it was. Henry said it was *touk-tahs*, a species of lizard, and I should have thought so too, if the little animal had been of a fleshy consistence. Cook said he *didn't know*, but he grinned a horrible grin which made my stomach heave a little, notwithstanding the deliciousness of the meal. In the evening we called Mr. Bazaar-man. " What did we have for dinner to-day?" " Were they good?" "Excellent." A tremendous explosion of laughter, in which the cook from his dish room joined as loud as he dared. "What were they?" "*Rats!*" A common servant would not have played such a trick, but it was one of the doctor's assistants who goes to bazaar for us. You know the Chinese consider rats a great delicacy,* and he bought them at one of their shops.

As for the house, it was very comfortable during the hot weather, for there is a brick floor overhead, but we suffer very much since the coming on of the rains. We are obliged to get directly before the window in order to see, and we suffer unaccountably from the damp air. We frequently shut all up, and light candles at noon. The doctor has severe rheumatism in his writing shoulder and constant headache, but his lungs do not trouble him so much as during the first storms. For myself, I am utterly prostrated; and, although I have taken care of everything and written a little, I have not sat up an hour at a time for six weeks. I have my table by my couch and write a few lines, and then lie down. The wooden ceiling overhead is covered with a kind of green mould, and the doors get the same way in two days if they are not carefully rubbed. Now, do you think I am in any way discontented, and would go back to America to live in a palace? Not I. I am ten times happier than I could be there. . . . And then we are so, *so* happy in each other. . . . We are frequently startled by echoing each others unspoken thoughts, and we believe alike in everything. You know I have always scolded, because nobody—minister nor people—was really *orthodox* in religious opinion. Well, he is strictly and thoroughly orthodox. At first I was a little annoyed by what seemed to me a taint of Guionism, Oberlinism, or something of that sort. I said nothing, however, but took to reading all those books with him, "for information." We went through all the numbers of the Methodist "Perfectionist;" took

* So it is said, and this story seems to lend credit to the saying. But Williams indignantly denies it as a general fact.—*Vide Middle Kingdom,* ii. 47.

story after story and weighed it with the Bible and common
sense; then we sifted Upham thoroughly, through all his growing and tiresome heaviness; and last of all, took up Madame
Guion. This last is really disgusting, and I consider her quite
as much a patient for Dr. Brigham as Joan of Arc or any other
monomaniac, though I believe, notwithstanding her very apparent
unamiability, she had grace. Well, the amount of all is, we
agree perfectly on all these topics. . . .

TO MISS C. SHELDON.

RANGOON, June 16, 1847.

Trouble on trouble—trouble on trouble! You could scarce
imagine, dear aunt Cynthia, people in a worse condition than
we are now. Last Saturday evening Dr. J. came into my room
with red eyes and a voice all temulous with weeping. " We must
be at the worst now," he said; "and in all my troubles in this
dreadful country, I never before looked on so discouraging a
prospect. We are hunted down here like wild beasts; watched
by government and plotted against by Catholic priests. The
churches at home have made no provision for our going to Ava,
the governor is importuned to send us out of the country, the
monsoon is raging, and we could not go to Maulmain if we
wished, and you are failing every day—it seems to me dying
before my eyes—without the possibility of obtaining either
medicines or a physician." It was all true except the last. I
have suffered severely from the rain, but people like me " die"
too many times to be much alarmed by anything that comes upon
themselves. But it is a very sickly time, almost everybody is
ill, and funeral processions pass our house every day. There
has been of late a funeral feast in nearly every house in our
neighborhood, and the constant tap-tap of nailing up coffins in
the night is dreadful.

I was speaking of Saturday evening. That same night Dr.
J. was seized with terrible pains in the bowels, etc., which he

thought was diarrhœa. On Sunday he took laudanum injections, and was easier; but in the night the disease showed itself a dysentery of the worst form which we could find in our books. He had never had it before, either himself or in his family, and was utterly at a loss to know how to treat it. No two books agreed, and you know there is no medical adviser in the place. I begged him to take calomel, and he would have administered it to any other person, but in his own case he procrastinated. He has taken various medicines, and thus checked the disease; but last night (to-day is Friday) he became alarmed, and for the first time took a dose of rhubarb and calomel. I am afraid, however, it is too late, for he is in a terrible condition this morning. The last resort is a sea voyage, which at this season of the year is a desperate thing. Nothing goes from this port but little native vessels, with no accommodations for a well man, much less a sick one; and they are frequently wrecked. It would be utterly impossible to find one large enough to take in me and the children (the latter must, of course, go where I do), and if he goes alone, I think of the terrible suspense which awaits me for four, five, or six weeks, and the sufferings to which he must be exposed. He says only a matter of life and death could induce him to leave me with the children, and the people who are only children of larger growth, in my present condition. (I do not sit up an hour at a time.) If he goes, he must take our most intelligent man, but he, alas! is a most indifferent nurse.

Yours, etc.,

By "too late," I meant too late for any thing but a sea voyage; of that we have strong hopes.

TO MISS ANABLE.

(Continued from Miss C.'s, about an hour later.)

DEAR ANNA MARIA,—

The Doctor is awake, but we can not tell yet whether he is better or worse. He is evidently *passing a crisis* of some sort. The music and mourners have set up their screeching and howling at a house nearly opposite, and men are busy decorating the funeral car in the streets. We seem to be hemmed in by death. Suppose it should come here; there would be only servants to bury the dead! Something is the matter with Edward. He was wakeful all night, and this morning he screams out suddenly when at his play as in pain, and runs to me as fast as he can. Poor little fellow! he can not tell his trouble. I have just quieted him, and take the moment to write while his head lies in my lap.

Saturday. The Doctor says "the back-bone of his disease is broken." If it is, I am afraid there are two back-bones, for I think I never knew a person suffer so severely. I have made Henry a little bed on the floor, and he is groaning in a burning fever. If he is ill he will be very troublesome. · I have given him a powerful medicine, and may get the start of the disease; it is Rangoon fever; he was seized suddenly and violently. Edward, also, was troubled some in the night, and acts as strangely as yesterday. He scarcely ever cries, yet screams seem forced from him as by a sudden blow. He runs to me, but recovers in a moment, and goes back to play. There is something very alarming in this, knowing the brave little fellow's disposition as I do.

Sunday Eve. It is out at last. Edward awoke this morning, his face so swollen that his eyes are nearly closed, shining, and spotted purplish. We could not imagine what was the matter, but he was very feverish, and I knew he must have something immediately. I consulted the Doctor and my Burman woman, but neither of them could give me the slightest inkling of the disease.

July 1. I was interrupted suddenly by my invalids while writing the above sentence; since then I have had as much trouble as my worst enemy could wish. I was about telling you that I gave Edward a dose of calomel at a venture in the morning, and that in the afternoon I thought of poor F—, and decided that the disease was erysipelas. The fever had by this time abated, and the spots on his face become red, instead of purple. I think my dose of calomel saved his life. I searched all my books and gave gentle remedies afterward; but the sweet little fellow is still a great sufferer. Both the Doctor and Henry were better that day. I went to bed late at night with one of my very worst nervous headaches. I was awakened from troubled sleep by Edward's screams; but as soon as I raised my head I seemed to be caught by a whirlwind, and fell back helpless. As soon as possible I made another attempt, and this time reached the middle of the room, where I fell headlong. I did not venture on my feet again, but crept to the bed on my hands and feet, and finally succeeded in soothing him. All this time the Doctor was groaning terribly, and he managed between his groans to tell me that he was in even greater agony than when he was first seized. I was unable to do any thing for him, however, and so crawled over to Henry's cot. Oh, the predicament that he was in! . . . I expected that both Edward and the Doctor would die, and you may imagine that I had one long cry before I began to contrive what I should do in case the worst should come. The vessel had gone off to Maulmain that very day, and it would be at least a week before another would sail. The amount of the whole is, that the Doctor had a most dangerous relapse, from which he has not yet recovered, though probably out of danger. Henry is left a pale, puny child, without appetite; and poor Edward, really the greatest sufferer, is still in an alarming situation. There is an abscess in his forehead and the acrid matter has eaten back into the bone, we can not tell how far; there is another immense one on the back of the head in a shocking state, and two lesser ones on his neck. We read our books and do the best we can; and are very grateful that we can keep the fever off, and that with this open house and damp air he does not take cold. He is the loveliest child that I ever saw; there is something which seems to me angelic

in his patience and calmness. He could not help crying when
his papa lanced his head ; but the moment the sharpest pain
was over, he nestled down in my bosom, and though quivering
all over, he kept lifting his eyes to my face, and trying to
smile, oh, so sweetly ! He watched his papa while he sharp-
ened the lancet to open another, and when it was ready, turned
and laid his little head on his knee of his own accord. Just
when we were at the worst my nurse was taken ill with fever.
She had it lightly, however, so that her husband (my cook)
took care of her, instead of burdening me with another patient.
You will say that I write of nothing but my husband and children. Of course not ; I *think* of nothing else.

NEMMY.

SKETCHES OF SCENES IN RANGOON.
WRITTEN FROM MAULMAIN.

MY DEAR MR. BRIGHT,—

. . . I do not know whether others find the sight of
eastern scenery and eastern men awakens fresh interest in the
narrative part of the word of God ; but really I would come all
the way from America for the sake of reading the Bible with
my new eyes.

"I have seen all this before !" was a feeling that flashed upon
me more frequently at Rangoon than here, producing a mo-
mentary confusion of intellect, that almost made me doubt if
"I was I;" and then came the reflections, when?—how!—
where? and finally it would creep into my mind; why I learned
about it in Sabbath school when I was a little child. The effect
was to annihilate time and bring the days of the Saviour very
near ; and the strength of the ideal presence has been by no
means unprofitable to me.

But there were peculiarities in my situation which I think I
have never yet mentioned. There I was in the identical town
of which I had read with such eager curiosity when I was a
little child away in the central part of New York ; and which
then seemed to me about as real as a city belonging to the

moon. And stranger still, I was actually associated with one of the movers in scenes, the bare recital of which had, in years gone by, thrilled on my nerves with greater power than the wildest fiction. Oh, how memory, and imagination, and various strangely mingled emotions wrought together in my mind, when I looked upon all that remained of that in which the first words of life that Burmah ever heard were spoken more than a quarter of a century ago. And you will readily believe that the baptismal waters which were parted by the first convert from this nation were to my eye unlike any other waters in the world. I could not, if I were to attempt it, give you any thing like an insight into my feelings as I stood under the shadow of the cocoa and lime trees on the banks of that beautiful pool, and gazed down into the clear waters. How angels must have rejoiced over that penitent! the first link in a precious chain which is to reach down to the remotest times!

With a similar, dreaming, wondering feeling, as though walking among shadows and skeletons, I wandered about the grounds occupied by the old mission house. The building was torn down after the war, and the place is now covered by a garden of betel, so thickly planted that it was with great difficulty we could make our way among the long creepers which had climbed far above our heads. This self-same soil had once been trodden by feet elastic with youth and vigor, and bounding with such hopes as God grants to those who trust their all to Him.

"The house must have been somewhere here," remarked one of those beings of the past (not a shadow), close at my elbow; "that mound was the site of an old pagoda, and I leveled it as you see. But there is a nice well somewhere—that will be a sure mark."

A plainly dressed, sober faced, middle aged Burman had been regarding our movements for some time with curiosity, and he now ventured on a remark.

"I am looking for a good well from which I drank water many years ago," was the reply. "It was close by my house, and was bricked up."

"Your house!" repeated the man with astonishment.

"Yes, I lived here formerly."

The Burman turned his eye on the tall betel vines with a kind of wondering incredulity; and then back upon our faces.

"It was in the reign of *Bo-dan-parah* (the fourth king from the present reigning monarch).

If, my dear Mr. Bright, some modern looking personage should walk into your parlor and announce himself as the "Wandering Jew," I doubt whether your smile and shrug would be quite so significant as were those of our new friend. There was the well, however, a proof against imposture; and the next moment it was evidently so regarded by the Burman, for he led the way to it without speaking. It was a large square well—the bricks all green with moss, or silvered by lichens— almost as good as new, and quite superior to anything in the neighborhood. It could not be looked upon without some emotion; and the man stood by us listening to all our remarks as though he hoped to hear something he might understand; and when we went away he followed a little, and then stood and gazed after us in wondering silence.

Another of our visiting places was the but half enclosed neglected English grave-yard. The first child of European parents born in Burmah had been buried there; and there was a strong tie between that mouldering little one and ourselves. Over the grave of *little Roger* stood, but slightly broken, the rude brick monument which was built thirty-three years ago; and a tall azalia, very much like those which perfume the forests of our New York, had grown out from the base almost overshadowing it. It was strange to stand and muse beside that little grave, with one parent by my side, and the other so irrecoverably a being of the past. Oh, how she had wept there!—and how *human* she grew—she whom I had formerly only wondered at —while my own tears started in sympathy. . . .

Most truly and sincerely yours,

EMILY C. JUDSON.

They were occupants of "Bat Castle" about seven months—months of many trials, but of deep and concentrated enjoyment, in which Emily was brought into most exclusive and close contact with her husband, and made most completely dependent on the stores of his rich experience, and culture, and ripened Christian character. Her spiritual nature was elevated in consequence, and her consecration to the work which absorbed his energies deepened. Mr. Willis' prophecy that her "husband's errand abroad would draw on the volcanic enthusiasm of her nature," was verified. She was becoming growingly dead to the world, and more and more anxious for a life of Christian usefulness.

For minute details—of the fire which consumed their goods left in Maulmain, of their missionary toils and government troubles, I must refer the reader to the "Life of Dr. Judson." But they could not remain. They were effectually precluded from any open missionary work at Rangoon, and had their faces and hearts turned toward Ava, when an unlooked-for obstacle interposed. Their supplies were cut off. They received word from Maulmain that the appropriations to the Indian mission had been curtailed, and that, in carrying out the plan of retrenchment, their brethren had not thought proper to make further provision for the mission in Rangoon. They, of course, had no further discretion in the matter, and were compelled, with bitter disappointment and anguish, to return to Maulmain, where, after much suffering on the part of Mrs. Judson, they arrived early in September.

CHAPTER XVII.

UNCLOUDED SUNSHINE.

"My life is like a river full and deep,
    And glowing with the light,
My other life submerging in its sweep,
    As morning buries night."

RE-ESTABLISHED in their old quarters, Dr. Judson devoted himself to his dictionary, and resumed a partial pastorship of the native church. His wife prosecuted the study of the language, and as soon as her health allowed, made herself growingly active and useful in the mission, conducting prayer-meetings, and instructing classes in the Scriptures.

On the 24th of December Emily Frances was born, whom she consecrated to a poetic immortality by the beautiful poem, "My Bird." This, with many other of her pieces, shows how the rod that smites the heart's affections opens the deepest well-springs of poesy, and how superficial was that old Greek conception which exiled the Muses from the sweet charities of domestic life.

MY BIRD.

Ere last year's moon had left the sky,
    A birdling sought my Indian nest,
And folded, O, so lovingly!
    Her tiny wings upon my breast.

From morn till evening's purple tinge
   In winsome helplessness she lies;
Two rose leaves, with a silken fringe,
   Shut softly on her starry eyes.

There's not in Ind a lovelier bird;
   Broad earth owns not a happier nest;
O God, Thou hast a fountain stirred,
   Whose waters never more shall rest!

This beautiful, mysterious thing,
   This seeming visitant from heaven,
This bird with the immortal wing,
   To me—to me, Thy hand has given.

The pulse first caught its tiny stroke,
   The blood its crimson hue, from mine;—
This life, which I have dared invoke,
   Henceforth is parallel with thine.

A silent awe is in my room;
   I tremble with delicious fear;
The future, with its light and gloom,—
   Time and Eternity are here.

Doubts—hopes, in eager tumult rise;
   Hear, O my God! one earnest prayer:
Room for my bird in Paradise,
   And give her angel-plumage there!

The year 1848 brought with it little of outward incident, and was one of almost unclouded happiness.
They were both in excellent health, and enjoying hourly
each other's society and their work. Dr. Judson was,
indeed, still looking toward Ava, and watching anxiously,
though vainly, the lifting of the cloud that rested on
idolatrous Burmah. In America, their friends the

Sheldons and Anables, transferred their home, and with this one of Mrs. Judson's "heart homes," from Utica to Philadelphia. I can select but three or four from the letters of the year.

MAULMAIN, February 7, 1848.

DEAR JENNY,—

I have seen my two fine boys safe in their nests, and taken a peep into baby's little swing-cot, and as the worser-half is out tea-ing it, I am all alone. All alone? Bless me, how indifferent we can be brought to feel to the presence of humans! There is Granny Grunter (alias wet-nurse, alias Mah Bya), who who does nothing but eat and sleep alternately (she is eating now) during the twenty-four hours, and who would invent a machine to lift the child and carry it to her breast if she were a Yankee. Then there is his impship, teetotum John, an old Bengalee dwarf, with a smoke-colored face, no teeth, a vermilion tongue, that looks precisely like a snake's, and muscles all on the outside of his dried-up body. No monkey ever practiced more grimaces, no goose was ever half so much of a fool, or hissed with more effect, and no other blackamoor, I am sure, *could* love "Massa" and "Missish" so well, or be so useful and faithful. In addition to all his other qualifications, our John (the missionaries named him John because his heathen name was too wicked to speak) is that wonder of wonders in this climate, an active man. Well, John is rattling the tea-cups on the veranda; and in my door, erect as a sentinel, stands Sir Oily Long-legs—a Bengalee of the first water—Jessingh by his heathen appellation, and lady's factotum, at least at present. He is a fine-looking six-footer, with a turban which makes him appear at least six inches taller. And what do you think he does—this magnificent specimen of humanity, with his quick eye, graceful figure, and smooth tongue? Why, any thing and every thing "mamma" pleases, and as deliberately and superficially as Jessingh pleases. He bathes the boys, dresses and undresses them, sweeps the floors, waxes the tables, puts "mamma's" things to rights, even in her dressing-room, runs of errands, and lastly, though far from least, sews on all needed strings and buttons. Isn't he a useful man, this Jessingh? Too costly, however, is he for common use, and so when Miss Frank is a week or two older, I shall have to dismiss him. Do you wonder why he stands there in the door so like a statue? Why, in these parts, where every man sleeps with a spear at his bed's head, women people do not stay alone as in your land of safety. So, when master goes out, Long-legs stands guard, and if mamma chances to want a pocket-hand-kerchief or string, searches creation over but it is found, and then presents it with such a reverence as you never saw in America. Such offices are what these fellows like, but all work they detest. What would you think, Jenny, of having this same Sir Oily hooking your frock, making your bed, and performing other like offices? Mind, I do not say that I so employ him; but if you want to learn to think just nothing at all of men and women, why, come out here and employ Bengalee servants. The Burmese are a little different.

February 10. The scene is changed since writing the above. It is just half past twelve and painfully light (nobody darkens houses here). I have just basted a hem for a Burmese girl— my only sempstress—and she is poking over it. Sir Oily has been missing since nine o'clock, and my mouth is drawn into scolding order. Wet-nurse asleep, as usual; factotum gone to buy dinner; little Master Henry at his lesson, which I must hear very soon; Edward rolling on the carpet, with his heels in the air, and spelling " b-a ba," with all his might; husband, as usual, digging at his dictionary, with his two assistants; and I by just such a confused, littered up table as you used to see at home, with baby asleep on my knees (baby is sick to-day, and I have been dosing her), my port-folio in a chair on one side, and a half dozen Burman books on the other. Do you think

you see us? Not a bit of it. The bare floors in every room
but this of mine, the unglazed windows, the high roof, through
which the daylight peeps so boldly, the frame-work of the house
standing out from the boards after the fashion of a barn, the
screen-like partitions, the strips of awning, hung here and there,
to answer the purpose of a ceiling, and waving in the wind—
these, and a thousand other oddities, I am sure you could not
see if you were to try.

"Not quite yet." That was not said to you, but in answer
to a call from the next room—"Lovey, will you have Ko-shway-
doke now?" Ko-shway-doke is my Burmese teacher, a fine,
gentlemanly fellow, who always covers his knees with his silk
waist cloth, and when he comes to my room sits in a chair.

Don't expect a decent letter from me, for I have scarce a
minute that I can call my own. Just before we left Rangoon,
I gave you a long description of the different costumes which I
saw in the course of the day—Burmese, Mussulman, Chinese,
Jewish, and Armenian. The Karen and Shan are very much
like the Burmese, and the Portuguese are caricatures of the
English. Think of men walking the streets with English panta-
loons, and jackets made of silk striped in crimson, yellow,
bright green, etc. The better sort of Armenian ladies adopt
English fashions, and procure *their go-abroad dresses* from Calcutta. They, of course, want the nicest articles out, and so get
party dresses. It is ridiculous to see one of these pretty, liquid-
eyed madams, parading our narrow, dirty streets, with a train
of Burmese women (lady's maids) at her heels, and arrayed
according to her extravagant taste. The richest silks, crimson,
green, gold, etc., are worn, but rich laces and lisses, with short
sleeves, low necks, and short over-skirts are most in vogue; and
would n't you laugh to see the mountain of a *bishop?* They
do not wear bonnets, but decorate their heads in various ways,
and load themselves with jewelry. A lady called on me in the
day-time, who would have been elegant in a ball-room, but
altogether over-dressed in a Utica party. . . .

MAULMAIN, March 20, 1848.

MY DEAR MRS. BRAYTON—

. . . I fully appreciate your kindness in "advocating my cause," but after all, my dear sister, of what consequence are the opinions of men? Why should I spend the few precious hours allotted me here in trying to convince people away in America that I am a good missionary? If I walk humbly and prayerfully before God, try to do all the good in my power, and leave my reputation in His hands, I am not afraid that I shall suffer. But for this trust I should scarce have ventured to put myself in a position to be criticized, as I very well knew I was doing when I consented to come to Burmah. Formerly I used the little talent that God had given me for what I believed a legitimate object, and I can but believe that I was blessed in so doing. As soon as that object was accomplished, He opened a wider field of usefulness, and I entered it. That I am unfit for the work I very well know; that I may be fitted for it I pray daily. But will it fit me any better—shall I be any more dilligent and prayerful, if I distract my mind and divide my attention between what Americans think of me, and what Burmans think of my Saviour? No, no, my dear sister; though many may think ill of me, I already have more credit than I deserve, and my little, small, insignificant self is not worth the ink that would be wasted on a vindication, explanation, or whatever you may choose to call it.

If you were here I could tell you many interesting—all of them to me interesting—stories of the children; but though my partial tongue may move very fast, I must put some restraint on my pen. Yet I will relate one little anecdote of Edward, which you may tell to Mary if you like. When you left, I believe the little fellow could not talk, but now he has become the veriest chatterbox in the mission. While we resided in Rangoon the children became great cowards (I suppose they caught the infection from us), and when we came over here I was obliged to take great pains to break it up. One night Edward, who slept in a little room by himself, called out that he was "afraid," and would not be comforted. I have never taught them a prayer to repeat, because I do not like the formality, but I assist them in discovering what they need, and then have them repeat the words after me. So I prayed with little E., kissed him good night, and left him apparently satisfied. Pretty soon, however, I heard him call out, as though in great distress, "O, Dod!" The poor little fellow had not sufficient acquaintance with language to know what to say next; but this up-lifting of the heart evidently relieved him, for in a few minutes after he again called out, "O, Dod!" but in a tone much softened. I stepped to the door but hesitated about entering. In a few minutes he again repeated "O, Dod!" but in a tone so confiding that I thought I had better go back to my room, and leave him with his Great Protector. I heard no more of him for some time, when I at last went in and found him on his knees fast asleep. He never fails now to remind me of asking "Dod to tate tare of him," if I neglect it, and I have never heard him say a word since of being afraid.

. . . I am very busy with the language, having got on but slowly during the past year. You know it is not every one who comes out that begins with a family of children, and so I am obliged to be doubly diligent. There is not much that is encouraging in the church or among the natives, and but for faith, I am afraid that the hearts of the missionaries would sink. By reports from Rangoon, Burmah seems more effectually closed against us than ever. But one thing we do know, that the day will come when "the earth shall be filled with His glory!"

Most truly and affectionately yours,

EMILY C. JUDSON.

MAULMAIN, May 29, 1848.

MY DEAR MISS CYNTHIA—

The rain is falling with a charmingly cooling sound to-night, a grateful sort of music with which we have been favored for the last two or three weeks. Would you have believed that *I* would ever like rainy weather, such as divides the streets into gutters, washes the color and perfume from the flowers, and mantles everything within doors with mildew? Yet I do. What a wonderful elasticity must the mind possess, which can accommodate itself to circumstances so readily! Mr. J. is digging at his tedious dictionary to-night, as usual; the three little people are fast asleep under their musquito curtains, and so, the day's work done, I am at liberty to come to you. And now do you see me, nestled down in the corner of the big couch, there where I have been a hundred times before? Not see? O, would that I could be there with eyes and tongue, as I am in spirit, for I want to look upon you once again, and to tell you a great many things. And first, I would tell you—for you would inquire—why my complexion and figure are so changed. I should scarce be called pale and thin now, I am so, *so* well! What do you think of a walk of three miles before breakfast? Is there no sound of health and vigor in that? Do not tell me that, in such a case, I have an additional talent to account for. I am feeling it most deeply just now.

But there are more interesting matters than any which pertain to my little self—just those things which it is impossible to write down. Since my first letters (all written *running*), I have been censured more than I deserve for being a negligent correspondent. Now, there are two special reasons why I write so little. The first is want of time. When I first landed I was a *spectator;* now I am a *worker*—in the smallest of all ways, to be sure, but still I am busy. Every moment seems inexpressibly precious, and how few the days before we shall be in the grave; and, Aunt C., I do want to be made the instrument of some little good before I die.

My other reason for not writing is, that I can not. I lack the power to paint to you things as they really exist. We breathe a different atmosphere from yours, and its peculiarities are not transferable, at least by my pen. If we attempt to present them to you, they fall in distorted shapes on your vision. I have felt this most painfully when sitting down to write to you. "How interested aunt C. would be in this story! But no. I must explain that—and that—and that; and then it would prove but a common-place bit of missionary intelligence after all." To be interesting, a writer must be met half way— half on the paper, half in the reader's heart. Now, though the great cause of missions is in your heart, and dear as your life, the special details are not there, and can not be put there. Imagination is a fine painter; but it is past associations, simple memories, that stir up feeling. "Give us light," one earnest generous-spirited correspondent writes to me, "and we will give you money." Now, if I believed it possible, by dint of severe labor, to furnish the necessary light, I would work much harder than in days gone by, when you used to come to me at midnight with the refreshing draught and kind words; for money is the thing just now most needed. . . .

If I were sitting by you, I could give you some personal experience. I would tell you of a time when we were hungry for want of palatable food; when we were ill, and had neither comforts nor physician; when we were surrounded by the spies of a jealous and unscrupulous government, without any earthly friend to assist us, or any way of escape. But there are circumstances in which even such trials assume a minor importance. My first *real* missionary trial—(you would believe me could you hear me speak the words, though it may sound common-place on paper)—was when, amidst sufferings such as I have described, a letter came telling of retrenchments. Schools, with the life already nearly pressed out of them, must be cramped still more;

assistants must be cut off; the workmen's hands must be tied a little tighter; and then, if they *could* succeed in making bricks without straw, the churches at home were ready to rejoice in their success. This intelligence, of course, reared a wall directly across our own path; for how could we carry out our plan of going to Ava, while we lacked even the means of remaining where we were? There was nothing left us but to retrace our steps; so we came back to good, comfortable, pleasant Maulmain, making a decided gain in the Egyptian "leek and onion" line. I do not wish, dear aunt C., to say an unkind word; but do, please, tell me your own opinion. Is not the great interest in missions, which makes so much noise at the present day, very much a matter of moonshine—more on the tongue than in the heart? It is not becoming in me, perhaps, to write of this; but I think, if some of our rich American Baptists could occupy our point of vision for a little while, it would plant a most salutary thorn in their consciences. I have only room, etc.,

E. C. J.

The following letter was addressed to Rev. Dr. Kendrick while he lay enduring the long agonies of his lingering death. When it arrived his eyes were sealed in death, and his spirit had gone to its rest:

TO REV. DR. NATHANIEL KENDRICK.

MAULMAIN, June 20, 1848.

MY VERY DEAR FATHER AND FRIEND,—

You have so long been apparently within a step of heaven, and have been so happy in that position, that you will not be shocked when I say I should have written you before, but that I supposed you would be beyond the reach of letters before mine could cross the ocean. God, however, has been very merciful to those who love you, and has kept you with them; and I can not but hope you will still remain much longer, though for yourself "to depart and be with Christ," is doubtless "far better."

Since, my dear Dr. Kendrick, you were the first, and indeed the only one to whom I communicated my early impressions with regard to missions, it is fitting that I should tell you something of my views since I have actually entered upon the field. I was very young when I opened my heart to you—full of the enthusiastic romance of girlhood, and the undisciplined zeal of a young Christian. When I remember this, I almost wonder that you should have spoken so kindly and encouragingly—indeed, your most judicious letter, though not understood at the time, was invaluable to me afterward. Your advice to "await the openings of Providence," had a calming effect; and I am glad I learned so long ago how good it is to *wait*, for this is a much more difficult part of Christian duty than to *labor*. God led me in a mysterious way afterward—perhaps to show me more of my own heart, and more of the completely unsatisfying nature of this world, even in its brightest guises, than I should otherwise have learned. My early impressions did not wear away gradually, as you would naturally suppose; but circumstances seemed to force me into another path of life; and so, not without a severe struggle, I deliberately gave up the hope—perhaps I should say dream—of years. But my regret was short-lived. I entered upon my new plans—every thing prospered that my hand touched—and I grew very worldly—so worldly that I used sometimes to laugh within myself at my own early folly, and to be ashamed to meet you, because I knew you were acquainted with it. In the midst of this, though I did not "*await* the openings of Providence," the door opened; but by this time it was like death for me to enter. *Of myself*, I never could have resolved on the great step, but God strengthened me, and after that first resolve, I found it comparatively easy to break the innumerable ties which I had been so long and so industriously gathering about me. And now I can not be too thankful that I am here. I do not know that God has given me any work to do—I am certain that I do not *deserve* any such honor; but I mean to stand ready, and I daily feel, more and more, that it is a precious privilege to be in the *field*. The work of missions is continually becoming dearer, and assuming increased glory and magnitude in my eyes; and now, though I am the least of laborers, too small to be included in the number, I would not exchange my position for any thing on earth.

The letter which, thirteen years ago, you slid into my hand as you were passing our door in Morrisville, tattered and somewhat faded, lies before me now. It opens with the remark, "The day is wonderful in which we live;" and the time that has elapsed since those words were written has only rendered their truth still more striking. The day is indeed wonderful, and each passing moment unfolds new wonders. Perhaps the strangest feature of all is that rulers and statesmen, and political revolutionists, without being in the least aware of it, are actually coöperating with the Church of Christ in setting up His kingdom; and as "the angel having the everlasting gospel to preach" wings his flight, they are opening the way before him. It is better to be a willing instrument in the hands of God, though it is to accomplish comparatively small things, than an unconscious one; and it is my earnest desire to have grace to "act well my part," whatever it may be. You used often to pray by the bedside of my now sainted sister Lavinia; will you not from your own bed of suffering pray for me also, since you know that I stand greatly in need of your prayers?

My dear husband joins in most affectionate regards.

EMILY C. JUDSON.

13*

CHAPTER XVIII.

GATHERING CLOUDS.

"'Then sorrow, touched by thee, grows bright
 With more than rapture's ray,
 As darkness shows us worlds of light
 We never saw by day."

THE year 1849 witnessed a marked change in their condition. The serious illness of Emily Frances at its commencement, was followed, upon her recovery, by alarming symptoms in Mrs. Judson. A trip down the coast to Tavoy was prescribed by her physician, and proved somewhat serviceable. Her worst symptoms gradually disappeared; yet she never entirely regained her previous robustness. And then toward the close of the year came the unlooked-for and crushing blow—that fatal illness of her husband which was ultimately fatal. Affliction, however, was proving a manifest blessing. The dark clouds which lowered upon her earthly lot beamed with brightness to her spiritual eye. God was evidently sanctifying her, and preparing her for the severe trials and struggles which awaited her. Her letters and journals breathe a growing spirit of Christian and missionary consecration:

TO MISS KELLY.

MAULMAIN, April 17, 1849.

MY DEAR JANE,—

You would have had my congratulations on the promising condition of your school earlier, but for extreme illness which has for a long time prevented me from using my pen. Aunt Cynthia writes that your dear mother and sisters (does your mother remember me?) are all with you, and also that you have Mary Barker, whom I know you love very much. How I should like to step into the dear old house once more and see it in its changes! It would make me melancholy, I know; but still I can rejoice in your bright prospects most sincerely. You have struggled against adversity nobly, and you deserve success.

Does Miss B. remember and speak of me? . . . Who conducts worship in the dining-room? Who takes charge of the compositions? And who are your music teachers? During my night fevers old scenes have come back to me with peculiar vividness, and O how I have longed to be set down in your school-room with my old composition class once again! Some of the pupils whom I loved have been married since I left, and some have gone down to the grave; the great body of them are scattered widely, while a few may be still with you. I should like to inquire for ——, and ——, and ——. Are they with you still, or have the older ones *finished* and gone? If you see them, please say for me that I remember them most lovingly; that I recall every feature of their faces, and even the tones of their voices. I shall never see them again in this world; but beg of them to meet me where, I doubt not, friends will recognize each other with more pleasure than we can now conceive—in heaven. Are they beautiful? Tell them to look on those who are but a few years older than themselves, and see how soon beauty will lose its attractive freshness. Are they accomplished? Accomplishments are more enduring; but in the grave, which, since I last saw them, has opened for many as full of health and hope as they, pleasant voices and the tones of music are not heard. There the bounding foot is stilled, the cunning hand is palsied; and there the star of worldly wisdom sets forever. Urge them strongly, dear Jane, to adorn themselves with such Christian graces as shall be transferred with their ransomed spirits to Paradise. Tell them how sweet to the Saviour is the incense of young hearts, and what a precious Friend He is under all the circumstances of life. I wish you would ask each one of them, and any others about you whom I may know, to write me, if but a tiny note. If you please, put all the notes into one envelope and forward to me. Now that our perils by sea, by fire, by robbers, and by a persecuting government, together with our first heavy illnesses, are over, my thoughts revert frequently to old scenes; and though I have a sweet, precious home, and am very happy in it, far happier than ever in my life before, I can not always keep back the tears. The past—*the past*—has in it a very saddening tone. Then I have to regret that I was not a more meek, prayerful, devoted Christian when with you; and I would gladly retrace my steps, and walk more becomingly as a child of God. Think of my own helpless little children, and of the ignorant heathen women that God has placed me here to guide, and pray for me.

That our Heavenly Father may bless and prosper you ever, is, dear Jane, the prayer of

Yours sincerely and most affectionately,

EMILY C. JUDSON.

TO HER SISTER.

MAULMAIN, April 19, 1849.

DEAR KATY,—

I should hardly write you this month but that you may hear I am ill and so be anxious. The whole truth is, I was attacked by a cough last December which kept growing more and more serious till into January. I strained my breast lifting Emmy Fan during her illness, and for about a week after she got well was considered "in danger," but almost immediately rallied again. We thought I was almost well, and purchased a pony so that I could get exercise on horseback, but I rode him only about a week. After that I went down very rapidly— cough, fevers, and night-sweats—until I got to be a mere skeleton and very weak indeed. We then became alarmed, and tried what a trip to Tavoy would do. Mr. J. could not leave

very well, so I took Henry and Frances and two servants, and
went off under the protection of a kind English officer, who paid
me every attention. Mrs. Bennett noticed my cough at once,
and sent for the doctor, who pronounced my case very critical.
I spent a week in Tavoy, but did not go out at all, and really I
believe they were glad to see me go (though extremely kind),
for they were afraid I should die away from my husband.
When I reached home again I was in a serious plight; but Dr.
Morton (our physician) thought the violent symptoms were to
be attributed to congestion of the liver rather than disease of
the lungs; in which, thus far, his opinion has proved correct.
He overcame the fever, pain in the side, and difficulty of breathing by degrees, so that I now suffer very little from either. I
still have some fever, which is kept down by daily doses of
quinine, but my cough is slight (I take medicine for it three
times a day), the night-sweats have almost entirely disappeared,
my appetite has been very much improved, and my strength is
daily increasing. We begin now to hope confidently that it is
not the will of our Heavenly Father to break up the family
again so soon. You may imagine that I have had many sorrowful thoughts about the poor children; but you can not imagine what a wrenching there was in the case of their dear
papa. However, there is every prospect now that my life will
be spared; and you may hear of us in a few months, *possibly* at
Ava. I don't know—and in truth I am not so very anxious
about it as I should be if my hands were not full here. I want
the privilege of doing a little for Christ before I die, and I leave
it with Him to determine where the work is to be performed
—though I must say I have a slight preference in favor of Ava.
However, my principal business now is to get well, and everybody seems to be trying to help me. The Houghs send their
carriage for me to drive out every morning for the present, and
as we find driving very beneficial, we have just made arrangements for purchasing a horse and buggy. And what do you
think? just as we were turning the matter over in our minds,

in came the mail with a present from Mr. Newton of New
York, which enabled us to make the purchase. So you see I
am quite set up. Tell Mrs. Wade to hurry back before I get
so well as to take to walking again; for Mr. J. hates driving so
that he usually makes me go out alone—so I shall have a seat
for her. (Going out alone is not here as it is in America—we
have a groom to lead the horse by the head.)

Did I tell you last month about the nice box I got from Philadelphia? It is valuable, and the articles, which are chosen
with great care, are just what we need. We hear by this mail
also that we are to have a box from Oliver street church, in
New York. The Philadelphians and New Yorkers consulted
with each others, so we shall not be overstocked (it is not very
easy to be overstocked with wearables in this country) with
articles of the same kind. These presents make us doubly glad
—glad for their intrinsic value, and glad because we and our
work are remembered.

TO REV. MR. GILLETTE.

MAULMAIN, April 20, 1849.

. . . "Mamma is as God pleases to have her," a native
Christian woman said to me a few days ago, when I was lament-
ing my inability to perform my usual duties; and it is that
consciousness which has, for several months past, kept me from
discouragement. If it pleases God to lay me on a bed of sickness, and thus stop my work and break up all my plans, shall I
put on a mournful face, and disobey the apostolic injunction to
"rejoice evermore?" That would be like a sulky child professing to want to help you, when you prefer it should be
quiet. . . . .

We don't need a comic almanac to make us laugh sometimes,
though we are away in heathendom; we have only to recall
scores of funny things some of which you know, and some you
do not know. You know we are neither of us *sad* people; perhaps not sad enough; but I believe that work which goes on

merrily and without groaning, is quite as acceptable to God as the other. The bearer of glad tidings should not carry a face to spoil his news—a fact of which the natives seem quite aware. However sadness is good, and rejoicings are good; and whether we have a weeping gift or a merry gift, let us strive to use it, as we are commanded to use eating and drinking, "to the glory of God." Possibly my doctrine may not be considered orthodox, but it is that of the New Testament. . . . .

TO MISS ANABLE.

MAULMAIN, April 20, 1849.

MY DARLING NINNY,—

I wrote, about two weeks ago, to Aunt Cynthia, but as I then supposed it would be my last letter, it is not suitable to send now. So she will excuse me for not answering her kind notes this month. I am decidedly better than a month ago, and there is now every prospect of entire recovery. The violent symptoms, it seems, were occasioned by congestion of the liver, and not by disease of the lungs, as was at first supposed; though the lungs are not yet perfectly safe from a bronchial affection contracted in December. Did Mr. J. write you that I took a trip to Tavoy in the steamer? I had a charming visit with good Mrs. Bennett, although I was confined to the house, and most of the time, to my bed. I do not wonder that Aunt C. likes her; she is one of the loveliest Christians I ever saw. I feel that I have made a great acquisition in adding her to my list of personal friends. She is a *real missionary*, always working quietly and noiselessly. "Great will be her reward in heaven."

This illness of mine has been a great interruption to my work. It is now nearly five months since I have been able to read aloud, either in English or Burmese, or to talk continuously, and I find that I have lost very much in the language. It is to be retained only by using the voice, not by the eye. What may be the intention of my Heavenly Father toward me

I can not know, but I think I feel submission to His will. When I was ill in Rangoon, I felt very impatient because I was *doing nothing*, but I have yielded that point now. I know that I do not deserve the privilege of laboring for Christ, and what right have I to repine? I have a right to pray, however; and I do pray, most earnestly, that I may be allowed to offer my mite, and that it may be accepted. A long life seems very desirable in a place like this; but the All-wise alone can tell whose life to preserve, and whose to take away.

I am not strong enough to mount my pony yet, and the physician says it will be long before the exercise is good for me. But the Houghs kindly send their carriage, and I drive every morning. I am about selling my pony; how I wish I could send him to you—a beautiful, black little creature, smooth and glossy; full of spirit, but gentle and obedient, and gallops, O, so charmingly. Do you not want him? We are negotiating for a horse and buggy, which is to be at my control. Do you think we are extravagant? "All that a man hath will he give for his life," or his *wife's* life. But just as we were revolving the matter in our minds—what do you think?—this very month's mail brought us a present from America which enables us to buy it. To us it seems providential. . . May God bless you, dear Ninny, all of you, and grant you much of His presence here, and a place at His right hand hereafter.

Lovingly,

NEMMY.

TO MISS ANABLE.

MAULMAIN, June 2, 1849.

MY DARLING ANNA MARIA,—

I have been thinking of three years ago, when you and I were at the little loggery in Hamilton, and somebody else, not a thousandth part so dear as now, was there too; and we were all anticipating a grand event in the evening. Then good old Dr. Kendrick was able to walk to our house; now he is shut in his coffin—no, not there!—resting in "the bosom of his Father and his God." Dear grandfather and grandmother occupied the comfortable basement room in Utica, which we used so often to visit of a Sunday evening; and dear Aunt Cynthia was the life of the household. Grandfather and Grandmother have since then found a *more* comfortable and a glorious home, where they are more tenderly loved than by us, or even by their own children; and the rest of you have found another home also, but a different one, where you must still encounter the ills of life, and turn over new leaves to be re-read in eternity. I have traveled half the circuit of the globe since then; taken upon myself new toils, new responsibilities, and new enjoyments; added one little spirit to the list of the immortals, and hoped and prayed for the privilege of adding many more of Christ's elect to the list of Christ's redeemed. Every thing is changed except our hearts; I trust they remain the same, only as they may have gathered spiritual influences about them, and adorned themselves with more beautiful Christian graces. I wish you were sitting by me now, here before my large open window, in a room, I will venture to say, as comfortable and as clean, if not quite so handsomely furnished as yours. The dark, glossy leaves of the Cape jasmin, just below the balustrade, are sparkling with rain-drops, and its magnificent white blossoms fill the house with their rich perfume. The trees, too, are all dripping with rain; and gorgeous birds, though not with the rich voices of our robin and bob-o-link, are singing in the branches; while the odd-looking native huts, that peep from the green beyond, add to the picturesqueness of the scene, just as a gnarled tree, or a particularly ugly stump, beautifies an American landscape. The bell has just done ringing, and the gayly dressed natives—the women with bunches of flowers in their black hair, and the men in snowy turbans—go streaming by to the chapel; and—wait a minute!—there, I have had my kiss, and the teacher, as usual of an evening, has gone to spend an hour with his flock. But I am not alone, for there

are merry tones rising from the veranda. Nurse is teaching
baby the Burmese alphabet, and her curious pronunciation makes
her little brothers shout with laughter. But I do not believe
you would do it much better; try, and see: *Kah-gyee, kah-
gway, ga-ngai, etc.* Finally, the woman comes to *tah-tha-nyen-
gyik*, which she pronounces very much as if it contained only
one syllable, and baby joins her shrill little voice in the general
laugh. She can not be induced to attempt its pronunciation.
I do wish you were here, darling, if only to see how God has
blest me with the sweetest of all human homes. True, we lead
a life of toil and self-denial; but all that we suffer is for Christ's
sake, and we know that our smallest sacrifice does not escape
His notice. And for every sacrifice we are receiving, even now,
" an hundred fold." I do not know how it is that we are *so* free
from every care; nothing can worry us, or make us anxious; and
I believe it is because the Saviour is making good His promises.
That is why I am not afraid to go to Ava, or any where. We
can not be unhappy while we lie in the hands of God like little
children; danger will not be danger, and suffering will be a
joy.

We are all getting well again. I drive out as often as the rain
will let me, and take my children with me, leaving one at home
by turns. I believe I have the trustiest servants in the mission,
for others find it very difficult to go out without taking all their
children. Mr. J. is looking, I think, much younger than he did
in America, and is so well as to be a proverb among Europeans.
For myself, I feel as though I had received the same blessing
that Hezekiah did, and I am anxious to improve it to the best
advantage. There was at one time scarcely the slightest hope
of my recovery, and the doctor commissioned Mrs. Bennett to
tell me so. But I feel very grateful for that illness. My
Heavenly Father revealed Himself to me as He never did in
health, and I trust that the influence will remain upon my
spirit for ever. I am grateful for recovery too. Even inde-
pendently of my family, I think that long life in this crisis of

the affairs of the world, and especially in a heathen land, is particularly desirable. O, how I wish that you could be here with us! It seems to me that I never loved you quite as well as now, when your new situation and prospects remove the probability of our meeting, except in heaven. But let us strive with all our might to do good, darling, that, when we meet there, we may make glad each other's hearts. Give love to Hatty, Fanny, and Mary, and believe me, darling,

Yours most lovingly,

EMILY C. JUDSON.

TO HER SISTER.

JULY 18, 1849.

. . . "The goodman" works like a galley slave; and really it quite distresses me sometimes, but he seems to get fat on it, so I try not to worry. He walks—or rather *runs*—like a boy over the hills, a mile or two every morning; then down to his books, scratch-scratch, puzzle-puzzle, and when he gets deep in the mire, out on the veranda with your humble servant by his side, walking and talking (kan-ing we call it in the Burman) till the point is elucidated, and then down again—and so on till ten o'clock in the evening. It is this *walking* which is keeping him out of the grave.

For myself, I am very well, indeed, though not so strong as before my late attack. We sometimes think that I have received a blow from which I shall never fully recover, though the only thing which makes us think so is continued sore throat and weakness at the chest. The doctor assures us that I am in no more danger from consumption than any other person of equal delicacy of constitution; but physicians are not in general over endowed with frankness.

We are having some encouraging tokens in the Church. Three have been lately baptized; one a trader from Burmah proper, who yesterday returned, in company with a friend, to his home on the Irrawadi. The friend also is, in all probability, converted, though he can not bring himself to be baptized. This may be the commencement of a Church (who knows) away up the river. The man appears well.

I should like nothing better than to write such letters as father wishes, about manners, customs, habits, etc., but you can have no conception of the busy life I lead. I am taking a very *thorough* course in the language, which the natives flatter me by saying I speak elegantly. The other day I turned the "Mother's Litany," in the memoir, into Burmese, to be sung at my maternal meetings; so you see I have made a beginning in poetry. I do not speak as readily as I write, however.

Lovingly, your sister,

NEMMY C. J.

During the preceding year she had completed her predecessor's series of Scripture Questions on the historical parts of the New Testament, and Dr. Judson mentioning this and other feats of the "young romance writer," hopes that "she will yet come to some good." Apropos of "romance" writing, the following extracts from a long letter, written July 18, to a friend, are in reply to some suggestions regarding her peculiar style. They are a just and forcible refutation of some natural prejudices, and show how close was her own mental analysis, and how accurately she discriminated between fancy and fiction :

. . . Though, as in the case of the late memoir, I sometimes embellish my *style*, I have never been guilty of embellishing *facts*, except when I have presented them in the guise of fiction. In the work alluded to (than which a more truthful narrative was never made), I had my reasons, and I believe them good and sound ones, for departing from the beaten track of compilers ; but if you will take the trouble to compare my statements with those of other writers, you will find mine always moderate, and where exactness is requisite, exact. . . .

You need never fear that I shall turn a pile of slate-stone into granite; but you may be sure, if I ever delineate a rock for you, that so far as my power of using language enables me to express myself intelligibly, you will have it as you would see it yourself—not its bulk, magnitude, and learned name merely, but every thing about it—its stains, seams, and fractures ; the trailing plant, the pendent lichens, the patches of moss, and the spots of sunshine playing on its surface. Allow me also to add that however free the use I make of nature's pencil, it does not necessarily follow that my touches lack mathematical precision, but I maintain on the contrary that flowers and herbage, so far from marring the correctness of the naked diagram, are necessary to its completeness.

You would have a tiresome task, indeed, if you were to set about finding Alderbrook at Hamilton; and why should you expect to find it there? The Alderbrook tales being professed fictions, can not be tried by the same rules as history, nor can they be classed under any of the definitions of falsehood, for they are not only destitute of the *intention* to deceive, but they are actually destitute of the *power*. However, I will acknowledge that I did not make the draft on my inventive powers which was my right. My localities are in the main correct, though, as I was under no obligation to be precise, they are sometimes altered and embellished to suit the occasion. My characters and incidents are mostly of the same order, having only a vail thrown about them to prevent their being recognized. About five miles from Hamilton is the little farm on which I was born, with a trout-stream bordered by spotted alders, running through it, and the very odd-looking house ("Underhill Cottage"), built by my grandfather, stuck in the side of the hill. It was one of the last places I visited before taking a final farewell of my native State; and Mr. J. accompanied me across the creek and up "Strawberry Hill," to gain a better view of the scenery on which twenty years had wrought so little change. About three miles north of this is the village where I was bred, and which, next to the old farm, shares in my memories of the past. I took the liberty in my little sketches to unite my two early homes, and the brook with its alders supplied me with a name.

The innocence or the usefulness of fiction, in at least one of its forms, does not lie open to discussion ; for the question has been decided by the Saviour Himself. But how far this mode of teaching should be used, at what point it becomes reprehensible, and when it degenerates into a vice, has puzzled too many wise heads to allow of my venturing an opinion. Justice to myself, however, impels me to say that although I have indulged somewhat extensively in poetry, novel reading has never been one of my sins. When I was a child, I waded through the voluminous histories of Josephus and Rollin, and afterward I took up the principal English prose writers in course, beginning with the author of " Utopia," and ending with Edmund Burke, whom I had not finished when I left America. I seldom more than looked into the light magazines, to which for about eighteen months I contributed, though I must own that my avoidance of them was less to be attributed to principle than taste. Those who have not confined their attention to books, or a select circle of good and intelligent persons, but have had a practical education in the world of men and women, will pay some regard to the wants of weak intellects ; and I will venture to assert that where one person is injured by insipid moral tales, a hundred persons are benefited.

Some superficial thinkers, disapproving of the popular magazine literature, unconsciously transfer their opinion of them to the individual contributor. If I have written immoral things, let me suffer as I deserve ; if not, do not let the odium of such writers as some magazine editors tolerate rest on me. But even my own productions, though I am answerable for all that is bad in them, furnish no criterion by which to judge my private character. In truth, no two persons could differ more widely on most points than the fictitious Fanny Forester, and the real author of the sketches. And in this I do not stand alone. Who would believe that the *venerable* author of " Proverbial Philosophy" was a young and handsome dandy ? or that the poet Young, who was perpetually inveighing against worldly vanities, at the same time crouched to the very dust before the great in order to gain church preferment, and actually went to his grave crushed beneath a load of mortified ambition? It is well known that Thompson was, to say the least, indifferent on the three subjects on which he seemed most to dote in his poetry ; and Lockhart asserts that " L. E. L.," who has excited so much sympathy on account of the doleful style of her writings, was an uncommonly light-hearted person. In my own experience as a teacher, I have observed that the gayest of my pupils usually wrote religious compositions, while the sober ones frequently chose light topics, as though the effort of expressing the thoughts threw the mind out of its usual track. One young lady in particular, singularly quiet and demure, and of unquestionable piety, always convulsed the school with laughter. I am not advocating these incongruities, nor will I attempt to explain them ; I only mention them as exhibiting a phase of human nature, of which, especially in forming an opinion of me through a work professedly fictitious, I ought to have the benefit. . . .

TO HER SISTER.

MAULMAIN, August 12, 1849.

My Dear Katy,—

I told you last month that I could not write the sort of letters father wished, for want of time ; but I have thought better of it ; and if he will promise not to expect more of me than could in reason be asked of a person who uses the pen on one subject, the thoughts on another, and the tongue on a third, I will see what my unguided " diamond point " will strike out for him of its own accord. First then to the dress, which he will say is always uppermost in a woman's mind, and with certain restrictions and qualifications " I canna althegither denee the truth o't."

The men invariably (to begin at the top) wear turbans, though not always the pure muslin of Moung Shway-moung and Moung Chet-thing, whose head-gear while in America you will doubtless remember. Turbans of that character, except on special occasions, are very scarce. They are a *gentlemanly* article, while those worn by "the great unwashed" are but little above the size of a pocket-handerchief, and disposed of in various fashions. The turban, however, I must say in short, varies from several yards in size to a wisp twisted like a cable, or a small fillet confining the hair around the brow. It is usually white, though sometimes red (which is not so nice); and I have seen some in Rangoon of lace and thin muslin spotted with gold. The hair, which is allowed to grow—the longer the better—is seldom disposed of in the folds of the turban, but confined in a knot or club on the top of the head, of the size of which they are very proud. The ears both of men and women have an immense hole bored in the soft part, through which a plug of gold the size of your finger, having a precious stone in each end, is thrust—that is, the wealthy wear this ornament; but the poorer classes use various substitutes, even to a roll of pasteboard or a bit of segar. And here I may as well say that the natives generally, even those who are poorest to appearance, own jewelry more or less! not merely for ornament's sake, but because it is convenient and portable, and they can raise money on it at any moment. Men shave more or less, and wear their beards—of which some of them seem to be as proud as their more civilized brethren—in every variety of fashion.

Their jacket or tunic (*engyee*, they call it), is usually of white long-cloth, with two or three pairs of strings in front by which it is confined at the throat and breast, and then allowed to follow its own way, parting and floating back, to my thinking, in a way very tasteful. There is a sort of stomacher or chemisette crossing the breast. Sometimes the tunic reaches only a little below the waist, sometimes down to the knees—usually it takes a medium between the two. Men seldom wear this when at labor, and frequently dispense with it even when they consider themselves *dressed*, arranging the waist cloth in a way to remedy the deficiency. The *waist cloth* is the great article of dress. And when I use this word for want of a better (the Burmans call it a pa-tso), I beg you will not think of the *bit rag* you usually see in pictures of the heathen. This cloth, which is usually of very gay-colored silk, is eight yards long when purchased. The only *making up* it requires is to sew the two sides together without cutting it, so that the width can cover the whole person from the waist to the heel, while the closed end serves as a bag which may hold the betel-box, etc. This garment is worn in a great variety of ways. It is knotted up before ; and sometimes falls over each leg like a pair of flowing trowsers, sometimes hangs from the waist like a woman's skirt, and is sometimes twisted into as small a compass as possible to allow free play to the limbs. Very commonly one end is thrown foppishly over the shoulder. A close observer will not unfrequently find in the mode of wearing the pa-tso a clue to the character of its owner. This silk is of Burmese manufacture, coarse, soft, of fast colors, and bears washing well. It is usually woven in checks or stripes. They have a way of making zig-zag stripes to appear like rays of light, a shading in of all the intermediate colors between pale lemon and deep crimson, which almost dazzles the eyes. I went one day to buy one of these for you, but could not get it for less than twenty rupees (about ten dollars), so I had to give it up. Cotton cloths are worn also, but a man would be a poor wretch indeed not to own a silk pa-tso.

The Burmans never wear stockings or any thing of the kind about the ankles. The most common kind of shoe or sandal is the one I sent father, though they are variously embroidered

14

and sometimes gilded. They have a piece of wood about an inch thick attached to the bottoms to wear as we wear India rubbers. They manufacture umbrellas very much like those of the Chinese, which I think you have seen, but rather coarser. The betel-box is *always* carried, either by the person himself or a servant, just as an old lady at home carries her snuff-box. Chewing betel and smoking cigars is universal among men, women, and children as soon as they are weaned. The betel grows like a vine. They use both nut and leaf, and spread it with a preparation the ingredients of which I do not know. I believe you have a lacquered box or two. Those used for betel would hold about a pint of liquid. I will for curiosity's sake furnish a betel-box and send it to you by the first opportunity. They put a small metallic box inside to contain the preparation I have mentioned.

August 20. I have just come in from my morning exercise, and the whole town is in a stir because it is a Moorman holiday. I wish you could have been with me. The Moguls and other Moormen dress magnificently. One dress will serve to give an idea of the whole, though there is an endless variety of colors, etc. A crimson satin tunic with wide sleeves open on the back and laced—cuff turned up with green satin facing, and edge trimmed with variegated cord. Tunic long, reaching to the ankles, and slashed in a way to display wide striped-silk trowsers, looking for all the world like a pair of rainbows wrought into loose drapery. Sandals—or rather slippers turned up nearly a quarter of a yard at the toes, and glittering with gold and silver embroidery. A gilded cap, or rather rimless hat, appearing as though braided of wide stripes of gold. Buttons, tassels, etc., in keeping with the rest of the finery. The children are all gorgeously dressed, and weighed down with bracelets, anklets, necklaces, finger-rings, toe-rings, etc. The streets are crowded with beggars, lepers, and all sorts of miserable objects, their feet or hands literally eaten off with disease. * * *

DEAR KATY,—

I am heartily disgusted with all descriptions, and if I had
not promised, the Burman women's dress might go to the dogs.
But luckily they do not wear much, and, as a stable boy would
say, "a short horse is soon curried." They are rather small of
stature, so much so that they look upon English ladies with
wonder, and say that Mrs. Moore and I are the only women of
the mission whose size is at all endurable. Their hair is straight
and black; it is carefully oiled, combed directly back from the
temples, and confined in a knot on the top of the head.
They are fond of decorating the hair with flowers. They wear
ear ornaments similar to those of the men, and those who are
able to afford it wear a half dozen different necklaces, magnificent ornaments for the head, finger-rings, etc. The chief article
of dress is the *ta-ming* (t'mĭng), a species of petticoat, of the
gayest colored silk, with a deep border at the bottom and a top
of crimson cloth, which is gathered in folds about the breast.
The *engyee* or tunic is very much like that worn by the men,
though sometimes made of thinner material—jaconet, gold-
sprigged lace, black lace, yellow gauze, etc. They usually fling
a light scarf, silk handkerchief, or small shawl over one shoulder.
Their sandals are mostly like those of the men. Burmans
always leave these outside the door, for, in their estimation, it
is as bad breeding to wear shoes into a house as, in ours, it is to
wear their hats. It is curious to see a Burman lady, a bride
for instance, magnificently dressed, and her great black feet
bare.

The dress of the Burman women is pretty and coquettish,
but decidedly objectionable on the score of modesty, if not of
decency. . . . The women are spirited, lively, fond of laughing and talking, and, although shockingly quarrelsome as wives,
in the main good-natured. They are as intelligent as could be
expected in their circumstances. Boys are always taught to
read—girls seldom. Children seldom wear any kind of cloth-

ing till seven or eight years old, though they are profusely
decorated with necklaces, bracelets, anklets, etc. I have seen
children with rich silk velvet jackets just covering the hips, and
no other article of dress, aside from jewelry.

Your loving sister,

NEMMY.

TO MISS ANABLE.

MAULMAIN, September 21, 1849.

MY DEAR NINNY,—

   . . . I will tell you as nearly as I can how I am, and
then you will be able to judge as well as we can of the result.
I have a slight cough, sometimes with bloody expectorations,
and a continued pain in my right side—the latter, Dr. M. says,
occasioned by congestion of the liver. My stomach is very
weak and so sensitive to the touch that I seldom wear a tight
dress, and my throat is shockingly ulcerated. I have a slight
difficulty of breathing, and just now can not read aloud at all. The
physician says that my lungs are perfectly sound, but admits
that there is more danger of their becoming diseased than there
would be if my throat was well, and every fresh attack on my
throat is worse than the last, although he succeeds tolerably
well in subduing the fever. I am not so thin as I was, and
some of my worst symptoms, such as night sweats, have totally
disappeared. I work little, study little, walk in the veranda
for exercise, drive out every day, and keep in excellent spirits.
I suppose it would not be a surprising thing if I were to die in
a few weeks, nor be considered a miraculous interposition if I
were to live to be eighty years old—so much seemingly
depends on accidental causes. . . .

   You ask how I felt when looking into the grave. We had
expected for some time previous to my going to Tavoy that I
was in a fatal decline, and I had endeavored to prepare myself
for it. I grew worse on the passage, but still did not think
myself in any particular danger till the physician at Tavoy

commissioned Mrs. Bennett to tell me what he thought of my
case. I was inexpressibly shocked; for it seemed doubtful
whether I should ever get back to Maulmain, or see my husband. Mrs. Bennett soon left me alone, and little Frances, who
was just beginning to walk, and very proud of it, toddled to the
side of my couch, and seemed disappointed that I did not laugh
and praise her. I put my arm around her, and she laid her
little soft cheek coaxingly on mine, as though she understood
that I was in trouble. Then was a struggle; it seemed that
my very heart would burst. I tried to tell Henry something
about it, but he could not understand, and only tortured me with
questions about the funeral, etc. I got a little better before I
left Tavoy, and Mrs. B. was somewhat relieved, though I presume she still considered me in a settled consumption. After I
reached home I became a good deal calmed, and quite reconciled
to leave both husband and children, if it should be the will of
God; but still I can not say that there was any time when I
should not have rejoiced at the prospect of recovery. You will
think it strange, but it is nevertheless true, that, during most
part of the time, I felt greater reluctance to leave my mission
work than to leave my family. Yet "we have been so, *so*
happy!" "and the time has been so short!" we used to say to
each other with aching hearts many times a day. Then I would
watch the poor children at their play, until the tears came and
blinded me. Sometimes I had enrapturing views of heaven, and
my heart bounded with joy (for I never had any doubts respecting my future state). The *horror* of death that I used to tell
you about was to a great extent taken away; but still death is
the curse of sin, and can not but be dreaded except as its hideous
features are lost in the glory of the resurrection. I believe a
long life to be a great blessing, and in this age of the world,
especially for a missionary, inexpressibly great. I pray daily
that I may be spared for many years to my husband, to my
children, and to my work; and I have no hesitation in putting
up this prayer, for you know we are commanded to "be anxious

for nothing; but in all things to make known our requests to God." If, notwithstanding this desire to live on my part, my Heavenly Father sees fit to remove me, He will do it in infinite wisdom and in infinite love—for my good and the good of His cause; and I can add most heartily, "His will be done." . . .

Affectionately,

NEMMY.

The reader of Dr. Judson's memoir will recollect the sad forebodings of some of his letters, regarding the results of her illness. "A dark cloud," he writes to Miss Anable, "is gathering around me. A crushing weight is upon me. I can not resist the dreadful conviction that dear Emily is in a settled decline." The cloud which thus lowered upon *his* prospects past away: but it soon gathered with triple blackness over hers. How happy, how "deliciously happy" a home this dark providence breaks up, is sufficiently evident from all their correspondence.

CHAPTER XIX.

SELF-COMMUNINGS.

"My soul and I."

THE following journal will shed an interesting light upon Mrs. Judson's religious history at this time. It shows at once her spiritual aspirations, and the tendency of her mind to abstruse, yet cautious speculation:

JOURNAL.

MAULMAIN, March 25th, 1849.

I have been for some time past steadfastly looking into my grave; with the expectation of being shortly laid there; and there left—in silence, and darkness, and loneliness, till the resurrection morning. Only the shell, the cast-off garment there! Ay, but it is a shell into which the Son of God has seen fit to send back the principle of life, and which He will render immortal. Death is a curse—the most awful curse that divine justice could inflict; and though the blessed Saviour has deprived it of its sting, has gained a glorious victory for us, the triumph can not be complete till bone is gathered to bone, and sinew to sinew, and we rise to meet Him in the air. We naturally shrink from death, as the wounded man shrinks from the hand of the surgeon. Can this shrinking be entirely overcome? Have men actually risen so high by faith, as in the dying hour to be insensible to the pain and shame of their punishment?

or are their beatific visions and their rejoicings to be in a degree ascribed to the peculiar state of the physical powers, the influence of the nervous system on the mind, in the moment of dissolution? It is a terrible thing to die! Am I, then, afraid? No, but I am filled with solemn awe.

March 27. Am I afraid to die? My husband will lay me in the grave, and return to his house, leaving me away in that cold place, alone, beside the half mouldered bones of little Charlie.* He will be very sad and desolate—O, *too sad!* and yet my image will gradually fade from his mind—keep fading —fading—the tones of my voice will be lost, and our *precious* little conversations will mingle with the gray of the past, and become pleasant dreams.

My children will look about for their mother, and perhaps cry; and then they will forget me. They will be in trouble, and I can not help them; they will sin, and I can not teach and discipline them; they will feel sorrow for their sin, and I can not pray with them and point them away to Christ. I am not afraid to die, but I am very sad.

March 28. Mah Zaat says I talk of death so calmly because my life has been so pure. Pure! Is there so great a sinner in the world as I? One who has sinned against so much light? Converted in early childhood, educated amidst a blaze of gospel light, prayed for by a numerous company now in glory, and still prayed for by saints on earth. I have no doubt but I shall get to heaven through Christ, but I have reason to believe that I shall occupy a very low place there. I can not condemn myself for idleness: mine has been a busy, working life; but such a waste of toil and vigor!—such a squandering of influence! How much good I might have done, if my heart had only been the dwelling-place of the Holy Spirit! I shudder and groan within myself when I think of it. Oh! to live a little longer and do good!

April 1. I am slowly gaining strength, and begin to weigh

* A son of Dr. and Mrs. S. B. Judson, buried at Maulmain.

the probability of recovery. If it is the will of God, I should wish to live. He can soothe my husband's heart and be the Guardian of my children, and He can dispense with my weak, puny efforts in the Church. He can also light the dark passage of the grave, and make the prospect of going to my rest delicious to my soul. But I should count it an invaluable blessing to be allowed to maintain my place a little longer—to do something for Christ before I die. Perhaps my Heavenly Father designs to grant me this favor; perhaps the draught which we have long been preparing to drink in tearful submissiveness, may be withheld. "If it be possible, let this cup pass from me; nevertheless, not my will, but Thine, oh, God! be done."

April 3. Mah Zaat has been asking about the *separate state*, and seems disappointed that I could tell her so little. I have had something like her feelings on this subject. If we had only been told as much about the dying as about the resurrection hour! This silence and mystery constitute much of the awfulness of death—horrible to the sinner, and a subject for the exercise of the Christian's faith. But since we shall be *with Christ*, what more need we to know? Sleep in Jesus! Perhaps it will be an unconscious sleep, and we shall seem to ourselves to step from our dying bed and weeping friends, to the glories of the resurrection. Perhaps it will be a conscious state of rest and subdued blissfulness—a baptism of the disembodied soul in Christ. We can scarcely suppose it a state of impovement or growth, or in any way a state of activity. Such a supposition would seem not in accordance with God's great plan. To be with Christ! My heart swells at the thought. I long to be with Christ—to rest in His bosom. We shall need a long rest, after escaping from the shackles of sin, before we are in a state to enjoy the full fruition of the redeemed.

April 4. Mah Zwoon came in to-day, and, after looking at me some time, shook her head sorrowfully and remarked, " I am afraid we never shall have the second part of 'Pilgrim's

Progress now." Since I told the women there was another part about Christian's wife and children, they have been very anxious to obtain it, and I promised to translate it as soon as I was sufficiently versed in the language.

April 7. The cloud is a little lifted. I am still growing stronger and stronger. Strange that my heart bounds back to earth so joyfully, when I have been accustoming myself to the thought of being with Christ, and being "like Him, for I shall see Him as He is." I do not love the world in one sense ; but the thought of leaving it does not make me joyous, nor have I acquired that indifference to it which Doddridge makes one evidence of growth in grace. It is not so much that my family ties are so strong ; but I can not but feel that my work is unfinished—the shock of corn would be cut down before it was fully ripe. I seem just on the threshold of the very kind of usefulness I have nearly all my life longed for ; and I ardently desire the honor of gathering a few sheaves for my Saviour.

"Not of works, lest any man should boast." Works, indeed! The very privilege of working is only an additional display of grace ; but I do so long for this privilege, for it is sweet to receive favors at the hand of Christ. The more I feel indebted to Him, the more I love Him ; but I know there are innumerable ways in which to increase my obligations. If He should prefer to take me to Himself rather than let me remain here longer, I shall see the wisdom of it hereafter, and praise Him throughout eternity for removing me from some unseen evil to come. If my Saviour call, I shall know that my work is finished, and go willingly ; but until He call, I pray for length of days, and a wide field of usefulness.

April 10. I am feeling very ill. The fever has returned, and my cough is worse. The appearance of recovery might have been one of those delusions to which persons in pulmonary diseases are peculiarly subject. Father in heaven, prepare me for cheerful obedience to Thy will.

April 11. I have been trying to recollect what I have done for Christ in the course of my long and toilsome life, and the retrospect is sickening. How soon I may meet my Beloved and my Judge I do not know, but the expectation covers me with confusion. Oh, it is a solemn thing to pass from one's probation —to feel that the last leaf is written and the book about to be sealed for the judgment.

April 24. Since my illness I have had some views on the subject of laboring for Christ, which, if not altogether new to me, are stronger and more definite than those I formerly entertained. Glorifying God, doing good to others, and receiving a reflex good, have chiefly occupied my attention, while I have scarcely thought, till now, of the peculiar honor conferred on the individual who is selected to be a co-worker with the Son in adding to the declarative glory of the Father. God has no need of us; He could establish His kingdom just as well without us; but, with infinite condescension, He has included our weak, imperfect, sin-polluted labors in His plan. How are we honored by such distinction! and how cheerfully and gratefully should we toil, feeling that our Father bestows a peculiar blessing on us when He trusts the meanest part of His glorious work to our hands. He gives it to us because He loves us—because He wishes to gratify us here, and to enhance our blessedness hereafter. And we should *watch* meekly for such work, and pray that it may be given to our hands. It is never sent in an obtrusive way; but it ever waits humbly before us; and many is the time we brush it rudely aside, or crush it beneath the bustling foot, because it seems trivial to us, and we do not see that it is from God.

April 27. I have just been unpleasantly struck by a remark on the first page of Payson's "Selections," etc.: "Look back to the time," he says, "when God existed independent and alone; when there was nothing but God; no heavens, no earth, no angels, no men." What reason have we to suppose that there was ever a point in eternity when God was such a solitary being? Is the idea that He has been creating from eternity

more difficult to conceive than the fact of His simple existence?
Our finite minds can not comprehend either. Neither can we
conceive how the works of such a powerful and benevolent
Being could have had a beginning; for wherever we place the
date, however far back in eternity, there is still an antecedent
eternity in which He was idle—in which, as far as we can see,
many of His attributes could not have existed. So far as we
can see!—and how far is that?—the circle described by the
sweep of a midget's wing. We know of the existence of God
in three persons. We know God the Father, because He is our
Creator and Preserver; we know God the Son, because He is our
Redeemer; and we know God the Holy Spirit, because He is
our Comforter. We know the angels, because some of them
seduced us to evil, and still follow us, heaping evil on our heads,
and because those that "kept their first estate" are "ministering
spirits" to us; and these are all the beings in the universe of the
omnipotent God of whose existence we have been informed.
We know nothing here except what concerns our poor, puny
selves, but hereafter we shall be taught the things of God. Oh,
what a glorious study!

April 28. To think that a God of infinite benevolence has
passed an eternity without *exercising* that beautiful attribute is
to me utterly impossible. We know that He delights in seeing
His creatures happy, and studies, if we may so speak, to render
them happy; and that He has been thus from all eternity is the
only view that seems to me consistent with His character. But,
on the other hand, if He has been eternally creating, there are
eternal creatures; and this seems like an absurdity. How do
we know but Lucifer was such a creature; and from this cir-
cumstance conceived the possibility of being able to compete
with his self-existent Creator? I lose myself in the maze of
thought, and my poor, little, narrow mind aches from being
stretched so far. Oh, what poor, contemptible creatures we
are!—not as God made us, but as we have, through Satan's
influence, made ourselves; and yet how we strut and swell, and

glory in each other's praises, till, if ridicule could take the place of pity in such benevolent minds, we should have all the hosts of Heaven staring and laughing at us. But no; like their blessed Master, they pity us, and because they know He loved us, notwithstanding all our follies, they hover about us, and whoever among us have truly received His mark, are sure to be continually encircled by unseen angel-wings.

April 29. I have had evidence to-day that holy angels are not the only "ministering spirits" we have. Satan too sends out his envoys, and they are quite as busy as the others, with the superior advantage of finding an answering voice within us. Little do we dream of the spiritual warfare continually carried on in our presence! The apostle does not represent the enemy of our souls as an inferior being, the dirty, contemptible being that we are accustomed to think him. He says we wrestle "against principalities, against powers, against spiritual wickedness in high places." Our adversary is no shadowy, half-apocryphal being, whose very existence may be suspected to depend on the evil in our own hearts. He is a real living creature, made by the same Hand that made us, and placed far above us at the head of the heavenly hosts. He is fallen now, and the whole strength of his mighty intellect is directed against us: he taxes all his power and all his ingenuity to compass our destruction, because of the bitter hatred he bears to Him who hath loved us from eternity. And with the company of once glorious beings that he drew away from heaven, he has ample resources at his command; and could doubtless at this very moment cope with any and all the beings in the universe, except the omnipotent God. Oh, how humble we should be, and how implicitly we should obey the lowest whisper from heaven, lest we should join our enemy, and try to defeat the benevolent plans of the Great General who has undertaken to conduct our otherwise desperate warfare!

May 3. I suspect it is not quite right to be strongly desirous of living, even though it be but to do good. True benevolence would make us as glad to see others employed in the active service of the Redeemer as ourselves; and if He chooses others to do the work, what claim have we to prefer? Why should we not go to our graves gladly, and leave our places to those whom He designs to honor above ourselves? And yet He loves to have us ask all good things of Him; and I know of no higher good than to be an humble instrument in His hands to promote the interests of His most glorious cause, and to save the souls of men.

March 5. The newspapers say the discoveries in California have made men mad. The same papers said three years ago that poor, little, insignificant "Fanny Forester" was mad—or *romantic*, which is only a pretty word for insanity. I wonder if they would class my madness and that of the gold diggers under the same head. O! that I may resemble the Californian madmen in all but the groveling nature of their object; and while they are laying up treasure on earth, may I be gathering gold and jewels which shall outshine the stars, and outweigh all the riches of this lower sphere—materials for a crown in heaven.

May 6. Mr. J. has been reading to me this evening Dr. Hopkins' second sermon on Canticles v. 16. At the close he remarked that the true reason why our love for Christ does not partake of the exclusiveness of human love, is that in proportion as His grace is infused into our hearts, we learn not only to obey the golden rule, but our brethren actually become as dear to us as we are to ourselves. And he added, that when we reach heaven we shall love others in precisely the same manner and degree as we love ourselves; so that the joy and happiness we have in Christ individually, will be multiplied by the whole number of redeemed souls that gather round the throne. How strange when we know that "God is love," and heaven is made by loving, and when we see how much bliss a little love creates below—how strange that this source of bliss is cultivated so little by the children of God!

May 23. I have been very busy since I began to get better —too busy I am afraid for my spiritual good. I have finished the notes to the memoir, and written a great many letters, and taken a short lesson daily in Burmese. To-day I resume my native female prayer-meeting. The women are delighted to see me so well, and expressed their joy both by smiles and tears. They are very anxious to have the Bible class commence again, and I have promised to gratify them as soon as I can use my voice a little better, but they are just like a parcel of children, and yet how vastly superior to the heathen about them! Grace makes a very visible change in them.

June 20, 1849. The notes to the memoir are finished at last, and are safely deposited in the post-office. To-morrow they will be on their way to Calcutta. I have re-written them all within the last month, and bestowed upon them a great deal of work and some prayers. I think they will give people in America more distinct and definite notions of Buddhism than they had before, without dragging them through all the rubbish and filth of idolatry. I do not see any use in filling books with the silly vagaries of heathenism, though an outline of the great systems with which the Church has to contend is doubtless useful. What am I to do next?

September 21. A person of strong, unwavering faith has already *entered into a rest* which the dissolving of the elements could not disturb.

September 25. It is not right for a Christian to be continually thinking of death—the coffin—and the grave. I am determined henceforth to look across this black gulf, and keep my eye fixed on Christ. He has trod the ground, and I know that He can, that He *will* lead me safely across; for even now do I feel assured He is preparing a place for me. Why should I fear?—and why should I try to harrow up my mind with fearful pictures, as though the flesh was not weak enough without? No; let ascetics keep their coffins to look at—I will look above the wooden box, and the cast-off clay, clinging, as

I hasten onward, with all my might, to the cross. Help me, O blessed Redeemer! and I shall indeed triumph over the grave—triumph most gloriously!

September 29. This earth is a mere speck in the immensity of God's creations; and yet is as dear to Him, as carefully watched over, and its inhabitants are as precious in His sight, as though this were His all. God is not man, that His interest should be divided and diluted by a multiplicity of objects.—I am less than a speck on the earth—few know of my existence, and soon I shall pass away and be forgotten. But if I have been truly washed in the blood of Christ, I shall not be forgotten of Him. I am as dear to Him as though I were the only intelligent creature in the universe—as though the only being God created, and the only being for whom the Son of God came into the world and died. If I am truly redeemed, I shall enter into that intimate relation with my Redeemer indicated by the scriptural phrase, "The bride—the Lamb's wife," just as entirely and completely as though, instead of being the minutest infinitesimal part of the Church triumphant, it consisted of me alone. These are overwhelming thoughts, and call for a serious, thoughtful, prayerful line of life. They are at once animating, ennobling, and humiliating·

March 12, 1850. The best way to bring the heart into a frame to love a person who has treated me unkindly or is in any way disagaeeable to me, is to pray for her. A *general* prayer will not do; I must pray for her success in the things that cross and mortify me most; and if I find my heart too rebellious to offer such a prayer, I have reason to tremble for my spiritual state. If, however, I persevere, I know that God will give me grace to triumph; and then—oh, how I shall love that enemy in heaven!

CHAPTER XX.

"Sunk though he be beneath the watery floor,
So sinks the day-star in his ocean bed,
And yet anon repairs his drooping head,
And tricks his beams, and with new spangled ore
Flames in the forehead of the morning sky."

WHILE Mrs. Judson's health was thus trembling in the balances, and she was contemplating the possibility of a speedy departure, there came another and unanticipated blow, terrible and decisive. "A look of age," observed by the physician, but not by her, had begun to creep over her husband, "the consequence of his shortened visit to America." In November, 1849, he was attacked by a violent cold, followed by dysentery, and prostrated for six or eight weeks. Rallying a little, he, late in December, took a trip down the coast to Tavoy and Mergui, and afterwards spent a month at Amherst for the sea air. His wife accompanied him, rendering to him all the attentions of devoted love ; yet in vain. In February, an extended sea voyage was pronounced by the physician the only thing that promised relief. A most serious objection to this was the delicate situation of Mrs. Judson, which rendered it impossible that she should accompany him ; and his strong repugnance to parting from

her and his family led him to delay it as long as possible.
By his bed-side Mrs. Judson composed her exquisite
little poem "Watching." The scene is thoroughly oriental; and the vivid truth of the portrait is surpassed
by nothing in the luxurious imagery of "Lalla Rookh,"
or the more simple and natural picture-drawings of Lord
Byron. The irregular metre is so delicately managed—
its variations adapt themselves so perfectly to the fluctuations of feeling, from the more abrupt "Sleep, love,
sleep" of the opening, down to the long drawn Alex-
andrine into which the exhausted emotion subsides at
the close, that the most fastidious taste can scarcely wish
this feature removed.

WATCHING.

Sleep, love, sleep!
The dusty day is done.
Lo! from afar the freshening breezes sweep,
Wide over groves of balm,
Down from the towering palm,
In at the open casement cooling run,
And round thy lowly bed,
Thy bed of pain,
Bathing thy patient head,
Like grateful showers of rain,
They come;
While the white curtains, waving to and fro,
Fan the sick air;
And pityingly the shadows come and go,
With gentle human care,
Compassionate and dumb.

The dusty day is done,
The night begun;

While prayerful watch I keep,
Sleep, love, sleep!
Is there no magic in the touch
Of fingers thou dost love so much?
Fain would they scatter poppies o'er thee now;
Or, with its mute caress,
The tremulous lip some soft nepenthe press
Upon thy weary lid and aching brow;
While prayerful watch I keep,
Sleep, love, sleep!

On the pagoda spire
The bells are swinging,
Their little golden circlet in a flutter
With tales the wooing winds have dared to utter,
Till all are ringing,
As if a choir
Of golden-nested birds in heaven were singing;
And with a lulling sound
The music floats around,
And drops like balm into the drowsy ear;
Commingling with the hum
Of the Sepoy's distant drum,
And lazy beetle ever droning near.
Sounds these of deepest silence born,
Like night made visible by morn;
So silent that I sometimes start
To hear the throbbings of my heart,
And watch, with shivering sense of pain,
To see thy pale lids lift again.

The lizard, with his mouse-like eyes,
Peeps from the mortise in surprise
At such strange quiet after day's harsh din;
Then boldly ventures out,
And looks about,

And with his hollow feet
Treads his small evening beat,
Darting upon his prey
In such a tricksy, winsome sort of way,
His delicate marauding seems no sin.
And still the curtains swing,
But noiselessly;
The bells a melancholy murmur ring,
As tears were in the sky :
More heavily the shadows fall,
Like the black foldings of a pall,
Where juts the rough beam from the wall;
The candles flare
With fresher gusts of air;
The beetle's drone
Turns to a dirge-like, solitary moan;
Night deepens, and I sit, in cheerless doubt, alone.

But Dr. Judson's case was becoming more critical, and yielding to necessity he allowed himself to be carried on board the French bark *Aristide Marie*, bound for the Isle of Bourbon, Mr. Ranney of the mission accompanying him. The ship being detained several days in the river, Mrs. Judson took a boat each morning and followed him down, spending the day with him, and returning at evening.

TO MISS ANABLE.

MAULMAIN, Dec. 25, 1849.

My DEAR,—

I can write you but a very short letter this month, for we have just now an unusual number of cares. My poor husband has been ill for the last six weeks. He took cold, which settled on the lungs, and produced a terrible cough, with some fever. This continued three or four days, when he was attacked with dysentery, and the physician had not quite subdued that when a congestive fever set in and took away the remainder of his strength. For about a month he had a burning fever twice a day, and yet he is now on the gain. So you may imagine that he has something of a constitution to grapple with disease. If he is well enough next week, he will take a trip down the coast. We feel very sad to have him go alone, but it is not absolutely necessary that I go ; we could not, therefore, in conscience ask it of the mission, and we can not afford the expense ourselves. Even Dr. Morton will not say that he can not go without me, though he says that the trip would do *me* immense good, and that I had better go by all means. The English think " Dr. Judson" a sort of bishop, and supposing our salary to be much greater than that of other missionaries, they never think of expense in our case. Trades-people always charge us higher, and our servant, being known in the bazaar, always expects to pay more for our food than others. You do not know, per- haps, that trades-people always charge the English in propor- tion to their rank. I have, once in a while, got some Burmese woman to go to bazaar for me, and she obtained articles for less than a third of what I usually pay. But in a day or two they discovered the ruse, and up went prices again. Are you not interested in my domestic matters ?

Mr. J., I say, is better, so much so that I took him a little drive last night (you must know I always hold the ribbons now- a-days), and though he returned excessively fatigued, I do not think it did him any harm. He will be well soon, I trust.

You speak of the affairs in Europe. Mr. J. does not think that real millennial glory will begin before the year 2,000; but thinks that the twelve hundred and sixty years of the Papacy will end in sixteen or seventeen years. God grant that we may all live to see its downfall ! In the meantime, he supposes that Europe will be the theatre of mighty wonders; and though he does not guess what these wonders will be, he thinks we may well observe the caution in Revelation xvi. 15. Have not the " unclean spirits" already "gone out," and is not the world "gathering to battle?" And *we* may not altogether escape! If England should be involved in a war with Russia, all India would be shaken; and if the latter power should even temporarily gain Constantinople, I tremble for all Eastern missions. But "the Lord God omnipotent reigneth;" and if we should be granted the honors of martyrdom, others will rise up, and the whole East in a few years be flooded with Christianity. It makes my heart swell to think of these things; but my notions are too vague to write down. Yet—have you ever thought of it— *you* may not altogether escape. The United States are peopled by Europeans, and, in all but the soil, belong to the old Roman empire. Nobody has yet been able to say who the two witnesses of Revelation xi. are, and they certainly have not been slain. If they were the Waldenses and Albigenses, they have been merged in something greater which (or who) is to be triumphed over for three years and a half. Who knows—(I do not say I think so, for it involves horrors such as I dare not think of)—that these two witnesses are not England and America? Well, we have nothing to do but *watch*.

Lovingly,

NEMMY.

TO MISS ANABLE.

MAULMAIN, April 15, 1850.

MY DEAR NINNY,—

I sit down to write you with a very heavy heart—indeed, heavier than I ever carried in my life before. I do not know whether my precious husband is still living, or whether he may not have already gone to heaven; and I shall have no means of knowing for three or four months to come. After I wrote you last month he continued to decline, but so very slowly that I was not much alarmed, till one evening, all on a sudden, his back gave way as he attempted to go to his cot, and he would have fallen if I had not caught and supported him. From that

night he never stood on his feet. About ten days after, he was
carried on board a French bark, bound for Bourbon, and laid
on a comfortable cot prepared expressly for him; but poor I
was not allowed to go with him. Every body said it would be
madness, and he too said I must not go; he would rather stay
here and die than have both our lives endangered. But may
you never know the terrible effort which the resolution to
separate, under such circumstances, cost both of us. The
doctor said that he could not possibly live if he remained here,
but that if he went to sea there was a chance—a very small
chance, indeed, he acknowledged. So the question became one
of duty; if it had been one of *choice*, all the world would not
have induced him to go. I had watched over him night and
day for five months, and it did seem at first as though we could
not breathe apart. "If it *should* be the will of God to let me
die here, what a mercy!" he repeated over and over many
times a day, as his strength very perceptibly failed. But it
was not, and the day before he went on board he revived considerably. The vessel was a long time in going out of the
river, and so every morning I took a boat and followed after it,
and at evening came back to look after my little ones. In this
way I was on board the greater part of four days, and had the
privilege of arranging everything for his comfort in the way
that I knew he liked. The officers were very kind, and treated
me with that delicate, winning politeness which the French so
well understand, assuring me that everything should be done
in their power—they were entirely at his command. Mr.
Ranney, the mission printer, was appointed to go with him,
and he took a most faithful Bengalee servant that has been
with us for two years. So as far as attendance is concerned, he
is quite as well off as if I were with him. The last day I was
on board he was much worse—so weak that he could not
speak above a whisper, and even that but little. When I parted
with him he moved his lips to speak, but made no sound; he
did not even open his eyes, though he returned my kiss. When

the pilot left, however, he seemed animated with the prospect of getting out to sea, which he always loved, and told Mr. Ranney to write me that he "felt too much life in him to believe he should die **at present,** and he had strong hopes of returning to us in as **good** health **as formerly."** Mr. Ranney, too, was encouraged, though less sanguine.

April 18. The mail has come in since I commenced this, and my cheerful American letters grated very harshly at first, but on a second reading they make me feel encouraged. I do almost believe that God will yet take pity on us, and let us have a few more years of happiness in this world. Oh, you do not know how desolate the house seems, and how I hear his voice calling me by day and by night. The worst of it is the uncertainty of getting intelligence. They arrive in six weeks, and in six weeks more I *might* get a letter, if a vessel should be coming this way—but I may not hear in four, five, or even six months. Can you imagine a more torturing state of anxiety? Ah, me! are we not brought into terrible straits sometimes? . . .

Ah, Ninny, you don't know how I want you to be here— how I want to get into your bosom and cry a week. After being loved and petted as I have been, it is so, *so* desolate to be alone! God is disciplining me, however; and I suppose I need something very severe. Sometimes I think it would have been *such* a mercy if I had died during my late illness; but then, who would have taken care of *him* during these tedious five months? No, it was a sweet privilege to be beside him all the time, and he has blest me over and over again for my care. Good bye, darling; I shall write again as soon as I am able.

Affectionately,

NEMMY C. JUDSON.

On the 22d of April, her **second** child (named Charles, from her father) was born; but he "brought no joy." She had not the happiness of recognizing any life in the perfect little form; and the stricken mother thus poured

forth her grief in **such** sweet strains as a mother's love
and a Christian's faith have rarely united in breathing :

ANGEL CHARLIE.

He came—a beauteous vision—
   Then vanished from my sight,
His wing one moment cleaving
   The blackness of my night;
My glad ear caught its rustle,
   Then sweeping by, he stole
The dew-drop that his coming
   Had cherished in my soul.

Oh, he had been my solace
   When grief my spirit swayed,
 And on his fragile being
   Had tender hopes been stayed;
Where thought, where feeling lingered
   His form was sure to glide,
And in the lone night watches
   'Twas ever by my side.

He came; but as the blossom
   Its petals closes up,
And hides them from the tempest,
   Within its sheltering cup,
So he his spirit gathered
   Back to his frightened breast,
And passed from earth's grim threshold,
   To be the Saviour's guest.

My boy—ah, me! the sweetness,
   The anguish of that word!—
My boy, when in strange night dreams,
   My slumbering soul is stirred;

15

When music floats around me,
  When soft lips touch my brow,
And whisper gentle greetings,
  Oh, tell me, is it thou?

I know, by one sweet token,
  My Charlie is not dead;
One golden clue he left me,
  As on his track he sped;
Were he some gem or blossom,
  But fashioned for to-day,
My love would slowly perish
  With his dissolving clay.

Oh, by this deathless yearning,
  Which is not idly given;
By the delicious nearness
  My spirit feels to heaven;
By dreams that throng my night sleep,
  By visions of the day,
By whispers when I'm erring,
  By promptings when I pray;—

I know this life so cherished,
  Which sprang beneath my heart,
Which formed of my own being
  So beautiful a part;
This precious, winsome creature,
  My unfledged, voiceless dove,
Lifts now a seraph's pinion,
  And warbles lays of love.

Oh, I would not recall thee,
  My glorious angel boy!
Thou needest not my bosom,
  Rare bird of light and joy;

Here dash I down the tear-drops,
　Still gathering in my eyes;
Blest—oh! how blest!—in adding
　A seraph to the skies!

TO MRS. STEVENS,

ON SENDING HER CARRIAGE FOR HER.

JULY 30, 1850.

My dear old Bible tells
How the tide of pity swells
　　Up above;
And hints at angel forms
That bow amid our storms,
　　Lizzie, love.

It puzzles me to know
How these angels come and go
　　On our sphere.
Do they cast their wings aside,
When with mortals they abide,
　　Lizzie, dear?

I have drunk my cup of tears,
I have known of griefs and fears,
　　Pain and care;
Then a footstep sought my bed,
And a form bent o'er my head,
　　O, so fair!

But since it can not fly—
Though I'm sure it's from the sky,
　　Lizzie, dear—
If you know, my pretty fawn,
Let the buggy and Bar-John
　　Bring her here.

EMILY C. JUDSON.

Many weeks and months now rolled away, during which Mrs. Judson endured the lingering agonies of hope deferred. Repeatedly she sent out missives to her husband, giving utterance to her fears and her hopes—now to the sad presentiment that their parting had been final —now to the cheering belief that God would, in mercy, return him to her arms—and adding such items of intelligence as would interest him, if he yet retained an interest in aught that was done beneath the sun. Her letters speak especially of the tender care—of the parental and sisterly affection and sympathy of her associates in the mission. Scarcely anything can be conceived more affecting than her present situation. The sods of the valley pressing her new-born child ; herself wasted to a skeleton and hardly able to rise from her couch ; her friends and relatives divided from her by half the circumference of the globe ; her husband withdrawn under circumstances which made it doubtful if he could survive even a week, and yet she compelled to wait four long months before her dreadful suspense can be relieved by the scarcely more dreadful tidings of his death ! Rarely are the fountains of sorrow in the human bosom more deeply stirred. Scarcely can we conceive a combination of circumstances more fitted to call forth that wail of a desolate spirit—that shriek of the soul— that cry of intense and concentrated agony which now embodied itself in the following lines to her mother:

SWEET MOTHER.

The wild southwest monsoon has risen,
  On broad gray wings of gloom,
While here from out my dreary prison
I look as from a tomb—alas !
  My heart another tomb.

Upon the low thatched roof the rain
   With ceaseless patter falls :
My choicest treasures bear its stain,
Mould gathers on the walls—would Heaven
   'Twere *only* on the walls !

Sweet mother, I am here alone,
   In sorrow and in pain ;
The sunshine from my heart has flown,
It feels the driving rain—ah me !
   The chill, and mould, and rain.

Four laggard months have wheeled their round
   Since love upon it smiled,
And everything of earth has frowned
On thy poor stricken child,—sweet friend ;
   Thy weary, suffering child.

I'd watched my loved one night and day,
   Scarce breathing when he slept,
And as my hopes were swept away,
I'd in his bosom wept.—Oh, God !
   How had I prayed and wept !

They bore him from me to the ship,
   As bearers bear the dead ;
I kissed his speechless, quivering lip,
And left him on his bed—alas !
   It seemed a coffin bed.

Then, mother, little Charlie came,
   Our beautiful, fair boy,
With my own father's cherished name,—
But O, he brought no joy,—my child
   Brought mourning and no joy.

His little grave I can not see,
  Though weary months have fled
Since pitying lips bent over me,
And whispered, "He is dead."—Ah me!
  'Tis dreadful to be dead!

I do not mean for one like me,
  So weary worn and weak,—
Death's shadowy paleness seems to be
Even now upon my cheek,—his seal
  On form, and brow, and cheek.

But for a bright winged bird, like him,
  To hush his joyous song,
And prisoned in a coffin dim,
Join death's pale phantom throng,—my boy
  To join that grisly throng!

O mother, I can scarcely bear
  To think of this to-day:
It was so exquisitely fair,
That little form of clay,—my heart
  Still lingers by his clay.

And when for one loved far, far more
  Come thickly gathering tears,
My star of faith is clouded o'er,
I sink beneath my fears,—sweet friend,
  My heavy weight of fears.

O but to feel thy fond arms twine
  Around me once again!
It almost seems those lips of thine
Might kiss away the pain—might soothe
  This dull, cold, heavy pain.

But gentle mother, through life's storms
  I may not lean on thee;
For helpless, cowering little forms
Cling trustingly to me.—Poor babes!
  To have no guide but me.

With weary foot and broken wing,
  With bleeding heart and sore,
Thy dove looks backward sorrowing,
But seeks the ark no more—Thy breast
  Seeks never, never more.

Sweet mother for the exile pray,
  That loftier faith be given;
Her broken reeds all swept away,
That she may rest in heaven—her soul
  Grow strong in Christ and heaven.

All fearfully, all tearfully,
  Alone and sorrowing,
My dim eye lifted to the sky—
Fast to the cross I cling—O Christ!
  To thy dear cross I cling.

At length, about the 28th of August, the dreaded
tidings came. Her husband was dead. Within two
weeks of bidding her adieu, amidst unspeakable physical
agonies, but in the utmost serenity of soul, he had breathed
out his life, and his body had been committed to the
deep, and his spirit gone to its reward. He had been
dead nearly four months, and he had not come and told
her. If there were any thing in "spiritualism" but a
foul and pestilent lie, or the subtle agency of the devil—
if the spirits of the virtuous and sainted dead could hold
legitimate intercourse with those whom they have left
behind, Mrs. Judson would not have been allowed by him

who loved her more than life to pine for four months in harrowing uncertainty, when a single whisper from his spirit lips had disclosed all. Sin has placed man in a state of judicial isolation, and hung a curtain of impenetrable darkness around his earthly abode. The great *moral* mysteries of the future are revealed to the eye of faith, but all that might minister to our curiosity—all that we do not *need* to know, is, even in the case of God's chosen ones, to be reached only through the portals of the sepulchre.

The intelligence of her bereavement was communicated by Rev. Mr. Mackay, of Calcutta. It was accompanied by expressions of deep sympathy, and a cordial invitation to her, should she decide on returning to England by way of Calcutta, to make his house her home during her stay there. He was of the Scotch Presbyterian church, and from him and his family Mrs. Judson subsequently experienced the most unwearied kindness.

TO MISS ANABLE.

AUGUST, 1850.

It is all over, Anna Maria, darling, and oh! do pity me. I am so, *so* desolate. He lived only four days after they left the river, and suffered so intensely that he longed for the release of death. And here for four long months have I been so anxious about him, when he was wearing his crown in heaven? I ought to rejoice and be glad that he is so happy and glorious: sometime, perhaps, I may get strength for it; but now I can think of nothing, and see nothing, but the black shadows that have fallen upon my own heart and life. Oh, it is a terrible thing to lose a friend and guide like him.

I can not write you any more, darling, for my heart is aching, and I am ill with grief. I do not feel as though I should ever be well again; but perhaps I shall—and then, perhaps—I do not know—I may try to bring my poor little orphans home. Write to me, however; for it is doubtful about my going at all —certainly not at present. It seems to me that I should like to die here, and be buried where my precious husband labored. But no matter; wherever we may be, we shall have no difficulty in finding each other on the resurrection morning. Oh, Anna Maria, you do not know how we have loved one another, and now, *I am alone.* In deep affliction,

Your poor

NEMMY.

TO HER SISTER.

MAULMAIN, August 20, 1850.

MY DEAR KATE,—

I suppose you will have heard before this reaches you, that the last blow has fallen upon me—that I am widowed and desolate. Oh, you can not guess how heavy my heart is—nor how dark and dreary my future appears. God help me! I can not write particulars now, I am too ill, and Mr. Ranney says he wrote from Mauritius. I can not say what I shall do. I have no plans, and no expectations. It was my husband's wish that I should go home with my poor little orphans, but the missionaries beg that I will decide on nothing hastily, and I feel as though America could never be a home to me again. Time will tell. In the mean time, pity me, dear Kate, for my poor heart is aching sorely.

Your afflicted sister,

EMILY C. JUDSON.

Love to father, mother, and Wallace.

TO REV. MR. STEVENS,

ON TRANSMITTING THE MSS. OF THE UNFINISHED DICTIONARY.

MAULMAIN, September 4, 1850.

MY DEAR MR. STEVENS,—

Parting with the manuscripts which were every day before my eyes during three happy years, almost carries me back to

15*

that sad morning in April when *he* passed from the door never again to return. But I well know that my Heavenly Father is ordering all these things, and I have nothing to do but submit —nothing to say but "Thy will, O God, be done!"

A few days before Mr. Judson went away, he told me, if he should never return, to place the Dictionary papers in your hands, and it is in compliance with that request that I now send them. I suppose that he would not have improved the English and Burmese part very essentially while carrying it through the press; and the second part, the Burmese and English is, as far as he had advanced, equally complete. The last word he defined was ——, and the corresponding initial vowel ——.

The only request he made was that there might be some distinct mark, both in the dictionary and grammar, to indicate where his work ended and yours commenced. The grammar was intended to preface the Burmese and English portion of the dictionary, but is complete only as far as through the cases of nouns—32 manuscript pages. I believe this grammar was on a somewhat different plan from the old "Grammatical Notices;" but I send a printed copy of that, in which he has marked several errors, as it may be of some service to you. In addition to the finished parts of the Dictionary, you will find the two old manuscript volumes which he had in use ever after his first arrival in Burmah ; and these I beg to have returned to me when the work is completed. Interlined and erased as they are, you will have great difficulty in deciphering them, and will no doubt find some parts quite illegible. I think I mentioned to you the plan of having Moung-Shway-loo make out, from the old printed Dictionary and his own memory, a list of words more or less synonymous, and I send the books, which, although not to be implicitly relied on, are, I believe, quite valuable.

There is one bound volume which I do not recollect having seen before ; but I think it must be a vocabulary arranged from an original Burmese one, as I have heard Mr. J. speak of having such a work. The remaining papers, consisting of two or three little vocabularies, and the like, are, I suppose, of no great value ; but I thought it best to send every thing in any way connected with defining words. I also put in with the rest the old proof-sheets, as he sometimes had occasion to refer to them.

And now, may the blessing of God rest upon this work— on you, or whoever else may finish it—on all who, for Christ's sake, study it, and upon poor Burmah, in whose behalf so much time and labor have been expended.

Very affectionately, your sister,
EMILY C. JUDSON.

Under date of September 20, Mrs. Judson wrote to her sister, Miss A. B. Judson, a minute and most beautiful account of the closing scenes in the life of her husband, and subsequently contributed most touching reminiscences regarding them, as well as other portions of his history, to the memoir, prepared by Dr. Wayland. The length of these precludes their insertion here, and they belong more strictly to his life than to hers.

CHAPTER XXI.

HOMEWARD BOUND.

"My visions fade behind, my weary heart speeds home."

THE question of her future disposition of herself and children, now pressed itself forcibly and painfully upon Mrs. Judson. Her heart was with the mission; her strongest wish to live and die amidst the scene of her now sainted husband's labors, and give her powers to the work whose glory had come gradually to absorb all the faculties of her soul. As her health slightly improved, it was her first purpose to remain at least a few years, in the hope of turning her knowledge of the language and her experience to account in some of the good for which she so ardently panted. But, with the setting in of the rainy season, she experienced a fresh relapse, which admonished her that a change of climate constituted her only prospect of contiuued life; and, looking both to her own health and the good of her children, she could not doubt that duty demanded her return to America. She writes thus to Miss Anable, October 20:

You will not think that I do not love you when I say that it is more painful for me to return to America—to leave *all* here—than it was to come away from you originally. But I have considered the subject prayerfully, have advised with the missionaries, and consulted the wishes of my sainted husband, and have no doubt in regard to duty. I must go back to America, and, if God spares my life, try to serve Him there. My heart is *here*—I love the missionaries, love the work, and love the precious Christians that have been accustomed to gather round me for prayer and instruction. They sobbed like so many children when I announced my purpose of returning. My knowledge of the language is too important to be thrown away, and my knowledge of the habits and character of the people is probably (from peculiar circumstances) greater than that of many who have been longer in the field. But the state of my health and the good of the children require a sacrifice of feeling which, from your distance, you will be unable to appreciate. . . . I am not permitted to raise myself in bed, for I am suffering from a relapse, brought on, the physician says, by writing letters.

TO MRS. NOTT.

MAULMAIN, November 16, 1850.

MY DEAR MRS. NOTT,—

I can not recollect positively whether I replied to your letter, written long since, or not, but I know it was in my heart to do so, though I may have failed in the accomplishment. For the last two years, "sickness and sorrow, pain and death," have been my constant attendants; and, in consequence of this, I have neglected many social duties and been deprived of many pleasures, among which correspondence with those I formerly loved is not the least. And now, though my hands are full of cares, and my heart heavy with its accumulated burden of sorrows, my thoughts still turn back to other days, and, even in the midst of pain, and weakness, and desolation, I find something not unlike a ray of sunshine left me from the dreadful wreck of all those bright hopes. God has given me a bitter portion, and yet, through all, even in the heaviest of my trials, His loving-kindness and tender mercy have never failed;

and now, though my path in life is darkened forever, He yet condescends to guide me, and I can not be wholly miserable. Heaven seems very dear to me, and very *near*, indeed, since it contains my sainted husband and the precious, precious little one that I had hoped to receive in his stead. And then, my own feet have been treading, for the last six months, close on the verge of eternity, so that trust in Christ has been my only resource, both for myself and my poor little orphans, and I have found it, indeed, a sweet dependence. Now my health is a little better, and the doctor says that if I return to America, I have a good prospect of recovery from the disease contracted here, though, on other accounts, a cold climate will be less favorable to me than a warm one. It is very painful to me to leave the mission just as I began to be prepared for usefulness, but it is of God's ordering, and I know that He will do what is best, both for me and for His cause. If I stay here I can not live ; if I go to America I may be permitted to be of some use to the children; so, there is no ground for question. I shall leave here for Calcutta in January, I think, and then take a passenger ship for England. . . . I shall probably reach England in June or July.

. . . It is my intention, if God spares my life, to gather the poor children (six in all) under one roof, and make a home for them in some place where they can have the advantage of good schools, and we can live economically. I can not yet decide where that will be. The three children here with me enjoy excellent health, and are delighted with the prospect of the voyage, but more especially the wonders they expect to meet in America. I shall also bring with me the Indian girl I have employed of late as a nurse, and a little son of Mr. Stevens, a brother missionary. So my party will consist of six, and don't you think they need a more efficient head than I? How different when I came out! Friends in America prepared my outfit and packed it, and my husband put everything in its place and watched me all the way, as mothers watch their infants. But the "Father of the fatherless and the widow's God" will go with us now, and I do not think I shall be afraid.

We heard of Dr. Nott's illness with much sorrow, and there was a time when my husband did not expect to precede him to heaven; but God had work for one and not the other, and "He doeth all things well."

With much love to yourself and Dr. Nott, as well as the Pearsons,   Very affectionately yours,

EMILY C. JUDSON.

TO RIGHT REV. BISHOP WILSON, LORD BISHOP OF CALCUTTA.

MAULMAIN, Dec. 17.

MY BELOVED FATHER IN CHRIST,—

I was so much overcome yesterday, both by a sense of the condescension of your lordship's visit, and also by the flood of mournful reminiscences which it generated, that I failed to say how warmly my now sainted husband reciprocated the affection you were pleased to express for him, and how deep were his respect and veneration. I also neglected to fulfill one of his last requests, made only a few days previous to our final earthly parting. It had been his intention to send you a copy of the memoir of his late wife, but the first editions were so defaced by typographical errors that he deferred it until we should receive a revised edition. This was expected daily when he went away, and he commissioned me to beg your lordship's acceptance of a copy *in his name*, so soon as I should receive it. My subsequent illness, together with my anticipated visit to Calcutta, has prevented the fulfillment of his wishes until now.

I also do myself the pleasure to add another memento—the accompanying engraving, from a portrait taken five years since in America. Those who loved him do not think it correct, but it is a very good representation of the face he wore in public.

Permit me again to express my warmest thanks for your kind gift—the Book of books—and to assure your lordship that this will be the copy which I shall hereafter read in my closet, and preserve among my choicest treasures.

Praying that our Heavenly Father may have you in His holy keeping, and spare you to the Church of Christ for many years to come ; and trusting that when you sometimes think of a saint in glory, you may remember also the widow and the fatherless in their desolation, believe me, my lord, with reverential affection,

Most sincerely yours,

EMILY C. JUDSON.

The following to Rev. Dr. Bright (the Home Secretary of the Missionary Union) is especially interesting as containing a brief but most just and beautiful delineation of the character of her deceased husband. It shows how thoroughly she understood him—how competent she was to do justice to his memory :

TO REV. DR. BRIGHT.

MAULMAIN, Dec. 23, 1850.

MY DEAR MR. BRIGHT,—

I have no words with which to express my gratitude for the kind sympathy of yourself and the executive committee in my afflictions, nor the pleasure with which I have regarded your manifest appreciation of a character now made perfect in glory. I would also, were it in my power, extend my thanks to all those Churches and individual Christians who have given me the support of their prayers during these dark months of trial; for surely the everlasting arms have been about me, and God—even the God in whom *he* trusted—has led me. In sorrow, in anxiety, in weakness, in the depths of desolation and affliction, I have found the blessedness of clinging to the cross of Christ, and though I have had my hours of trembling and despondency, I have also had glimpses of the eternal world, and of a crown radiant with the glory of the redeemed, which have made me rejoice that I am permitted thus to suffer, while the suffering is *mine alone*.

After my illness of 1849 (by which my prospects of usefulness in the mission were greatly impaired), my husband expressed his desire that, in case of his death, I should return to America and assume the guardianship of the children. A few days previous to his embarkation I took occasion to allude to the subject, inquiring if he had any objection to my remaining here until I had accomplished certain objects for which I had been striving to prepare myself, provided it should seem in my own eyes the wisest course, and should meet the approval of the Mission and the Board. After some little hesitation he replied that it would be very sad to leave me in such circumstances, and he should feel far happier to think of me in the position he had so often pictured in my native land, but added, " I do not wish you to feel under the least restraint from any thing I have said ; act as your judgment dictates, and I am sure that God will guide you to a wise decision." I felt, therefore, that it would not be a violation of his wishes for me to remain until the age of the children made my return necessary ; and for a little time, with the kind concurrence of the Mission, I decided accordingly. But God ordained it otherwise, and, as you have already learned, left me without a choice. The physician who has attended upon me for the last three years has expressed his decided conviction that I shall never be equal to the performance of active missionary duties ; and there is much reason to fear that loss of life might be the penalty of remaining through another rainy season. The manner of effecting my return has been a subject of great anxiety to me. A merchantman, with no female friend or medical adviser on board, presents but a forbidding prospect ; and I have not felt at liberty (looking to your treasury for disbursement) to incur the additional expense of more suitable accommodations. Even in this, however, God has fulfilled His promise to those who put their trust in Him. A few friends in Bengal have proposed making up a small purse as a tribute to the departed, which I hope will be sufficient to defray all expenses over and above those usually incurred by returning missionaries. I therefore propose leaving here in the January steamer for Calcutta, and thence taking an English passenger ship to London, which port I hope to reach early in May. May I be assured of your prayers, both in my own behalf and in behalf of my fatherless children?

I need scarcely say that the action of the Board on the subject of the proposed memoir meets my most cordial concurrence. . . .

The choice of a biographer I consider to be a question of great difficulty and delicacy, and one on which I can not but hesitate to express a decided opinion. The common tendency, I think, would be to place the subject at a cloudy distance, and divest him of those attributes of humanity the lack of which no heroism or saint-like quality should ever be thought sufficient to compensate. Besides, Dr. Judson possessed a strongly marked character, and one writer might seize upon one view, another upon another, and a third upon still another; while each representation would be as incomplete as the description of a multiform edifice from the survey of a single side. He needs a biographer capable of grasping his whole character at once, and of reconciling and harmonizing its singularly diverse elements—its delicacy with its strength, its almost unparalleled tenderness with its uncompromising sternness, its sensibility with its stoicism, its ardent enthusiasm with its cool severity of judgment, its frank, genial socialness with its tendency to asceticism, its discreet and quiet caution with its bold fearlessness, its patience in study with its promptitude in action; its impetuous earnestness, its graceful play of fancy, its humor, with its serene dignity, its mock seriousness, the simplicity of its devotion, and its constant aspirations after holiness. The work had better never be performed than marred by weak hands; the character had better remain undelineated till the judgment day than be crippled to suit the powers of a mind less capacious than his own. In addition to this, his life has been such a complete exposition of the age in which it began and ended, that a rapid but comprehensive glance at these times will be an essential requisite to a full development of the subject. The unseen influences which had been so long in operation, and gradually tending to the finally bold conjuncture; the Spirit of God brooding upon the dark waters until they were finally stirred beneath it; the new-born light, flashing forth in the Old World, to be caught up and reflected from the walls of Andover; the progress of the wondrous work, girdling the whole earth with its slowly advancing glory; all this requires to be connected and interwoven in such a manner as to exemplify the dealings of God in the mightiest movement which marks this age of wonders.

Pardon me if I write too earnestly. I do not wish to overstep the bounds of modesty, but it is a subject on which I have a right to feel the deepest interest; and yet I can truly say that I am less solicitous for my husband's honor (which I believe would be safe in any hands) than desirous that his death should subserve the interests of the noble cause to which his whole life was devoted.

The Committee will be pleased to learn that the mission so far anticipated their wishes with regard to the monument at Amherst as to obtain a grant of the ground from government, so that whatever changes occur, the spot marked by the hopia tree will remain undisturbed.

Again thanking both you and the Committee for your courteous consultation of my wishes, your kind sympathy, and your expressed interest in my welfare, believe me, my dear Mr. Bright, with the highest respect and esteem,

Most sincerely yours,

EMILY C. JUDSON.

Weary and desolate—weary, worn, and desolate—oh, Anna Maria, my path is mantled by the very " blackness of darkness." I am on the eve of embarkation; one day more, and I leave my loving, sympathizing friends here to plunge into the midst of strangers. How well fitted I am for the long and lonely voyage you will imagine, when I tell you that I have not been able to enter the nearest mission house since that fatal April but once, and then (two weeks since) it brought on a relapse, from which I am still suffering. My Calcutta friends write me kindly—tenderly even—and though they are stranger friends, God may see fit to turn their hearts toward me—I don't know. It is better, of course, to look altogether above the world, but that is scarcely possible while in it. O, for the rest of the people of God? I sometimes feel that it would be delightful to share *his* grave—but then the children.

On the 22d of January, 1851, Mrs. Judson, with aching heart and tearful eye, bade adieu to Maulmain, the scene of her happiest and of her wretchedest hours. It was like death to tear herself away from the place hallowed by so many delicious and sacred memories—from the spot where with *him* she had so long lived, and hoped, and labored ; from the missionaries who were to her more than brothers and sisters ; from the native Christians, whom she loved as children. Early in February, with slightly improved health, she reached Calcutta, and found a most hospitable welcome and delighful home in the family of Rev. Mr. Mackay. They are the " Wayside friends" of the Olio. Her health, however, again declined. She was prostrated by the slightest exertion, and unable to fulfill her anxiously cherished wish to visit the mission of Serampore, and the grave of a child of Dr. Judson that was buried there. She received here, besides innumerable other kindnesses, a testimony of respect to the memory of her late husband, in a liberal donation of three thousand rupees (fifteen hundred dollars), made by Calcutta gentlemen, without distinction of religious sect.

She writes thus to Rev. Dr. Bright:

CALCUTTA, February 23, 1851.

MY DEAR MR. BRIGHT,—

I am just now on the point of embarking for England, after spending some three weeks in this place, waiting for the sailing of the vessel. I am in the family of the Rev. W. S. Mackay, missionary of the Free Church of Scotland, a fine scholar, a warm hearted Christian, and altogether one of the most noble and chivalrous characters I ever met. Through him, I have made the acquaintance of a large circle of friends, not only of his own church, but Episcopalians, Independents, etc., and have also met with all the English Baptist missionaries in town. I have been too ill to visit Serampore, which I regret exceedingly, for I consider it, apart from family associations, a place of deep missionary interest. "The Judson Testimonial," a subscription by "the friends and admirers of the late Dr. Judson" (as they style themselves), for the benefit of his family, amounted to about three thousand (Company's) rupees; and from this it is my intention to defray all the expenses of my passage home, above what the Board would have to pay in the *Washington Allston*. That somewhat unfortunate vessel entered the mouth of the Salwen just as the steamer was leaving it. I, however, saw Dr. Dawson, and received a very hurried note from Mrs. Wade, whom I was distressed to pass without seeing. At this place I had the pleasure of meeting the Kincaids and Mrs. Vinton; the latter looking very well, but poor Mrs. Kincaid had almost a ghostly appearance. They seemed very glad to learn that I was going in an English vessel, and the very one which brought them from the Cape. I have taken my passage (a small upper-deck cabin) on the *Tudor*, Captain Lay, bound for London, *via* Madras, Masulipatam, and the Cape. As she touches at so many places, I anticipate rather a long voyage, but there is every prospect of its being a pleasant one, at least so far as accommodations and society are concerned. There will be at least two pious families on board, perhaps more. I pay for myself, three children, and a servant girl, fifteen hundred rupees, which is thought to be a very moderate sum. I was very much benefited by the change when I first came to Calcutta, but it soon passed away, and since then I have been growing more and more poorly every day. The doctor whom I have consulted here says there is no hope for me but in a long voyage, and thought it a matter of regret that the vessel should be so long delayed. Then, although I have received company here mostly on my couch, I know it has injured me, and I anticipate great benefit from the quiet of the vessel. I know it is on account of the respect for my sainted husband that I am received so well here; and I can assure you the evidences of esteem for him which meet me on every hand are deeply gratifying to me. The Missionary Conference (Scotch Free Church) has addressed me a beautiful letter, and private testimonials are almost number-less. I send you with this the *Calcutta Review*, a quarterly edited by Mr. Mackay, and containing an article from the pen of Major Durand, formerly commissioner of the Tenasserim provinces. He was a personal friend of my husband and the second Mrs. Judson, and has also shown great kindness to me. Through Lord Ellenborough, with whom he is a favorite, he possesses much influence, and the whole of it is exerted in favor of pure, genuine Christianity. It will be a blessed thing for missionaries, and for the heathen, when there are more such men in the East.

I feel like setting up an Ebenezer in this place before I go, for surely the Lord has thus far helped me; but I still go on my way with fear and trembling, not knowing what is before me; though I do know that God, even *my* God, is on the sea as on the land. It is not very probable that I shall reach England before the end of June, which will bring me to America at a very favorable season—the hottest of the year. Do not forget to pray for me while on my trackless way, and also for my poor little ones, that however desolate in other respects, we may have the presence of our Heavenly Friend.

Sincerely and affectionately yours,

EMILY C. JUDSON.

On the 24th of February she embarked with her three children and nurse in the ship *Tudor*, Captain Lay, for London, to retrace, under circumstances how sadly altered, the way which, five years before, she had traversed with a heart filled with hope, and an idolized husband by her side. But she met with kindness everywhere. The captain was unweariedly attentive; her fellow-passengers courteous and respectful; and a Mrs. Thomas especially, though a brilliant woman of the world, yet by her unaffected sympathy and warm-heartedness, as well as by her intelligence, won a large place in the heart of the stricken widow. Mrs. Thomas' husband was not with her, and Mrs. Judson wrote for her—as an address to him in his absence—the little poem, "Alone upon the Deep, Love." She gazed sadly upon the receding shores of India; caught for the last time "the spicy breezes" that blow from those groves of balm and islands clothed with eternal summer, and once more the southern cross looked down upon her—but with a deeper, sadder meaning than when she first gazed on it through the glowing atmosphere of hope. Its strange blended lesson of severity and kindness she thus sweetly interpreted:

TO THE SOUTHERN CROSS.

Sweet empress of the southern sea,
   Hail to thy loveliness once more!
Thou gazest mournfully on me,
   As mindful we have met before.

When first I saw the Polar Star
   Go down behind the silver sea,
And greeted thy mild light from far,
   I did not know its mystery.

My Polar Star was by my side,
   The star of hope was on my brow;
I 've lost them both beneath the tide,—
   The cross alone is left me now.

Not such as thou, sweet Thing of stars,
   Moving in queenly state on high;
But wrought of stern, cold iron bars,
   And borne, ah me! so wearily!

Yet something from these soft warm skies
   Seems whispering, "Thou shalt yet be blest!"
And gazing in thy tender eyes,
   The symbol brightens on my breast.

I read at last the mystery
   That slumbers in each starry gem;
The weary pathway to the sky—
   The iron cross—the diadem.

The opening of their voyage had been unwontedly
propitious—so that Mrs. Judson felt "ashamed to own to
sea-sickness;" but they encountered very heavy gales before reaching Cape Town. They arrived here about the

26th of May, and remained a few days, Mrs. Judson
having greatly improved in health, as is shown by the
following to Mrs. Stevens :

Would you not be astonished to see me getting ready for a
dinner party, three miles out of town, at the fashionable after-
dark hour? They have a joke on board the ship that the
fairies have changed me; for I am not the same person that
came on board at Calcutta. And they are right. I am not fat
yet, as you will readily believe, but my complexion is entirely
changed, my appetite is enormous, and nothing that I can eat
or drink does me the least harm. I did not improve much
until we got in sight of land which was about five weeks before
we actually landed. The first gale, which was frightful, nearly
killed me while it lasted; but as soon as it was over, I came
out a new creature, and from that moment up to this, I have
been steadily improving. You never saw me when I was so
well as I am now. Dear, good Captain Lay watches my face.
and notices every change, and it is "now you have a head
ache," or " I shall not ask you how you are this morning—your
face tells," or " now you need this," etc. His kindness is almost
incredible. Every morning after I got well enough to go on
deck, he would come to my cabin door, and tell me whether I
had better come out or not, what shawl to wear, etc., and during the gales, when we were all shut up in our darkened cabins,
he took my boys and Mrs. Thomas's into his cabin to relieve
us, and—but there is no use in trying to enumerate—he does
EVERY thing. His attentions to us who have no protectors, are
not merely the attentions of a courteous gentlemanly commander, but the thoughtful watchfulness of a brother or husband.

"I beg," she says in a letter to her sister, " that you
will never call the English cold-hearted any more. So
far as I have seen here, they are *all* heart ; and even

you and Mrs. Stevens could scarcely be kinder to me than six or eight of the prominent passengers on the *Tudor.*"

About the first of June they left Cape Town, and reached London about the middle of August. "I find my health," she writes to Dr. Peck, "improved by the voyage, long and stormy as it was, and the sallow Indian cheeks of my children are beginning to glow with English roses." She took quiet lodgings at the West End, but the kindness of her English friends soon drew her from them, and gave her fresh tokens of that large English hospitality which she had so often experienced in the East. She made her stay chiefly with W. B. Gurney, Esq., and with Rev. Joseph Angus, of Stepney College. Her stay in London, though fatiguing was very delightful. Besides visiting the principal objects of interest to a stranger, and being "introduced to a wide circle of English acquaintances," and forming "ties which death will not have the power to dissever," she also met Rev. Messrs. Oncken and Lehman, from the Continent, and expresses her peculiar pleasure in meeting "many who have hazarded their lives for Christ, and others, their still dearer reputations."

CHAPTER XXII.

"Dear mother, in thy prayer to-night
There come new hopes and warmer tears;
On long, long darkness breaks the light—
Comes back the loved, the lost for years."

BUT her heart was hastening homeward, and the generous kindness of her British friends could detain her but little over a month. On the 20th of September she embarked from Liverpool, in the steamer *Canada*, for Boston, and early in October, 1851, set foot on her native shores—a little more than five years after she had left it for the East. How different the present from that hour of weeping gladness! Yet the welcome she now received was undoubtedly more deep and heartfelt than the tumultuous God-speed which had accompanied her departure. Then, misgivings existed in many minds that would not utter them, lest the brilliant romance-writer might fail in the practical qualities and self-denying duties of the missionary. She had gone through the ordeal, and come out, like gold from the furnace, approved and refined. She had proved a faithful wife to Dr. Judson, and a most competent mother to his children. She had entered zealously, intelligently, and efficiently into his labors; had overcome all prejudices, and won the hearts alike of the native Christians and of her associates in the mission. She had shown great natural cour-

age, tempered and exalted by Christian principle. She
had borne up under her crushing weight of sorrow with
a high, heroic heart; and, now that she brought back
her deceased husband's children from the scene of his
life-labors, the enthusiasm of her reception might well
be "not loud, but deep," and the welcome which greeted
her, not from the lips of the many, but from the hearts
of the few. Among others was her daughter Abby Ann,
and her faithful friend, Miss Sheldon, came on from
Philadelphia.

The fatigue and excitement of landing, however, were
too much for her frail constitution, and she was immediately attacked by an illness which confined her several
days to the bed. She had intended making an immediate visit to Miss A. Judson, at Plymouth, but was
obliged to forego it, and proceed with the least possible
delay to Hamilton. She had previously to make a disposition of the elder sons, Adoniram and Elnathan, and
of Abby Ann, all of whom were placed at once upon
her hands. Her slender health rendered impossible her
assuming the care of more than the three younger ones,
whom she had brought from India. She was relieved
from her anxiety regarding the two elder sons by the
kindness of Dr. and Mrs. Bright, who received them as
members of their own family; Abby Ann she determined to place with Miss Anable, assured that she would
be watched over with equal judiciousness and affection.
These arrangements made, she proceeded to Hamilton—
Miss Sheldon and Abby Ann accompanying her. The
meeting with the loved home circle I shall not attempt
to describe, nor the emotions with which she recrossed
the paternal threshold. With a deeper emphasis and a
profounder meaning might she now have said:

A welcome for thy child, father,
   A welcome give to-day,
Although she may not come to thee
   As when she went away.

It was now, not the poetry, but the reality, of change. "Long years—long, though not very many"—had written their record of stern experiences on her brow and heart. Providence had falsified her predictions, and brought them together again on this side of the final meeting-place. Little was changed in the outward aspect of her home, and the years that had been so eventful to her had glided tranquilly over the heads of its inmates. But her mother's form had lost much of its erectness; time had plowed deeper furrows into the cheek of her father; and her brother Wallace had matured and changed beyond her recognition; but the old affection glowed in the hearts of all. She had sought and found the ark once more, and into the bosom of maternal and sisterly love she could pour out all her joys and all her sorrows.

She had received on landing the intelligence that Elnathan was rejoicing in a newly found hope in Christ. No tidings could be more joyful to her than that her late husband's children were walking in the truth. With her joy, however, she mingled discretion, and wrote to him, advising a little deferral of a public profession by baptism. She adds, however: "In the meantime, do not forget that you have 'put on Christ' in deed and in word; that you are, as we humbly trust, a member of His spiritual, though not yet united to His visible Church: and strive to honor Him in all things. Let 'the beauty of holiness' be continually visible in your charac-

ter, and try to win Adoniram to the shelter of the same
cross, not so much by words (though words are sometimes necessary), as by showing him what a lovely thing
it is to be conformed to Christ."

An early object of attention was the securing of a
memoir of her late husband, such as should meet the
public demand, and do justice to such a life. The Executive Committee of the Union, whose servant he
had been for many years, proffered their utmost aid in
its accomplishment. Through their agency, Rev. Dr.
Wayland was engaged to prepare the work, Mrs. Judson
undertaking to collect and arrange the materials. With
generous benevolence Dr. Wayland proposed to execute
his part of the work without compensation, leaving its
entire profits to the widow and children. This arrangement made it necessary for her to pass the winter in
Providence, after a brief visit to her daughter and
friends in Philadelphia.

Another attack of illness (her steadily intermittent
friend), and she proceeded early in November to Philadelphia. She found Abby Ann happily situated. The
meeting with her friends of so many years—the dearest
out of her own father's house—whose faithful love and
sympathy had followed all her checkered fortunes, could
not but be deeply affecting. They had watched the
dawning of her literary reputation ; with them she had
shared all her sweetest and bitterest experiences ; and
the renewal of her friendship with them was among
the dearest joys which she could now promise to herself on earth. Her stay with them, however, was short ;
and having refreshed herself by the communion of friendship, and made the needed arrangements for her daughter, she hastened on to Providence to the work which

she felt among her most immediate and sacred obligations. She took lodgings for herself and the three children that had gladdened her Indian home ; the elder
boys were with Dr. Bright in Roxbury, and Geo. D.
Boardman, a member of Brown University, was able
to beguile many of her desolate hours with conversation
and reading.

On the first of December she sent out her missives in
all directions in quest of materials. Her efforts were not
very successful. Dr. Judson's utter disregard, or rather
morbid dread of posthumous reputation, had secured the
destruction of all papers illustrative of his life, over
which he had any control ; and time, fire, and water had
done an effectual work on the bulk of his correspondence.
The ample records of the mission rooms were placed at
her disposal ; some valuable documents were furnished
by individuals ; and her personal reminiscences would,
of course, abundantly illustrate that portion of his
history with which her own was linked.

Thus armed with her documents, she went to work,
reading, selecting, copying, digesting, commenting, and
where her own knowledge availed, filling out the deficient materials, and thus pioneering the path of the
biographer. The industry and judgment with which she
performed her task were alike remarkable. So ill that
she could write but a few hours a day, and then suffering from a pain in the side which made writing a torture, she wrought steadily on, bending into shape and
preparing for use the intractable materials.

"Whatever value this memoir may possess," says Dr.
Wayland in his preface, "must be ascribed in no small
degree to the assistance which I have received from Mrs.
Judson. She arranged for me all the letters and papers,

furnished me with information which no other person
could possess, and has communicated notes and reminiscences which will be found among the most interesting
portions of the work."

Dr. Wayland's reminiscences of Mrs. Judson at this
time, and his general estimate of her character, he has
kindly furnished to me in the following interesting and
most just article :

PROVIDENCE, Aug. 1, 1860.

REV. AND DEAR SIR,—

In compliance with your request, I cheerfully send you
a few reminiscences of the late Mrs. Emily Judson. I regret
that they are so brief and imperfect. I commenced them some
time since, but an attack of illness obliged me to lay them
aside, and now I am unable to do much more than transcribe
what I had then written.

My acquaintance with Mrs. Judson hardly commenced before
her return from Burmah. I had seen her for a few minutes
on two previous occasions, but had no conversation with her
beyond the interchange of ordinary civilities. I had been led
to suppose that she devoted herself exclusively to light literature, and though I have heard her spoken of as a person of
sincere piety, had formed no exaggerated anticipations of her
success as a missionary. During her absence, I learned with
some surprise that she had acquired the Burmese language with
almost unprecedented facility ; that she was able to use it in
conversation and in devotional meetings with the natives; and
had composed some hymns in this difficult tongue, for the worship of the sanctuary. It was soon told of her how she had
surpassed the anticipations of her friends ; how in delicate
health she had distinguished herself by self denying labors for
the salvation of the women of Burmah, and had cheerfully
accompanied her husband to Rangoon, where she would be iso-
lated entirely from European civilization, and be exposed to the

ragings of a fanatical mob, and the caprices of ignorant and despotic power.

Shortly after her return, it fell to my lot to prepare a memoir of Dr. Judson, and in this labor I was permitted to avail myself of her assistance. For this purpose she came to Providence, and resided for several months in my immediate neighborhood. I of course saw her very frequently, and was in the habit of conversing with her with the utmost freedom respecting missions in general, and the missions to the East in particular ; and, in fact, on almost every subject connected with the progress of religion in the world.

The first thing that struck me, upon becoming acquainted with Mrs. Judson, was the remarkable contrast that presented itself between her material and spiritual nature. She had been ill during almost the whole of her residence in Burmah, and was incurably sick on her arrival in this country. I think I never saw a person, able to walk across a room, whose motions indicated so great a degree of physical debility. It seemed as though she would have fallen to the floor, if any person had accidentally jostled against her. She was generally unable to rise before ten o'clock in the morning, and was confined to the couch for the greater part of the day. She was, for a time, a member of my family, and I strongly urged upon her slight exercise in the open air. She took my advice and made the attempt. I however found immediately that I had mistaken her case, and that an effort which I considered very slight, was wholly beyond her strength. I was perfectly willing, afterwards, to allow her to judge for herself in all matters respecting her health. I would not convey the idea that she was always at this point of extreme debility. She was at times slightly invigorated, but each alternation of improvement and decline left her more thoroughly prostrated, until she entered into rest.

But in the midst of this exhausting debility, her intellect retained a vigor which I have rarely seen equaled. So complete a victory of mind over matter it has never been my good fortune elsewhere to observe. Over that feeble and attenuated body she exercised a perfect control, and all that it was possible for it to do it did at her bidding. Though sinking steadily into the grave, she was able to accomplish more than most women in perfect health. She was actively employed in arranging for my use the voluminous letters and papers from which her husband's memoir was compiled. At the same time she felt it necessary to write for the press, and prepare her works for new editions; her correspondence was extensive; and the care of her husband's family, which had devolved upon her, was exercised with incessant vigilance, and a soundness of judgment and tenderness of affection which I have rarely seen equaled. Those who knew of her only as the author of pleasant tales for the young, could hardly believe that the power of condensed thought, the logical acuteness, and the indignant sarcasm which marked her letters to a certain New York publisher, could have proceeded from the pen of Fanny Forester. Those, however, who knew her intimately, perceived in them nothing but the workings of a mind which they knew to be equal to any emergency, intensified by the necessity laid upon her of guarding the character of her husband from misrepresentation, and of defending the interests of her children, soon to be left orphans, from what she believed to be a selfish and cruel injustice.

Her religious character was elevated and equable. Her faith rarely faltered, even in times of the sorest extremity. She had formed the habit of relying on her Father in heaven as a living and ever present God, who had always cared for her as beloved child, and she never doubted that He would do so to the end. Conscious that she in all things submitted to His will, and desired in all things to serve Him, she relied in implicit faith on all His promises. That God would help her in every extremity, and guide her by His wisdom to correct decisions, seemed with her a thing taken for granted. Yet it was not a boastful and loud-spoken trust that animated her. It revealed itself only to her most intimate friends, and to them only inci-

dentally. It was a guiding and directing power that responded
to every prayer, but of which she only spoke when the particular occasion seemed to render it appropriate. Such occasions
might occur when she differed in opinion on some practical
matter from her counsellors. They then saw that there was
an unerring Guide, on whom she relied in preference to all the
wisdom of this world; nor was her trust often disappointed.

Her piety was, besides, of the most cheerful character. She
seemed habitually to live on the borders of the unseen world,
and almost within sight and hearing of its glorious realities. The friend whom she loved best was already there, and
she seemed ever in the enjoyment of his society. She knew
that their separation from each other must be short, and while
on earth she was intensely desirous to complete, as far as possible, the work which he had left unfinished. This idea expanded
itself over every thing that pertained to the cause of the Redeemer on earth. She was sustained in every labor by the
thought that she was coöperating, not only with the good on
earth, but with the holy in heaven, and suffering for Him who
is the Captain of our salvation.

Nor was there in all this any thing dreamy or mystical. She
was an eminently practical woman, and a most accurate judge
of character. In this latter respect her sagacity was unerring.
Her administrative talent was remarkable, and would have easily
placed her in the front rank, whenever she was called upon to
coöperate with others.

To all these, which rank among the stronger elements of
character, she added exquisite feminine delicacy, and great per-
manency and strength of affection. No person could possibly
have been rude or unfeeling to a woman of so refined sensibilities. Her poetical address to her mother presents a true picture
of her affections. To her mother she was attached with more
than filial love, yet the outgoings of the same sentiments were
manifest to all that she had ever loved, or who had ever done
her a kindness.

For several of the last years of Mrs. Judson's life, she resided at so great a distance from Providence that I did not often see her. Her final sickness and death were, however, in all respects similar to her life. I count it a special blessing that I had the pleasure of her acquaintance, and that I was permitted, in some humble manner, to alleviate her sorrows, and assist her to bear the burdens which our Heavenly Father saw fit to lay upon her.

I doubt not that the memoir which you have prepared will make it evident that I have in no manner exaggerated the remarkable elements of the character of Mrs. Judson.

I am, reverend and dear sir,

Yours truly,
F. WAYLAND.

CHAPTER XXIII.

THE RESTRUNG HARP.

"My gentle harp, once more I waken
  The sweetness of thy slumbering strain;
In tears our last farewell was taken,
  And now in tears we meet again."

TOWARD the close of the winter, having completed the heaviest part of her labor on the memoir, she turned to authorship on her own account, and commenced the preparation of a volume of poems, consisting of some of her earlier pieces, and such of her later ones as were unpublished, or floating in the public journals. She called it an "Olio of Domestic Verses," "as," she says, "I am not a poet, and am not going to claim to be one on my title-page." It was sent in May, "after innumerable touchings and polishings," to Mr. Colby of New York for publication. There doubtless are some pieces in the volume which can claim to be only "verses;" others which are poetry, though unfinished; but others which are the sterling article, and which, in spite of her disclaimers, vindicate for her that "glance of melancholy" which is the "fearful gift" of the poet. I reserve more specific remarks for the notice of its publication.

Mrs. Judson had been much tried in regard to her permanent arrangements for herself and children. Her favorite idea had been to gather them under one roof and commence housekeeping; but hitherto the miserable state of her health had almost cut off the hope of realizing her desire. Her health had latterly improved, and she again began to contemplate the measure, and balance the claims of different localities. Warm and cherished friendships, a mild climate, and city advantages for her children, concurred in recommending Philadelphia; but its expensiveness formed, with her limited resources and delicate health, a serious objection, and after all her heart turned back to Hamilton. The home of her parents, with its quiet rural beauty, and excellent school advantages, attracted her thither. She purchased a larger and more commodious house, with the purpose of removing her parents into it, and, if unable to spend the entire year there herself, of making it a summer residence, and an occasional gathering place for the children.

Before leaving Providence in May, she had contemplated making a visit with her children to Miss Abigail Judson at Plymouth, and had fixed the day for her going; but her life-enemy prevented. A fresh attack of bleeding at the lungs (she had repeatedly raised blood during the winter, and had cough and pulmonary fever) prostrated her; and it was deemed madness for her to go, at that season, into so rough a climate as that of Plymouth. As soon, therefore, as she rallied from her attack she proceeded to Hamilton, whither also she was called by the serious illness of her mother. In June, she took possession of her new house and commenced housekeeping.

Early in August she had a family reunion—all the surviving children who had sustained blood or legal relations to her late husband and herself, being gathered into one group. Being on the eve of departure for Europe,

I now spent a few days at Hamilton, and had the pleasure of seeing them together. The house which they occupied had formerly been my home, and many painfully pleasing associations clustered about it. It needed but a glance to see that they were a very happy family, and that the mother, with no natural tie to either of them but one, moved among them as a superior spirit, gentle, affectionate, intellectual, swaying them with the sure mastery of knowledge and of love. They had an evening gathering of many village friends, at which they exhibited a series of tableaux, arranged under the presiding skill and taste of the mother. The scenes were mostly oriental ; and veritable oriental costumes brought the strange and picturesque life of the East vividly before the eye, while they must have crowded her heart with at once happy and tearful memories.

I had not before seen Mrs. Judson since she moved among us a happy bride on the eve of her departure for India. "Time had not blanched a single hair" that clustered around her smooth and ample forehead. It had but touched her features with a soft and mellowing hand, and rounded her slender form into somewhat more of matronly fullness and dignity. The varied experiences and larger intercourse of life had given ease and polish to her manner ; and the companionship of her noble husband, and the inspiring scenes with which she had been conversant, had lent a deeper light to her eye, and depth and ripeness to her whole tone of thought and conversation. Altogether she was a rare specimen of womanly loveliness ; not handsome with any commonplace prettiness of feature ; but her dark eye and intellectual countenance beaming with those spiritual graces which lend her highest charm to woman. Her conver-

sation, turning on many topics, was free and vivacious ;
with none of the slight tinge of affectation which in earlier
years timidity had sometimes forced upon her ; but replete
at once with feminine delicacy and masculine good sense ;
while the exceeding feebleness of her health scarcely lowered the buoyancy of her spirits. I parted from her,
strongly hoping that the delicate flower, so manifestly
blooming for Paradise, might shed its fragrance through
many earthly summers ; I returned a little more than a
year later to find it already drooping on its stalk, and
bending toward the tomb.

"My health," she writes to her friend Miss Haven,
"is better than when I saw you last winter, and if I
could only get strong enough to sit up all day, I would
keep my children all together. The little warning cough,
however, haunts me still, so the will of God be done !
. . I do not feel anxious about the memoir, but a
good deal discouraged. The lost papers and the nameless grave seem to me just a part of the oblivion he
courted." Her discouragement, I need scarcely say, had
respect exclusively to the scantiness of materials.

The family gathering, delightful as it was, could last
but a few weeks. Early in September, Abby Ann left
for Philadelphia, and on the Sabbath preceding Mrs.
Judson had the satisfaction of seeing Adoniram and
Elnathan baptized into the communion of the Church.
She writes, September 9, to Miss A. Judson :

"You may be assured, my dear sister, that to me it was a
day of mingled rejoicing and trembling. The boys will remain
with me until I can secure them some good place. They are
getting so old now that board and the proper care while they
are fitting for college will cost me many days and nights of
hard labor ; but if it be God's will that I should live to care for

them, to labor and suffer, it is all that I ask. To train up the six children committed to my care for usefulness in this world and happiness in the next, is all that I can hope to do. Abby left under more serious impressions, probably, than she ever had before in her life. May God bless the conversion of her brothers to her own conversion."

September 11 she writes thus to Abby Ann :

"I have just wiped up eyes after reading your tear-provoking letter. . . . —— has been very kind to you, but, my dear child, do not let your serious impressions evaporate in gratitude toward him. Think how infinitely more the Saviour has done for you, is doing for you even now ; and how He stands pleading with His Father to spare you yet another year. Do not, my darling, allow these feelings to pass without any result except the hardening influence which such feelings are sure to produce unless they soften. . . . Meanwhile, my daughter, try to be conciliating. Adopt your father's motto, 'Sweet in temper, face, and words.' Another of his mottoes was, 'Sweetness is the blossom, love the root, and kindness the fruit of true virtue.' "

During the summer Mrs. Judson contributed occasionally, as her health allowed, to *The Macedonian*, a small monthly sheet of the Missionary Union. In August the "Olio" appeared, accompanied by a modest and graceful preface, deprecating severe criticism, and stating that some of the pieces were written in early childhood. This is very well, yet "a book's a book," and no amount of deprecatory prefacing, probably, can or should shield a writer who comes voluntarily before the public from an impartial estimate of its merits. The reception of the "Olio," though favorable, was not enthusiastic. Its plan, as a collection in part of her juvenile pieces, while it might gratify her friends, and mark her intellectual progress, stood yet in the way of its general popularity. It would have been wiser to pitch the tone of the book and her poetic claims higher, inserting nothing but what was worthy of her matured powers, and leaving the gleanings from her portfolio to another and later hand. Some of the pieces, too, whose merit warrants their insertion, should have been subjected to a severer criticism. The two or three epigrams have not sufficient wit and point to redeem their want of dignity. "The September Rain" is an obvious imitation of the "Last Leaf," but with none of the mingled humor and pathos, and the delicate finish of that exquisite *jeu d'esprit.* "Peter" is modeled upon Longfellow's "Skeleton in Armor;" but the wild and somewhat rough structure of the verse is less adapted to the subject than to that of the weird Scandinavian legend : still, with some faults of execution, it is a poem of much picturesque and descriptive power. "Samson" is a sort of rude torso, containing the elements, imperfectly worked up, of a fine poem. Some of the lighter pieces, as "My Bonny Sleigh," "Thou hast left me alone," etc., are replete with the delicate and airy grace of the genuine song writer. "Stern Duty" is spirited and brilliant—an outgush of excited and lofty feelings. Its difficult structure makes success in it a greater triumph ; and the noble strain of the poem, and the perfection of parts of it, make us doubly regret the lack of polish in the rest. "The Choice" is an ideal representation of the youthful Judson turning away from the lures of science, poesy, and eloquence, that he may devote himself to the divine work of bearing the message of spiritual life to the nations. The conception is happy, and though written because she was too ill to do any thing else, it is wrought with no little poetic power. The "Wan Reapers," though one of her later pieces, and on a favorite topic, is one of her least successful ones. The prosaic harshness of such lines, as

For laborers, for laborers, we pray;

and the tautological tameness of a line, like

There the rose never blooms on fair woman's wan cheek,

should have laid them under the ban of a taste less severe than that of Mrs. Judson. Woman has been "fair" ever since the days of Eve and Helen, and we need not be told that the cheek is "wan," upon which the "rose never blooms," besides that "fair" and "wan" stand in almost incongruous relation.

But while open to these criticisms, it is but justice to add that the volume evinces throughout much poetic feeling, power of language, and skill in versification; and that some of the pieces, especially those which turn on her heart history, are, in conception and execution, almost faultless. "Love's Last Wish," "My Bird," "Contentment," "Watching," "Angel Charlie," "Sweet Mother," "The Southern Cross," are poems in which the deepest emotions of the heart gush forth in a tide of purest song, and which, while taste and feeling live, will be reckoned among the Muses' choicest breathings. They are the distillation of the life-drops of a most sensitive and exquisite nature, and have the merit which belongs to the blending of the finest powers of fancy and feeling. Though feeling is her deepest fountain of inspiration, and she is most successful in themes dictated by the heart, yet even in these the passionate

element is by no means exclusive, nor always predomi-
nant. Her imagination idealizes the creation of passion,
and taste, instinctive and unerring, presides over their
joint creation. Thus, in **several** of **her** pieces, the
rhythm, the metre, the structure of the stanza, the imagery, all unite harmoniously in one common impression.
"Contentment" is a beautiful, though not the most striking example.   In " Watching," the lines swell and undu-
late to the passing emotion with the elasticity of air ; the
elements which make up the picture of an oriental night
are happily selected ; and the same power of imagination
which makes Lear reproach the heavens for storming on
his aged head, "for that ye yourselves are old," makes
the very shadows to sway to her eye

> With gentle human care,
> Compassionate and dumb.

   "Sweet Mother" is even more remarkable—a piece
over which the very "blackness of darkness" seems to
brood, scarcely illuminated at the close by some glimpses
of light, enough to relieve the intensity of gloom, but
not to impair the general keeping. of the picture. The
imagery is all harmonious ; the successive elements are
poured drop by drop into the bitter cup of her misery ;
the intensified repetition of each closing line (finer in
this respect than that in Hoyt's " Old") sounds like an
echo from the sepulchre, while the opening—

> The wild southwest monsoon has risen
> On broad, gray wings of gloom—

is at once one of the finest of images, and forms a fitting
prelude to the dreary monotone of woe which follows.

These, with several pieces written subsequently, must take their place among the precious poetical gems of our literature. Their emotional intensity and strictly individual character may, perhaps, keep them from being bandied about in school-books and volumes of elegant extracts. We shrink from playing with heart-strings, and regaling our ears with even the most melodious utterances of real woe. When, however, sorrow is idealized, as in Milton's "Lycidas"and Mrs. Judson's "Angel-Guide"—when passion puts on the drapery of imagination—we may gratify our tastes without reproaching ourselves with invading the sanctity of grief.

The first edition of the "Olio" was soon exhausted, and a second was called for in September. Still her moderate expectations of profit from it were not more than met. She had a heavy charge upon her hands—really not less than ten persons—for whose support the income from her deceased husband's property, from Alderbrook, and from the memoir of Mrs. Sarah B. Judson (which, since her return, had been made over to her by the Executive Board), was, even with the rigid economy which she knew so well how to practice, entirely inadequate. The provision made by the Union for the widows of missionaries, she had, from motives of delicacy, declined receiving, and felt the necessity of exerting her powers to the utmost.

She now prepared a volume which might at once supply her deficient income and aid the cause (dearest to her of all) of foreign missions. It was made up of missionary essays, written for the *Macedonian,* and of several other essays and poems, hitherto unpublished. It was entitled the "Kathayan Slave," from the opening narrative of the book, which recounts a scene of horrible cruelty and torture that occurred in the prison at Ava, during the English and Burmese war of 1826. It was published by Ticknor & Fields, of Boston, but failed of a reception corresponding with its merits. Its elements of interest were too remote, perhaps, for popular apprehension and sympathy ; but I doubt if anything from her pen gives to the thoughtful reader a higher impression of her genius. Its picturesque and dramatic talent is the same that enlivens the pages of Fanny Forester, while the chastened and sustained diction is suited to the position of the writer and the gravity of the themes discussed. The "Kathayan Slave," the "Legend of the Maizen," and "Wayside Preaching," are all wrought with admirable simplicity, beauty, and pathos. The "Madness of the Missionary Enterprise" finds its text in several diatribes of journals and reviews on the reckless waste of life in modern missions, while it draws its *occasional* inspiration from the tomb of Ann H. Judson, beside which it was written, during her month's stay with her sick husband at Amherst. It is a most beautiful and eloquent plea for missions—an argument of masculine cogency, distilled in the alembic of a woman's heart. It exhibits the so-called infatuation of the votaries of missions in a light which assures us that it *must* spring from some higher than earthly principle ; finds that animating principle in *love*, and closes with a glowing prediction of its destined triumph. It is argument running molten in a tide of holy passion.

Of the poetic pieces, the Lines to Rev. Daniel Hascall, are a tribute to a man of rare personal excellence, who, as a leading founder of the seminary that has sent forth such a host of missionaries, had wrought powerfully, though indirectly, on the mission cause. One of the finest little pieces in the volume delineates a most touching scene connected with the death of Boardman. It is a sketch full of life and beauty, redolent of the fragrance and glowing with the sunshine of an Oriental landscape. It is a fit companion-piece to " Watching," reproducing, like that, with great vividness, the peculiar features of the Orient ; like that in its beautiful blending of the physical with the moral ; and, like that, shedding the charm of verse over the dying agonies of a Christian hero.

In November, Mrs. Judson, having placed her older sons with Rev. Mr. Aldritch, of Middleborough, Mass., to be prepared for college, went again to Philadelphia, to avoid the rigors of a New York winter, visit with her friends there, and watch over the rapidly developing character of her daughter, Abby Ann. Henry and Edward she left in Hamilton, under the care of Mr. Osborne, a student in the University, in whose piety and discretion she reposed much confidence. " My Bird" went with her.

The reader will remember that just seven years had elapsed since, in this very month, Fanny Forester, then in the full flush of her new found reputation, had come to the same place on the same errand, in part, as now—the enjoying of a milder climate. How had that coming controlled her destiny ! Thither Providence soon after brought Dr. Judson ; and thence on, through the intervening seven years, what a rush of unlooked for and strange experiences had swept over her outward and her inner life ! The wife of one of the world's moral heroes —five years spent among dark faces and darker hearts, amidst luxuriant nature and a dwarfed civilization, on the opposite side of the globe—widowed under circumstances of fearful agony, and now (broken in health and—no, not blighted in spirit)—again at home, the mother of six fatherless children, and again in the city where she had met the dear departed, and vowed the vow that had linked their destinies for eternity ! What emotions crowd upon her as she thinks of the now and the then, and the tide of experiences that roll between ! Does she question her own identity ? Whether she, the bereaved one, that, " with weary foot and broken wing," seeks now the sheltering bosom of love, is the laughing, buoyant Fanny Forester of that earlier day ?

And what verdict does she pronounce on the past—on the choice which then linked hers to a missionary's lot ? Would she turn back to the cup of sweetness which mantled to her lips, from that cup of bitterness which she has drunk ? Would she turn back to the path which lay so bright before her, from the thorny way which she has trodden ? Would she clutch at the chaplet of earthly fame, that promised to grace her brows, and fling aside the " iron cross—the diadem," which is her pledge of immortality ? Did she ask herself these questions, and can we doubt what was her reply ? Can we doubt that her heart swelled with grateful joy to the Saviour who had ordained her lot with such severity of kindness ; who had turned her from the phantoms of earth to the realities of heaven ; who had linked her life, however short and troubled, with those great moral movements which, as certainly as the truth of God, are to open out into the consummated glories of a world's redemption ?

CHAPTER XXIV.

THE MOTHER.

"Still with thoughtful care providing,
Sweetly ruling, softly chiding,—
Such the mother's gentle guiding."

MRS. JUDSON spent the winter with her friends, Miss Sheldon and the Anables. On her arrival in Philadelphia she found that Abby Ann's religious seriousness had ripened into a confirmed Christian hope, and she had the pleasure of witnessing her public profession of her faith in Christ. In reference to her coming baptism she writes to the boys:

It will not be as pleasant as last summer—but God will accept the act of public consecration all the same. I did not wish Abby to hurry matters; but to neglect so grave a thing as taking a decided stand for Christ among her schoolmates, simply because it would be more gratifying to defer the act of obedience, made me fear that if God did not punish us all by clouding over our next family meeting, He might withdraw some of His sunshine from her heart. It is better even in the smallest things to obey God than to please ourselves; or rather, it is better to find our pleasure and happiness in obeying Him. It was decidedly Abby's preference, in view of all things, to go

17

forward now. She is very steadfast, as well as very gentle and lovely.

We have all been suffering from influenza. Eddy has recovered, but poor little Emmy is making a fortnight fever of it, and I am not much behind her. I chanced to hear Abby remark, the other day, that she wished, if her brothers sent her any Christmas presents, they would send *something of their own manufacture*, and not buy. Perhaps you are not aware how much more valuable, in the eyes of those who love you, such gifts are, than those that come out of a shop. "A word to the wise," etc.

Elly, you know that I am no enemy to "corn and chestnuts," except as my own weak stomach might soon cry "enough." . . . You are no great capitalist now, to be sure, and are not likely to be, if you become a minister or missionary; but always consider yourself the steward of God, even if you have but a penny, and use your penny conscientiously. Have under all circumstances, even if it should be your lot to be subjected to poverty and sickness, a little sacred fund, etc., etc. You know all I would say, and a great deal more than I can say in so small a compass. And I do not write all this because I am afraid you will fail in being generous and charitable, but because I want you to have some system in your benevolence, and never to regard giving or not giving as a mere matter of preference. Neither do I, as I said before, think corn and chestnuts *wickedness*. Bread and butter may be made wicked, under certain circumstances. Now even chestnuts are indifferent matters—to be had or not had, as things may go—but your mite for the Lord's treasury is not a thing of indifference. . . .

I am glad you skate—only look out for a safe place, remembering that the shallowness of the water would contribute little to your safety with your head under ice. I like to have you engage heartily in all these winter sports, and with equal heartiness in your studies. "A healthy mind in a healthy body" is beyond price. My dear boys, you do not know how thankful

I feel to our Heavenly Father for all His kindness to us in our desolation, and especially for having taken so many of the family, as I trust, into His own great family. . . . Abby sends a hundred *somethings* of love, and Emmy something which seems to stick half way between *kitties* and *kishes*.

FROM A LETTER OF **A LITTLE** EARLIER DATE TO ABBY ANN.

My DEAREST ABBY—

I have been amused, pained, pleased, and deeply interested, by your frank, open-hearted letter, received this morning.

> "Standing with reluctant feet,
> Where the brook and river meet,
> Womanhood and childhood fleet;
>
> Gazing, with a timid glance,
> On the brooklet's swift advance,
> On the river's broad expanse :"—

There is where you are, my dear child; you are too old to be a little girl any more, and you are not yet prepared to be a woman. This is an awkward point in the life of most girls. R—— L—— has passed gracefully over it, because (that is, in my hasty judgment, for you know I have seen but little of her), she is of a natural temperament too serene to be disturbed by *any thing*. With you it would naturally be otherwise, but never mind that; you will be in the broad, deep river soon, and then I expect to see you, if not a model woman, a very intelligent, agreeable, useful one. You need not apologize for writing me *such* letters. I want heart letters—all your little troubles, and big ones, too—your resolutions broken or kept. I think, though some would disagree with me, that it is better to make a resolution and break it, than not to make one at all, just as it is better to try to be good, and fail, than never to try. I am glad you " knew what I would say," even though you are so faithless. Prayer is your only hope, connected with constant effort. The whole of life is a struggle with the evil that is in us, and God is our only efficient helper. Do you not believe that I would lift you out of all your embarrassments in one moment if I could? Christ loves you infinitely more than I do—more than your own sainted mamma, even—and will not He afford you assistance? But He is so much wiser than I that He knows how much self-culture, how much discipline, how much faith and trust you need, and He is watching and waiting to assist you in the most efficient manner. It is not His purpose to make you a passive recipient of His bounty—a mere machine—and in your wiser moments you would not wish that. Persevere, then, in resolving, and praying, and endeavoring, and so sure as the promise of God, you will be successful. But do not think, my dear child, that the only place to pray is on your knees in the closet. This ought to be done, formally, at least twice every day; but this does not fulfill the apostolic injunction, "Pray without ceasing." Whenever temptation comes in your way through the day—when you feel anger rising—when you go to study a lesson, but, more particularly, when you enter the recitation room, let your ejaculation rise from your heart, though your eye may be open and your lip smiling; "O God, help me!"— "Make me wise!"—"Make me calm!"—"Give me the right feeling!"—"Control my tongue!"—"Give me patience!" Any thing that you feel you have need of, ask in a single thought, and it will soon become habitual to you. This practice you will find a source of great power.

I certainly do not think a young lady "who never read a novel in her life" the best person to direct your reading. I would not object to a volume of Scott for you in vacation, and neither, I think, would Miss Anable. I would rather, however, you would do but little reading in term time, for the reason that I suspect your general reading already to be in advance of your school education; and you will have plenty of time to read when you get too old to attend school. Scott is a healthful writer, both of prose and poetry, and Campbell's poetry is a

thing for you to read and re-read when you get time from school
duties. But I do not like to have you read Moore. Lalla
Rookh is exceedingly beautiful; but a girl reading it is very
much in the condition of a fly in a pot of honey—a girl of feeling and imagination, I mean. I dare say there are girls so
insensible as not to be injured by it. . . .

I give these simply as specimens of the very large correspondence which Mrs. Judson carried on with her
children. It would be impossible, without far more
copious extracts than my limits would allow, and impossible even then, to do justice to the unwearied care,
the judicious and patient fidelity with which she discharged her relation to them as a mother, and watched
over all their interests. Nothing was too minute for her
vigilant eye ; nothing deemed unimportant of the thousand elements that might go to form their characters and
determine their destiny. Her care extended to all points
of manners, habits, mental and moral culture and growth,
while, at the same time, she studied carefully their
diversities of temperament, and cherished, rather than
repressed, their buoyancy of spirit. There was nothing
narrow, or obtrusive in her care. She discriminated
clearly between the essential and the non-essential ;
made large allowances for the natural thoughtlessness
of youth ; knew how to allow a generous liberty for
all that was innocent, and yet to guard sedulously
against the first encroachment on the forbidden or
doubtful region. Hence she exercised over her children,
through all stages of their culture, an almost unbounded
influence. They felt that her hand was equally gentle
and firm ; that her care was equally affectionate and
discriminating ; that she looked down into the depth of
their natures, and understood better than themselves

both their motives and their interests. She was thus
exceedingly successful in her training, and even those of
the children who had passed the impressible period of childhood, felt, during their brief visits with her, powerfully
her influence for good. And especially her ardent desire
and her unwearied effort was to lead them into the path
of piety. Few of her letters but that urge upon them
affectionately their spiritual duties—upon those who had
made no profession of piety, the duty of seeking the
Saviour—upon those who had, the duty of growing Christian consecration.

During December and the early part of January, Mrs.
Judson's health so far improved that she half indulged
the hope of permanent recovery. "I am getting," she
writes, "*so* well, I do not fear the cold weather;" and
she was meditating a return to Hamilton during the
winter. But these bright prospects were suddenly over-
clouded. She was seized, about the middle of January,
with congestion of the lungs, which confined her to her
room, and much of her time to her bed. She wrote
to George Boardman:

My pen is not very busy. I can not take it up but I get a
genuine scolding. I am afraid I shall never write any more,
and so we shall have to take to *starvation* for a living. But
what *can* you mean by complimenting my skill in polemics?
I never wielded a lance except once, to ward off the attack of
dear, good ———, and then I put a feather pillow on the end.
I have rather taken to rhyming than fighting, and mean to
take out a patent for my machine. The "Kathayan Slave,"
the title of my forthcoming work, is nearly half through the
press."

Here an ominous gape in the letter shows that the

coil of disease was drawn still tighter around her, and that her prospects of labor were even more seriously broken in upon. Her letters to her children, however, were never neglected while she could hold a pen, and they always breathe the same cheerful, loving, Christian spirit.

Her literary labors were, of course, in a great measure suspended. Still, besides carrying the "Kathayan Slave" through the press, she found time and strength to draw up that touching little memorial of sisterly affection, "My Two Sisters," subsequently published by Ticknor & Fields. She also wrote some very sweet pieces of poetry : among them, "The Child of Sin," a touching ballad, founded on fact ; "St. Valentine's Eve," exquisite in its finish, and "My Angel Guide." The following little piece was addressed to Abby Ann, in connection with a Christmas present of a bracelet made from a lock of her mother's (Mrs. S. B. Judson's) hair, with the word "Mother" engraved on the clasp, and on the reverse her own initials, "E. C. J." The reader will, of course, remember that Abby's mother was buried in the Island of St. Helena.

THE BRAID OF GOLD.

TO ABBY.

I bring my child a braid of gold
   To mark this Christmas morning,—
But rather round thy heart to fold,
   Than for thine arm's adorning.

Its gleam first caught thine infant eyes,
   When, far beyond the water,
A meek saint bent in love's sweet guise,
   And soft lips whispered "daughter."

Thou saw'st it last on that wild night,
    Forgotten never—never!
When Death's black shadow crossed thy light,
    And orphaned thee forever.

Now round where rests its golden twin
    Wild mournful waves are sweeping;
And o'er the roof that shuts it in
    A peepul tree leans weeping.

The saintly head which wore this tress—
    Too oft a crown of sorrow—
Bows but to regal blessedness
    Through heaven's eternal morrow.

So wear, my child, this golden braid,
    Thus doubly stamped with mother;
And while upon my bosom laid,
    Love, reverence *the other.*

Early in June, 1853, she bade adieu to her friends in Philadelphia, and proceeded to Providence, where her aid was needed in some matters relative to the memoir, now nearly completed, especially in settling the question of a publisher. She was the guest of Dr. Wayland, and by his request read over the manuscript which he had prepared. Her letters express the highest gratification with the labors of the biographer.

From Providence she went to Newton, where she again enjoyed the hospitalities of the family of Mr. Gardner Colby. She formed the acquaintance of Miss Ella Covell, the lovely and gifted young lady, to whom her son, George D. Boardman (then in the Newton Theological Seminary), was affianced; and making her long anticipated visit to Miss Judson at Plymouth, had the moutnful pleasure of communing with her over the memory of him whom they both so tenderly lamented.

The latter part of June found her again at Hamilton, giving what of time and strength disease allowed chiefly to the forthcoming memoir. Illness in his family had compelled Dr. Wayland to commit almost entirely to other hands the task of carrying the now completed work through the press. This was performed by the joint labors of herself and Rev. Dr. Bright. Dr. Bright carefully read over the first proofs, and then sent the sheets to Mrs. Judson, who, on her sick bed, went anew over the whole. How great a labor this imposed upon her in her invalid state can be judged only by those who have gone through a like task. But she had the satisfaction of laboring for a noble end, and of feeling when it was done that a work had been produced worthy of its subject, and a noble monument reared, not only to the memory of her late husband, but to the power of that Christian principle which had inspired his labors.

The little book which she had prepared while in Philadelphia she had not then sent to the press ; she now put to this also the finishing hand. It is a little volume of one hundred and twelve pages—a beautiful and feeling tribute to two characters of uncommon loveliness. It is written with that peculiar felicity and grace so natural to Mrs. Judson's pen, and by which she gave a charm to the most common-place incidents. But Lavinia and Harriet Chubbuck were no common-place characters, and this little record, added to the history of Mrs. Judson, shows concentrated in this family a rare wealth of mental and moral endowments. The work was issued in the winter.

The memoir of her husband was published in September. The reputation both of its subject and its

author was alike a guaranty for its intrinsic excellence
and interest, and for its favorable reception with the
public. Mrs. Judson, besides procuring and arranging
the materials, and contributing to it valuable reminiscences, had aided largely in carrying it through the
press, and might naturally look forward to its sale as
a source of permanent and needed income to the large
family whom her husband had left dependent upon her
—and all the more needed, as her steadily declining health
warned her that they would soon be left wholly orphans.
But while trembling between life and death, her prospects
were threatened by an event as unanticipated as it was
painful. On her landing in Boston she had received
from a publishing house in New York a copy of a memoir
of Dr. Judson prepared after his death, and proposing to
pay her fifty dollars on each thousand copies sold. The
proposition Mrs. Judson quietly declined, not wishing by
any act to sanction this as a final and authoritative
memoir of her husband. The gentlemen who had made
what they undoubtedly intended as a liberal proposal
were not united with her by denominational ties, and
she neither deemed the matter surprising, nor requiring
any special protest. But she was now called to deal
with a different matter.

In October, just as the work of Dr. Wayland was fairly
coming before the public, a Baptist publisher of New
York advertised as about ready a cheaper memoir of Dr.
Judson, in a single volume, for the benefit of Sabbath
schools, and of those who should be unable or unwilling
to purchase the more voluminous and expensive work of
Dr. Wayland. On what principle of morality or courtesy
the author of this project could justify to himself this inva-
sion of the moral rights of Mrs. Judson and her family, it

is difficult to see. He probably argued that his proposed publication would circulate chiefly among a class whom the larger and more elaborate work would not reach. Yet it required but a fraction of an ordinary publisher's sagacity to know that, if the work which he issued was really well done, it would present an alternative to thousands who would at all events furnish themselves with some reliable memoir of that great man, and would, in fact, therefore, restrict seriously the circulation of the other. And if he deemed a smaller work demanded to meet the popular wants, common decency, to say nothing of any higher obligation, demanded that he should wait a reasonable time for it to be prepared by those immediately interested, and only when assured that the religious interests of the public were to be sacrificed to the sale of a large and expensive book, could he be justified in interfering, and even then only after consultation with the family.

But it is needless to argue a matter which was decided by an instant and unanimous verdict of the public, from which there can be no appeal; and I shall dwell upon it no farther than is absolutely necessary to do justice to Mrs. Judson. Her first intelligence of the project reached her in a letter from Dr. Bright. In what condition it found her will be seen from the following to Abby Ann :—" My cough has returned, and keeps me awake the greater part of the night. I have also had a hemorrhage of the lungs which has weakened me exceedingly. I should like to go to New York this winter, but am afraid I shall not even leave my bed." To George Boardman she writes under the same date :—" I am quite too ill to write. Let me hear from you. God bless you and Ella both, and grant, if it be His will, that we may meet again in this world; if not, that we may share the same Paradise."

Under these circumstances she writes to Dr. Bright, December 2d, in regard to a suggestion about reducing temporarily the price of Dr. Wayland's work, to foil the new project:

It will, of course, interfere somewhat with the sale of the memoir, perhaps alarmingly for a few months; but it will be an ephemeral thing, while the other will be perpetual. "Wayland's Memoir," people know to be genuine, and though they may cheat themselves with something cheaper at first, they will in the end buy the book which they know can be relied on. Now you and Dr. W. have more wisdom, and the publishers more practical knowledge in one little finger than I have in my whole head; yet it would be only in deference to your opinion that I would consent to a reduction in the price the book. My own judgment, or perhaps my womanly instinct, tells me it would be a bad measure; that, however suited to a temporary purpose it would injure the interests of all parties concerned, but more especially the holder of the copyright, in the end. The book was thought to be fairly worth two dollars, and every candid person acknowledges that the price is not high. At two dollars, then, let it stand. I think it more dignified, knowing we are in the right, to stand firm, and let the lamb-clothed robber see what he can effect. I have been brought to stands similar to this several times in my life, and by going straight onward and avoiding what I believe to be an almost fatal course, *shaping my policy to other people's policy*, I have come out unharmed.

But duty to her orphaned children—soon about to be doubly orphaned—called on her to make a vigorous effort to avert the blow, by appealing directly to the publisher. As a professed Christian and of the same denominational faith, he could not, she deemed, refuse to listen to her request that he should abandon his unrighteous purpose, and persist in wronging the offspring, under pretense of honoring the memory of the dead. From her couch of sickness and pain she wrote to him as follows :

HAMILTON, N. Y., Dec. 3, 1853.

DEAR SIR,—

I have been confined to my room a helpless invalid for about three months, or I should have taken the liberty to write you earlier. I make an attempt to use my pen now, simply to request you to abstain from publishing the book about my husband which you have advertised. Why should strangers make matters of traffic of the virtues of a holy man, while those who loved him remain to cherish the sacred legacy?

I entreat you not to do me and the orphans of my sainted husband this great wrong. Be assured that " the Father of the fatherless, and the Judge of the widow " will never bless you in such a course. You may gather up a few handfuls of money, but that money will not make your pillow easy, nor your heart light. You may at this present moment bolster up your purpose by sophistical arguments and well planned excuses and evasions, but the time will come when these will be torn away, and you will see this thing without a mist before your eyes.

Will you suppress the book? May the Holy Spirit guide you in the ways of righteousness, and many hearts will be glad at the announcement. But if, blinded to the right, you still persist in your cruel purpose, why, then, may God have mercy on you in your hour of darkness.

EMILY C. JUDSON.

MR. F.'S REPLY.

NEW YORK, Dec. 8, 1853.

DEAR MADAM,—

Your letter of the 3d instant has been received, in which you request me to refrain from publishing a proposed " book about your husband," and denouncing upon me the judgments of God in the event of my refusal.   I am happy in believing, however, that the disposal of all events is in the hands of One who judges not after the manner of selfish mortals, and who may even *forgive*, through the Great Redeemer, the sins of His erring children, when truly repented of, and who requires us to forgive others as we wish to be forgiven—depriving us of any vindictive rights.

Your letter attributes to me a contemplated WRONG upon yourself and the children of Dr. Judson.   That no wrong is involved in the publication of this "book about your husband" is my sincere and undoubting conviction.   The public life of a public man is public property ; and the record of a man's life, or of a nation's annals, is the privilege of any historian who chooses to embrace it.

Divest yourself for a moment of personal interest in this matter, or suppose an analogous case, and let me ask you to decide it.   Suppose that you were impressed that you could prepare a memoir of Daniel Webster that would benefit a class not reached by the great "authorized" edition (as Mr. Banvard has already done), would you for a moment think of consulting the "bereaved family ?"   And, not doing so, how would you regard a requirement from Mrs. Webster of abandonment, coupled with an accusation of wrong ?

And, while I believe that in this case there is no infringe-ment of rights, there does appear a positive duty.   The abandonment even of an important publication, as of the ministerial or missionary work, may be inadmissible by the conscientious Christian.   It is not a severe faith that sees more good to the world in the history of Judson than what he actually accomplished in his lifetime; and when no provision is made or proposed for the thousands of little country Sabbath schools and poor families, I believe this work to be called for by the Great Taskmaster.   The highest of all obligations, therefore, forbids its relinquishment.

My estimate of the demand is corroborated by many who canvassed for Dr. Wayland's work, and now engage in this, going over again the same field. Thus each work will find the place for which it is adapted, giving to the former the advantage of earlier publication.

A principle of *courtesy* would prevent me forestalling the market, by anticipating other arrangements, or by taking advantage of a vitiated copyright (by copyrighting in England). I gladly leave all the great advantages your work possesses, pursuing a course sanctioned by long usage.

My views of the moral question are sustained by some of the wisest and best of Christians—men who never wrote a line they ever afterwards wished suppressed. Some who claim to be your personal friends have been my advisers in this. Doctors of Divinity, who ought to understand the moral principles of this undertaking, have given me their written approval, and offered every assistance in their power. And the principal author of the work you would hardly visit with denunciation. I am also joined by the different publishers of our denomination, all of whom, I think, will take an interest in the circulation of this "book about your husband." Indeed, not a note of disapprobation has reached me, except from those personally interested or an immediate friend.

The consideration of charity a family so well provided for pecuniarily, will not urge. The engagements I have made and expenses incurred form another reason against a compliance with your request, which compliance would probably only result in a change of publisher. Still I will comply and give up my own part upon condition that you will yourself prepare a work of the same plan and scope, and allow it to be published by some Baptist publishing house, saving me from loss in the out lay already made.

As I have a wife who may be a widow, and children who may become orphans, I hope to be sufficiently sensitive to the rights of such, and, when destitute, disposed to succor. And I

pray you, if you must think me wrong, to believe me mis-
takenly so, and capable of better than sordid motives.

Very respectfully yours.

To Mrs. Emily C. Judson, Hamilton, N. Y.

MRS. JUDSON'S REPLY.

HAMILTON, December 14, 1853.

SIR,—

If you will do me the favor to look again at my note of
the 3d instant, you will see that it contains no denunciations.
Unless I am greatly mistaken, I commended you to the *mercy*,
not the "judgments" of God.

It will be a heart-sickening task to wade through your long
letter, to note the different points in your sad system of morality, but still I suppose I ought to do it.

1. You say—"The public life of a public man is public property." I am not prepared to dispute this maxim, but simply say
that it is entirely irrelevant to the case in question. My husband was not, in the true sense of the word, a "public man"—
he was not a statesman, a diplomatist, a military or civil commander, or any thing of the sort. He took his commission
from no human government, and he labored mostly alone, under
the eye of his Master. Therefore, unless your book is false to
the character of the man, it will be far more a record of private
than of public life. Indeed, unless I am greatly mistaken, your
book, so far from confining itself to public acts, peers into the
most sacred privacies, going even to his closet, and picturing
him on his knees before God. If you really can not discern
the broad difference between a life like his and the official position of a statesman like Daniel Webster, I could wish that you
had at least left the public and myself to settle the question of
property.

Your "analogous case" is a very extreme one; but still, by
a supposition or two, we may make it do. If Mr. Banvard had
had the slightest reason to infer, from Mrs. Webster's previous
habits, that she was at all likely to have an abridgment of her

husband's life suited to Sunday schools in the course of preparation, he was bound, both as a gentleman and a Christian, to consult her wishes before entering on his own work. If Mrs. Webster owned the copyright of her husband's life, and were to write me that a book I was publishing for the good of Sunday schools was interfering with her interests, and actually doing her a positive injury, I would as soon (I regret to write it, but you asked me)—I would as soon steal her purse, hoping to benefit Sunday schools by the contents, as to go on with the work.

2. I dread to reply to this paragraph, because there are sentiments in it positively shocking. *Your* duty, while I am out of my grave, to look after the memory of him whose inmost thoughts and feelings I have shared, and over whom I have watched through so many weary hours of pain, and suffering, and sorrow? Yours—a stranger's duty? Where is his wife? Where is his own beloved sister, the playmate of his childhood, and correspondent of his later years? Where are those noble-hearted men who have cared for and watched over his helpless, desolate ones, as fathers and brothers watch? *Your* duty! Alas! alas! And do you really think " The Great Taskmaster" *requires* of you to seize on the orphans' birthright, because not secured by human law, and, putting the avails in your own coffers, stand before the world as a man who has acquitted himself of a " positive duty?" No, no; be assured the day will come when you will find this act was called for by a very different taskmaster. But you do not stop here. You go further, and even profess to be too conscientious to abandon this scheme, lest the public, forsooth, should lose some prospective good. Why, do you not know, that just so far as you prevent the sale of Dr. Wayland's book, by substituting an inferior one, you are doing a positive harm? Some men " do evil that good may come," and are justly condemned for it; but this looks to me very much like doing evil that good may be prevented.

How came you to know that no provision was being made for Sunday schools and poor families? Did you ask any one likely to know—the family of Dr. Judson, his biographer, the executive officers of the Missionary Union? or were you afraid to ask, lest you should learn certain facts which would spoil your speculation? Those who looked after the memoir for the churches, were not likely to forget the Sunday schools.

3. Do you mean to say that nothing but "courtesy" kept you from seizing on my copyright, which you happen to fancy is not good? Verily, if this be true, I should be sorry to be your neighbor in Patagonia, where there is no law for the protection of life and property, and where, courtesy not being fashionable, many proceedings are "sanctioned by long usage," that would be, to say the least, inconvenient to the weaker party.

4. You say your views are sustained by Christians, wise and good. I know nothing of that matter (except by the piles of correspondence on my table, which would astonish you), but I do know that they are not sustained by Christ, and so will not stand in the great day. You also say that some of your advisers claim to be my friends. Very likely. I never doubted that I had my share of false friends—men who fawn and flatter, while, in order to serve their own purposes, or even to gratify some petty spite, they would not hesitate to crush me as a fly; but the servant is not above his Master—so was it with Him who died by a traitor's connivance—so is it with Him still.

Your principal author may be, for aught I know, a man who stands up in the sacred desk, and is zealous against vice—both from that position and from the press—but he is himself guilty of an act that no high-minded worldling would stain his honor with. I would not denounce him any more than I have denounced you, but I would denounce his sin precisely as I have yours. You give me startling ideas of the system of morality adopted by Baptist publishers, and then ask, or rather demand of me, to employ them! No, no; there are honorable men among Baptist publishers who would scorn this thing. If all the D.D.'s that human colleges have ever made were your advisers, and all the Baptist publishers in America your accomplices, it would not change the color of this deed one whit—it is as black as midnight, and all the honorable names on earth can not whiten it.

5. Charity! No, sir, I do not come to you for charity. I ask only *justice* at your hands; I ask you to let alone what belongs to me and to my children. And whether, through the mercy of God, I have a decent provision, or am left to starve in a gutter, it need concern you in no way whatever.

6. I am sorry you have incurred expenses so recklessly; but business men do make mistakes, and recover (I rather think) more readily by an honorable course than by a dishonorable one. The conclusion of your defense is but the rumseller's excuse— "If I do not make this man drunk, somebody else will."

Having gone through with these somewhat singular arguments, you come to me with your "conditions." I can not, without compromising my self-respect, go over these in detail, and so would simply say that I acknowledge no dictator in my own affairs, and that I beg leave to decline all interference with yours. If you conclude to desist from the wrong you are doing, well and good; if not, the Lord judge between us.

In conclusion, you ask me to think you "capable of better than sordid motives." What saith the Scriptures? "By their fruits," etc. You have furnished me with a cluster of as sharp thorns as were ever planted in a sick woman's pillow, and it is all the "fruit" of yours that I have ever seen. I can not imagine these to be the refreshing grapes so grateful to a female lip. I know too well what they are. Still they may have been hung upon your vine by some foreign hand—those blind leaders of the blind, who have advised you to commit a wrong. It is not mine to judge you, and I will not. I leave it all to Him who knows the hearts of men completely.

The writing of this letter has been a sorrowful task to me. It has made my heart ache. If any thing in it seems harsh, it is the harshness of truth, not of ill-will. If I had been alone in the world, I should probably have borne this injury in silence;

but I am the guardian of six orphan children, whose rights it is my duty to try to protect. I have now done for them what I could, and commit them to their Father's care.

If you persist in your work, there will be no further occasion for writing between us.

May the Lord forgive you, and give you a better mind.

EMILY C. JUDSON.

Her efforts to arrest the proceeding were ineffectual. The proposed work was published under the title of "Burmah's Great Missionary," but was soon after consigned by the moral sense of the public, to oblivion. To give the matter additional notoriety, the publisher, with a sort of judicial infatuation, brought it afresh before the public by instituting a libel suit against Mr. S. B. Norton, for an expression contained in a letter from Rev. Dr. Wayland, published in the *Literary Gazette*, of which he was proprietor. This suit occasioned the reading in court of the correspondence above given, which being copied into the papers, sent over the country a fresh thrill of indignation at the course which, under Christian pretenses, could strike at the orphans' inheritance through the grave of the father, and the agonies of the dying widow. The suit was brought in February of 1854, but the trial which, from the character and the parties involved in it, awakened great interest, and in which the defendant was triumphantly acquitted, did not occur until a year later, when Mrs. Judson's ear was deaf to the tumults of earth, and her aching heart had found repose in the grave.

CHAPTER XXV.

REST.

"There are mansions exempted from sin and from woe,
But they stand in a region by mortals untrod ;
There are rivers of joy, but they roll not below ;
There is rest, but 'tis found in the bosom of God."

TRUE to her nature, Mrs. Judson labored on to the last. She had contemplated an abridged memoir of her husband, chiefly for Sabbath schools and for the young ; and such a work, had she been able to complete it, she could scarcely have failed to make deeply interesting. Illness compelled her to change her plan, and about the 1st of January, 1854, with the concurrence and advice of Drs. Wayland and Bright, she commenced an abridgment, chiefly by the scissors, of Dr. Wayland's book, exscinding its larger documents and incidental discussions. Even this, however, she speedily relinquished, and, January 31, she writes to Dr. Bright : " I have not written a word of the memoir, and am afraid I never shall. I am very sick now, and rapidly failing. The doctor says there is but the slenderest hope possible of my recovery, though I suppose I may live a couple of months or so. I may *possibly* get out again, but not *probably*. Be it as God wills ; I would not interfere if I could." The proposed abridgment was, at her request, committed to the accomplished pen of Mrs. H. C. Conant, then of Rochester, who, in her "Earnest Man," has produced a book combining the merits of an abridgment with the results of independent investigation, and given a most beautiful delineation of the life and character of the Christian hero, which will impart fresh light even to him who has read the more elaborate work of Dr. Wayland.

Of the month of February Mrs. Judson's letters furnish no records—an ominous hiatus indicating that she was writhing in the gradually tightening grasp of the Destroyer. For her to live was to write: her pen had been so long the ready minister to her thoughts that we need no other evidence than its silence of the powerlessness of the hand that had wielded it. When she next breaks the silence it is through the ministry of another: she was prohibited from writing even the briefest note.

The letters of her brother Wallace, written at her dictation, through the months of March and April, chiefly to Dr. Bright, show her unceasing care for her children, and how active was her mind in other necessary matters. With May 20 they close, and her brother writes: "I fear that 'the last of earth' is speedily approaching for my sister. For the past few days her weakness has materially increased, and she is likely to drop away with but a brief warning." She was now too close on the borders of the dark valley to give any more public tokens of interest in aught beneath the sun. Death, that had long been making his gradual and intermittent approaches, now laid upon her an iron grasp that would no longer be cheated of its prey. His coming was neither unexpected nor unwelcome. She had long been familiar with his tokens, and she panted for the hour of release. Her form was wasted to a skeleton; fever was drinking up the springs of life; and her ulcerated lungs made the effort to speak a torture. But she lingered till June, her own favorite season, and on the first of that delightful month—the month of the bursting gladness of nature—on the day preceding the anniversary of her marriage, she passed into the fadeless bloom of the Heavenly Paradise, and in her robe of spotless white joined the train of the Heavenly Bridegroom.

Her death was in keeping with her life. Patience, resignation, cheerfulness, a placid serenity of spirit and trust in her Saviour, marked her entire illness. From her sister Catharine's reminiscences—her affectionate nurse during her illness—I condense a few particulars of her sojourn on the borders of the spirit land. The first formal announcement that she could not live long, occasioned something of a struggle, not so much on her own account as that of her aged parents, and the orphans dependent on her care. "There is *one* who will be inconsolable," she said, referring to her little Emmy. But from this she soon recovered, and assured of her approaching end, she set about her arrangements with the calmness of one going to visit a friend. For herself, nothing marred the serene composure with which she looked forward to her rest in the bosom of her Saviour. *Rest* was that for which she panted. "It is not," she said, "the pearly gates and golden streets of heaven that attract me; it is its perfect rest in the presence of my Saviour. It will be *so* sweet after a life of care and toil like mine—though a very pleasant one it has been, and I am only weary of the care and toil because I have not strength to endure them.

This lack of strength is dreadful. I have been wasted to a mere skeleton, and suffered the most excruciating pain, but it was nothing in comparison with my present sufferings." To her sister's expression of a wish to relieve her sufferings, she replied : "No, I have not one pain to spare. I feel sure that God will never send a pain that I do not really need to fit me for the rest I hope to enjoy in heaven." "Not brilliant, but very peaceful," she said, when asked regarding the prospect before her. "It is bright either way," she said with sparkling eye to a friend who expressed the hope that God might yet restore her.

Early in her illness she was haunted occasionally by thoughts of being laid in the cold, dark grave, away from her friends. But these feelings she gradually surmounted, and succeeded in looking to the grave but as the "wardrobe locked" which would contain the "cast off dress" of the beatified spirit. With this thought she consoled her mother. "Do you not believe," she said to her, "that when I get home to heaven, I shall be permitted to look down upon you here with the same tender care and solicitude with which you look upon me now? Never think of me in the cold grave; for really you know I shall not be there; but look upward, and think of that happy meeting when all our cares and sorrows will be forgotten, and God will wipe all tears from our eyes."

Her sickness illustrated beautifully the grace of patience. "Kate," said she, "tell me honestly if I am patient." On being assured that she was, she replied : "I am *so* glad that you think me patient. For consumptive people are so often fretful and complaining that I have greatly feared that I should get so too, and it would be sad and indeed wicked, I am so nicely cared for." "You do not know," she continued, "how glad I am that I am at home. Formerly when I visited Laurel Hill and other beautiful burial places, I thought it would be pleasant to lie amidst such beauties. But I have lost all that feeling now. O, it is sweet to die at home! I could not bear the thought of being buried elsewhere than here where you all will probably rest by and by at my side." She directed a lot to be purchased and enclosed, and a plain marble stone to be procured for her husband and little Charlie; and wished the same simplicity to mark the selection of her own tombstone.

She evinced the most affectionate concern in the comfort of all about her, and would not allow her sister to tax herself with watching with her during the night. She, however, insisted on being dressed each morning and carried down stairs that she might be with the family as much as possible, though she said that it seemed to her that each day *must* be the last. When very near her end, after enduring dreadful agonies from suffocation, she said, "O Kate, how I long to be at home—to be at rest! I am so weak all the time that I can scarcely *think*. I love you all as dearly as ever, and try to be interested in whatever you are doing. But in spite of myself I have felt for two or three days that I cared very little for you; and you know, Kitty, when it comes to that, *I must be very far along.*"

She had from the first desired to die in June. It was the month of flowers, and flowers were always her especial delight. Her sister Lavinia had died in that month; she had been married in it. About a month before her death she said to her sister very confidently, "I shall die in June." On the morning of the first of June she was roused by her sister with the question, "Emily, do you know that it is June ?" " Yes," she replied, "my month to die." She was dressed and carried down stairs as usual ; but in the afternoon one of her terrible attacks of suffocation came on, occasioned by the utter wasting of her lungs. She lingered until ten in the evening in great agony ; the pain then subsided, and after a few minutes, sweetly and tranquilly, without a groan or the movement of a muscle, she breathed out her life on the bosom of her sister.

She had requested that her funeral sermon might be preached by Rev. Dr. Wayland. In the event of his absence, by Rev. Dr. Eaton, president and theological professor in Madison University. Dr. Wayland being unable to be present, Dr. Eaton preached before a crowded assembly, from 1 Cor. xv. 6 : " But some are fallen asleep."

Her little Emmy she had committed (her sister having charge of their aged and infirm parents) to the motherly care of her bosom friend, Miss Anna Maria Anable ; Edward had found a permanent home in the family of Rev. Professor Dodge, of Madison University. For the other children she had secured comfortable temporary homes. She had appointed Rev. Drs. Edward Bright and James N. Granger executors of the estate and guardians of the children. In Dr. Bright she had found, ever since her return from India, a most faithful friend, a judicious counselor, and an indefatigable co-worker in all her plans and labors.

The provisions of her will are worthy of special mention. She left a life annuity sufficient to insure a comfortable support to her aged parents. She left to the faithful Malayan woman Nancy, who had accompanied her from India, a sum considerably more than sufficient to defray the expenses of her voyage back to the East. In providing for her children, she made no discrimination in favor of her own daughter Emily, but placed her on precisely the same footing with Dr. Judson's other children. All the children were to receive a liberal allowance until their education, both literary and professional, should be fully completed—no legitimate expense being spared for this purpose. If anything should remain after this was accomplished, it was to go to the treasury of the Missionary Union.

The reader may be grateful for one word respecting the present state of the family that Mrs. Judson had thus watched over. Abby Ann, having completed her education, is now teaching in the seminary of Mr. A. M. Gammell, of Warren, R. I. Adoniram and Elnathan were graduated from Brown University (the educational home of their father) in 1859. The former is now pursuing the study of medicine ; the latter studying theology, preparatory to the work of the Christian ministry. Henry and Edward enter college the present autumn.

In the cemetery of Hamilton stand, side by side, two neat and simple head-stones ; the one placed by Mrs. Judson's order, a little before her death and inscribed,

"TO MY HUSBAND

AND

ANGEL CHARLIE."

The other placed by parental, and brotherly, and sisterly affection, and inscribed,

"DEAR EMILY."

A few feet distant are the graves of both her parents, who, since her death, have gone to add two more links to the domestic chain, broken on earth, to be reunited in heaven. There the tear of affection is daily shed, and the flowers which Emily loved in life blossom above her grave. The footsteps of many a pilgrim, to whom genius and virtue enshrined in lovely womanhood are sacred, linger reverently about the spot. "Dear Emily:"—that is a heart record. Bright as was her genius, her virtues were still brighter. The lustre of her intellect was outshone by the purity of her heart. The laurel wreath of literary fame would have faded, but entwined with the chaplet that crowns a beautiful and heroic life, both shall bloom together in undying fragrance.

CHAPTER XXVI.

THE RETROSPECT.

"Once more ye laurels, and again once more
Ye myrtles brown, with ivy never sere,
I come to pluck your berries wild and crude,
And with forced fingers rude,
Shatter your leaves before the mellowing year."

"The autumn wind rushing
Wafts the leaves that are serest;
But our flower was in flushing
When blighting was nearest."

WE have followed Mrs. Judson to the close of her short, but eventful career; it remains that we cast back our eye for a moment, and seek to gather up its impressions, and bring the living woman before us in a brief estimate of her personal and literary character. I am not unaware of the great delicacy and difficulty of the task. To fix her Protean features—to catch their fleeting and changeful hues—to develop the elements of a nature so singularly gifted and so admirably balanced, at once so strong and so tender, so firm and so elastic, so heroic and so womanly, I feel to be beyond the capacities of my unaccustomed pen. I shall merely attempt to sketch a few lines of the picture, leaving the filling up and coloring to the reader's imagination.

Let us glance first at what meets the physical eye. In person, Mrs. Judson was about the middle height, but giving the impression of great delicacy of structure, and a highly nervous organization. Her general appearance was graceful and pleasing, and especially so as the timid shyness of her earlier manner gave way, in the larger intercourse of later life, to a quiet self-possession and dignity. Her residence abroad, while it gave elevation and maturity to her character, wrought a corresponding improvement in her outward bearing. Gentle, genial, and dignified, she impressed one at once as full of soul and sensibility. Her face, in repose, would scarcely be called handsome, but easily lighted up into an expression fascinating, if not beautiful. The likeness which accompanies the present volume does admirable justice to her countenance, especially in her more thoughtful moods. The philosophic depth, the calm decision and self-reliance, the playfulness lurking in the corners of the mouth and just ready to flash out from the eye, can not fail to strike one who looks at it a second time, while they but truly represent the living personage. In reality, so much of the interest of her countenance depended on its play of expression, that any picture could do it but inadequate justice. The dramatic vivacity of her intellect shadowed itself on her face. The philosophical, the poetic, the practical, the girlishly sportive and half mischievous elements portrayed themselves in rapid alternation on her flexible features. Her broad, deep, and finely-shaped forehead, indicated a large development both of the logical and ideal elements. Her dark eye, somewhat too small and not sufficiently liquid for beauty, yet glowed with spirit and intelligence, now sparkling with mirth and humor, and now, in her more thoughtful moments, seeming to penetrate the depths of the subject she was considering. Her nose, perhaps a little sharp, was prominent and finely outlined ; her mouth rather large, but well-formed ; while her thin and delicate, but slightly compressed lips, indicated at once strength and sensibility. The entire cast of her features betokened clearly that union of intelligence, refinement, and energetic will which marked the living character.

In proceeding to notice her intellectual and moral traits, we may mention as among the most obvious, the union of poetic ideality with downright common sense and practical efficiency. While picking wool in the factory, at the age of eleven, she was framing visions of distant climes, and dreaming dreams of ideal happiness and splendor. This dreaming faculty followed her through life, and constituted a part of her heritage as a child of genius. It enabled her to tinge every object with the hues of romance, and to clothe external nature with a beauty born of her own spirit. Yet her dreams never distracted her mind, never dulled the edge of her intellectual perceptions, nor disqualified her for the work actually in hand. Her powers of fancy and imagination were balanced by a strong practical sense which met the exigencies of every position. Her " life" was thus eminently " twofold." While she reveled in poetic dreams and fancies—while she wandered at will in the enchanted realm which the wand of genius is so potent to create, she was never for a moment unfitted for the duties of the every-day world in which she moved. She was none of those helpless children of genius who own " principalities in Utopia," but are condemned to starve on our vulgar planet; who build magnificent castles in the air, but are incapable of gaining a firm foothold and a comfortable abiding place on *terra firma*.

This practical efficiency showed itself in her first vigorous wrestling with the destiny which was drifting her toward a life of mere material toil. " I went away," she says, when her mother put to her the perplexing question what she would do, " *to think*." And she did think, and thought to purpose. At an age when most children would have thoughtlessly yielded to the maternal wishes, or as thoughtlessly rebelled, she quietly reasoned out the matter, formed her plan, and executed it with a resolution which bore down not only outward obstacles, but the still mightier obstacles of her own constitutional sensitiveness and timidity. This early act tells—as it partly, perhaps, determined—the story of her life. A mingled thoughtfulness and energy—an energy resting on thoughtfulness and sustained by an iron force of will, fitted her for any practical emergency, and made her equal to any amount of endurance and any acts of heroism.

A like happy union of qualities marked the workings of her intellect. They were characterized by equal elegance and strength. Her mind moved with a natural and spontaneous grace ; it glowed, as Mr. Wallace expressed it, with a certain " soft brightness" which naturally generated the impression that softness and beauty were its leading qualities.

It seemed scarcely possible that a mind of such exceeding delicacy and refinement to which the lighter play of fancy was so thoroughly congenial, could be equally endowed with the sterner and more masculine attributes. And yet such was the fact. The play of her intellect was not more graceful than its workings were vigorous.

The airy movement of her fancy no more than kept pace with the measured tread of her reason. The lighter elements of her genius rested on a solid basis of sterner qualities. From childhood she evinced a most various and many-sided mental activity. She "lisped in numbers," and inspired her friends with no unreasonable assurance of her poetic promise. Yet her mind was even more busy in other directions, remote from the paths of poesy. She displayed an eager thirst for knowledge, great capacity of intellectual acquisition, and a special delight in those solid processes which call forth the sterner powers of the soul. Her procuring the " Age of Reason," and noting down its arguments, that she might examine and refute them ; her joining not only the youths', but also the older peoples' Bible-class, that she might listen to their discussions of the profounder problems of Scripture ; her success in mathematics, and other more difficult branches of learning—all are but proofs of the solid structure of her mind, and early foreshadowings of that love and habit of vigorous mental action which followed her through life. While she delighted in poetry and wrote elegant fictions, she delighted equally in those forms of labor which demand patient research and philosophic generalization. She spent weeks in preparing herself to write two or three short notes on Buddhism, in the appendix to the Memoir of Mrs. S. B. Judson. She went with her husband patiently over the pietistic and mystical writers, and her shrewd comments and criticisms probably contributed not a little toward removing a slight mystical and ascetic taint from his religious opinions. She entered with hearty sympathy into his dry dictionary labors, and not only solaced his hours of relaxation, but aided with her acute suggestions in

18*

resolving many a knotty word-problem ; while she herself attained a practical mastery of the Burmese language, and even an elegance in writing it, entirely beyond
what could have been anticipated from the exceeding
slenderness of her health, and her engrossing domestic
cares.   Her journal of 1849 shows upon what profound
and far-reaching subjects she adventured her bold and
yet cautious speculations ; how her intellect followed
her faith across the confines of the spirit-world, touched
some of the profoundest mysteries of the invisible, and
yet held the conclusions of reason strictly subordinated
to the teachings of the only standard.   And on the
great practical questions with which our East Indian
missions were so rife while she was abroad, she formed
decided views, influenced no doubt by those of her husband, but reasoned out for herself, and held with the
clearness and decision of independent convictions.   In
one word, she had a mind of great speculative and analytical power, that loved to go to the bottom of things,
and that was quick and keen, in any abstract or practical
matter, to strip off the disguises that sophistry might
have flung around it, and hold it up in its genuine features.   Her soul swelled with the intellectual and moral
grandeur of the missionary work, and her essay on the
" Madness of the Missionary Enterprise" is a fine specimen alike of the grace and the power of her mental
movements.

Mrs. Judson again united the warmest and tenderest
affections with great independence and force of character.   Whatever course her judgment decided upon she
pursued with inflexible decision and unwavering courage.
Both the breadth of her intellectual views, and her high
moral sense supported her in the path of right, and en-

abled her to go forward in the teeth of almost any opposition. Yet all this sprung from no stoical apathy, and no indifference to the views of others. She trod the path which she pursued, not because she was insensible to the judgments of the world, not because she did not feel keenly both its censures and its approval, but because she valued more than either her own innate sense of right and duty. Her heart was full of tenderness, and her nature most affectionate and confiding. None lived more in the smiles of friends ; none yearned more intensely for affection ; none repaid it with a more enthusiastic and constant devotion. Yet her affection, like her other feelings, did not expend itself mainly in words and protestations. She did not ordinarily indulge in vehement professions, but left her regard in large measure to the utterance of action. And of action there was no stint. She gave herself to the service of her friends with the most unselfish and generous devotion. Indeed it is hardly too much to say that her life, from its beginning to its close, was a continuous sacrifice upon the altar of affection. Whatever of prejudice she incurred as a magazine writer was incurred in obedience to that holiest of all merely earthly principles, filial love—the necessity of paying for a home purchased for her aged parents. And her sacrifices were made ungrudgingly, uncomplainingly, almost unconsciously. She seemed almost wholly unaware that she was playing the heroine, or doing any thing not demanded by the simplest dictates of duty, and the spontaneous impulses of love. Sacrifice was to her not sacrifice, for she was moving in simple obedience to the great law of her affections.

Mrs. Judson's character thus evinced a remarkable

and most symmetrical union of seemingly opposite qualities. With all the keen susceptibilities of genius she
united the most downright common sense. Brimful of
romance, she contemplated every subject from the most
practical point of view. Masculine in her force of character, she was almost more than feminine in its tenderness and delicacy. Her strength of mind was without
a particle of strong-mindedness; for none observed more
scrupulously all that belonged to the peculiar sphere of
woman, or exhibited more of the fascinating loveliness
of a true woman's character. With a high spirit, that
would not brook wrong or meanness, she combined a
temper meek, gentle, and forgiving; with a most generous liberality, the strictest business habits and syste-
matic economy. Either of her traits might easily have
been in excess, but that it was balanced by others equally
decided. She might have gone to Burmah as an enthusiastic dreamer; but in fact she did go there with as
clear an eye to the realities that awaited her as if the
element of romance had not been in her composition.
She had, as she herself terms it, "a certain dollar and
cent mode of looking at things," which might have de-
generated into a sort of hard, Gradgrind spirit, but this
was utterly precluded alike by the largeness of her intellect, the warmth of her affections, and the richness of
her enthusiasm. She had spirit enough to make her a
heroine—to lead her to plunge into any dangers and
endure any hardships—but no hair-brained audacity,
and no love of encountering peril for peril's sake. She
weighed the sacrifice and the results, and went forward
because reason and affection bade her go. She was in a
great measure regardless of conventionalisms; and yet
her instinctive sense of what was due to the relations

she sustained, guarded her against any taint of eccentricity. She knew how to lead; but she led so that she seemed to follow. She was a shrewd and unerring judge of character, but as kind and indulgent as she was discriminating. In short, the delicate flower of her genius and sensibility blossomed on a granite basis of character; but her mental movements were so easy, so graceful, so spontaneous, that but for the oppositions which she met, the hardships she endured, the stronger elements of her nature would have been scarcely suspected.

Her disposition was thoroughly cheerful, and she possessed a buoyancy of spirits that easily rose above the pressure of any ordinary adversity. She had a keen sense of the ludicrous, and a playful humor, often supposed to indicate a shallow nature, but in fact almost an universal attendant upon a deep one. There was in her disposition no taint of asceticism; no austerity of temper; no feeling that it is a sin to let the lightness of the heart mantle the face with smiles, or a virtue to gird with a hair-cloth mantle a grieving or a merry heart. Her sympathies were broad, generous, and diffusive. She loved the merriment of childhood and the gravity of age; she rejoiced in the humblest joy, and she had a tear for the lightest sorrow.

Her religious character, as well as many other of her traits, has been most justly portrayed in the admirable analysis of Dr. Wayland. I shall merely add a few supplementary suggestions. Her religion rested on a basis of early, deep-seated conviction, and a thorough study of the Scriptures, with which she had been conversant from her childhood. Her religious views were evangelical, and her familiarity with the New Testament made her competent to their defense. She had great confidence in the efficacy of prayer and an humble and constant trust in an overruling and directing Providence. If her religious zeal for a time declined, and she half questioned the genuineness of her christian experience, yet it was speedily rekindled, and her after life was a beautiful exemplification of the power of a spiritual faith. Her religious character, indeed, partook of the general structure of her mind. There was no cant— little demonstration—little outward profession—but the graces of faith, and patience, and consecration wrought themselves into her life, and when the vail was incidentally lifted upon her spiritual nature, one got a glimpse of the depth and fullness of the fountain out of which such streams were flowing.

All the relations of life Mrs. Judson fullfilled with exemplary fidelity. As a daughter she so deported herself that she might well feel that she had no occasion to fear retributive undutifulness from those children whom Providence had committed to her care. As a sister, she was affectionate and tenderly thoughtful ; as a wife, she displayed unlooked-for and admirable qualities. It was fortunate for her that Providence gave her a husband whose capacious intellect and noble heart could draw forth all her powers of love and reverence, and nurture and develop the faculties which, in a less happy marriage, would have turned in upon themselves, and it was no less to her credit that she appreciated her advantages, and opened her whole mind and heart to the ennobling influence of such companionship. That her husband and herself were " deliciously happy," was a natural result of the union of two natures at once so prodigally endowed, and so thoroughly congenial.

As a mother, it is scarcely possible to overstate her merits. Affectionate, watchful, patient, judicious, impartial, carrying ever a firm but gentle hand, fathoming thoroughly the diverse dispositions of her children ; at once alluring them into the path of virtue and leading the way, she guided them with a judgment and affection which shielded her from even any suspicion of error.

As a missionary, she entered heartily into the work ; was assiduous in learning the language, and as soon as it was mastered, hastened to make herself useful in every department of effort open to her—conducting the female religious meetings, instructing in the Scriptures, guiding inquirers, and aiding the new converts to larger spiritual attainments.

Her literary character I have perhaps sufficiently discussed, and can now only glance at. It is when we turn to this, and compare what she did with what—had life and health been given her—she might have done, that we feel the full force of the sentiment contained in the lines at the head of our chapter, and mourn that the leaves and blossoms of her genius were shattered " before the mellowing year." That she can never take the place in literature which her high endowments should have won for her, grows, we fear, out of the very nature of the case. The child of poverty and privation—her life one long struggle with disease—pressed with engrossing cares and toils—and finally cut off just as the blossom of genius ordinarily ripens into fruit, she could give little more than specimens, first fruits of what would have been the harvest. But these specimens are of exquisite quality, and augur most favorably for that harvest had sunshine and dew been permitted to bring it to perfection. Her stories, racy, original, truthful, springing from the very core of her heart, originated a partially new school of magazine writing, and from their intrinsic excellence will always find admiring readers. They are genuine of their kind, and therefore no changes of literary taste and fashion can render them wholly obsolete. When she leaves the paths of fiction, her style, losing little of its sparkle and nothing of its grace, assumes a simple dignity befitting the themes it discusses.

In poetry, Mrs. Judson wrote enough to show her ability to achieve a high place in female authorship. That many of her pieces have but little more than ordinary merit we may readily grant, without disparaging her poetic powers. Many of them were written when very young ; most of them before time and trial had developed all the depth and strength of her genius. It is a recognized and just rule to judge the artist not by his inferior productions but by his best ; for these alone show the actual measure of his endowments. The swiftest runner may lag in the race, but the tortoise is condemned to inevitable slowness. The wise man may sometimes utter folly, but only a miracle can cause the words of wisdom to distil from the lips of a fool. Homer sometimes nods ; but no sleepless effort can convert an ordinary rhapsodist into a Homer.

Applying this principle to Mrs. Judson—judging her by her best poems—and of these there is a sufficient number to show that they are not literary accidents, but that the soil in which they sprung was as deep as it was genial—we must ascribe to her poetical capacity of a high order, and lament that her early death snatched from us not only a beautiful life, but many a sweet strain that was already quivering on the exquisitely strung harp of her genius. These strains, unheard, unborn on earth,

it is delightful to believe blend their **untainted** music
with **the** melodies of angels. The specimens **contained**
in this volume make good our claim for her genius, **and**
show taste and feeling, passion **and** imagination, beautifully combining for high poetical effect. I add **one**
more piece in which she portrays, in exquisite imagery,
the great joy and the great sorrow of her life. The closing
stanza of "My Angel Guide," has been enthusiastically
and justly admired ; but it is not the finest in the poem.
The leading thought in the stanza may be regarded possibly as partaking slightly of the nature of a conceit ;
but the third, fourth, and fifth stanzas are as faultlessly
as they are exquisitely beautiful. Each one furnishes a
picture for an **artist.** And with this we drop the curtain, and leave the child of sorrow to her **dawning joy**—
to the beckoning of that "one steady star," soon to fade
before the "Bright and Morning Star," whose radiance
shall bathe her spirit through eternity.

MY ANGEL GUIDE.

I gazed down life's dim labyrinth,
　A wildering maze to see,
Crossed o'er by many a tangled clue,
　And wild as wild could be ;
And as I gazed in doubt and dread,
　An angel came to me.

I knew him for a heavenly guide,
　I knew him even then,
Though meekly as a child he stood
　Among the sons of men,—
By his deep spirit-loveliness
　I knew him even then.

And as I leaned my weary head
　　Upon his proffered breast,
And scanned the peril-haunted wild
　　From out my place of rest,
I wondered if the shining ones
　　Of Eden were more blest.

For there was light within my soul,
　　Light on my peaceful way,
And all around the blue above
　　The clustering starlight lay;
And easterly I saw upreared
　　The pearly gates of day.

So, hand in hand we trod the wild,
　　My angel love and I—
His lifted wing all quivering
　　With tokens from the sky.
Strange, my dull thought could not divine
　　'Twas lifted—but to fly!

Again down life's dim labyrinth
　　I grope my way alone,
While wildly through the midnight sky
　　Black, hurrying clouds are blown,
And thickly, in my tangled path,
　　The sharp, bare thorns are sown.

Yet firm my foot, for well I know
　　The goal can not be far,
And ever, through the rifted clouds,
　　Shines out one steady star,—
For when my guide went up, he left
　　The pearly gates ajar.

ADONIRAM JUDSON.

A Memoir of the Life and Labors of the Rev. Adoniram Judson, D.D.,
By FRANCIS WAYLAND, D.D.

Illustrated with a fine Portrait of Dr. Judson. Two volumes 12mo. Price $2.
Or two volumes in one. Price $1.25.

"We are glad to see this valuable biography of one of the most remarkable men of the age in which he lived, in one volume, and at a price so low that its circulation must be very extensive. Dr. Judson was a man of undaunted resolution, wonderful natural gifts, high attainments, and earnest and self-denying piety. He was exposed to many dangers, and passed through many perils for the love he bore to his Saviour, and the souls of men. When Judson first went out to India, many regretted that one of such fine abilities should engage in such a work. But his name will never disappear from the history of the world, and only eternity can reveal the effects of his labors in the salvation of souls, and in awakening the missionary spirit in the churches."—*Presbyter. Banner.*

"This biography is so well known that we need only say of the copy now before us, that it is a cheap edition, giving the two volumes in one, and thus placing the book within the reach of all. None interested in missionary enterprise, none able to appreciate the life of a great man doing a great work nobly, ably, and with much self-denial, should fail to read it."—*Philadelphia Journal.*

"It is one of the noblest monuments to true worth that the world has ever produced. Though dead, yet in these printed volumes his spirit will live and speak to this and coming generations, in strains of power and eloquence such as his own tongue could never give birth to. It is an occasion of gladness to all the friends of missions, that one so well qualified for the task has embalmed all this on the printed page. A sublimer theme could not be furnished any man since the apostles. Let the *Memoir* find its way to every family in the land, and it will not fail to create new sympathies, and enlist fresh zeal in that cause to which Judson gave his all."—*Philadelphia C. Chronicle.*

SERMONS TO THE CHURCHES.

By FRANCIS WAYLAND, D.D. 1 vol. 12mo. Price 85 cents.

CONTENTS.

I.—THE APOSTOLIC MINISTRY.
II.—THE CHURCH A SOCIETY FOR THE CONVERSION OF THE WORLD.
III.—CHRISTIAN WORSHIP.
IV.—A CONSISTENT PIETY THE DEMAND OF THE AGE.
V.—SLAVERY TO PUBLIC OPINION.
VI.—THE PERILS OF RICHES.
VII.—PREVALENT PRAYER.
VIII.—RESPONSIBILITY FOR THE MORAL CONDITION OF OTHERS.

"It grapples with living evils and errors, and will make a practical impression."—*Cincinnati Christian Herald.*

"This is a book truly worth printing, and worth reading. They are discourses on important topics, admirably written by a noble Christian."—*American Presbyterian.*

"Dr. Wayland is a clear thinker, and a strong and elegant writer. His Sermons are models worthy of study."—*Christian Intelligencer.*

"They are emphatically sermons for the times. The plowshare of Christian truth and duty is driven with unrelenting hand into the festering evils of our popular Christianity, and there are some passages which should make the ears of professing Christians tingle."—*Southern Presbyterian.*

SWITZERLAND.

By S. Irenæus Prime, D.D., author of "Europe and the East," "Power of Prayer," "Bible in the Levant," &c., &c.

Illustrated with six choice Views of Swiss Scenery. 1 vol. 12mo. Price $1.

ILLUSTRATIONS.

Interlachen and the Jungfrau.	Hospice of St. Bernard.
The Monument at Lucerne.	Chamouni and Mt. Blanc.
The Devil's Bridge.	Under the Giesbach Falls.

"Dr. Prime never knew how to write a dull sentence, and prompted by such natural beauty as abounds in the path of the Swiss tourist, he has here presented an account of his journeyings worthy of himself and his theme. The publishers increase the attractive appearance of the book by incorporating with the text some well executed illustrations of prominent scenes."—*Boston Post.*

"The impressions received from a Summer's ramble among the mountains of Switzerland are familiarly described in this agreeable volume. In addition to numerous lively pictures of the sublime scenery of that region, the volume contains sketches of personal adventure, accounts of people met with by the author, incidents of domestic and social life, and recollections of celebrated historical events called forth by the localities in which they occurred."—*New York Tribune.*

"Dr. Prime has delineated the characteristics of Swiss scenery and the interest of Swiss history, *con amore*, and therefore made both attractive. To those who have sailed on the Lake of Geneva, or traversed the Alps, this volume will prove a delightful memorial; and to those who have yet this experience to anticipate, the work will yield valuable information in a most agreeable way. It is cleverly illustrated with wood cuts."—*H. T. Tuckerman.*

"Every tourist can engage our attention when he describes, discourses, rhapsodises, with them for a theme; and Dr. Prime, a tourist of more than common education, intelligence and experience, is sure of increasing even his wide circle of readers by the publication of this pleasant and instructive volume."—*Boston Transcript.*

THE NONSUCH PROFESSOR

In His Meridian Splendor; or, The Singular Actions of Sanctified Christians Laid Open. In Seven Sermons.

By William Secker.

With an introduction by C. P. Krauth, Jr., D.D.

1 vol. 12mo, cloth. Price $1.

"We are almost prepared to endorse the judgment of a distinguished critic, who speaks of this as 'a beautiful little book, worth its weight in gold.' It comes of the Puritan age, and first saw the light in 1660. But the quaintness of its style, rich in striking thought, will scarcely make it less acceptable now than then. We might select whole paragraphs, where each successive sentence is characterized by the terseness and weight of a proverb."—*New York Evangelist.*

"It abounds in striking epigrams and happy conceits, and its thoughts are often set over against each other in antitheses and contrasts, after the style of the age; but these peculiarities and quaintnesses only serve to make the book the more attractive. It is read with best effect a little at a time—and will prove to the reflective reader a rich mine of thoughts for each day, and of topics for devout meditation."—*New York Examiner.*

"It contains, however, much of common sense and practical importance, and it presents a fine opportunity for young preachers of this day to gather suggestions which may be of advantage to them in the composition of their weekly discourses."—*Boston Post.*

SUMMER PICTURES FROM COPENHAGEN TO VENICE.

By Rev. HENRY M. FIELD.

1 vol. 12mo.   Price $1.

"A delightful book. The writer, who is the senior editor of the *New York Evangelist*, makes a summer tour with a joyous and genial companion, through the most picturesque and interesting parts of England and the continent, and coming into graceful contact with eminent personages, and refined society, his ' pictures' are a succession of scenes, that are surveyed by the reader with constant entertainment and satisfaction. The author is observant of men and manners : he is intelligent and candid : his historical and literary references and illustrations are copious, apposite and instructive, and his style lively and piquant, so that it is a pleasure to go with him from place to place, or linger with him in Venice or Vienna, in Denmark or Sweden. We are indebted to the author for a pleasant hour of railroad travel with his book in hand, and we commend it to our readers as one of the happiest summer books they can take in hand, by the way or in the shades of home."—*New York Observer.*

" Our excellent and well-beloved brother, Rev. Henry M. Field, of the *Evangelist*, in a series of entertaining and instructive letters to the journal which he so ably edits, gave, last year, outlines, or sketches, of his European tour. These letters have been re-written, amplified, and prepared for the now eager demand for intelligence respecting the scene of the present war. Mr. Field's pictures have been drawn with a graphic pen, and the book, we doubt not, will be everywhere wanted."—*New York Intelligencer.*

" We have *read* this book with unfeigned gratification. It is written in a sprightly, graceful style, and gives graphic descriptions of scenes of travel in 1853. Many of these are now scenes of great interest, on account of the stirring events transpiring in connection with them. These lively and vivid descriptions can not fail to entertain the general reader, while they impart useful knowledge of places, and personages and events, worth knowing something about, as seen in the light of the author's observations."—*Vermont Chronicle.*

" The readers of *The Evangelist* have enjoyed the sprightly and instructive communications of its editor from Europe ; but we are glad they are not to have a monopoly of such good things. Mr. Field is an observing and genial writer, and his recent observations upon countries which are now conspicuous in the movements of war, will have just now a timely value. It is a very attractive book, combining the historical, the descriptive, and the narrative in a pleasing and graceful style."—*Independent.*

THE "PRECIOUS STONES OF THE HEAVENLY FOUNDATIONS."

By AUGUSTA BROWN GARRET.

1 vol. 18mo.   Price $1.

"A book of great beauty, and full of attractive discourse on heavenly and divine things."—*New York Observer.*

" The articles are brief, and include many choice specimens of prose and poetry. It is especially adapted to lay on the center-table, or elsewhere, for the casual reader."—*Congregationalist.*

" The book is a suggestive one, and needs but a slight examination to become a favorite with the religious portion of the community."—*Boston Post.*

" Most of the pieces are original, but some are selected from congenial authors. Among the gems in the book are a series of reflections on some of the figurative external beauties of the Heavenly City. The writer dismisses her labors with the prayer that they may be the favored medium of calming the tempest in some troubled minds, of healing some stricken hearts, and of lifting the soul to the contemplation of heaven. We cheerfully commend the book as worthy a place in every family library "—*Waterbury American.*

THE WIFE'S TRIALS AND TRIUMPHS.

One volume. 12mo. Printed on Rose-tinted Paper, and handsomely

bound. Price $1.

From the Philadelphia North American.

"The characters are distinct and well-sustained—the incidents natural and varied—the style unambitious, but graceful. There is no display of learning—but ample knowledge and high culture are everywhere unconsciously visible. The book is handsomely 'got up' in its externals, and ladies especially will find it good reading."

From the Boston Journal.

"It is an English tale, descriptive of the aristocratic class, and is of more than ordinary interest. Its characters are life-like and are brought tangibly before the mind of the reader. The incidents are truthful and subserve the purpose of the tale, and the interest is very well sustained."

From the N. Y. Courier and Inquirer.

"The tone of the work is excellent, for, though not a religious novel, it is pervaded by a religious spirit. The publishers have issued the book in an exceedingly neat manner."

From the Salem Register.

"This is a story of English life, and well worthy of the beautiful dress which the publishers have given to it. To say that it is equal in interest and high moral tone to the author's previous works will be praise enough to those who have read the productions named in the title-page."

From the Troy Arena.

"The tale is simply and delightfully told, and its teachings are as correct as they are practical and impressive."

LIFE IN TUSCANY.

By MABEL S. CRAWFORD.

1 vol. 12mo. Price $1.

From the New York Tribune.

"The accounts given by the author of the religion, the manners, and general society of Tuscany will be found, to a high degree, instructive and entertaining."

From the New Orleans Delta.

"The aim of the author of this volume is to go out of the beaten track of sketch-writers about Italy, and to give the reader glimpses of the inner life and every-day habits and characteristics of the people as she saw them during a residence of ten months in Tuscany. She writes with earnestness, and often with considerable grace and graphicness."

From the Congregationalist.

"A book far above usual volumes of travel-sketches in its style, and in the interior details which it gives of Tuscan life. It is worthy of reprinting, and will repay careful reading. We wish all publishers who reprint London books would make their works come as near as this does to London excellence of typography."

From the New York Observer.

"It presents vivid sketches of the most noteworthy places and things, with the men, women and manners, arts, religion and reminiscences of that classic and beautiful country. Those who have visited Italy will recognize the fidelity of the sketches, which convey to the reader a fair idea of the attractions of the most delightful country in the south of Europe."

THE CHINA MISSION,

Including a Sketch of the Geography, Natural History, Customs, Language, Laws and Religions of China, together with a history of Christian Missions in that empire, including also Biographical Sketches of about fifty Missionaries, male and female, who have died in the service of that Mission.

By WILLIAM DEAN, D.D.

1 volume.   12mo.   Price $1.

From the Albany Statesman.

"'The China Mission' seems something more than the record of a spiritless existence among the strange people. The author appears to have realized that the extension of the kingdom of Christ was to have been achieved by study, observation and adaptation—that the voice of the Lord, if heard from mortal lips, must be pitched in cadence with the mortal ears and understanding to which it was addressed."

From the Christian Advocate.

"It is unnecessary to say a word in favor of this book. The title will excite a desire to read it, and the name and opportunities of the author will be sufficient assurance of the quality of his work. The book contains a most interesting, and doubtless reliable account of that curious people, in whom the world is now taking so much interest."

From the New York Observer.

"Dr. Dean writes with a free, graphic and facile pen, impartial in his judgments, strong in his convictions, and honest in his purposes. The records of such a mission as that of China in the hands of such a man as Dr. Dean are of permanent value to the church and the world."

From the New York News.

"The biographical sketches, with which the work fitly closes, are very interesting and touchingly executed."

From the Halifax Provincial Wesleyan.

"Its biographical sketches are full of interest, and throw great light on what the gospel has already achieved there."

THE GOSPEL IN BURMAH.

By Mrs. MACLEOD WYLIE. 1 vol. 12mo. Price $1. (In press.)

Notices from the English Press.

"The work is written in a clear and simple style, abounding with happy Scripture mottoes and pertinent quotations; while the story itself possesses an interest so deep and so fascinating as to enchain the reader's attention till its close."—*Nonconformist.*

"Mrs. Wylie has accomplished her work with much distinctness and literary ability. The order of the narrative is admirably maintained, while the incidents selected are characteristic of general features, so that the historical plan is never lost sight of in details. We cordially commend the book to the perusal of our readers."—*News of the Churches.*

"A more agreeable book on a missionary subject it has rarely been our lot to meet—more full of attractive information on its theme, more scriptural in its tone and substance, and more unaffectedly graceful in its style."—*Calcutta Christian Intelligencer.*

"Mrs Wylie has performed a most acceptable service; sincerely do we thank her for her trouble."—*Freeman.*

"A charming volume, which we would recommend to all who are interested in this singular people."—*Book and its Missions.*

THORNTON'S FAMILY PRAYERS;
PRAYERS ON THE TEN COMMANDMENTS, Etc.

To WHICH IS ADDED A FAMILY COMMENTARY ON THE SERMON ON THE MOUNT,
BY THE LATE HENRY THORNTON, M.P. EDITED BY BISHOP EASTBURN.

1 vol. 12mo. Plain, 75 cents. Fine edition, red edges, $1.

From the Episcopal Recorder, Philadelphia

"This collection of family prayers is placed in England as the most faithful and reliable that can be used, and we cheerfully unite in this opinion. The present edition is neat and complete."

From the Christian Witness, Boston.

"This is a new and neat edition of one of the best volumes of family prayers which has been published. It has been long and favorably known in this country. Probably no published volume of family prayers has ever been the vehicle of so much heartfelt devotion as these. They are what prayers should be—fervent, and yet perfectly simple."

From the Echo, Toronto.

"The prayers are expressive of deep piety tempered with a sound judgment, the language being forcible and concise, keeping always within the limits of sober humility, and never inflated, or running into exaggeration. They appear to express what most Christians would desire to say when kneeling before the throne of grace, and what most would deem appropriate to their daily wants and circumstances both of body and soul."

THE PRICE OF SOUL LIBERTY,
AND WHO PAID IT.

BY HENRY C. FISH, D.D.

1 vol. 18mo. Price, 40 cents.

From the New York Chronicle.

"This little book contains a condensed record of the various cases in which the Baptists have in various ages suffered for their radical idea of religion, as a 'matter of intelligent conviction and voluntary choice.' As a denomination, they have from the apostolic age repelled the idea of a religion imposed from without, by the act of parents, by hereditary succession, priestly manipulation, or any thing apart from the personal individual self of the actor or worshiper, in repenting, believing, and consecrating his life and services to Christ, by a voluntary submission to baptism. This view of Christianity has in all ages been the great antagonism to Church and State establishments, restraint upon personal freedom in matters of worship or of belief, and to the union of those born after the flesh and those born of the Spirit in outward Church organizations, as the great source of corruption and apostacy to the so-called Christian world. And as the opponents of this Baptist view of soul-liberty have always been, and are to this day in the majority, our denomination has in every age suffered persecution, and are still the objects of general dislike and distrust. Though the book is a compilation, it is none the less valuable, and we commend it to the universal and impartial attention of the public."

WAY MARKS TO
APOSTOLIC BAPTISM;

OR, HISTORICAL TESTIMONIES DEMONSTRATING THE ORIGINAL FORM OF THE RITE AS ORDAINED BY OUR LORD JESUS CHRIST, AND ADMINISTERED BY HIS HOLY APOSTLES.

1 vol. 18mo. Price, 35 cents.

www.ingramcontent.com/pod-product-compliance
Lightning Source LLC
Chambersburg PA
CBHW030954110726
47900CB00004B/1266